BRIERLEY REVIEWS:

<u>Edges of Time</u> "Brierley's writing is so vivid I felt I was there. His words paint a picture that transports the reader to that time and place. After 30 plus years working with writers developing scripts, I have known few who can translate vision to screen. Brierley is one of those few. I love everything he writes."
              --- Gay Gilbert, Casting Director and Film Producer

"<u>Timeless Interlude at Wounded Knee</u> is a finely crafted tale."
                    ----Clive Cussler, author of <u>The Spy</u>

"Barry Brierley is the Tom Clancy of Indian historical adventure. His diligent research shows through on every page." --- Marshall Terrill, Author of <u>Steve McQueen (Portrait of an American Rebel)</u>

"<u>Timeless Interlude at Wounded Knee</u> is one of those wonderful books that is read in one sitting -- not because it has little to say, but because it's said so well that it's hard to put down. The book is so well researched that Brierley's Lakota Sioux leap to life in the reader's eye as they face their darkest hour."   --- The Writer's Showcase

"<u>Wasichu</u> is a remarkable tour de force, bold in concept and brilliant in theme. An excellent read of what the West has become."
                            --- Clive Cussler

"In <u>Yesterday's Bandit, (Butch Cassidy's Last Ride)</u> I believe that Brierley has captured Butch Cassidy's true character. It is a fun read for young and old. I especially encourage the younger generation to read this book to help give them insight about morals, justice and family values."
              ---Bill Betenson, great nephew, researcher of Butch Cassidy

EDGES OF TIME

For Mary and Dan
with warm regards!

Barry Brierley

ALSO BY BARRY BRIERLEY

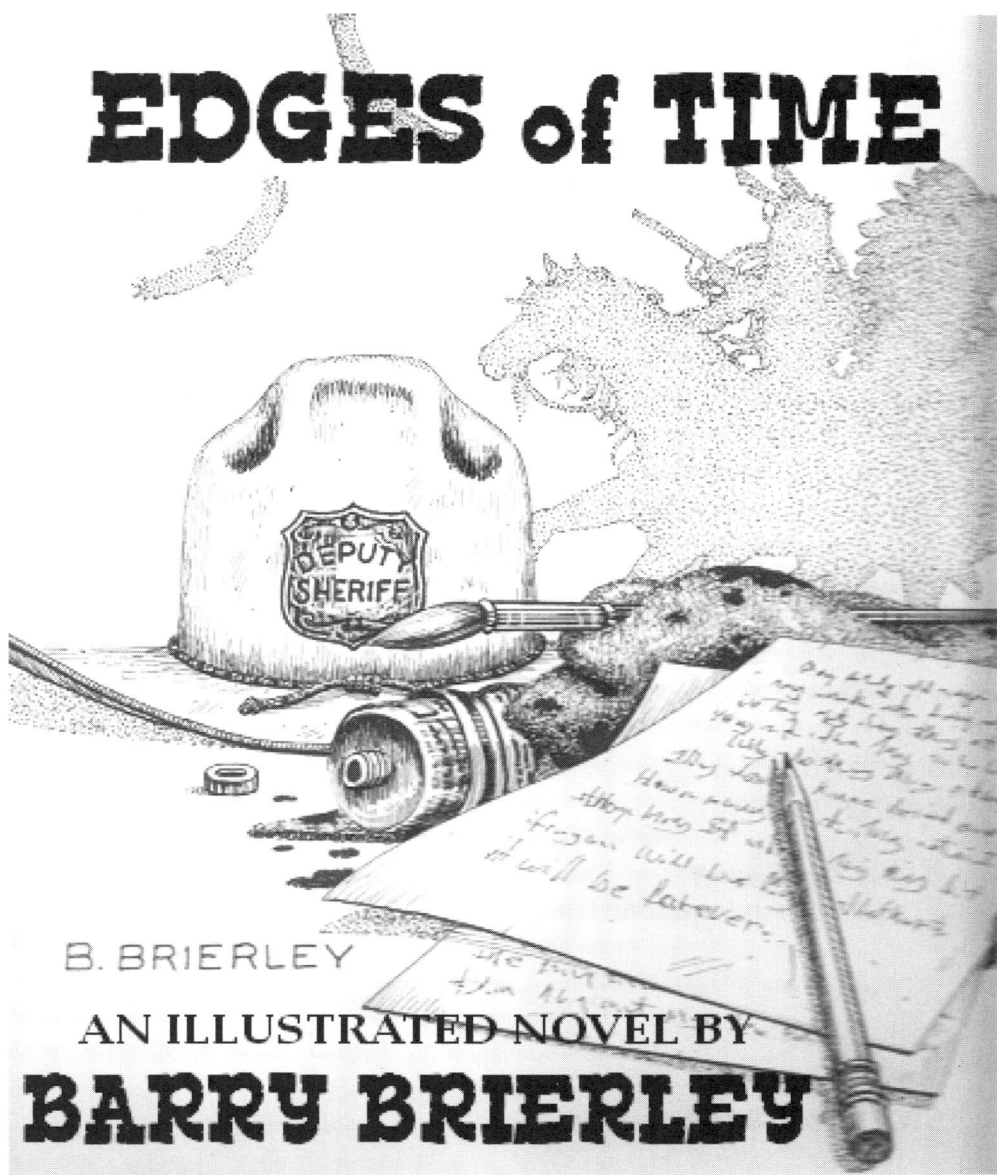

EDGES of TIME

B. BRIERLEY

AN ILLUSTRATED NOVEL BY

BARRY BRIERLEY

BEAR BOOKS

Copyright © 2010 by Barry Brierley.

Published by
BEAR BOOKS
115 E. Main Street
Florence, Colorado 81226

Printed in the United States of America.

Cover art by Barry Brierley
Designed and illustrated by Barry Brierley

www.barrybrierley.com

Reprinting of Timeless Interlude at Wounded Knee, Written and illustrated by Barry Brierley 1995

This is a work of fiction. Names, characters, places and incidents are the product of the author's imagination and are used fictitiously.

FIRST EDITION

ISBN 978-1-889657-16-5

Acknowledgments

As everyone probably knows a writer almost never accomplishes the writing of a novel alone. Other influences and inspirations are involved. That motivating force in my writing and my art is my wife, Barb, who not only gives me encourage-ment, but critiques me to the limit. I must thank her for the presentation of this novel, with her editing and insightful suggestions.

It must also be noted that the enthusiasm of fans of my books when I tell of the storyline of Edges of Time. Thank you for all my fans of *Timeless Interlude at Wounded Knee*. I promised you a sequel. As the first edition was sold out, and it was only a novella, I decided to print it again and include the sequel with a prologue. Hope you enjoy this complete book of *Edges of Time*.

This novel is dedicated to all the native people who unjustly suffered from government and military persons who had the power to make their lives insufferable and to change their way of life which was their given rite of passage.

A special dedication goes out to all who had participated in the Lakota ceremony 'Wiping of the Tears' honoring those who had perished in the massacre at Wounded Knee and their surviving ancestors.

Note from the wife: All of Barry's books float you into another place and time with magical story lines and unforgettable characters. *Edges of Time* will take you to places you will never forget, and the chills will start all over again … remembering.

Let your life lightly
Dance on the edges of
Time like dew on the
Tip of a leaf.

Sir Robindranath Tagore

JOHN NIGHTHAWK

B. BRIERLEY

PROLOGUE

TIMBERLINE

Stepping down from his Jeep Cherokee, Deputy Sheriff John Night-hawk moved away from his vehicle with an easy natural grace. His eyes swept across the clearing and scrutinized the area's dozen or so deserted cabins searching the autumn tree-line for movement. Nothing moved.

The thirty-year-old Minneconjou Sioux was lean in appearance. His bronze skin and cropped, blue-black hair appeared out of place in the Lakota County Sheriff's Department. Many South Dakota locals would take one look at Nighthawk's dark face and come to the unjust conclusion that the man had no right to wear the uniform. In reality, John Nighthawk did his job and did it better than most. He had an almost obsessive quality about upholding the law. Not that he lived by the letter of the law, only that he would always try to do what was right. During his youth John Nighthawk had seen every wrongful act known to man. From the very first day he pinned his badge on, he had made himself a promise that he would always try to do what was morally just no matter what the cost.

Deputy Nighthawk eyed the sheriff department's cruiser parked nearby and wondered at the whereabouts of the driver. While speculating he let his gaze slowly scan what was once a thriving logging community called Timberline.

A heavy but pleasant scent of pine hung in the air. He watched a breeze stir the yellow leaves of the aspen and cause the tops of the ponderosa pine and the thick boughs of blue spruce to sway and undulate with the power and grace of powwow fancy dancers.

John relished any excuse that enabled him to spend time in the more secluded portions of the Black Hills. To the Lakota the Black Hills has always been a holy place. Because of the Lakota belief that Mount Harney (highest point in the Black Hills) is the 'Center of the Universe' many consider it to be sacred ground.

He looked again at the log homes and thought of the prefab housing on the Rez. Like his peoples' reservation dwellings, each cabin was the same in appearance as its neighbor, but the Timberline log homes were of a much sturdier construction. He wondered briefly how many people used to live in the isolated logging community. A number of years ago the camp was an area full of activity. Located in one of the most remote regions of the Black Hills, it had in recent years become almost uninhabited.

At the moment the camp looked totally deserted to Nighthawk. He did know, however, that at least one person lived there. A man claiming to be a custodian at Timberline had phoned the sheriff's department twice in as many days. Both times he had reported that his friend was missing.

A sudden movement near the western edge of the clearing caught Nighthawk's eye. A large, bearded man, dressed in worn bib overhauls, stepped into the clearing and seeing Nighthawk, he stopped and stared. Pondering the whereabouts of Deputy Mix, Nighthawk waved and casually approached the man, as he covertly unsnapped the strap that secured his Browning 9mm automatic holstered on his hip. A scatter of leaves, propelled by an errant gust of wind, skipped and bounced ahead of him. Drawing closer John could see that the man was huge, at least three or four inches over his own six-foot frame and easily forty pounds heavier. He appeared to be in his late forties. The man's eyes were red and sore looking as though he had been weeping. The man met his gaze, then looked away and pulled a large bandanna free from his jeans, blowing heartily into it before folding it and tucking it behind the bib of his overhauls. John noticed a curious sprinkle of what appeared to be black-heads around his red-rimmed eyes and protruding forehead. Catching the man's roving eye, Nighthawk gave him a slight nod and smile.

"What's your name?" Nighthawk queried.

"James Frump," the man growled in reply.

Keeping his right hand on his automatic, John gestured toward the cruiser with his left.

"Where's the deputy?"

"He's with the body."

Although the death came as a surprise, John Nighthawk immediately sensed that the death was a violent one. He felt a hollow spot form in his stomach as he remarked, "Last I heard the problem was a missing person."

Frump briefly met John's gaze. His eyes blinked repeatedly.

"After I called the sheriff early this morning, I had me an idea. Bob loved the woods and he was always wanderin' off some place. One of his favorite places was the falls. I was on my way there and found him lyin' on the trail ..."

The big man's blue, reddened eyes found Nighthawk's. Tears were evident as he continued.

"He's dead. Some bastard killed him with an arrow."

Had John been a horse, his ears would have been standing tall and quivering with anticipation. As it was he practically blurted, "An arrow?"

Rubbing the moisture from his eyes, Frump turned his head and mumbled, "Yeah, shot in the back ... probably killed by that Injun."

"Indian? What Indian?"

Even before Frump's angry reply, John knew what his answer was going to be.

"Redfoot! That God-damned wild man done it."

For years there had been reports of a naked, wild man running loose in the Black Hills. Nighthawk hadn't put much stock in the stories, thinking they were just a South Dakota version of the Bigfoot legend. A lifetime of prejudices and injustices allowed a fleeting bitterness to pass through his mind. Only around these parts, he thought, would they turn Bigfoot into some kind of wild Indian by labeling him 'Redfoot'.

With a practiced ease John shelved his resentment; he then removed a notebook and pencil from his shirt pocket.

"What was the victim's last name?"

James Frump turned his head, and remarked, "White, his full name was Robert White."

Nighthawk recorded the information.

"How long were you and Mr. White friends?"

The big man shuffled his feet.

"Hell, we go way back. We used to ride together. He's been livin' here at Timberline with me now for over two years."

"Ride?"

3

Barry Brierley

Frump's head swiveled and his red-rimmed pale blue eyes pinned John's black gaze.

"Harleys, Man. We rode bikes together."

"You have any idea why anyone would want to kill him?"

"Naw, Bob never done much socializin' … besides, I told you who must a done it."

John pocketed his notebook.

"All right, Mr. Frump. Would you take me to Deputy Mix and the body?"

The man took another swipe at his eyes, and then he led the way into the woods.

"I know it was that Redfoot 'cause Bob was always snoopin' around in out-of-the-way places. I don't think the wild man would like that."

The caustic words were thrown over a meaty shoulder as Frump, finding the trail, lengthened his stride.

Nighthawk, knowing that the man posed no immediate threat, again secured his holstered automatic and lengthened his own stride to keep up. John breathed in the mixed aroma of pine, aspen and the assorted grasses that covered the Earth Mother. The rich, mountain air stimulated him and helped divert his thoughts from the grisly sight that he knew awaited him.

At the sight Nighthawk silently studied the red clay path and grassy area surrounding the body. The babble of a nearby stream and the rush and hiss of what sounded like a small waterfall added a melodious background to the ugly scene. The deputy's roving gaze quickly located the stream and falls. Once again looking at the tracks in the clay surrounding the body, John's previous suspicions were confirmed. The crime scene had been compromised. The Lakota deputy's black eyes lifted to the lounging form of Deputy Harlan Mix, leaning against a rock and picking his teeth. It was obvious that Harlan had carelessly trampled the whole area around the corpse ruining any chance of finding a clue among the tracks. Feeling Nighthawk's eyes, Harlan looked up. Seeing the disdain in the deputy's gaze, Deputy Mix responded with a sullen anger.

"What? I didn't do nothin'."

Nighthawk dropped his gaze and put the deputy out of his mind.

The victim was lying face down on his stomach; his arms were outstretched over his head as though in supplication, or prayer, toward

4

the stream. Like Frump had said, an arrow was sticking out of his back. Twelve inches of the shaft rose from a spot between the shoulder blades, just to the left of the spinal cord. Heart shot, he thought. Knowing that the man was probably dead, John still placed his palm against the protruding notched end of the shaft and paused. Nothing. Sometimes, with an animal, if it is still alive you can feel vibrations from the heartbeat.

Nighthawk knelt and without touching carefully examined the arrow.

The appearance of the arrow and its implications caused Nighthawk to create an interim while he put some thoughts together.

The shaft and fletching (feathers), and the method of attaching the feathers to the shaft, were done by hand and made in a primitive Native American form of craft. The style and colors painted on the shaft called cresting did not indicate any particular tribe that was familiar to Nighthawk. But the use of gooseberry wood for the shaft and the high plains style of fletching both indicated Lakota. Could Redfoot be a possibility? The thought came out of nowhere, breaching reality with its foolishness. Nighthawk scoffed at his own gullibility.

Curious, Deputy Mix straightened and moved closer.

"How long you think this sucker's been dead?"

Not answering the deputy's rude question, Nighthawk raised a quieting hand so suddenly that Harlan stopped his approach and stepped back.

John glanced at James Frump. The big man's eyes flicked toward him before fastening on Mix with an open hostility. Deputy Mix returned to his indolent posture and resumed picking his teeth.

John immediately noticed Frump's body language. Or, he asked himself, was it merely coincidence? The man appeared to have positioned himself between Deputy Mix and himself, blocking the path leading to the stream.

The Lakota deputy shelved the thought for later and stood up. Purely out of habit, he watched where he stepped and moved away from the body. Nighthawk's searching eye noticed how the somewhat rocky terrain climbed above the falls for a short distance until it crested onto a grassy, treeless dome. The stream apparently cut straight through the treeless hillock. Reluctantly, John's gaze returned to the body.

Barry Brierley

The victim's mouth gaped in a silent scream; the horror of what had happened was clearly defined in his protruding eyes and bared teeth. The body was lying in a slight downhill position so that blood had flowed past his face and outstretched arms until absorbed by the rocky turf just inches short of the stream.

Turning to Deputy Mix, Nighthawk flipped him the keys to Mix's cruiser. The deputy at least had the grace to look sheepish about his negligence. John said, "Call the sheriff and tell him what is going on and what is needed here. Afterwards, secure the grounds, stay by the radio and wait for instructions. We do not want tourists nosing around, and I need you up there to direct the sheriff to the scene. Understand?"

Harlan nodded but didn't leave. He sucked on his toothpick, moving it with his tongue and stared at the corpse until he noticed that Nighthawk was watching him. The deputy straightened and was about to throw his toothpick down when he saw Nighthawk's expression and changed his mind, pocketed the sliver of wood and turned to leave. Seeing that the giant Frump was still watching him, Mix made a swing around him and started up the path toward Timberline. Mix stopped and looked back.

Mentally dismissing Deputy Mix, Nighthawk focused on the body. He noted that the victim was a male Caucasian who appeared to be in his late forties, early fifties, brown hair and eyes, well groomed, of average height, and compatible weight. He was dressed in typical local attire: blue jeans, flannel shirt, hooded sweat shirt and boots. What is it about the boots, he mused.

"Hey, chief, how long you think he's been dead?" Harlan asked.

Nighthawk's black eyes glittered with anger. His gaze swung up the trail and sighted in on the lingering deputy.

"How many times have I told you not to call me, chief?" Not waiting for a reply, Nighthawk added, "Forensics will answer your questions more accurately than I can. Now how about doing as I asked?"

Turning away, Nighthawk listened as Deputy Mix's footsteps slowly moved on up the trail. Taking his time, and being careful not to move the position of the body, the deputy lifted one side and looked beneath him. He then thoroughly searched through all his pockets; no I.D., money or anything else was to be found. Glancing at the hulking Frump, Nighthawk asked, "Did you touch the body, or take anything from his pockets?"

6

Edges of Time

The big man slowly shook his head and sat down on a nearby boulder. Nighthawk noticed that his legs still blocked the path leading to the falls.

Eyes focused on the ground, John bent at the waist and slowly began to circle the body, gradually widening his circle as he went. When he was a good twenty feet from the body he stopped and straightened, placing his hands on his hips. His eyes lifted and met Frump's gaze.

"Mr. Frump, I would like you to go to your cabin and wait for the sheriff. He will want to look at everything that belonged to your friend and will need all the information about him that you can come up with."

Nighthawk waited until the quiet giant moved out of sight before bending over and picking up a small, blue piece of paper that had been partially hidden by the grass. He examined it and then pocketed it, as he murmured softly to himself, "Interesting what people leave lying around."

Judging from the position of the body and the angle of the arrow's entry, Nighthawk was able to get an approximate idea where the killer might have stood when he launched his arrow. He made a quick search of the area, starting with the path leading to the stream. Other than the fact that the path was well traveled, he found a partial heel print near some aspen about thirty feet from the body. What bothered him more than he wanted to admit was the fact that the heel-print wasn't from a boot, or shoe ... it was made by a moccasin.

After completing a sweep of the area encompassing the body, Nighthawk took an out-of-the-way deer trail and followed it back toward Timberline. He made an effort to prepare himself for his forthcoming encounter with his boss, Sheriff Irwin Hoage.

Forever at odds with the irascible sheriff, Nighthawk fervently hoped that Hoage had the sense to leave his young clone, Deputy Triplet, at the department to catch any other calls. One redneck was bad enough to put up with, the two together made Nighthawk seriously consider the pros and cons of starting another Indian war by taking their hair and stretching their scalps on a willow hoop.

After deliberately avoiding the falls area, John Nighthawk stopped at Frump's cabin and asked a few more questions. Finished with the questioning, he went back into the woods and made a general sweep of the wooded area before returning to the Timberline buildings. Moving out of the trees, John entered the log cabin community at a spot several cabins away from Frump's dwelling. He stopped and stared in surprise. A paramedic's 4X4 vehicle was parked near the cabin. Nighthawk was amazed that the emergency vehicle had already arrived. They must have been in the area, he thought, when the call came in. There was no one in sight near the unit. Assuming that its crew was already busy with White's body, the deputy momentarily relaxed and let his gaze sweep the clearing.

As usual he heard the sheriff before he saw him. When he did see him, the big-bellied sheriff was standing on the dirt road that led to the cabins bellowing something incomprehensible at the spineless Deputy Mix, who was standing up by the paved road in what was probably an assumed attitude of confusion.

John was almost within touching distance before the sheriff gave a small start and acknowledged his presence with his customary charm. With a smile that didn't quite reach his narrowed eyes, he said, "Where'n Hell you been? I been wonderin' where my pet Injun had disappeared to."

Nighthawk ignored the sheriff's racial remarks and said, "Well, I been snooping for clues in the woods. Did you question James Frump?"

Sheriff Hoage removed a notebook from his shirt pocket. Hitching his sagging trousers up over his belly before checking his notes, the sheriff frowned.

"Peers that Robert White and Frump had lived here together for 'bout two and a half years."

"Is that right?"

He decided not to bother telling Hoage that he already had gotten the information from Frump before he made his reconnaissance. Nighthawk then asked to see the sheriff's notes which the sheriff reluctantly handed over.

There wasn't much there that Nighthawk didn't already know, but he quickly memorized the pertinent facts.

"Where is Frump?" John asked, as he returned the notebook.

Pocketing the book, the sheriff shrugged.

"Hell, I don' know, said somethin' 'bout having to check somethin' or other."

The deputy turned away. He had the strange feeling he was being watched. Over his shoulder he said, "I'm going to look around a bit more." Sheriff Hoage smirked.

"Well, hell, I already did. But, suit yourself ... you always do."

Nighthawk walked to the shed-like building attached to the cabin and went inside, showing no sign that he felt someone watching.

From the shadows just inside the trees, a silent figure watched the building that Nighthawk had entered. The man in the trees remained absolutely still; his form becoming as one with the surrounding pine. He waited and watched with the same quiet assurance and patience as the man he watched.

Time passed and the deputy left the shed. Writing something down in his small notebook, he moved across the clearing toward the sheriff, who was once again busy hiking his uniform pants higher on his non-existent waist.

As usual, Nighthawk's approach was silent. The sheriff jumped when he saw him. He was about to make an angry remark when John asked, "Where's Deputy Triplet?"

"You know damn well he's coverin' the phone at the office," Hoage complained.

Returning his notebook to his pocket John suddenly felt uneasy. The hackles raised on the back of his neck. Someone is still watching me, he thought.

Without appearing to do so John's gaze swept the perimeter. Beneath the brim of his hat, his relentless eyes searched for that which did not belong. He saw a small gust of wind scoop several leaves into the air and scatter them across the clearing. A bird alighted on a nearby pine bough, while another shied away from a quaking aspen. A small animal with mottled, brown fur scurried across the road behind a totally unaware Deputy Mix, who strolled back and forth at the edge of the paved road.

While Sheriff Hoage perused his notes, Nighthawk moved slowly away from him, strolling casually about within Timberline's boundaries but keeping a sharp eye. He hoped for a glimpse of whoever was spying on him. Time stood still for the Lakota deputy as he peered from beneath the brim of his hat; his critical eye searched for and found every nook and cranny within range. When the hunted feeling eventually left, Nighthawk relaxed and rejoined the sheriff who was standing with his hands clasped behind his back, rocking back and forth on his heels.

Movement picked up by Nighthawk's peripheral vision pulled his gaze to the edge of the woods. He watched as Frump stepped lightly from the trees. The burly man looked in neither direction, simply moved in a straight line toward his cabin. Just before moving out of sight, Frump turned and looked at him. John didn't know what to make of the bearded James Frump. Something about him bothered him. Maybe, John thought, what I'm sensing is that the man just doesn't like Indians.

Suddenly aware that the sheriff was speaking to him, Nighthawk interrupted him.

"Sheriff, I think you had better talk with Deputy Mix. I think he has more to tell you than he's letting on."

"What's that, Nighthawk ... you saying that Mix knows somethin' we don't?"

Nighthawk turned away before the sheriff saw his smile. While he watched the sheriff huff and puff up the grade he moved quickly toward his Cherokee. John threw a glance to where Mix was still standing guard at the mouth of the driveway. Seeing that Mix was completely unaware that trouble was swiftly approaching from the rear, John grinned and opened the jeep's door. Before climbing into his jeep, Deputy Nighthawk removed his hat and threw it on the passenger seat. Scooting behind the wheel, he put on a pair of Ray-bans and drove up the dirt driveway where it connected with the paved county road. He smiled as he saw Sheriff Hoage tongue-lashing a bewildered Deputy Mix. As the Cherokee breezed by, John stuck his head out the window and spoke loud enough for them to hear over the engine noise.

"I'll meet you back in Rapid, Sheriff. I have to check on something."

With a grin and a wave, Nighthawk rolled his window up and cut off Hoage's angry reply in mid-sentence. As he began his drive down and away from the derelict logging camp, the deputy watched the side of the road with a sharp eye. He had only driven a short distant before spying what he was looking for and turned onto one of the many dirt logging roads that were scattered across the Black Hills.

When John was in the trees far enough, and was certain his vehicle couldn't be seen from the county road, he stopped and shut the motor off. The natural quiet settled over him like a weightless comforter. He removed his sunglasses, pushed the seat back, and fully relaxed. He checked the location of the sun before putting his head back and closing his eyes. His thoughts began drifting. For some reason they tumbled

10

back over the years to when he had been hired. John chuckled, remembering the shocked faces of his fellow employees when he had showed up for his first day at work.

Sheriff Hoage's racial prejudices were not allowed to become a factor in Nighthawk landing the job. An Indian would never have been the sheriff's choice. As it turned out, he needed more than encouragement to hire Nighthawk. It took a considerable amount of political pressure to get the job done.

When the deputy position had become available an incident had occurred at about the same time that had made the sheriff's preference unimportant. Almost overnight, John Nighthawk had become a local hero.

A small girl had wandered away from her family's campsite in Custer National Park and disappeared into the forest. John had volunteered to help find her and, he had done so after all others had given up. His phenomenal tracking skills were very instrumental in her safe recovery. He had found her inside a small, stone-walled cave where she had instinctively crawled to get out of the elements.

The incident had been picked up by the Associated Press and John Nighthawk became a brief shining star in the national limelight. Letters and petitions poured in, each and every one, persistently encouraging Sheriff Hoage to hire John Nighthawk. The final incentive was a personal phone call from the governor who threatened, come election time, to use his influence to see to it that the sheriff's job wound up going to someone else. John Nighthawk became the first Native American peace officer to be hired by Lakota County.

Nighthawk's wandering thoughts returned to the murder. He knew it would be a day or two before they got the lab report on the arrow, and at least a day on the autopsy; in the meantime there were things that needed looking into. The last thing the deputy wanted was Frump's looming presence while he searched around. He had several questions for the caretaker that needed answering, but they could wait. Thoughts of the hulking Frump were pushed aside as John concentrated on clearing his mind so that his relaxation would be complete. He closed his eyes and waited.

It was almost sunset when Nighthawk decided that enough time had passed for all outsiders to be clear of Timberline; he removed his half-boots and put on a pair of old moccasins. Removing his hat, badge, sunglasses and anything else that reflects light or could create an unnatural sound, John left his vehicle and began to circle back through the woods. He moved easily through the trees. Ever so often he would stop and listen. Near the edge of the Timberline clearing, he paused beside the paved road. Nothing moved among the deserted cabins. There was no sign of Frump, and all the county vehicles were gone. Nighthawk welcomed the solitude. He listened to the many voices of the forest that signified the approach of day's end. Everything seemed normal. With extreme caution he moved into the open. Keeping a low profile, he crossed the road with the swiftness of a mountain lion and silently slipped behind the cabins. John flowed through the woods, trying to attain the grace and assurance of a creature that was in his natural element. Like the wolf, the Lakota deputy's lean form moved in a way completely harmonious with nature.

His elder mentors had taught him that when the wind blew, everything in the woods moved in the same direction; anything that moved in a conflicting manner would become immediately visible to a person with knowledgeable, searching eyes.

By the time he neared the site where the body was discovered, Nighthawk felt as though he had become a natural part of the forest and in tune with the Earth Mother. John moved into the open beside the stream and looked back. His gaze lifted beyond the waterfall to the rocky incline above. He did not know why but something intangible pulled his attention to the top of the knoll. Only a patch of golden sky was visible at the top of the treeless hill. Once again Nighthawk shook off the eerie feeling of being watched. He continued walking parallel to the path as it moved downhill. He approached the base of the hill where a smaller waterfall appeared. At the bottom of an abrupt incline a small pool had formed. Shaded by the nearby trees golden, aspen leaves floated on its glass-like surface. Dark and light reflections created mosaic patterns across the water and surrounding terrain. A stone ledge hovered just above where a stream of clear water gently cascaded into a free-fall from a rock projection and landed with a soft, musical discord in the pool below.

With an inexplicable foresight, John knew that there was something in the trees beside the hill that did not belong there. He unsnapped the strap that secured his pistol and slowly moved forward. The area was out of sight of the pool and opposite the path so Nighthawk was very careful as he moved around the side of the hillock. Once he realized there was no killer lurking nearby, only inanimate objects, he relaxed.

Hidden among the trees and bushes were several mining tools. In addition, a small generator and a hydraulic jack-hammer leaned against the rock face. An air hose was coiled in the grass. Being in the shadow of a rock it looked like a long, red snake. Nearby, a man-made opening was carved out of the rocky hillside; it was a shaft large enough for a grown man to walk inside. The excavation was as carefully concealed as the tools and mining equipment. Instead of investigating the inside of the mining shaft, Nighthawk hurried back to the pool. When he had walked past it on his way to the discovery of the mine, something in the sandy soil near the falls had caught his eye.

A scatter of leaves that covered a patch of sand didn't look normal, nor did the leaves look as though they belonged there. Kneeling, the deputy carefully brushed the leaves aside. In the dispersed light the sand was mottled with darker patches that looked like something had been spilled and then brushed in an effort to cover the stains.

Working quickly, John brushed at the dry sand until he had revealed a large patch of discolored soil. He sat back on his heels Lakota style and studied the stain. His fingers touched one of the dark areas of sand. It was cool and still retained some dampness; several grains of sand stuck to his fingertips. To confirm his suspicions, Nighthawk got on his hands and knees and smelled the darkened sand. The scent of blood was unmistakable. As he got to his feet, John knew that he had found the real scene of the murder.

Earlier in the day after examining the body, it became clear to him that Robert White had been killed elsewhere. The lack of blood spilled and the absence of red clay on the murdered man's boots were indicative that the body had been moved. The path where he was found was almost entirely composed of red clay. It was a type of soil that was moist enough to leave visible deposits on any type of footwear.

John was suddenly alert. He had heard something but wasn't certain of its source. He turned. There was a whisper; a familiar flutter of sound. A solid blow struck him high on his left chest! He staggered, as much from surprise as the impact of the blow. With an instant awareness of what had happened he realized that an arrow had penetrated deep into his young body, immediately causing excruciating pain and shock. The trauma took away his legs and he collapsed onto the sand near the pool of water.

Dizziness had his thoughts swirling like a prairie dust-devil. The trees closed in on him, tall soldiers sealing off his escape from the darkening forest. Shadows moved and motley patches of light joined forces with the ranks of marching trees. Panic was creating chaos within his mind. John shook his reeling head but to no avail. The pain made it difficult for him to focus on the problem at hand. Survival ... the word surfaced and swam through the waves of agony into his awareness. Knowing he had to move or die, he cursed softly under his breath and braced himself. With tremendous resolve, Nighthawk lunged out of the clearing into the bushes. He landed hard, sliding behind the cover of a ponderosa pine deadfall. The agony from his effort exploded in his shoulder like a hand grenade. He snatched a branch off a dead limb and rammed it between his teeth and bit down, stifling an involuntary outcry. John's head swirled as he fought against the increasing pain and the frightening possibility of a blackout. In addition, another battle was being waged within himself to find the cerebral strength not to welcome the relief of unconsciousness.

While he silently grappled with the hurt and shock, clarity of thought returned with a grim reality. Nighthawk speculated what his attacker might do. He could sit back and wait for the arrow to do its work, he thought, hoping that I'll pass out or bleed to death, or he will come down here and finish me. If he does wait, he thought, I know I'm a dead man. The warm sensation of blood running down his chest added a grim footnote to his latter thought. Either way, he knew the end result would be the same. John Nighthawk would begin his final journey to the Spirit World much earlier than anticipated.

Determined not to give up without a fight, the young Lakota spat out the acrid, bitter tasting stick and waited, conserving his waning strength. He knew that in a very short time he could be in a fight to the death with a determined, desperate killer.

Time seemed to pass with agonizing slowness. Nighthawk watched the shadows form geometric designs across the bronze color of his skin while the setting sun's warmth did its best to relax him. Squeezed in a vice of discomfort, he waited with the inherited patience of his ancestors as they had waited in ambush for hated enemies, or listened for the soft, subtle sounds that would tell them that game was near and that their band would soon have sustenance.

While he waited, Nighthawk's thoughts drifted back and forth like a shifting wind whirling through a time tunnel. Reality became a scarce commodity until finally, the present returned. Recalled terror tapped back into his befuddled mind and brought with it a grim determination not to die. His inherent ability to concentrate helped him channel his thoughts and prepare himself mentally for whatever was to come.

When the golden sunlight had turned to orange, John heard the sound of something moving furtively through the bushes and grass. The noise had come from behind.

Biting down, to bolster against the pain, Nighthawk's right hand slowly went to his holstered automatic. It was gone! He hadn't secured the weapon in its holster. It must have dropped out with his fall. Without moving his head, Nighthawk's eyes frantically searched the leaf-covered ground. The covert sounds evolved into footsteps that grew ever closer. A shadow loomed. Through his pain, the first thing Nighthawk saw was a pipe tomahawk. The hatchet's steel blade glistened where orange light touched its burnished surface. The painted haft was in the grasp of a large, powerful hand. Hating to move and disturb the debilitating pain, the deputy forced himself to lift his head. A maniacal gleam glittered from beneath James Frump's prominent brow as he stared down on the helpless form of John Nighthawk. A mirthless smile appeared within the shaggy beard. A hand-crafted bow dangled from his other hand; a quiver of arrows, brothers to the one found in Robert White's back, peeked from behind a muscular shoulder. The display of hand-crafted Native American replicas confirmed Nighthawk's earlier suspicion that Frump was either a member of a black powder club or one of their rendezvous vendors.

"I didn't have you fooled at all, did I? I had a feeling you'd show up tonight."

Frump's voice rumbled with a new menace and his hand holding the tomahawk tightened.

Nighthawk pushed his fear aside and looked Frump in the eye.

"No, you didn't."

The deputy's simple, matter-of-fact answer seemed to infuriate the giant Frump. John saw the meaty hand flex on the tomahawk's shaft.

With the inherent patience of his forefathers he waited. Frump managed to regain control of his rage.

"None of this would've happened if the damn fool would of just let things be ... we could've pulled a small fortune out of this hill."

"Gold?"

John's voice was tight with repressed anguish.

Frump nodded. His eyes narrowed as memory brought back his anger.

"If the stupid bastard would've just agreed to keep his mouth shut ..."

The big man's face seemed to crumple into planes of sorrow.

"You don't know the whole story, Indian." His eyes softened as he paused, then added, "If only my ..."

Whatever Frump was going to add withered and died. Then the anger returned in force.

"This bein' state land, if Bob talked, we would've lost it all!"

Unexpectedly Frump lashed out with his foot and kicked him in the ribs. Agony exploded in Nighthawk's shoulder! The pain was so intense he feared he would pass out; a white-hot anger surged, strengthening his resolve to live and to reap revenge.

"What in hell did you find in my cabin?" Frump roared.

With a concentrated effort, John pulled himself together. Purely to buy himself some time, he told him of his finds.

"A glue gun and some slender gooseberry sticks that could be used to make arrow shafts."

John paused and with a new found intensity, he foolishly added.

"Listen carefully to my words, *wasichu* (white man). If you think clearly, you will see ... there is no chance you can get away with this. When the lab work is done, it will show that the epoxy used on the arrows will be the same as in your shed, not evolved from animal hooves and horns, as the old ones used."

Frump's rage smoldered.

"Caught by a God-damned Indian ... never thought I'd see the day ..."

John saw Frump's knuckles whiten as his grip again tightened on the tomahawk. With blazing eyes, he shuffled even closer. The big man bent from the waist until his face was inches from Nighthawk's. With a barely restrained violence, he whispered, "They still won't have any proof,

Injun. All I got to do is get rid of those things you were so dumb to tell me about."

A bright flicker of light caught John's roving eye. His pistol was lying almost within reach! Frump's foot must have nudged it clear of the leaves when he moved closer. Now his mind was searching desperately for a way to reach it.

"... after I'm finished with you, I'm home free. That sheriff's dumb as a post, he won't be no problem."

John stared, incredulous. His eye had picked up movement beyond the pool and above James Frump's bulky form. He couldn't believe what he was seeing!

On top of the treeless hill, framed against the patch of darkening sky, was the near naked figure of a man. He was standing motionless watching them. The wind caught his long black hair and whipped it across his lean dark face. Redfoot! The name ignited in his brain and seared away his former disbelief. The wild man was holding something long and narrow in his hands. Frump's menacing voice intruded into his spinning, bedazzled thought process.

"... all I got to do now is snuff out yer spark, Injun."

As though witnessing a dream, John watched the distant Redfoot raise his arms. He had a bow and arrow! From the corner of his eye he saw Frump raise the tomahawk. His body tensed. Even as Nighthawk's mind registered the fact that Redfoot had released his arrow, he knew the distance was too great for accurate shooting. Again Nighthawk heard the frightening flutter of approaching death. There was a wet, meaty "Thud!"

Frump screamed!

The arrow had pierced the thick muscle leading from his neck to his shoulder. Frump swore loudly, dropped his bow and yanked viciously at the bloody shaft.

Blood spattered Nighthawk like scarlet rain. He ignored his throbbing wound and dove forward toward his automatic. Frump grabbed at him and missed! John's hand closed over the Browning. He rolled onto his back. Frump loomed above him with the hatchet raised overhead! Nighthawk's thumb automatically cocked the hammer, pointed and squeezed ... three times, the automatic bucked in his fist! The tomahawk was already descending as the three rounds slammed into James Frump's massive chest. Nighthawk tried to get out of the way, but

17

it was too late. The tomahawk smashed against his skull! His head obliterated into splinters of pain, then ... nothing.

Within the silent forest, the bark of the 9mm had been deafening. The triple echo slowly faded until consumed by the encroaching trees. Once again silence prevailed.

***

Excruciating pain awakened him. The pounding ache in his head had almost made him forget about the pain from the arrow in his shoulder. He was alive, and he began to realize that the hawk's blade must have turned, striking him with a flat side instead of the edge. All at once he was aware that there was no feeling in his legs. He couldn't move them!

Nighthawk fought down a rising panic. Fear of what he would discover kept him from opening his eyes. He heard movement. He was having trouble remembering the sequence of things ... then in a rush of terror it all returned. Again, he heard something. Cautiously, he opened his eyes to mere slits and peered through the blur of his eyelashes. Redfoot! In the fading light all he could see was the man's dark legs, cross-hatched here and there with thin white scars, plus new scratches still red with clotted blood. He saw the muscles tense on the dark, sinewy limbs. Suddenly, feeling rushed back into his lower body and he felt a cramp in his leg! Nighthawk silently rejoiced at the pain. He watched, as though peering through curved glass as the nearly naked man finished lifting Frump's great weight off his legs.

An unexpected vortex of pain twisted through his impaled shoulder and pulled him into its black center and he swiftly began to lose consciousness.

'KA-POW!'

The gunshot tore through his ebbing perceptiveness with startling effect. Once again he was fully aware and cautiously peered with disbelief through the slits of his narrowed eyes. A waft of burnt gunpowder tingled Nighthawk's nose, but he didn't notice. His gaze was pinned on the wild-looking, crouched figure in front of him.

Redfoot's back was to him. Naked but for a hide loin-cloth and moccasins, the man was crouched over Frump's body with John's gun in his hand. The deputy peered into Frump's glazed, dead eyes while his befuddled mind wondered, why? Why did he shoot him again? Was

18

Edges of Time

Frump still alive? Through John's pain-induced perceptions his questions remained unanswered. Flashes of clarity surfaced but never stayed. He still hadn't seen Redfoot's face, but through the ensuing gloom Nighthawk could clearly see that he was Indian. He also saw that his moccasins, though crudely made, were put together in Lakota style. Nighthawk's eyelids drooped, and suddenly they were so heavy he couldn't keep them open. Rough hands pulled at his shirt. Pain washed over him in waves as he felt his left side being raised and then carefully lowered back down. Suddenly, agony exploded in his shoulder and he knew no more as he once again slipped away and 'walked in darkness' (Lakota term for being unconscious).

John Nighthawk opened his eyes. It was almost dark. His shoulder throbbed mercilessly. Without moving his head he used his side vision and saw that the arrow was gone. A steady pressure had replaced the shaft but managed not to release the pain; it gnawed at his shoulder with unrelenting savagery. Suddenly, he sensed his presence. He was so close that John felt the warmth of his breath on his ear and could smell his wild scent. A soft, sibilant voice came from directly behind him as the man uttered a strange remark.

"For me, the circle has finally closed. I am at peace."

"Who are you?" Nighthawk rasped.

"You will know ... in time."

Barely conscious, John Nighthawk listened to the man's breathing. A beguiling scent of wood smoke, leather, burnt sweet grass, and sage hovered nearby. With a voice that was barely more than a whisper, the man spoke again'

"I have been watching these men."

John waited. Just when he thought the man was finished talking, he continued. Harshness had entered the man's voice.

"They have been digging into the Earth Mother's skin desecrating our sacred ground."

In his struggle to remain conscious, John was unaware how much time had passed before the voice spoke again. He thought that Redfoot had spoken again, but he wasn't sure. When he did hear him clearly it could have been ten minutes or ten seconds later ... he would never know.

"Rest, Deputy Nighthawk, but remember this ... I was never here."

Barry Brierley

Pausing a moment, he added, "Someone will come for you."

In Lakota, Nighthawk whispered, "*Pila maya, kola.* (Thanks, friend)."

He heard no more except a softly intoned "Hgun, hgun" (Lakota courage cry). But later he thought perhaps it had been merely a murmur of the wind.

***

When Deputy Nighthawk opened his eyes again he was in a bed in a pristine hospital room with sunlight shining through his window. An I.V. was in his right arm. Sheriff Irwin Hoage was looking out the window while busily hiking his sagging trousers up over his mountainous belly.

"Sheriff Hog. How long I been here?" Nighthawk croaked.

The sheriff spun around and fastened his beady, porcine eyes on his deputy.

"God-damn it, Nighthawk … it's Hoage, not Hog!"

The sheriff waddled over to John's bed and plopped his bulk into a flimsy chair beside it. The chair creaked in protest and threatened to collapse as the sheriff adjusted his buttocks inside the narrow fit and fixed Nighthawk with a stern look.

Not up to their usual exchange, John hoarsely said, "Sorry, Sheriff."

Hoage nodded.

"You should be. It's 'bout time I got a little respect outta you."

Nighthawk gestured toward a glass of water on a nearby tray.

Sheriff Hoage grabbed the glass and passed it to John. After washing the dryness away, Nighthawk handed the glass back, feeling somewhat refreshed but tired.

The sheriff settled back in his chair. He cleared his throat, ran his hand over his perspiring face and short cropped hair.

"I got me some questions I need answered."

"How long I been here?" Nighthawk repeated.

"Oh ... ah, couple a days. Say, if we hadn't got that phone call you'd still be lyin' out there ... dead, more'n likely. Serve you right for not tellin' me what you were up to."

"Who called?" John interrupted.

The sheriff blinked and stared at him.

"I was hoping you could tell me. Fella wouldn't give his name. Said he was hiking and found you with an arrow stickin' outta you. And old Frump lyin' dead beside you. If this fella hadn't pulled that arrow out and stopped the bleeding with a bunch of leaves, you would a' bled to death."

Nighthawk's mind was swirling with unanswered questions. Trouble was, there was no one who could answer them except someone who 'did not exist.'

"What'n hell made you go sniffing around down by them falls, and why'd you suspect Frump?"

Hoage's questions pulled John's mind away from his frustrating speculations. He shifted on the bed and felt a twinge of pain in his shoulder and a throbbing reminder from his head. For the first time he noticed how heavily bandaged he was. Strangely, stymied by the question, Nighthawk paused. When he met the sheriff's questioning gaze it all came back. As he began his story, John looked past the sheriff. His gaze passed through the window to the hills towering just beyond the hospital grounds. It was as though in his mind he was once again walking near the empty cabins at Timberline.

"At first it was little things that made me wonder about James Frump. When I first talked with the man he had strange, tiny black marks around his eyes. I didn't want to stare. If it had been something important, and he saw me staring, it would put him on guard, perhaps give him time to think up a story."

"What'n hell was it, blackheads?"

With the question the sheriff pulled a bandanna from his pocket and swiped at his neck and face.

"Jesus H. Christ! Don't they have any air conditioning in this dump?"

Nighthawk, his mind focused on answering the first question, didn't pay any attention to the sheriff's outburst. He looked at Hoage.

"In a way, some might have been blackheads. In his shed I found a couple of black powder flintlocks and many things used by members of Buckskinner Clubs. I know that sometimes when firing replica flintlocks, powder in the frizzen pan can flare up, sometimes back into your face, imbedding under your skin. That's probably where some of those black spots came from. But later when we were with the body, some of the spots were gone."

The sheriff was now getting interested.

"Well, what in hell were they? Where'd they go?"

John smiled.

"They were snuff particles ... or ground tobacco, whatever. What he did was rub some snuff in his eyes to produce a few tears and redden his eyes. Guess he wanted us to think he was upset over his friend's death."

Sheriff Hoage stood up and began to pace and tug at his pants. He stopped and peered over his shoulder at Nighthawk with a comical leer.

"Are you sure, Nighthawk ... or is this some of that Injun voodoo stuff?"

John ignored Hoage's ethnic ignorance.

"I do not know if this is fact. I'm telling what made me suspect James Frump. I also found a blue paper that is used to seal Copenhagen snuff tins. It wasn't far from the body. I realize this is all circumstantial, but it no longer matters."

"That's right!" Sheriff Hoage proclaimed.

"The murdering sonuvabitch's dead and we can close the case."

Sheriff Hoage stood up, hiked up his pants, cocked a curious eye at Nighthawk and smiled.

"I think you're gonna have to spend some time at the pistol range once ya get kicked outta here."

Puzzled, Nighthawk asked, "Why is that?"

"Hell, Boy. Ya put three rounds dead center, then jerked the last shot so bad you only got a piece of the top a Frump's shoulder."

Once again, in his mind, Nighthawk heard the fourth shot and saw Redfoot standing over Frump's body, gun in hand. Now he understood. The final shot was to cover-up the arrow wound Redfoot had inflicted in Frump's shoulder.

"Or was it the first round that went wild?"

Hoage followed his query with a bemused look.

Obvious to John that Hoage didn't believe that everything happened as it appeared, he continued to play dumb.

"Sorry, Sheriff, I don't remember."

Hoage noisily cleared his throat and moved toward the door.

"When am I getting out of here?"

Nighthawk's question halted the sheriff's departure.

"Don't worry about it. The doctor told me in a day or so."

Sheriff Hoage opened the door and paused in the doorway.

Edges of Time

"Get well now, hear? By the way, your personal stuff's in the night stand drawer. Another thing ... I didn't know you carried that voodoo stuff around in your pockets. You keep that crap outta sight! Can't have folks thinkin' one of my law officers is toting somethin' like that around."

When the door shut behind the sheriff, Nighthawk continued to stare at the space the sheriff had vacated. The deputy's mind raced, tumbling in its hurry to make sense of the sheriff's remark. Whatever could have been in his possession that the sheriff would consider spiritual ... or voodoo, as he would call it, was beyond John's recollection. Nighthawk carefully eased himself toward the right-hand edge of his bed. Ignoring the sharp twinge of pain in his shoulder, he reached to pull the night stand drawer open. Unable to see inside he slipped his hand in. At first all he felt were coins and his billfold. Something tickled his palm, and his fingers closed around a flat, smooth object. When he saw the object, he no longer felt the pain in his head or shoulder. The room began to spin and he feared he would pass out. The feeling passed and Nighthawk stared at the object clutched in his hand.

Lying in the center of his palm was an arrowhead made from pipestone that had been worn dull and smooth as glass by much handling over the passage of time. A hole had been bored through the blunt end, a small eagle plume tied to the stone with rawhide.

Nighthawk stared at the talisman; the legend of Redfoot now became a reality. Several years earlier, right after the war in the Gulf, he had arrested a young Lakota for drunken assault. The story he eventually pried from the young man was a grim one.

The young soldier had returned from Desert Storm to discover that his whole family had recently been killed in a car accident on the Rez. He no longer had a single living relative. His family had not been a traditional one so he had no spiritual ties and very little knowledge of his peoples' heritage. Devastated by his loss the young man had turned to alcohol and welcomed the resulting oblivion, and had ended up in jail. After his release, John Nighthawk had spent many hours with him trying to find a way that would help him find himself and give him a reason to live. Nothing worked. Finally, John had taken him to a blind Lakota elder named Weasel Bear. The sightless elder took it upon himself to teach the young Lakota the special pride he should feel at being a

Barry Brierley

Lakota. Repentant because of his past behavior, the young man listened to the old one's teachings. He was impressed with the blind elder's knowledge and his happiness in spite of his handicap. Eventually, the young Lakota began to respond. He found great peace whenever he and Weasel Bear made offerings on the sacred mountain, Bear Butte. The man's transition had its setbacks, however. He had great difficulty with the rigors and disciplines of reservation life. Especially trying were his encounters with racial prejudice. In time, the young man became reclusive and chose to spend most of his time alone. But the traditional values stuck and Nighthawk heard of no other problems with alcohol or the law, and his public life faded into obscurity. The deputy had forgotten about him ... until now when the pipe stone arrowhead reappeared.

Nighthawk stared at the smooth, sharp stone, remembering giving it to the troubled young man after his release from the county jail, hoping he would find some comfort in the ancient artifact. His adopted grandfather had been given the stone many decades ago by an Oglala medicine man, and he had passed it on to Nighthawk. He remembered Weasel Bear telling of the youth's new found pride in his heritage and of his love for his lost family.

The deputy smiled and leaned back against his pillows. He admired the subtle colors in the eagle plume and carefully stroked it while he thought about life and Redfoot's new compassion for his culture. Random ideas came at him from all sides. John wondered if Redfoot had found the eagle plume, or had acquired it in the time honored Lakota way by pulling it from the body of a live eagle. He liked to think that the latter was true. Unexpectedly, he felt himself break free from the white man's' world and become filled with spirituality. Suddenly, he wished he could shape-shift, become an eagle, and fly from the two story window. He would soar above the Sacred Hills and swoop effortlessly down through the valleys and canyons. Perhaps he would see a naked figure running wild and free across the Earth Mother's bountiful body. Yes! In his mind's eye, John could see Redfoot running free as the wind, happy in his solitary, unfettered life. In his heart, John Nighthawk soared above him on eagle's wings showing him the way.

Edges of Time

Barry Brierley

BOOK ONE

TIMELESS INTERLUDE
AT
WOUNDED KNEE

NATHANIAL STARR

B. BRIERLEY

STAR WATCHER

B. BRIERLEY

Barry Brierley

CHAPTER ONE

BLUCKSBURG MOUNTAIN ESTATES
AUGUST 21, 1998

The sheriff and his two deputies left their vehicles and approached the bottom of the winding wooden stairway. Sheriff Irwin Houge, a large man with a prominent beer-belly, decided to stop and admire the view of the distant prairie below. One of the deputies, who could have been the sheriff's clone, stopped and joined him.

Tuning out the other lawmen's conversation John Nighthawk ignored the view and knelt beside a scramble of footprints. While he studiously examined the bare ground near the stairs for any sign of recent visitors he felt a twinge of pain high in his left chest.

Involuntarily his right hand reached for the healing wound. It had been several months since the murder case up at Timberline. The wound he received from Frump's arrow had healed on the surface but John would still occasionally experience twinges of pain from damaged nerves.

Refocusing, John once again studied the jumble of footprints at the bottom of the stairway that led up to the log house they were about to investigate. He saw how the edges of the tracks had all dried and crumbled inward. The crumbling edges and the many insect trails across the prints testified that it had been at least several days, probably much longer, since the prints were made.

Hoage's loud, sarcastic basso interrupted John's concentration.

"Well, Little Beaver, find anythin'?"

Nighthawk looked up at the smirking sheriff and his sniggering sidekick. Keeping his face expressionless, he nodded.

"Maybe."

31

Ignoring their derisive laughter he climbed the twisting stairway of the beautiful log home. At the top he stopped and looked north over the rolling prairie. He wondered if on a clear day you could see all the way north to Eagle Butte on the Cheyenne River Sioux Reservation.

Far below and to his left was the geological wonder known as Bear Butte which has always been a spiritual place to the Sioux, Cheyenne and Mandan Nations. The Lakota call it 'Mato Paha' (sleeping bear mountain). They see the mountain as a place of visions and prayer and make a pilgrimage there at least once every year.

The rambling log home was perched on a pine-covered ridge located on the northern edge of the Black Hills. The house belonged to the artist Daniel Starr. Lately, he had become as famous for his reclusive life-style and his disappearance as he was for his realistically rendered historical paintings.

John glanced down at the sheriff and his brown-nosing flunky. The two men continued to chat as they slowly lumbered up the open stairway. He turned away disgusted. They gossip, he thought, like two old women who have no family and no respect for others. He mused briefly about Deputy Mix getting fired after Timberline and thinking how it was about time, but now he had to put up with this clone of Sheriff Hoage who used to stay in the office and take calls instead of working in the field.

Facing the ornately carved door, Nighthawk wondered what they would find inside. The man, Starr, had not been seen for months; he hadn't picked up his mail, nor had he been seen at the restaurant where he habitually dined on the weekends. The few friends he had in town hadn't seen him either. Their phone calls and messages had not been answered. Most importantly, his agent had called the sheriff's department from Los Angeles and was concerned about foul play. Starr was past due on a deadline for a painting, and according to the agent the artist was never late.

Deputy Nighthawk faced the wheezing arrival of his fellow officers and waited for the insult that he knew was forthcoming.

Red-faced from the exertion the sheriff leaned against the deck railing and glared at Nighthawk while he caught his breath. The clone, Deputy Triplet, kept glancing back and forth between the two. He had a little smile on his face while he waited to hear what witticism his beer-bellied hero was going to come up with next.

Edges of Time

"Well, 'Beaver'... ain't ya gonna knock on this Starr fella's tipi an' see if he's here?"

Nighthawk turned away before the sheriff could see the anger forming in his eyes. While knocking on the door he thought of the sheriff's referral to Starr's tipi which was an obvious implication that the artist was Indian. He had never met the man but had heard a rumor that the man was part Crow.

He hammered on the door one last time. When he turned the doorknob the heavy door swung inward. John started inside. The sheriff rudely squeezed his sweating bulk past him and bellowed.

"Hello ... anybody home?"

His voice echoed throughout the large house. Both deputies followed him inside and stared at the attractive, rustic decor that was evident everywhere.

The sheriff glanced over his shoulder.

"Ya know this here is just another wild goose chase. This rich asshole has done this shit before. Several years ago he disappeared for ... God knows how long. When he showed up again, he couldn't come up with any answers 'bout where he'd been. I was just a piss-ant deputy like you all, so I didn't get the whole story back then. But people were pissed-off 'bout it all."

The sheriff stared off into space, thinking. Suddenly turning, he glared at them.

"Are you two gonna stand an' gawk all day? Get your asses movin'!"

Leaving the sheriff with the difficult task of hiking his trousers up over his mountainous belly, the deputies split up.

Nighthawk moved slowly toward the back of the log house. He stared in awe at the many Native American artifacts and the beautiful leather furniture. One wall was covered with plaques and other awards. There were also photos of the missing artist taken with local and national dignitaries. He stopped. A breathtaking, realistic painting almost covered one wall. It was a rendering of a fight between two groups of horse-back Indians. In the far background, John could see soldiers dressed in blue scurrying about. He looked at the hair styles and war paint and realized that the Indian warriors were Sioux against many Crow and Shoshone. Moving closer, he read the inscription etched into the brass plate that

33

was screwed into the wooden frame: 'On The Rosebud' by Daniel Starr.

Shaking his head in admiration for the artist's work he moved on. Just before stepping outside, he discovered a cozy little alcove that must have been the den. The room was octagon in shape, and three fourths of its walls were windows with a great panoramic view of the Black Hills that lay to the south. Its interior was full of Western and Indian artifacts, antiques, and other décor; the only furniture was a wing-back leather chair with a reading lamp and an old roll-top oak desk. Perched on top of the desk's scarred surface amidst a stack of papers was a replica of a kerosene lantern that ran on electricity.

Moving into the room, Deputy Nighthawk felt uneasy. He sensed that something out of the ordinary had occurred within its walls. Except for the papers covering the writing surface of the desk, everything seemed to be in place, so he tended to rule out violence as being the object for his uneasiness. He moved straight to the desk and stared at the stack of papers that were in disarray across its surface. The first two papers were hand-written, done in the same hand. He picked up the top sheet, which was the shorter of the two missives, and began to read.

My tears come no more; they have dried and blown away. They are gone as surely as the years have flown swiftly by, leaving me a mere shadow of the man I once had been. I sit for hours and stare at her painting ... thinking of how it was between us, remembering.

Nighthawk carefully laid it down and picked up the other loose sheet of paper. Beneath the two handwritten sheets was a bound sheaf of typed papers that looked like a manuscript. Fascinated, he began to read the final handwritten paper.

I remember the first time I saw you; the sky was a bright cerulean blue, and the rolling land was covered with the gray-blue hues of a winter landscape. The green tree-line far behind you was almost black, grayed with distance. The varied colors of many blankets relieved the stark black and white of the snow-dappled ground. Splashes of orange, red, and yellow color erupted from the Hotchkiss cannons' mouths and joined the scarlet of the bloodied bodies. The vivid primaries added horror and realism to the scene. Your hair wasn't in braids and was flying about your head and face as you ran. The tattered red blanket you clutched to your body billowed out like a cape as you raced through the snow. All around you were the dead and dying. Defenseless women and children were mixed in with the orchestrated chaos of desperately fighting men. The man reaching for you with a gauntlet-clothed hand was dressed in the dark blue blouse of the U.S. Army, but he was wearing buckskin trousers tucked into beaded, knee-high moccasins. His face was still blank of features. Although you wore an expression of terror, you were still the most beautiful woman I had ever seen or created on canvas. I miss you terribly. Each remaining breath that I have will be shared with a thought of you and our time together. I remember it as though it were yesterday.

"Hey, Chief!"

Nighthawk bit down on his resentment and replied.

"Yeah?"

"Find anything?"

"No!"

"Sheriff says were leaving ... let's go!"

John stared at the papers for a moment and realized that he couldn't just leave ... at least, not yet. He returned the deputy's shout.

"Go ahead, I'll be right down!"

He listened. Hearing the deputy's boots out on the stairs, he hastened through the house until he could see the sheriff and deputy going down the long staircase, then covertly watched from the window as they traversed the last of the open steps and walked over to their vehicles. He hurried to the front door and started down the stairs. The sheriff and deputy were climbing into their Blazers when John stopped and yelled at them.

"Hey, Sheriff! I'll meet you back at the station; I forgot to lock the doors!"

Giving a disgusted wave of his hand, the sheriff and his clone drove off leaving a cloud of red dust hovering in the air. Nighthawk ran up the stairs and rushed back to the den; he felt he had to read more. Something deep within compelled him to find out more about the mystery man,

Barry Brierley

Daniel Starr. He picked up the manuscript and began to read.

CHAPTER TWO

I leaned back from the canvas and rinsed my brush. I couldn't take my eyes off the young Indian woman's face. I was captivated by my own creation, a virtual prisoner of my own design. It was the strangest thing that had ever happened to me in nearly thirty years as a professional artist.

For years I had been nationally recognized as one of the best 'realistic' painters of the Old West, my specialty being recreating actual historical moments out of the past. An example of my work can be seen hanging in the Cowboy Hall of Fame in Oklahoma City. It is an acrylic rendering of the Battle of the Little Big Horn which took place in June of 1876.

It was the painting that triggered an almost obsessive passion for me. Perhaps a portion of the passion came from the family secret. For years there had been hearsay that there was some Indian in our bloodline, either Sioux or Crow. Nevertheless, my artist's zeal focused on the history of the Sioux, including their language and culture. That was several years, dozens of paintings, and two books ago.

This, the most important chain of events in my life, began late in December of 1990. I had been following the local news and the progress of the Lakota Nation in their efforts to organize a ceremony called washigla (wiping of the tears) in memory of those Lakota who had died at Wounded Knee back in 1890. The final ceremony was to be the fourth annual horse-back ride starting at Sitting Bull's camp at Standing Rock. From there they would travel southwest to Big Foot's campsite on the Cheyenne River, and finally south to Wounded Knee, covering the same ground at the same time of year as Big Foot and his band of

Barry Brierley

Minneconjou had done that led to their fatal encounter with the revenge-minded Seventh Cavalry.

Perhaps it was my interest in the Big Foot Memorial Ride that was the catalyst for the events that followed, but I will probably never know. I do know that for the first time in my life I felt driven to do a painting. Never before in my life had I started a painting without doing research beforehand. This painting was very different. Strange as it may seem I started this painting without really knowing my subject matter. Even more bizarre was the fact that my painting, the actual applying of paint to canvas, was out of control. It was almost as though it was painting itself.

I remember as I once again sat down before the canvas, there was something especially compelling about the woman I had painted in the foreground. The woman was running for her life, her face was twisted with terror, and she was clearly beautiful. I forced my gaze away from her and looked at the rest of the painting. The action and blood-letting were more graphic than I usually painted. My hand trembled. Suddenly, I applied paint to my brush and began to wash in the blank features of the long-haired man who was reaching for the Indian woman. I couldn't believe what was happening. My hand was painting in the face without my brain controlling the strokes

Mesmerized, I watched closely as the features developed. My head began to spin as I realized what was happening. I stared in horror at the face of the long-haired soldier/scout. I felt myself begin to move. All at once, I was caught in some type of invisible vortex. I felt myself rise into the air and begin to spin. This was followed by a gut-twisting maneuver that allowed me to catch a final glimpse of the freshly painted face and somehow gave me the opportunity to gaze down upon my empty chair and contemplate my fading sanity. The face in the painting that was frozen in an expression of distress and determination was my own.

***

The noise was deafening: screams, gunshots, shouts of anger, and fear surrounded me. I felt the bite of the wind and the bitter

38

cold. In contrast, a bright sun was shining as though God wished to illuminate the horror for all to see and remember.

Beyond my outstretched hand the Lakota woman looked back at me, her running stride abruptly faltered. I immediately noticed a scar, or maybe it was a birth-mark, high on her right cheekbone. Curiously, it had five points like a star. The mark did nothing to mar the wild beauty of her youthful face; it merely enhanced it.

Fear seemed to leap from her eyes, prompting me to swiftly exclaim in Lakota.

"Wait! Do not be afraid, I will help you!"

Something wondrous then happened to erase the frightened look. I do not know what caused the change in her, but she slowed enough to enable me to grasp her arm. Instinct caused me to jerk her in another more westerly direction.

A nonstop assortment of gunshots, shrieks, and screams of the dying and bereaved filled the air. The stench of cordite, blood, and gun-smoke attacked my sense of smell. Combined, they became hedonistic messengers from hell. Everywhere I looked, I saw unarmed Indians, many of them dressed in ill-fitted white-man's clothing, wrestling with soldiers and trying desperately to pry their guns away.

The roar of cannons, the hum of bullets and the occasional hiss of an arrow added speed to our flight ... I ran through the murderous carnage and the struggling combatants with the speed of a man who knew where he was going. Unfortunately, I didn't have a clue where to go. I didn't even know where I was! While we ran, my gaze swept those who were fighting and those running for their lives. I was baffled. Never in all my years of research had I read about soldiers fighting Indians who, for the most part, were dressed in thread-barren clothing. I was shocked to see how poverty stricken and destitute they looked. After my educated eye picked up the color of an occasional ghost shirt, I realized that the desperately fighting Native Americans were dressed from a period toward the end of the last century and were probably Sioux.

Pushing aside my pointless, silent queries the most

immediate concern was for us to get out of the line of fire and away from the killing frenzy of the soldiers. Perhaps the experience I had during my early years with the Marines was what guided my instincts. Whatever it was, we broke clear of the fighting and ran west toward a distant ridge. We were crossing an open area when I saw a mounted trooper appear behind us. Miraculously he didn't immediately see us.

Foolishly I hesitated. Looking beyond him, the vivid colors slashed across the killing ground, and the clamor of the cannons and other gunfire was dazzling but also frightening. Somehow it all reminded me of an elaborate movie set. If it weren't for the winter cold and the warm reality of the strong, brown hand clenched in mine, I would probably have been waiting for an exhilarating sound track to kick in.

Upon spying us, the cavalryman spurred his horse into a gallop. Pistol held at the ready, he charged! By the time he closed the distance between us, we were still several strides away from the relative safety of the stunted pine trees. Steam and vapor exploded from the horse's mouth and nostrils with each labored breath. Pushing the woman behind me, I pointed directly at the horse and rider. My hand jerked in accompaniment with a loud, flat clap of sound, and the trooper threw his arms in the air. Blood sprayed from his chest as he toppled backwards off his big cavalry horse. He landed at my feet as his mount thundered by, splattering me with icy mud and slushy snow. I stared in horror at the man's bloody shirt and staring eyes. Steam rose from the scarlet maw in the center of his chest. Through the hazy veil of my frozen breath I gaped and stared at the smoking revolver clutched in my gauntlet clothed hand. As my mind worried over the mystery of the pistol's surprise appearance, I realized that I had just killed a man.

I felt a sharp tug on my sleeve. The Lakota woman was shouting at me.

"Come! We cannot stay here! The Bluecoats will kill us!"

Stumbling, I followed her lithe form into the trees that rimmed a twisting, dry gulch that still retained several patches of snow. Quickly, we covertly slipped into the gully. Having reclaimed the lead, I ran through the trees until suddenly, the Lakota woman's hand was violently wrenched from mine.

40

Edges of Time

Sliding to a stop I looked back.

A leering trooper had the woman around the waist. Having pulled her blanket aside he was ripping at her cotton dress with his other hand. She was fighting courageously but ineffectively. I felt myself become rigid with shock. Seeing my stare, the soldier grinned, then snarled, "Looks like she prefers my company, don't it, Buck?"

I stared frozen in horror as he threw her to the snow-dappled ground, striking her in the face with his gloved fist, ripping off her clothing with his other hand. I don't even remember moving across the ground that separated us. My leather-clad hand slapped away his bear-fur hat; I'd recall hearing his scream as my fingers grasped and twisted his greasy hair. Using every bit of my strength, I ripped him off her and flung him to the ground. He got as far as his knees when he stopped. Horror widened his milky blue eyes when the blue-black muzzle of my revolver bumped against his white forehead. I could smell his fear as it seeped through his pores. He became very still. He reeked of stale liquor and sweat. I wanted to kill him, but something was holding me back. From the corner of my eye, I saw the woman struggle to her feet and straighten her clothing. There was blood smeared across her face, the exact color of her blanket. Seeing the blood dripping from her nose, I nearly changed my mind. My thumb tightened on the hammer.

"Come. We must run away from here."

The soft, musical lilt of her voice made the metallic cocking of my pistol sound brittle and hard. I glanced her way as she grabbed some snow and held it to her bloodied nose. Pinned by the intensity of my gaze, the trooper began to tremble. He was pleading with his eyes. I jerked the muzzle away and he collapsed onto all fours. Drool oozed from his gaping mouth and darkened the snow.

Leaving him I grabbed the woman's hand as she grabbed her blanket and we ran swiftly up the gulch. Instinct made me stop and hide among some trees. We watched the opposite rim of the gully as nearby cavalrymen rode back and forth shooting down at dodging, running Lakota. Most of the Sioux ran while others tried to hide in the meager shelter of some scrub trees. We waited for the right moment and then ran deeper into the long, twisting gully.

We unexpectedly, burst into an open area surrounded by pine amidst patches of snow. We both stopped and stared in horror. Two soldiers were grappling with two Indian women; another Lakota woman was sprawled on the frozen ground, obviously dead. One of the troopers was on the ground viciously raping one of the two still alive. The woman being attacked was sobbing in anguish. The other soldier, standing nearby, was holding the reins of their horses and forcing the remaining woman to watch his comrade rape the other. She stared immobile as he used one hand to tear and pull at her drab clothing.

We were as of yet unseen and I felt my stomach heave as realization hit me. The son-of-a-bitch closest to me was about to rape a woman who was clearly a withered, old lady. In one lightning motion I pushed the young woman away from me, lifted the long, steel barrel, and cocked the revolver.

Too late, the trooper heard the hammer click as it was pulled to full cock. He glanced over his shoulder and his eyes widened in terror. I felt the solid kick of the recoil in my palm as the trooper spun away from the old woman. The horses tossed their heads and tried to pull free from his grasp. Shot in the throat he choked and staggered backwards. His free hand clutched at his throat, as though trying to staunch the steaming red flow of bright red blood. Frantically he clutched at the hole in his throat, while his face darkened as he hopelessly struggled for air. Making gurgling sounds, he toppled face-first into the snow. Still clasping his throat the stained fingers fluttered, then were still.

Beyond him, the rapist had clumsily gotten to his feet. His pants were rolled over the tops of his boots revealing legs that were as white as his frightened face. While he teetered to keep his balance and raise his pistol at the same time, the brave young woman beneath him reached up and clawed at his exposed groin, distracting him.

Before I could get a shot off, he changed his aim and shot the grasping Lakota woman in the chest.

My first bullet shattered his elbow, and encumbered by his rolled down pants he stumbled. The second round struck him in the center of the chest; he toppled backwards, dead before he hit the ground.

Rushing forward, I moved past the older woman. She still gazed in horror at the naked woman at her feet; steam was rising from the bloody hole in the woman's chest. I stared in disbelief at her resolve as she raised herself up and reached her arms out to one side. As I knelt by her side she hemorrhaged, shuddered and died. Her out-flung arms were pointed at a blanketed bundle lying in the snow where it had apparently been thrown. Curious, I started to rise.

"A-ah!"

The Lakota warning cry twisted me around in time to see the young woman, red blanket flapping, fly through the air and crash into a deadfall. The trooper, who I had spared earlier, had shoved her aside and he was crouched in the middle of our back-trail aiming his revolver at me. I dove to the side as his gun bellowed and belched fire and smoke. I heard the heavy bullet smack into flesh as my own pistol bucked and barked twice. I cocked and fired a third time, but the hammer fell on an empty chamber. The third shot wasn't necessary. The young woman's would-be-rapist, shot through the head, had crumpled to the ground as though his legs had suddenly vanished. The instant my gaze left the soldier, it found the body of the old one. I felt my throat close with sorrow. The old woman, who had apparently been frozen in place with shock, had been struck in the back by the bullet intended for me.

As I rose slowly to my feet, I saw that the old Lakota woman was dead; her thin, frail form looked child-like in her tattered dress and blanket. The near and far sound of gunfire was a reminder that time was short and I needed to get the young woman away from the killing and raping mania of the soldiers. At least, I thought, the cannons have stopped firing.

Instinctively, I turned back to the small, blanketed heap the dying woman had tried so desperately to reach. But before I could reach it, the young woman was there. Her breath formed a white halo around her head as she knelt in the snow and *carefully parted the blanket's edges.*

When I allowed my glance to slide toward the pair of spooked cavalry mounts, an unexpected sound erupted from the bundle. Startled, I foolishly raised my empty revolver. My gun hand fell to my side as I stared in wonder at the red, wrinkled face of a newborn baby.

CHAPTER THREE

While the young woman quickly looked the baby over for injury I kept on the lookout for soldiers. As I continued to watch and listen my thoughts turned to the baby's mother; apparently, the infant belonged to the Lakota woman who had just been raped and murdered. Stunned by the horror of it all, it took me an instant to realize that if we hadn't stumbled into that clearing when we did, the baby would also be dead. My gaze touched the crumpled forms of the other two deceased women. I felt a knot twist in my stomach. I knew without a doubt in my mind that the older of the two was the baby's grandmother. In a matter of minutes the two troopers who I had shot could have wiped out three generations. Suddenly, I stopped my vigilant lookout for danger. I felt the neck hairs rise on the back of my neck. Someone was watching me; I could feel the eyes.

I looked down and discovered that pair of the blackest, liveliest eyes ever created was minutely examining my face. The baby gurgled and flapped its little arms. The young woman's gaze fastened on me with the most happy, joyous expression I had ever seen. In the middle of all the death and horror, the young woman absolutely glowed with happiness. Hating to risk wiping the joy from her beautiful face, I said, "We must leave. And we must do so now."

While the woman finished bundling the baby, I slowly approached the dead troopers' horses, a bay and buckskin. The first soldier I had shot still had the reins clutched in a death grip. Just moments before, the horses had dragged the dead trooper across the clearing to the edge of the trees. They were still skittish because of the smell of fresh blood and the random gunfire.

The sudden discharges of pistol and rifle shots close at hand almost sent me diving for cover. Spooked again, the horses dragged the dead cavalryman even further away.

They watched me from the bogus security of the trees at the edge of the clearing. Rolling their eyes, they tossed their heads and snorted at my advance but still allowed me to get close enough to pry the reins free of the death grip. Leading the two mounts, I stopped walking and stared at my hands. Without thinking about it, I had wrapped the reins around my forearm and began to expertly reload my pistol. I had never fired a revolver in my life, yet alone reloaded one. All my handgun experience had been with automatics. My mind blanked as I struggled to cope with my escalating state of befuddlement.

Adding to my confusion, I noticed that I was wearing a gun-belt. The belt loops were nearly full of brass cartridges and a well-oiled leather holster was set up on my left hip in a cross-draw rig. A very large Bowie knife with some type of bone or ivory handle weighted down my right side. Even more disturbing, a sudden gust of wind-driven snow made me avert my face and I noticed how my long, black hair whipped in the wind.

I don't have long hair! If that wasn't frightening enough, I had pulled my gauntlets off and didn't recognize my hands. The ones staring back at me were several shades darker than my own and were more youthful!

My senses went into a stall and I probably would have stood there in the snow staring at the hands that were not mine forever, if the woman had not snapped me out of my trauma with her sharp, disturbing words.

"Crow warrior, you must help me get this baby away from here."

Her words were punctuated by a gunshot that was so loud, it sounded as though it could have been fired within our clearing. The horses tossed their heads and pulled hard on the reins. The nearby explosion blew away the shock of my disturbing new identity and reminded me of the very real danger lurking nearby.

Edges of Time

Shelving my mental anguish I holstered my revolver and returned my fingers to the gauntlet's warmth. Moving quickly I jerked repeatedly on the reins; simultaneously, my head was on a constant swivel so that we wouldn't be caught off guard. Hastily, I led the cavalry mounts toward the woman. The big horses followed me in a docile manner, yet the steam gushing rhythmically from their nostrils gave them the unworldly appearance of a pair of earth-colored dragons.

In mere seconds I was at the young woman's side. Without further ado, she thrust the bundled baby into my arms and relieved me of one of the horses. She grasped the bay's bridle with one hand and unbuckled the belly girth with the other. In almost a single motion the Lakota woman pulled the saddle off, grabbed a handful of long mane, and leaped upon the reddish brown horse's shaggy back. Her ebony eyes searched my face as she held out her arms for the baby. Our eyes met and she captivated my soul with the gift of a dazzling smile. As she took the squirming bundle, she asked, "Why do you have white eyes, Crow? Are you part wasichu (white man)?"

Besides the smile, her reference to my blue eyes had surprised me, causing my response to her second question to be an open-mouthed nod like that of a love-sick school boy. Embarrassed by my childish handling of the situation, I quickly leaped on the back of the leggy buckskin. Having regained my manly equilibrium, I spun my horse and with misplaced confidence again faced the beautiful Lakota woman.

"What is your name? I am called Starr."

As I made ready to ride and perhaps die for a complete stranger, her eyes widened and then locked with mine. Another smile touched her lips.

"Star Watcher."

Barry Brierley

CHAPTER FOUR

I could hear the troopers up on the rim of the dry wash shouting and calling to each other. A drum-roll of gunfire that came from the edges of the gulch encouraged me to pray that our horses' hooves remained quiet. Confused and disoriented by it all, I relinquished my lead and followed close behind Star Watcher as we rode east, back toward the main killing ground. Since the baby had entered the picture, I had decided that it would be wise to follow Star Watcher's lead. Star's first concern was for the infant. She had informed me that it was a boy. She also said that the Lakota needed all the warriors they could get, so before she could leave the Bluecoat's killing ground, a wet nurse must be found for the newborn.

Without the slightest hesitation I rode with her back into the killing zone where I was more than likely already a wanted man for the soldiers I had shot. The risk could not be avoided. There was no possible way that I would let her go back alone, unprotected.

Having asked young Star Watcher where we were geographically and which band of Lakota she was from earned me a very puzzled look. Thinking fast, I made up a story that explained my ignorance and it seemed to satisfy her, at least for the moment.

She told me that she was an Ogallala from Pine Ridge and had been visiting some Minneconjou friends in the North when news of Sitting Bull's murder had reached them at Cherry Creek.

49

Fearing reprisals, their chief, Big Foot, of the Minneconjou decided to unite with Red Cloud at Pine Ridge. She went on to say that the wasichu soldiers had stopped her band on their way south to join the Ogallala.

This struck a chord in my memory. I knew there was another historic event connected to Sitting Bull's death but for the life of me I couldn't name it.

But it was the rest of her answer that had me dizzy and my stomach twisted into major-sized knots ... she told me that the Bluecoats had then made Chief Big Foot have his people camp near Wounded Knee Creek.

Wounded Knee! Just the name was enough to give me goose bumps. I briefly wondered if my interest in the Lakota Nation's recent ceremony, Washigla (Wiping of the Tears), had anything to do with my predicament. I instantly stopped my new train of thought, hopefully without endangering my mental health any further. While desperately trying to keep a grip on my sanity, I vividly remembered reading about the slaughter that took place on December 29, 1890. Most of all, I remembered a quote from Bury My Heart at Wounded Knee *by Dee Brown: 'One estimate placed the final total of dead at very nearly three-hundred of the original three-hundred and fifty men, women, and children. The soldiers lost twenty-five dead and thirty-nine wounded, most of them struck by their own bullets or shrapnel.'*

I remembered having done a small amount of research for a painting about Wounded Knee but had decided that it was too depressing, and the available information was too sketchy.

For the moment, painting was the farthest thing from my mind. I had become so used to the constant sound of gunfire that the danger had become almost incidental. It wasn't until a bullet whipped by my ear like an enraged hornet that I again became aware of my frail mortality.

Pulling the buckskin to a stone and mud flying halt, I shouted a warning at Star Watcher and spun my horse in a circle as I looked for the sniper. I spotted him at once ... a Bluecoat crouched in a patch of snow! He must have thought that my blue cavalry blouse was captured goods. I aimed the buckskin at him and viciously pounded his ribs with my moccasined heels. The big, yellow horse squatted and lunged forward. He was into a full gallop within three strides. The trooper was crouched halfway up the north side of the gulch, frantically trying to reload his rifle and watch my thunderous approach at the same time. As the distance between us rapidly shortened, pulsating bursts of white vapor came from the buckskin's flaring nostrils and joined the flying clods kicked up by his driving hooves.

When he dropped his cartridge, the blood left the soldier's face, realizing that he would not have enough time to reload. The fear in his youthful eyes removed my finger and thumb from the revolver's trigger and hammer. As the buckskin carried me past the terrified youngster, my pistol's long, blue barrel swung in a short, controlled arc and struck his head a glancing blow. He staggered then fell to the cold ground unconscious. I wheeled the big horse and galloped toward the waiting Star Watcher. Immediately after joining her, a sudden flurry of gunshots came from up ahead. We quieted our mounts and carefully wove our way through the stunted pine.

Breaking clear of the trees and brush, we forced our horses up the northern side of the gulch near some gnarled pine and looked to the east and north for danger. The scene that awaited us was heartbreaking. Across the winter plain were the dark, bloody forms of dead Sioux who hadn't made it to the relative cover of the gulch. Beyond the scattered bodies, a group of Lakota women and children were huddled beneath a clay bank. Several cavalrymen were pointing their guns at them. I saw the pale blobs of the soldiers' faces as they all abruptly faced to the right. Following their line of sight, I felt a sudden jolt in my solar plexus. I was staring at another scene right out of the pages of history.

A band of about twenty horse-backed warriors had appeared on a low ridge. These Indians were very different in appearance from those I had seen die in the snow and mud. They looked like warriors out of the past, painted for war and bristling with assorted weapons. As we silently watched, their brave hearts were about to exchange the tragic day's raw heartache for a brief example of unselfish heroism.

As one, they raised the weapons overhead and began to sing.

Barry Brierley

I couldn't make out all the Sioux words but I did hear, "A thunder being nation I am!" This was repeated several times followed by a loud, "Hokahey!" Swinging their quirts and brandishing their weapons, they swept down off the ridge and charged the soldiers. As they rode, they chanted, "You shall live! You shall live!"

The wild riding Sioux were such a spectacular sight that my breathing faltered, and I was swept away by the courage and beauty of the moment. It wasn't until then that I realized that the horse-backed Indians had to have come from the reservation on Pine Ridge. Big Foot's people had their horses already taken away before the killing.

The cavalrymen fired repeatedly at the oncoming Sioux but failed to slow their charge. Although they had fired several rounds, they didn't appear to hit anyone. As the Lakota closed with the soldiers, panic swept through the blue ranks. Losing their nerve the soldiers ran away to the east before the two groups could come together.

While the jubilant Lakota celebrated the soldiers' retreat, I thought it a good time to show ourselves. For some reason, Star Watcher hesitated to join the Pine Ridge Lakota. Perhaps it was because of me, not knowing what kind of reception I would receive.

We watched as the rescuers gathered the women and children and pointed them in a north-westerly direction. When they had the small group of survivors well on their way toward safety, they rode back toward us. Situated as we were beside a small clump of pine, I don't believe they saw us. They rode by but did not, to my knowledge, look in our direction.

The lead warrior's face was painted red and he was wearing a single eagle feather in his hair. There were also eagle feathers fastened to the wrists, elbows, and shoulders of his colorful ghost dancers' shirt.

Star Watcher glanced my way and our eyes met. Her eyes glittered like obsidian; they bewitched me with their intensity. Enthralled, I imagined that her eyes emitted an invisible matter that entered my skull and saturated my brain with the very essence of her being. I returned her consuming look with what I hoped was a look of equal passion. Neither of us smiled. Perhaps it was then that our souls entwined and we became one. To this day, I have no explanation for the chemistry that took place between us. It was such an instant, cohesive blend that was, and still is, totally inexplicable.

With Star Watcher still in the lead, we started moving our horses in the general direction of the warriors. Suddenly, a larger group of soldiers emerged from behind a low hill in the east and began firing at the Sioux warriors. It looked like the cavalrymen the Sioux had chased away had found some help. Before Star Watcher and I were able to make a decision as to what we should do, the leader of the Lakota waved his men to stay put and encouraged his horse, a red sorrel, into a full gallop. I stared in awe as he single-handedly charged the soldiers!

The cavalrymen had dismounted and were lying down to steady their aim when they fired their weapons. As we watched, the hard-riding Lakota leader thrust what looked like a slender bow out in front of him like a shield. Arm straight he grasped it in one hand, knuckles up. The man had no arrows for his bow; he was unarmed! He rode straight at the soldiers as though the bow were magic and would ward off their bullets. Apparently it did, because he rode right through their powder smoke and was in among the dismounted cavalrymen who continued to shoot at him. He swiftly spun his golden horse and rode back the way he had come. As far as I could tell, he didn't get a scratch. When their leader returned unharmed, the Lakota began to hoot and holler and jeer at the soldiers. Discouraged, the soldiers mounted up and rode off in search of easier prey. The Lakota continued to celebrate until they heard more gunfire coming from the west. Led by the red-faced warrior, the party of Sioux rode down into the gulch looking for others in need.

Clutching the wrapped baby to her breast, Star Watcher grinned at me and kicked her bay into a gallop. Sensing that she was going to confront the Lakota, I felt worms of fear squirm in my belly as we followed the Sioux warriors into the gully. I became more than a little concerned about my blue cavalryman coat becoming an Indian target.

After just a few abrupt twists and turns we unexpectedly caught up with the small band. We burst into a large clearing and had to pull our horses to an immediate stop. The Sioux had their backs to us and were staring at the aftermath of what must have been an amazing feat of courage. The warriors were spread out in a line and were staring silently at two young Lakota boys, armed with bows and arrows. The boys were standing in a natural shallow depression. It was obviously the place where they had made their stand. Scattered around the two small youths were the bodies of several soldiers, whom they had killed while defending themselves and their fleeing relatives. It was a classic example of a military rear action delaying maneuver.

Unexpectedly, the haunting, guttural growl of the Lakota courage cry came from the line of horseback warriors.

"Hugn ... hugn ... hugn."

The two boys smiled shyly and touched their left brows in respect. Approximately half the band swarmed down on the boys, engulfing them with praise and embraces.

My horse snorted and shied sideways. I looked down and saw a crooked stick that he had probably thought was a snake.

"Heyah (No)!"

The alarm in Star Watcher's voice made me bring my head up. I found myself staring into the muzzles of several rifles and at the business ends of numerous arrows. I very slowly raised my arms.

Star Watcher began speaking in such a rapid, forceful Lakota that I was only able to identify a word or two of her whole desperate tirade. As she finished, a pall of silence settled over the clearing except for some distant gunfire. My eyes were locked with the leader of the band. And it wasn't an easy task. I found that it was very disconcerting to try to stare down someone who has his entire face painted red.

The leader broke our eye-lock and turned back toward the boys and the warriors with them. As he spoke to them, I noticed that the entire back of his brightly painted shirt was covered with the design of a stylized spotted eagle with wings outstretched. He abruptly reined his pony around so that he was again facing us. For the first time I noticed that vivid, red lightning bolts were painted on his shirt's front.

Star Watcher moved her bay closer to me and to show her trust, handed me the baby as she turned back toward the Lakota.

Edges of Time

She said, "Hear me, Black Elk, Holy Man of the Ogallala; this man is a friend of the Lakota. Twice he has saved my life, and he has rescued this baby from two murdering soldiers."

Star Watcher said more, but I wasn't hearing her words. The name Black Elk was still burning its way through my skull and putting its brand on my brain. Even the threatening moves made by some when Star Watcher handed me the baby couldn't diminish my awe. I could not believe that I was staring at the man who was the most famous Native American of American literature.

At the end of her appeal I was stunned to hear her say that I had killed five troopers during the fight. Not realizing that there had been that many, I was surprised at my lack of shame.

Black Elk interrupted my thoughts when he heel-thumped his pony's ribs and moved closer. Behind the vermilion paint, I saw the face of a man who probably wasn't even thirty years of age. My admiration increased in leaps and bounds. For a man of his tender years to have the charisma and leadership to command the respect that I had just witnessed was amazing. Also memorable was the intelligence and compassion that radiated from his black eyes. With silent pride he showed the confidence of a man who was certain of his rightful place in the universe; it practically oozed from his pores.

"Why are you doing this, Crow Bluecoat?"

The Holy Man's voice startled me out of my ruminating. Thinking carefully, I handed the baby back to Star Watcher and unbuttoned my blouse. I removed my beaded, gauntlet gloves. I then savagely pulled the cavalry blouse off and threw it into the snow. Although the sun was shining the cold air instantly attacked my upper body with fingers of ice. Steam passed through the thin cotton shirt that I wore beneath the army blouse. While my brain scrambled to come up with the right thing to say, I pretended to ignore the cold and slowly put my gauntlets back on. Softly, I spoke in lyrical Lakota.

"My heart is on the ground. My people continue to follow the selfish ways of the wasichus. I thought that by scouting for the Bluecoats, perhaps I would be able to do some good for myself

Barry Brierley

and for my people. I see now that this was not possible. These Bluecoats were looking for revenge for the Greasy Grass (Little Big Horn). My mother was a Crow; my father is white. In spite of his white skin, he has always been on the side of the Indian. I was raised not to fight for a flag ... or for the color of a man's skin ... or the name of his tribe. I was taught to do what is right. I do not kill women or children, nor do I scout for anyone who does. That is all I have to say."

I became frightened again but not a fear of physical pain or death. At that moment my concern was again focused on my mental health. Not all of those words that spilled out of my mouth with such certainty were my own! At the time I wasn't even aware of who I was supposed to be, not to mention the mystery of my parents' identities.

Seeing a glint of friendship and a flicker of trust in Black Elk's eyes encouraged me to make a silent vow; above all else I must get Star and the infant to a place of safety.

Black Elk gave me a thin smile. I saw the sadness that lurked behind his eyes. Instinctively, I knew that the sadness had nothing to do with me or Star Watcher but was in fact a lament for his people on this day of infamy.

As Black Elk became occupied with adjusting the blanket and robe across his legs, I noticed that the gunfire had all but stopped. He then pulled his blanket free, caught my eye, and handed it to me. When I took the red and black blanket from him, the Holy Man gestured for me to wear it. Wrapping its warmth around me, Black Elk said, "Waste. (Good)."

The young medicine man raised his right hand to shoulder level and then kept the index and middle finger extended upwards as he brought his hand up beside his face. It was the Plains Indian hand sign meaning friend.

A renewed burst of gunfire began turning Lakota heads and making for nervous Indian ponies. Black Elk gestured and spoke quickly and about half the band moved off into the gulch to look for survivors. Before leaving, one of the warriors leaned from his pony and scooped my army blouse from the ground, and handed it to me.

Having dispatched his warriors to investigate, Black Elk ignored the shooting and spoke to me again.

Edges of Time

"We are in your debt, Warrior. How are you called among the wasichus?"

Not knowing what else to say, I replied, "I am called Starr."

The youthful medicine man's eyes widened and his gaze rested on Star Watcher for an instant. There was a twinkle in his eye as he held out his arms for the baby. He took the boy child in his arms as gently as a woman. The twinkle was still there as he glanced at both of us and remarked, "With your name Starr and her name Star Watcher, I think there is much medicine here. I think perhaps Wakan Tanka is trying to tell you something."

I threw a glance at Star Watcher at exactly the same time she looked at me. Our eyes met and we both quickly turned away.

Black Elk and a few of the warriors laughed aloud. The Ogallala became serious and faced Star Watcher as he said, "These are terrible times for our people. We cannot be sure how they will react to this man. Take this Crow warrior away from here where he will be safe. I will find someone to care for the infant. Whenever it is safe to do so, come to me and I will take you to the child. I have already sent some of the people to hide in the O-onagazhee in the Badlands."

Star Watcher nodded her approval, and then swiftly explained to me that the O-onagazhee was a sheltering place, an elevated plateau that was virtually inaccessible to enemies.

Turning from me, she urged the bay in alongside Black Elk's pony where she spent a moment being certain that the baby boy was fully protected from the cold.

Star Watcher's voice was melodious as she thanked the medicine man, "Le mita pila (many thanks), Black Elk. We will go now."

With a final nod and raised hand, Black Elk and his warriors rode down into the dry gulch. Black Elk cradled the baby safely in
his arms as though he'd been doing so all his life.

The shooting had again become very sporadic, but I could still see soldiers here and there. I pulled the blanket tighter around my upper body and looked in all directions to be sure of our immediate safety. I glanced at Star Watcher. The young

Lakota woman was staring at me. She had a look in her eyes that I couldn't fathom.

"Crow Man. You are a very brave and fierce warrior. I owe you my life and that of the baby. Come with me and I will take you to a place that is known by only a few. It will be the perfect place to hide. As you know, the Bluecoats will now be hunting you, also."

Star Watcher smiled and added, "Hopo. (Let's go)."

She pointed her bay northwest, then with a glance over her shoulder at me, she urged him into a canter.

Keeping an eye out for soldiers, I followed. Without knowing it, I was riding toward the happiest interlude in my life. I would be spending it with the one woman in my life for whom my love would be timeless.

CHAPTER FIVE

We were not challenged as we left the killing place. Far to the east I saw soldiers both on horse-back and on foot. Many of the dead and wounded were in piles among the tipis or scattered over the stark terrain, the colorless bundles of the dead too numerous to count. In the distance their formless bodies gave the appearance of a handful of raisins spilled across a rumpled and stained table-cloth. Depressed by the horrible scene I looked away and concentrated on watching out for trouble of a more immediate nature.

Following Star Watcher's lead, we circled back and rode until we were well past the so called battlefield. After riding several miles we crossed a wagon road and entered a line of scrub pine that did little to conceal us. When the cover began to thin even more, we stopped and stayed hidden among the fragrant pine.

Far in the distance I could see a few buildings. I suspected it was the Pine Ridge Agency. I seem to remember from research that it was approximately three or four miles from Wounded Knee Creek.

After a more intense scrutiny I could make out a flurry of activity surrounding them. When I glanced at Star Watcher, her face was a picture of dismay.

"What is wrong?" I asked.

She appeared nervous and confused.

"I do not know why I came here. It is too dangerous. We will need food and supplies where we are going and without thinking I just naturally came to the trader's store."

As she backed her big horse further into the trees, she added,

Barry Brierley

"It is too dangerous for you; we must find another way."

"Wait."

As I grabbed her mount's bridle I was calculating the danger potential.

"Where else can we go for supplies? Can we not hunt for food?"

She shook her head in dismay.

"The place we are going is in the Badlands. Many of the people are already near there; there will not be enough game for everyone. Come, I will think of a place."

A strange feeling interrupted my thought process. Somehow, I knew that if I were to take the risk and brazenly walk into the turmoil of activity around the store, everything would be all right, and I would be able to pull it off. Something was telling me that it was essential I take that chance. Perhaps I would learn more about who I am, or at least who I am supposed to be.

I released the bay's bridle and met Star Watcher's troubled look with a smile and a voice filled with bogus confidence.

"Heyah. It will be all right. I will ride in and be out so fast they will not see me. I will become a wanagi (spirit) and fly away like the wind."

My grin caused the doubt in her eyes to diminish. I quickly threw the red blanket across my legs and put the cavalry blouse back on. Relishing the added warmth of the wool, I buckled my knife and holstered my revolver over the shirt's tails. Swiftly I searched my pockets until I found a small, heavy, beaded pouch that gave off a musical jingle. Not having a clue how much items would cost, I didn't bother looking inside the pouch. One thing certain, I thought, I'm not going to look and show my ignorance in front of her. I knew that I had already been acting pretty strange. No sense in letting her think that I'm such a fool that I don't know how much money I have.

"Will you wait here for me?"

Star smiled softly and nodded yes to my inane question. I tore my eyes away from her allure and urged the buckskin into a trot. Leaving the trees behind, the cavalry mount moved into a canter and carried me onto the open ground that paralleled the road. I felt anxiety climb my spine and firmly lodge itself in a slot in my brain labeled 'pointless worry.' With my eyes hidden in the shadow beneath the wide brim of my hat, I watched the come and go of Bluecoats around the buildings.

Between me and the larger building I saw a stone-walled well. Some soldiers were just leaving it as I approached. Beyond them I saw a group of men who, in spite of the chill in the air, caused sweat to form a light sheen across my face. They had long hair and dark faces but were wearing dark blue soldier blouses and an assortment of fur and felt hats. *They have to be scouts, or maybe interpreters,* I thought. *Does my straight brimmed, high-crowned hat set me apart from them? Who in God's name am I supposed to be?* My questions were becoming flagellant and paranoid.

My silent query went unanswered as the buckskin carried me unerringly to the stone well. A cluster of soldiers standing nearby gave me the eye. Nerves tingling, I ignored them and stepped from the saddle. From the shadow of my hat brim I saw several civilians as well as army officers hanging around, many of whom were either going in or coming out of the smaller of the two buildings, which was made of logs. *Must be a telegraph or post office,* I mused.

Keeping a cautious, covert eye on all the activity, I dropped the wooden bucket into the cistern. The hollow, distant sound of the splash was somehow soothing to my frayed nerves. I cranked the wooden pulley and wound up the rope until the brimming bucket appeared. I hefted it up onto the sandstone lip of the wall. My mouth was dry with fear; it seemed like I would drink forever. When finished, I removed my fringed gauntlets and splashed water onto my face. I was immediately sorry. Although the winter day had become unseasonably mild, I forgot that it was still too cold for such activity. The shock of the cold water, however, did help to wash away my doubts and reestablish my confidence.

After the buckskin had his fill, I dropped the bucket back into the well. As I turned away and began to lead my horse toward the front of the store, an angry shout spun me around.

"Hey! Gawd-damn it. What'n the hell ya think yer doing?"

I stopped. My heart was in my throat as I watched a short,

burly soldier, wearing corporal stripes on his blue blouse, swagger toward me.

"Damn it! How many times I gotta tell you mutts to leave the bucket up on the wall?"

I fought down my anger and struggled to find the key that would unlock the cerebral solution to do and say the right thing. I quickly averted my eyes so that the red-faced corporal wouldn't see the anger in them.

I mumbled, "I am new here. I was not told."

"You, fer gawd-damned sure, are bein' told now, Bucko!"

Still averting my eyes I nodded and moved back to the well. I felt the hatred ooze from the man's gaze and it was not a pleasant feeling. It was my introduction to a first-hand experience with racial prejudice ... and I didn't like it.

I cranked the bucket back and left it setting on the wall. Still leading my horse, I ignored some hostile white stares and walked the short distance to the clapboard building, half expecting to hear the corporal's challenging shout.

In front of the store, soldiers in blue were talking in pairs and small groups; civilians dressed in tweed suits and overcoats had formed noisy little clusters full of whoops of laughter and strange conversations. While tying the buckskin to the hitching rail, I overheard one civilian fellow say something that didn't make any sense.

"... so I said to the Nancy Boy, I'll be the huckleberry to your persimmon if you will imbibe one more smile before parting."

The listeners all laughed heartily. I mentally shook my head at the confusion of it all and moved toward the steps leading up to the porch of the trader's store.

"Nathanial!"

Somehow I knew that voice was addressing me. Fear for Star Watcher's safety pushed me forward; I started up the steps.

"Nathanial Starr!"

I stopped. The man's use of my surname, Starr, tolled like a bell inside my head. Feigning a casualness that was pure fiction, I turned to face my destiny. It was at that moment that the true horror of my predicament hit me. My breath caught in my throat as the reality hit home ... I was reliving one of my ancestor's lives! Thinking of my dark skin and long black hair, I began to comprehend that the family 'rumor' was in truth, fact.

An Indian wearing an army blouse and a big hat congruent to mine stepped away from a cluster of similarly dressed Indians. He was smiling at me. Because of a missing front tooth and flattened nose, his smile was ludicrous.

"Nathan, where have you been? We sure could've used you to help us track a traitor."

I felt my throat close with dread and my heart turn to ice. The smiling Indian continued to speak as he walked toward me. It wasn't what he said that was so frightening ... it was the fact that I understood every word! The man was speaking in a different language, probably Crow. Then to my horror I knew he was Crow, because I knew his name. He was called John Crow by the soldiers.

Luckily I mustered up a quick reply.

"I was chasing some throat-cutters (Sioux) to the south"

My head began to spin. Time stood still as my mind recoiled at the comprehension that not only did I understand Crow, I spoke it!   "Aah," he grunted.

The Crow stopped at the bottom of the steps. A gust of wind bent the brim of his hat and stirred the scout's long, black hair. Something in my perception of the man told me that he couldn't be trusted. What he said next snapped me out of my dazed state and made me more alert.

"It don't matter. One of the white-eyes saw an Indian wearing a soldier shirt shoot a horse soldier. He then ran toward the gully with one of the Lakota women."

The older scout peered deeply into my eyes before he lifted a gloved hand and turned away. Somehow, I knew that this man was not a friend and was capable of committing heinous crimes. He threw a parting, narrow-eyed glance over his shoulder as he said, "Of course, the blue soldier didn't know which scout or interpreter it was since we all look alike to them."

It wasn't very incriminating news but was enough to frighten me. Just knowing that I had been seen was bad enough.

I nodded, forced a smile, and then took the remaining steps two at a time. In spite of the late afternoon chill in the air, a fresh

Barry Brierley

patina of sweat covered my body. I stopped at the doorway and tried to regain my composure before entering the store. I leaned against the door frame and faked a coughing fit while I secretly peered through the glass window.

A pair of civilians hovered near the warmth of a pot-bellied stove that was situated in the middle of the store's large room. A uniformed, mustached officer wearing a wide-brimmed hat and, of all things, a scarf, was standing nearby. The bright, multi-colored woolen cloth was wrapped around his neck in a very non-military fashion. He was talking to a man who was either the clerk or owner. They were standing next to a broad counter that covered three of the four walls.

My gaze rapidly scanned the large room. Just about everything imaginable was either hanging from the walls and ceiling or was stacked on the counters and dumped into open wooden barrels.

I felt a trickle of sweat slide down my ribs as I straightened, opened the door and stepped inside. All four faces turned toward me as I stepped into the overheated atmosphere of the store. I stopped. They all stared at me. My heart began to hammer in triple-time.

"Shut the damn door, Buck. Where were ya born ... in a tent or what?"

The smart-ass remark came from one of the civilians, a leering middle-aged man sporting a beard, a bowler hat, and a malicious gleam in his eye. His wit set off a hoot of laughter from his side-kick and pulled a sneering grin from the clerk. The officer simply stared; it appeared he wasn't inclined to participate in civilian banter.

Fear kept me from being affected by the remark. I stepped to the door and carefully shut it. I thought of the fifty-odd men just outside that same door; each of them would enjoy the opportunity to hang me from the nearest tree limb if they knew who I was and what I had done. I avoided eye contact with the men in the store and began to collect the needed items.

"You there."

The clerk was extending a flour sack toward me while trying not to sneer with distaste. Averting my eyes, I took his offering, grunted an unintelligible response, and stepped away. I dropped

64

a box of sulfur matches and a tin of corned beef into the bag and moved on to some open barrels.

I found a barrel of what looked like salted pork. Later, I was sorry that I took some. God only knew what it really was; it left such an after taste. I remember vowing to go hungry rather than chance it a second time. I added some bacon and canned peaches, a tin of apple butter, and a small sack of wheat flour. Dried fruit was strung on strings and hung from the rafters in multi-colored groups. After selecting some dried apples and apricots I moved on. A stack of tablets and a cup full of pencils stopped me in my tracks. Being the artist I was, I couldn't resist. After grabbing several of each I stuffed them into the bag, along with some canned beans and a pair of small loaves of what looked like corn bread. Not having any idea how long we had to hole up, I finally decided that I had enough.

While concentrating on getting what we needed, I hadn't noticed how quiet it had become. Every eye in the room was watching me except for the army officer. He was busy scanning through a magazine or catalogue. I fought down the tremors rising inside of me and stepped to the counter. The clerk snatched the bag and dumped its contents onto the counter. My back was to the men by the stove, but I sensed one of them move in close. His breath was warm on my ear as he reached down across me and snagged one of the tablets out of the pile and said, "What you want paper 'n pen for? Am I going to have to worry about my job as correspondent with the Chicago Tribune?"

Everyone laughed.

The other reporter leered encouragement.

"Eh, Buck ... is that how it is?"

I faced the man. Alarmed by my unexpected move, he quickly stepped back. His small pointed mustache was nearly twitching, as he slipped his hand under his suit-coat.

Knowing that his hand was on a gun, I pointed at the tablet and pencils and said, "I learn to write white talk on these thin, talking skins."

Everyone tittered at my expense. Looking relieved, the newspaperman stepped forward again. Just as the man with the

Barry Brierley

twitchy moustache was about to speak again, help arrived from an unexpected source.

The soldier, a captain with a snide look and a nasty tone of voice for the reporter, interrupted.

"Do you people realize that by ridiculing this man, you are in fact making a mockery of the United States Army?"

Blinking the sweat out of my eyes I pretended to ignore the officer's lecture, pulled out my bag of coins, and swiftly dumped them on the counter. The sound of coins on the wooden counter captured the clerk's immediate attention. Not having any idea of the cost I gestured to the man to take what he needed for payment. A sly look passed over his features and then just as quickly was gone. Oh shit, I thought, he's going to cheat me and there isn't a damn thing I can do about it. The greedy clerk began to tabulate my provisions.

I listened with half an ear to the reporter's whining voice as he presented his redneck rebuttal to the captain.

"What I don't understand, Captain ... is this. What in the hell's the difference between the savages you killed today ... and this greasy devil standing right here?"

'This one here works for the army. He's either Crow or Shoshone... not Sioux. They do what we tell 'em to; the Sioux don't. It's as simple as that."

Not daring to create a disturbance, I watched helplessly as the man scooped up several silver dollars and a few small gold coins. The small ones had FIVE D. embossed on them. I also saw two that were bigger that had TEN D. embossed beneath an eagle with spread wings and crest on his chest with a banner with 'In God We Trust' flying overhead.

Suddenly, I was forcefully shoved aside! The officer's white gauntlet covered hand was clamped onto the clerk's wrist, and his sweeping mustache was inches from the man's pasty face as he grated through his teeth, "Damn you, Clem! It's people like you cheating these Indians that brings about all our problems."

"Make damn sure you count it out right this time!"

The captain let go of the clerk's arm and angrily gestured at the money.

Clem's hands shook as he put back nearly all of the gold coins.

66

Edges of Time

As the officer made his final point, it was clear to me that things haven't really changed that much in a hundred years.

"They would probably be happy just lying around eating government beef if it wasn't for the likes of you, cheating them every chance you get."

After grabbing the rest of my coins I nodded my thanks to the officer. A glint formed in the captain's green eyes as he quietly returned my acknowledgment. I pointedly ignored the other men as I collected my bag and moved to the door. I could feel their eyes on me as I slipped outside and faced a cloudy sky with a new chill in the air.

Much of the activity around the buildings had diminished, and many of the soldiers were gone. I moved swiftly to the buckskin and tied the bag of supplies to the saddle. While doing so I noticed that the Indian scouts had also left. Feeling a little more safe, I relaxed and took my time adjusting the bulging pack.

I couldn't seem to shake free of the captain's words. After being rudely reminded for a second time of the fact that I had Indian blood, it made me much more aware of the plight of the Native American. It made me think of something that I had been conscious of all my life but had never really addressed: how a basically good people refuse to accept that some Native Americans cannot be happy living under the same culture and values as white people. It seemed to me that in most cases all the Indian ever wanted was to live his life the way he had always done and to do so, on his own land.

I climbed down from my mental soapbox and stepped up into the saddle. The buckskin read my mind and headed west from where we had come. The sun was noticeably absent. I glanced at the sunless, overcast sky and hoped that Star Watcher's refuge was both warm and safe.

As the buckskin cantered past the stone well, I noticed that someone else hadn't returned the bucket to the top of the wall. My voice had a bitter edge to it as I muttered aloud.

"Probably some cocky little mutt wearing corporal stripes left it down in the water."

Barry Brierley

CHAPTER SIX

As the buckskin carried me near the spot where I had last seen Star Watcher, I became nervous. I almost felt like a starry-eyed school boy again. Not only did I miss her, I longed for the sight of her. Her wild, unconventional beauty took my breath away in a manner that a woman's looks had never done before.

A gust of wind tugged at the brim of my hat and reminded me of the changing weather. I took the blanket Black Elk had given me and draped it over my shoulders. The broad sky had become a gun-metal gray. Clouds began to move as turbulence stirred the atmosphere into an upheaval of pending violence. Where is she? I worried. An unexpected vision of rape and murder interrupted my thoughts and filled me with unwarranted fear.

"Washtay (Greetings), Crow warrior."

Following close behind her soft words, Star emerged from the shadows of a copse of stunted pine. She was seated on the bay looking cheerful in spite of the savagery of the day. I realized then and there that it would take an enormous amount of personal calamity to break her spirit.

Relief that she was safe left me weak and speechless. All I could manage was a wimpy grin and a silent thank you to whatever God had watched over her.

There was nothing weak about Star's answering smile; it did its usual number on my sensibilities. I relaxed and felt happily tethered, tied to her body and soul as securely as man has ever been captivated by a woman.

Barry Brierley

She swung the bay alongside my buckskin. Our legs brushed together and her gaze met mine.

"Come, we must hurry."

With a final glance at the impending storm, Star gave me a look that was so full of promise I reacted like a mute, timid schoolboy. Had I been standing, I probably would have looked down, kicked a clod of dirt and murmured, 'ah, shucks.'

With a grin and a husky, "Hopo (let's go)," she tapped the bay's ribs with her heels, and the horse lunged forward. Eagerly my buckskin followed in her wake.

Moving northwesterly at a ground-eating canter, we quickly disappeared around a small clump of trees. Just as quickly I rearranged my thinking into a more protective, cautious mode and closed the space separating our mounts.

I had no way of measuring the distance we traveled or the length of time it took for us to get there, but it was obvious that we had arrived. The Badlands spread out before us in all its strange, rugged beauty. We both reined in our horses. I pulled the ends of Black Elk's blanket close together against the increased chill as a quiet moment settled in between us.

Living in the Black Hills, I had been to the Badlands before. When I had first seen its unusual grandeur, my initial thought had been that when God had made South Dakota, He became bored. Perhaps, in an effort to liven up the scenery, He had thrown in the Black Hills. When that didn't seem like enough He broke off a hunk of Arizona's Painted Desert and planted it east of the Hills for some variety.

In reality, the Badlands are different than the Painted Desert. Many of the rock formations rise from the arid ground like giant stalagmites on the floor of a roofless cavern.

Everywhere I looked the strange, rugged terrain extended for mile upon mile. Star and I stared, lost in our own thoughts, at the eerie landscape. I was thinking how different her thoughts must have been compared to mine when she spoke and confirmed it.

"Wakan. (Holy)."

She looked at me.

I met her gaze as she quietly continued.

"The Stronghold is a very holy place. There are many spirits that dwell there."

Edges of Time

"Why do you call it the Stronghold?"

She shrugged and looked to the south.

"It has always been so. Perhaps because of the many hiding places and good shelters from which to make a good fight where the Bluecoats cannot reach us ... such as the place, O-onagazhee."

Star glanced at me, then stared back toward where Pine Ridge must have been located. When her eyes returned to mine, they were full of shadows and doubts. Tears brimmed as her words unexpectedly changed course. They, along with the tears, took me by surprise.

"Do you think the soldiers will kill more Lakota?"

Her midnight eyes beseeched me with their intensity as she continued, "I fear for the baby at Pine Ridge."

Somewhat taken aback by her question and new found fear I hesitated before I responded.

"There will be no more revenge. The baby will be all right."

Her tearful gaze pierced my skull and searched for the truthfulness of my words with such focus that I felt compelled to explain.

"That was the Seventh Cavalry back there; they were getting their revenge for Long Hair and the Greasy Grass. There will be no more reprisals."

"How do you know this, Starr?"

My heart plummeted. How in hell do I explain something like that?

Knowing that most Lakota believed in dreams or visions, I rapidly whipped up what I hoped was a convincing story.

"While my horse followed yours to this place, I dozed and had a dream. My vision was of a hawk that came at night. It took me into the homes of the Ogallala and showed me the baby sleeping peacefully with two women caring for his every need."

She stared at me in wonder. I could see that she wanted to believe me. Quickly, I placed my hand on her arm and tried to convey absolute conviction as I said, "Please believe me, Star, and the baby will be all right. If danger were to come near, wouldn't those that protect him run for the Stronghold?"

Begrudgingly she nodded.

Barry Brierley

She peered at me in a shy, embarrassed manner.

"You are right, Starr. He will be all right; it is you that I must hide and shelter."

Being a painter I became momentarily mesmerized by the gift presented to me by the day's end. It was a picture that I knew I would one day paint. The sun had set and the last splash of color added orange and gold to the pale copper of Star Watcher's face. A gust of wind caught a tattered edge of her blanket and placed a swath of its redness against her burnished cheek. Raven hair, loosened from its plaits by our flight, whipped free into a filigree of flowing, black lace.

Star turned her cavalry horse and broke the magic of the moment, yet the image stayed with me long enough to be deeply etched into my brain.

Looking back over her shoulder, Star's smile dazzled as she urged the bay into a canter.

"We must hurry, Crow warrior, before our bath gets cold."

My hand was just in time to catch my hat before the wind carried it east toward Pine Ridge. When I looked back, Star Watcher's bay was pulling away, forcing me to urge the buckskin into a gallop. Her last words must have been snatched away by the wind; I could have sworn that she had said something about a bath.

The driving snow was a punishing force that pushed and pulled us onward, completely obliterating my sense of direction. With the wind-blown snow forever in our faces I could no longer tell our changes of direction. We could have traveled in a circle for all I could tell. The bone-chilling cold had taken away any interest I might have had concerning our whereabouts. At the moment all I cared about was finding shelter for us and our horses. At least, I mused, we don't have to worry about our enemies searching for us in a blizzard.

Star Watcher led me through a maze of towering rock formations and formidable cliffs. The spires and plateaus appeared ghost-like within the swirling clouds of snow and ice. Time soon became an important factor, not the time people usually associate with the word like clocks and watches, but in the truly important sense ... survival. One question had managed to work its way to the top of my list of priorities. How much time can the human body take being exposed to a raging blizzard and below zero conditions?

I had no idea how long we had been riding in the storm; the lack of feeling in my lower extremities told me that it had been too long. With my blanket clasped shut over my nose and mouth I was wrapped in a cocoon-like bundle oblivious to my surroundings. Most of the time I had my eyes shut, letting my horse follow the bay's lead, so when I felt something strike my leg my stomach twisted into a knot. It took me a moment to realize that the blow to my leg had been Star Watcher's way of getting my attention. Because of the wind's howl I could barely understand her shouted words.

"You will have to lead your horse. The opening through the rock is not high enough for a rider."

My legs were so cold I was half afraid to swing my right one over the saddle in fear that it might crack and break off. My fears, however, were unfounded, and I could almost feel my feet as I stumbled behind the bay's broad rump. All at once, what light there had been was snuffed out as we entered what must have been a tunnel or cavern in the rock. As we left the cold wind and snow behind, the relief was instantaneous. There was a crackling noise as I pulled the icy, snow-caked blanket away from my face and army blouse. Thankfully, I breathed in the ice-free air. The air in the cavern was anything but frigid. There was a strange hint of sulfur and moistness in the atmosphere, but it was far from being unpleasant. I couldn't see my hand in front of my face, but the channel was so narrow it didn't really make much difference. There were no wrong turns to take or decisions to make. The only way I could go wrong would be to turn around and go back.

The darkness lessened in density as the trail widened, and we came to an alcove that was wide enough for the horses to move and browse; what rough ceiling it had was far out of the reach of man or beast. The floor was mainly sand and weed, although there was some brush and a stack of cut grass for fodder. Within the alcove there was a strange luminous glow that illuminated the place. High above I could see an opening in the rock where gusts of wind pushed an occasional cloud of snow inside. Puzzled, I watched as a plume of snow came through and drifted downward only to melt before it reached the bottom. Where, I wondered, is the warmth coming from?

My silent question was destined to be forgotten, because Star Watcher appeared in front of me and then moved in close, very close. The pale oval of her face was turned up to me. The mark high on her right cheekbone appeared black in the weak light. I couldn't move; I actually felt the heat radiating from her body. A smile was on her lips and shining from her eyes.

"You will be safe here from your enemies, Crow warrior. This haven will not keep you hidden forever ... for now, you will be safe with me."

My breath caught in my throat as Star's hand slid up my chest and touched my cheek. Her hand paused there as her ebony eyes probed mine in the weak light. I don't know what she saw in my eyes, but her hand left my cheek and her gaze slid past me. She reached for our bundle of supplies tied to the buckskin's saddle. Speechless, I helped her free the muslin bag and lower it from the horse's back. Star clutched our bag of goods and moved further into the cave toward the black unknown. She stopped and slowly turned and faced me once more. In the gloom her features were indistinct; her face was merely a lighter spot among various shades of gray. She said nothing, simply stood there for a long moment, then gracefully turned and moved away until she disappeared into the shadows. During that moment she had not said a word, but in my mind her voice rang with the clarity of a new bell; although delivered in a silent manner it relayed her message in a code known to all lovers since the beginning of time.

CHAPTER SEVEN

I unsaddled the buckskin and removed the bridles from both horses as though in a daze. I shook the moisture from my blanket and removed my beaded gauntlets and hat before I stepped forward into the narrow passageway. Immediately, the strange lighting disappeared. I moved cautiously with a hand extended for protection against my blindness. Slowly, the passage through the rock began to widen. As I increased my pace the temperature began to rise at such an unbelievable rate that I began to perspire. I couldn't for the life of me understand how it was possible to have all that heat in the middle of a full-scale Dakota blizzard.

The same strange light that was in the horses' alcove appeared to grow brighter with each step and gradually illuminated the passage. Finally I rounded a corner; I stopped and stared in amazement.

I was standing in the opening of a wide cavern with a curved roof covered with cone-shaped stalactites, but most incredible of all was the black pool of water in front of me. Steam was slowly curling up from its smooth as glass surface. Hot springs! I couldn't believe it. Stepping closer to the water I discovered that it wasn't black after all. I peered into the pool; a soft greenish, luminous glow came from deep in the water. That same aura of light gave the cave an illumination that was almost magical.

I then dropped to my knees beside the mirror-like surface. I stared in horror at my reflection. Or did it belong to someone else? Discounting the dark skin and long hair, the face looked a lot like mine; but what truly frightened me was that it belonged to a person thirty to thirty-five years younger!

75

Barry Brierley

A rapid movement in my peripheral vision swung my head in time to catch a glimpse of long, coppery legs and firm buttocks as they disappeared with a subtle splash into the pool's dark depths.

I stared mesmerized as Star Watcher's grinning face rose to the surface. She slicked her black, glistening hair away from her eyes and gestured for me to join her.

"Come, Warrior. Can you swim?"

A sudden exuberance swept over me.

"If I can't, I'll just have to drown."

Star's musical laughter was resonant within the hollow confines of the cavern and echoed in secret corners of my heart.

In less time than it takes to tell about it, I was undressed and had put aside my fear for my sanity in lieu of my newly acquired youth. Seeing Star Watcher's shy glances made me aware of my youthful body. Her manner of being both shy and bold was maddening but had a certain charm that I found fascinating. An old-fashioned term called coquettish came to mind. Whatever it was that she was doing, if her goal was to capture my interest and desire, she was certainly going about it in the right way.

I dove in. The water enveloped me within its limbs of liquid warmth. The sensation was breath-taking. After riding for hours through a blizzard, the soothing effect of the heated water was very therapeutic; its ability to placate the frigid cold spots and hard to reach areas of the body was uncanny. I surfaced. After smoothing my wet hair away from my face, I kept my eyes closed and breathed in the warm air. While my legs automatically treaded water to keep me afloat, caressing hands of liquid silk moved across my body. My eyes opened. Star Watcher's face was but inches from mine. With a mind of their own my hands reached for her. Her skin felt molten to my touch. She moved willingly within the circle of my arms. Gently, I pulled her close but only for an instant. Our thrashing legs wouldn't permit a longer embrace in the water. Star smiled invitingly and pushed away from me. I watched her swim away and then disappear into the rising steam. It wasn't until then that I realized that we hadn't spoken a word. Not one word had passed our lips since I had entered the water. Staring at the point of her vanishing act, I was compelled to follow and allowed myself to sink beneath the surface.

Edges of Time

The water's warmth seemed to lessen as I entered a channel through solid rock that was in absolute darkness. Ahead of me I could see a faint glimmer of light that made the rising mist ghostly. The pale illumination increased as I swam closer. I rounded a pinnacle of stone and saw a narrow strip of sand that led to a cave-like alcove carved from the rock walls by millions of years of erosion. Of course, at the moment, that was the last thing on my mind. The reality was that there was swiftly approaching me the most beautiful woman I had seen in my entire life. She was waiting for me in all her unabashed nakedness. A copper goddess lying on a dark robe spread across the pale sand: wet and alluringly desirable.

I pulled myself up beside her and stared in wonder at her breath-taking beauty. She was reclining on a furry animal skin of some type. It was very soft and comfortable ... again, this is something that I noticed later. At that moment, my eyes were devouring every naked inch of her. That's how I was captured by her unusual beauty; nothing was left to my imagination. She was totally, gloriously nude. The star-like mark high on her cheekbone was a rising hue of red. Her arms reached; her eyes implored; her mouth beckoned. I slipped into the circle of her arms as though it was the most natural place in the world for me to be. There was no hesitation or shyness; it seemed that the moment was predestined and that we were simply meant to be together. What followed was the most enchanting and gratifying experience that had ever happened to me.

In my previous life I had slept with many women; some were meaningful relationships, most of them were not. I had never been married, had never wished to be. Over the years, family members began to speculate; they thought something was wrong with me. Some went so far as to wonder if I'd been spending my time hiding in a closet. This subtle insinuation, of course, was pondered behind my back. The final analysis came in with the old belief that all artists are 'weird.' Happily, I settled for that and went about my business never realizing that Star Watcher was destined to be in my future and was going to become the most important part of my life.

Barry Brierley

I remember how every single explicit detail of what occurred between us was perfect. Even our movements whether in passion or with tenderness seemed to have been choreographed by a god or goddess of love. During that first time, neither of us spoke a word. We conversed by touch; whether tender or rough it conveyed our wishes or desires with an immediacy that surpassed thought. We made love with intensity and passion unlike anything either of us had ever imagined could happen. Ours was the complete fulfillment of both of our wants and desires that went far beyond our expectations. We had become one; our union soared to a level that attained the status of mystical or spiritual experiences.

Limbs entwined we slept, while the blizzard raged and others less fortunate searched for shelter and solace without the comfort of their murdered loved ones.

CHAPTER EIGHT

I awoke to a very moist warmth that lingered in the air like a living presence. I opened my eyes and saw a plume of steam waft above; then it evaporated like liquid smoke and by doing so restored the dormant memory of my whereabouts.

There was a new light source that furnished a diffused golden glow that seemed to come from everywhere. It was then that I realized that it must have been daybreak. Listening carefully, I could hear the shriek and howl of the storm's voice.

A hand smoothed my hair away from my face. I was suddenly captured by Star Watcher's gaze. Once again I noticed the star-shaped mark. My finger lightly traced the blemish, which to me was more of a decorative, beauty spot than anything detrimental. With its five distinct points and pleasing color I thought of it as a sign that we belonged together.

We stared into each other's eyes like two dewy-eyed teens. Neither spoke; for the moment we were content just being close to one another. I kissed her softly on the lips. She didn't act surprised or startled as I expected. I surmised that at some point in time she had seen white people kiss, so she was unafraid. With the second kiss she responded with enthusiasm and in no time at all, kissing wasn't enough.

I have no idea how long we stayed in our hideaway nook, but it took hunger to get us to leave. I had awakened a second time and found Star gone. At first I was alarmed. When I felt the hollowness of my own stomach I realized why she had left. Before following in her footsteps, I explored a portion of the alcove. There were shelves chipped out of the rocks and the stubs of candles and burnt matches lying on them. Several small bowls were also present; I used one to slake my thirst with water from the pool. Although strange tasting and smelling slightly of sulfur, the heated water did serve my purpose.

This time I eased into the pool. The warmth of the water seemed to reach deep inside of me and touch the place reserved for soothing aches and pains. I felt almost too relaxed to swim, but knowing that Star Watcher awaited me beyond the darkness became a definite source of motivation. I entered the dark area and childishly reminded myself that darkness was merely the absence of light. Encompassed by the warmth and closing walls of stone, the darkness swiftly changed into a glow that grew into light that pulled me toward it as surely as a bee is drawn to a flower.

When I swam into the light, the rising steam and the pointed cones of rock hanging from above gave the chamber an unearthly appearance. The air was moist and warm as I pulled myself out of the pool. A small stab of apprehension jabbed me when I became aware that Star wasn't in the room. Upon investigating our food supplies I discovered that she had taken some dried apples. Swiftly I dressed. Instead of bothering with my shirt I grabbed Black Elk's blanket. Revolver in hand, I stepped through the rock opening that led to the outside. Claustrophobia's walls of fear began to close in on me as I rushed headlong through the narrow passage. Light from the horses' alcove brought with it relief and encouragement. My heart sank when I discovered that Star Watcher wasn't with them. I had hoped and prayed that she would have been busy tending to their needs or had simply brought them the apples. Worry and fear pushed me beyond the horses and into the darkness once more. I backtracked the only way left to me, toward the waiting blizzard. I had already begun to feel cooler air when I sensed that I wasn't alone in the narrow, rock passage. I stopped and waited.

A shadowed form materialized out of the darkness. My eyes had begun to adjust to the dimness, and I stared hard, desperately trying to make something out of the animated shape. It moved swiftly toward me and grew in size with each beat of my heart. I reached out with my left hand, ready to grab, and kept the pistol close to my hip with the right. If it was an enemy I didn't want him to be able to knock my gun aside.

I cocked the revolver.

"Dho!"

Star's startled voice sent waves of relief down my spine.

"It is I, your Crow warrior," I said, softly.

Her sigh of respite was in conjunction with my left hand touching her shoulder.

"I was frightened for the baby. It was important for me to see if the storm was still blowing."

Under the folds of her cotton dress her skin was hot beneath my fingers. I felt her breath quicken and she trembled softly.

"What is wrong?"

"Warrior, you frightened me. I ..."

I clenched the smooth fabric of her dress and gently pulled her to me. My lips found hers and we clung to each other as though there was no tomorrow. She trembled again as my hands passed over her body. I touched her unbound hair and covered her face with tender kisses. When her hands discovered the warmth of my bare skin, her grip tightened and she pulled me flush against her. I removed the blanket from my shoulders and placed it behind her to protect her back from the cold, rough wall. We made love standing in the narrow rock passageway. This time it was truly different from the first. Not only did we speak, our voices and the sounds of our love-making echoed down the stone corridor, only to be disseminated by the driving winds of the blizzard.

We returned to the main room on unsteady legs. Shyness momentarily seemed to strike us both. I don't know what caused it, but even that seemed to have a purpose. I quickly ate a hunk of jerky in silence, as my mind actively formulated a drawing. While Star began rummaging for food, I found the pencils and tablets and did several rough sketches of my Lakota lady and her wonderful hideaway.

Later, when Star had finished eating, she came and sat beside me. I put aside my sketch book and resumed one of my newfound hobbies, watching the only true love of my life. She was quiet and pensive. At first I was concerned that she was unhappy with me for some unknown reason. When I asked, she looked at me with such irrevocable love that I felt shame for having worried. Star pulled me close and held me tight as though at any moment I might jump to my feet and run out into the blizzard. Still holding me she looked into my eyes and captured my soul as well as my heart.

"Please understand. My love for you is as certain as Wi (the sun) will take his daily journey across the sky. What is not certain is the fate of my people. I worry that they will all perish under the fist and gun of the white man."

Trying not to be too knowledgeable, I assured her that after the horrible incident at Wounded Knee, the Bluecoat wasichus would probably be so ashamed of their behavior that they would finally leave the Lakota alone to live in peace.

It was obvious that Star wanted to believe my words to be true. The fine lines of her face and the curves of her posture suggested dismay and worry, yet her eyes betrayed her love as well as her hope and happiness. My arms tightened around her as my love for the woman grew in leaps and bounds.

"What is your other name?"

Her question was so unexpected I felt like I'd been punched right between the eyes. I couldn't think! Then, I remembered the scout, John Crow, calling to me.

"Were you not given another name? I know that it is a practice of the wasichus and you being half-white, I ..."

"Yes, I do have another name. It is Nathanial or ... Nathan."

"Nay-thon ... I like that," she said with a smile.

Sometimes it's the little, inexplicable things that fuse a man and woman into a powerful bond of love. When Star smiled and called me 'Nay-thon' which isn't even my real name, my stomach did flip-flops. I could almost feel an emotional fault-line forming across my heart. At that moment my love for her became a living thing, something to be nourished and protected ... but most important of all ... to remember and cherish.

Star threw me another heartbreaking grin, scooting forward so that her legs could dangle into the water. She looked back at me and coyly announced, "I believe I will name the baby Nay-thon ... and perhaps I will use part of your dream also."

At first I didn't know what dream she was talking about. But *then, to my embarrassment, I realized that she meant the dream with the hawk that I had fabricated to ease her fears while on the trail.*

Feeling Star's eyes watching me, I met her inquisitive gaze with one of my own. My heart went out to this woman who for some unknown reason had chosen to share herself and her love with me.

"Would you mind, Nay-thon?"

My stomach began doing acrobatics again.

"Of course not ... I am honored."

"Would you write it for me? It will need to be put on the 'rooster' at the reservation."

At first, I stared at her in confusion. When I realized what she had said and why, I laughed aloud and heard my laughter echo across the vaporous, hot springs and into the rock-lined labyrinth of our cavern.

Star stared at me as if I had gone mad.

When I explained that the English word she meant to say was 'roster' and explained what a rooster was, she also laughed.

I wrote her name beneath a small sketch of her, and I wrote "Nathanial" off to one side. When I tore it from the tablet and gave it to her, her eyes widened.

"Dho!" she exclaimed in surprise, "you are a shadow catcher."

At first I was surprised by her reaction; then I remembered that photographers were called 'shadow catchers' by Native Americans. I was flattered ... I would gladly have my sketches mistaken for photos any day.

"I am pleased. Someday I will have both mine and Nay-thon's shadow caught for you."

Happy to see her so easily pleased, at the time I didn't realize the staggering importance of her remark.

After I ate some dried fruit, we went for another swim. This time we stayed within the perimeters of the main room. After we dried each other with our blankets we didn't bother to dress; instead we cuddled and affectionately caressed each other until our intimacy led to a more gratifying culmination of our needs. Afterward, Star and I drifted off to sleep, wrapped within each

Barry Brierley

other's arms and lost in dreams of the future.

CHAPTER NINE

I awoke to an unexpected coolness. Much of the light was gone, so I assumed that it was night. Star Watcher was snuggled next to me as though for warmth. Without disturbing her slight form, I was able to reach the other blanket. After wrapping her in its thick folds, I gently enfolded her in my arms and thought of tomorrow, as sleep again took control of my lagging volition.

My eyes sprung open as though my lids were on springs. I had no idea what had awakened me. I rubbed my eyes. It was morning; diffused light was everywhere. I closed my eyes and listened. There. I could hear the faint howl of the wind as the blizzard raged on. Star was curled into a ball and sleeping soundly. Carefully, I disengaged her arms from my neck and stood up.

I stretched mightily and gazed about me. When my roving eye fell on my sketch book I left Star's side and retrieved the tablet. Happily, I glanced at the sketches that I had done. With Star resting it gave me an opportunity to do some more drawings and to make the others more detailed. Stretching out on a slab of rock I began working. I sketched furiously for what seemed like several hours. I know that it couldn't have been that long, but I was so inspired that before I knew it, my tablet was completely full.

Tired of drawing, I let Star Watcher continue sleeping while I did some exploring. I got dressed and began a careful examination of the cavern's sloping walls, almost immediately finding another narrow corridor that had been partially hidden by a large, odd-shaped boulder. I returned to my gear and quickly buckled on my gun and holster. Grabbing a fresh pencil

85

and pad, I stooped for the low entrance and carefully slid into the narrow passage. It wasn't as dark as the main one, but it seemed to be closer to the outside and narrower. I could clearly hear the blowing winds, yet it still stayed warm within the rock-encased path. It was so narrow I was forced to make my way sideways and with my limited vision snakes came to mind.

The tapered passage finally widened and opened up into a miniature room. I stopped and stared. The walls were covered with ancient paintings: animals, men hunters, symbols, and signs. All the petroglyphs left me breathless!

After staring in awe for what seemed a long time, I silently vowed to do a painting of Star Watcher in that room. Using my tablet, I did several rough drawings of the room. Afterwards, I moved around the room looking for anything unique. Something about the shadows from one of the rocks led to the discovery of another narrow path that led further into the stone maze. Excited, I ducked and slipped inside the wide crevice and edged my way forward. Turning a sharp bend I felt the first chill of the storm and heard the wind howl like a banshee. I entered a frigid cavern and through an opening in the wall saw the snow-covered walls and towers of a neighboring cliff. As I watched, the scene disappeared in a frenzy of wind-driven snow and ice that whipped a draught of cold air inside. The abrupt change in atmosphere was enough to send me scurrying for my crease in the wall like a rat for his hole.

With bumped knees, scraped knuckles, and other superficial injuries to my body I made it back to the main cavern. After the brief encounter with the cold I found the place to be stifling with humidity. Star Watcher still slept, so I quickly undressed and slipped into the water and then out again, hoping that the moving air in the cave would feel cool on my wet body. Quickly but quietly, I found something to eat and excitedly began to plan several paintings. I tried not to worry or speculate about what was waiting for me in the future.

For some reason, I decided to quit drawing and spend my time studying my sketches and outlines. Afterward, I committed the sketches to memory. I have no recollection as to why this was done. It wasn't something that I had never done before; it just didn't seem necessary at the time. In the past, while working in

Edges of Time

the field, I had memorized roughs but never detailed drawings. This time, I had to remind myself that my mind was much older than my body. Who knows, I mused, perhaps senility had moved in quicker than anticipated.

Later, Star Watcher's body stirred beside me. I felt her soft breath on my back just before her moist, warm lips pressed against my skin. Her caresses were a pleasant but mortifying reminder of my recaptured youth. Putting my sketches aside, I pulled Star into my arms and rolled over until her willowy body was on top of mine, covering the object of my embarrassment. Her raven hair cascaded down around my head like folds of black satin and shut out the pale light. To my ears, her soft cries of passion were lyrics from a love song, sung for me alone. Wrapped in each other's arms we stayed until motivated by sustenance, which bid that we 'rise and go forth'.

Time passed quickly for us on that final, full day. We swam; we ate; we talked incessantly and spoke of our love. I showed Star the findings of my exploration; when we returned to the alcove she had a surprise for me.

After we rediscovered the warmth and comfort of the buffalo robe, she led me back into the cave past the shelf that I had found earlier. There was a definite chill in the air, and the light was getting brighter when we stopped, and I saw her surprise.

The walls were covered with delightful petroglyphs. Star Watcher showed them to me with an ancestral pride that was both charming and beguiling. They were beautiful, far more detailed than the batch I had found. Taking me by the hand, Star led me deeper into the cave's dwindling channel. The cold increased to a point where, naked as we were, it was time to retreat. We scuttled back to our hot springs and savored the tingling warmth of the water. In time, we returned to the main cavern where we dallied away the remains of the day.

That night our love making was especially sweet and tender. I believe that we both instinctively knew that our love tryst was destined to end soon. We spent most of the night wrapped in each other's arms as we shared our dreams and spoke of a life together for all eternity.

Barry Brierley

CHAPTER TEN

Something woke me. I listened hard without hearing a thing. I tried holding my breath, but all there was to hear was the untroubled breathing of Star Watcher. It was then that the truth dawned on me. The storm! I couldn't hear the wind; the blizzard was over. Excited, I rose from my blankets, careful not to awaken Star. Although the security of the cave had made it possible for me to enjoy some of the happiest days of my life, I was eager to breathe some fresh air and to see the aftermath of the storm.

While getting dressed, I occasionally stopped and listened but invariably the silence prevailed. As I buckled on my gun and holster my mind began fluctuating with the inconsistency of a tumble-weed; thoughts kept vacillating in and out, moving here and there. I didn't know whether to be happy or sad. Most importantly, I didn't have a clue what the future held for me. Furthermore, being a mixed-blood I didn't know how I would manage to take care of Star, raise the baby, and maintain a livelihood in the nineteenth century. It was exciting but also very frightening. My mind became a whirlwind of half formed ideas and fully developed fears. I knew that a new career was a must. Half-breed artists weren't too marketable in the 1890's. A sudden thought brought a ripple of pleasure across the still waters of my improbable future. Horses! I've always loved horses. Encouraged by the unlimited potential of this idea, my spirits lifted.

Happy, but still concerned, I stepped into the passageway. Suddenly I stopped. Removing my gauntlets I hurried back inside. What if she awoke and I was gone?

At that moment my thinking wasn't at all rational. I don't know if I was just excited that the storm was over, or what. At a later date I would decide that my subconscious had to have been concerned with both: being pursued by the army and trying to accept the fact that I was in South Dakota in the last decade of the previous century. Besides being dazed over the latter, I was also irrevocably in love.

Quickly, I grabbed a tablet and printed:

DO NOT WORRY, I WILL RETURN.
I LOVE YOU.

Nathan

It wasn't until I was leading the buckskin from the alcove that I realized what I had done. First of all, I had left a note for someone who probably could not read. Secondly, I had left my hand drawn star that I sometimes used as additional signature. I stopped in my tracks and wondered at my stupidity.

Already, I could feel the cold air coming down the stone corridor as the impatient buckskin bumped me in the back with his nose. It was as if he were telling me to get a move on. Thinking I would be right back I ignored my concern and tried to refrain from worrying about the confusing note.

It was almost magical how the yellow horse's breath gradually turned to vaporous clouds of frost as the air became more frigid. Nearing the cavern's opening to the outside world, I shielded my eyes with a gloved hand as we rounded a corner and moved into what appeared to be a brand new pristine world. The sun's rays were blinding. The land was so white beneath the bright blue sky it was painful to look at. Out of necessity, my squint was so tight I could barely see. After my eyes adapted to the glare, my gaze swept a terrain that was nearly featureless; snow was everywhere. Behind and below me cliffs towered ... nonconformity became commonplace. Snow impacted or covered every rock, crack, and crevice as far as the eye could see.

I stepped into the stirrup and swung up. The leather squeaked as I settled into the saddle. Each and every minute sound was loud in the still atmosphere.

Edges of Time

Feeling frisky in the brisk air the buckskin gave a couple of half-hearted bucks before he settled down. Afterwards, a little prancing and snorting plumes of white vapor satisfied him.

Pulling my hat brim lower against the reflected light, I touched my heels to the buckskin's ribs, and he lunged forward into a lope. The air was cold and fresh as we cantered through the pristine winter terrain. The absolute whiteness covered everything with its illusion of purity. A quiet had settled over the plains that was disconcerting. It gave me the strange feeling that I was alone on a planet completely devoid of life. As far as I could see there was not an animal track, a bird, or even a form of plant life. The buckskin loped around a lofty rock abutment.

A solid blow to my left side sent me reeling in the saddle! The sound of the rifle shot was loud in the winter quiet. My eyes shot left as I grabbed for the buckskin's black mane and fought for my balance. The quick glance had been enough to identify the bushwhackers; their image was burned onto my retina. I shelved that picture for later and dug my heels into the yellow mount's ribs. He squatted and thrust forward as though shot from a gun. Pain knifed through my body as a shout and more shots followed the first. With each rapid heartbeat, adrenaline pumped through my veins and hardened my resolve. I urged the buckskin to an even greater speed.

Like the ground-nesting meadowlark which will pretend to be injured, and lure predators away from her nest, I was determined to lead my pursuers away from Star Watcher. When I looked back, John Crow and two other scouts were riding hard about a hundred yards behind. The cold wind forced tears from my eyes and made it difficult to see. A wave of dizziness swept over me and I felt myself sway in the saddle. Leaning left I crouched over the bobbing neck; sensing my urgency the yellow horse lengthened his stride. The pain in my side was a growing presence that throbbed with a searing rhythm that refused to be ignored.

Through my icy, wind-induced tears, the open prairie beckoned; its shining whiteness blended and fused the land into a featureless, undulating blanket. I clutched the horse's flying,

Barry Brierley

black mane and felt the wind sharp against my face. When I turned and looked back, the buckskin's mane whipped and mixed with my own mane of raven hair and momentarily blinded me. My gauntlet clothed hand brushed away the clinging hair. My vision cleared and my heart soared with joy. The soldier wolves had fallen behind, and they appeared to be slowing their mounts.

Happiness moved through my body with an all encompassing fervor. I knew that with each lunging stride my yellow horse was pulling me and John Crow's scouts further away from Star Watcher and our Badlands hideaway.

Suddenly, the buckskin threw his head back! The muscular neck caught me on the cheekbone and jaw with stunning force. Bright colors flashed before my closed eyes and I hung on with blind determination. Muscles bunched and legs stiffened as the big horse struggled to come to a halt. My gloved hands scrabbled for purchase as my buckskin jolted to a sliding stop. I sailed over the rigid neck in a graceless sprawl. Pain exploded through my body as I struck the snowy ground with a jarring impact and slid forward until stopped by a jutting boulder that dangled over a hidden, snow-covered abyss.

Breathless, motionless with pain, I stared down at the snow-capped, jagged rocks far below. Because of the shroud of fresh snow that covered virtually everything, I had not realized that my pursuers had chased me up onto a long, high plateau that ended with a lethal drop of what looked like hundreds of feet. The pure white of the new snow made depth perception almost impossible.

Through the mist of my gasping breath I watched the yellow army horse, neck arched and head held high, trot away from the cliff's edge. Clumps of snow and ice flew from the horse's hooves as he left, taking my only chance to escape with him. Through the pain, the realization hit me that if I didn't kill the three scouts my life was over. Along with that depressing reality came a fierce resolve to save Star Watcher at whatever cost.

The three scouts were charging toward me in a single file. Their big cavalry chargers were galloping hard; flying snow from their hooves was bright against the blue sky. John Crow was already smiling in anticipation of his big coup when the first shot from my revolver missed him but snapped back the head of the scout directly behind him. He tumbled off his army mount as though some god-like hand had miraculously plucked the bones from his body. His tumbling lifeless form fell directly into the path of the following horse, causing him to stumble and make a sudden swerve. His rider, surprised, lost a stirrup and fell into the snow. He jumped to his feet just in time for my second shot to find his heart. The Indian dropped as though his legs had been swept from beneath him; hope surged as I shifted my aim toward the towering presence of the hard-charging John Crow.

A solid blow struck me with the force of a two-handed hammer swing! I felt the bullet go deep into my chest. My vision dimmed and I knew no more until a sudden new pain attacked my scalp and brought fresh tears to my eyes.

John Crow's fetid breath assailed my nostrils as he yanked once more on my hair.

"Stand! Rise and point to where your Lakota bitch makes her den, you spineless, half-breed dog."

His bray of laughter sent a chill up my spine. Its maniacal pitch carried a hint of madness and brought with it a recollection from the past. The vision was there for mere second ... flash-like images of him savagely beating and raping a woman. The startling, brief disclosure was an obvious memory of Nathanial Starr.

Knowing that I was but seconds away from death, my love for Star Watcher put the strength of desperation into my legs. In spite of John Crow's grip on me, I staggered painfully to my feet.

The Crow scout clutched me to him and cackled in my ear, "Point to where I can find the bitch! Why waste time tracking when I have you."

He shook me and yanked at my hair as he added, "Bitch in heat that she is, she will welcome a wolf to replace her tame dog. Show me the way!"

His words of fury were the catalyst I needed. From some deep reservoir of strength I managed to twist free. Lunging forward, my arms became steel cables that wrapped around John Crow; my fingers, interlocking metal clamps. I ignored his raging voice and frantic struggles as my moccasin enclosed toes *searched for a foothold beneath the new snow. Finding solid ground, I again tapped my fading reserve of power. My legs drove him backwards with a pile-driving force that was motivated by a frenzy of pure rage.*

Together, we toppled over the edge of the plateau! The snow-covered rocks loomed below, growing larger with each heartbeat.

Suddenly, I was soaring above the falling John Crow and my own lifeless form. I watched as the two bodies, one soundlessly shrieking in terror, and my own, limp and without life, smashed onto the jagged rocks far below.

Within my newly found silence, I felt myself drift upwards into an enveloping cocoon of nothingness; there was no light or dark, nor heat or cold. I felt no pain or sorrow only a serenity that encompassed everything. A bright light appeared that seemed to beckon to me. An overwhelming urgency pulled me toward it, or it was approaching me. I reached out.

CHAPTER ELEVEN

BLUCKSBURG MOUNTAIN ESTATES
AUGUST 21, 1998

Deputy John Nighthawk stared in disbelief at the last page. His mind rebelled. Starr could not have died, he thought. Foolishly, he glanced at the back of the typed page as though there would be more typed there. Sheepishly, he smiled as he realized how ridiculous a turn his train of thought had taken. Of course he didn't die, he mused, if he was dead, how could he have written the manuscript and told of his own death? It was at that moment, having shifted in the desk chair, that he spied the piece of paper. It had apparently fallen off the desk and lodged between it and the paneled wall. Nighthawk grasped the corner that was exposed and pulled it free. It was another handwritten page in the same hand. His heart began to beat with renewed vigor as his eyes tracked across the cursive sentences.

I could smell the dust in the carpet and felt its feather touch against my cheek and fingertips. My eyes opened to a sun-bathed room. The first object to catch my eye was the familiar sight of the back of my left hand. The noticeable age spots loomed large and frightful on the back of my hand's skin as they told me that Star Watcher and Nathanial Starr were no more. I had lost her.

I was lying on my stomach in front of my easel. My head was turned to the left facing my bent left arm and hand. I felt a tear slide across the bridge of my nose and follow several wrinkles and crevices before disappearing into the forest of the shag carpet. Through the blur of tears my artist's eye saw how the

Barry Brierley

rays of the sun brightened my surroundings and made pockets of warm light. Needless to say, the sun did little to lighten the pall of gloom, or chip away the ice of despair that had pervaded my heart.

The bullet that had ended Nathanial Starr's life had also destroyed my connection with my first and only true love, leaving Star Watcher an unknown personage of our country's history and me to resume my life as the aging, lonely artist that I was before Star entered my life.

Days turned into weeks. I passed the time painting and thinking of her and our tryst. At first my thoughts of Star Watcher were full of guilt. What will she think of me for deserting her? Eventually, I reasoned that her love for me would prevail and that she would know that it was something beyond my control.

My thoughts of Star Watcher were as positive a recollection as a hard-core alcoholic remembers and savors his last drink. When I wasn't painting I was thinking of her while plotting and scheming, trying desperately to find a way of rejoining Star and our foundling child.

Weeks turned into months as my painting became obsessive and filled with bitter-sweet memories of our brief time together. When I tired of painting, research filled my hours as I continued to search relentlessly for a way of rejoining my lost love. My obsession took me to libraries, museums, and booksellers all over the country as I pursued my elusive dream.

Ironically, the answer to my dilemma was so close to home that at first I couldn't believe my eyes. It happened at the Crazy Horse Monument Museum near Custer, South Dakota where I found several photos on display by a photographer named J.C.H. Grabill. Some of the photos were of Sioux at the Pine Ridge Agency that began after the Indian Wars and continued on through the years to 1900. Within these photos were clues that set in motion a search that resulted in my victorious discovery of information and photographs in a book that I believe will enable me to return to Star Watcher and our adopted son.

I have yet to ascertain if my plan will work, yet the things I have uncovered are burned into my soul and have made me a firm advocate of the spiritual, if not the whimsical. Destiny,

96

Edges of Time

kismet, karma ... call it what you will, if you don't believe, perhaps after you compile the facts, as I have, you too will come to believe the impossible.

Well, dear reader, bid me adieu or farewell, but be certain of this, if I am no longer on these premises, you will find me happily dreaming away the day and thinking of tomorrow while enclosed in the arms of my one true love.

Nighthawk stared at the five-pointed star that was left in lieu of a signature and thought of the hurried note that Starr had left for Star Watcher. Curious, he paged back through the last pages of the manuscript until he found where Starr had drawn the star signature. He looked from the handwritten page to the manuscript ... they were exactly the same! The beginning and ending of the lower left hand point of the star he had overlapped. Both hand-drawn stars were almost exactly alike as only an accomplished artist could make it. Why the same, he wondered? His eyes dropped to the bottom of the page at the handwritten post script.

I must add, dear reader, if ever your common sense leads you to doubt my accomplishment, study the work of the 'Shadow Catchers.' I owe them a great deal. Perhaps, in time, my support will repay them in a small way and inform you of my existence in the past.

Puzzled by the man's words, Deputy John Nighthawk replaced the manuscript on the desk and got to his feet.

Feeling a slight twinge in his upper chest, his hand unconsciously rubbed the healed area. He glanced out the window and noticed that the sun was lowering in the western sky, and that inside bars of sunlight were beginning to penetrate the shadows throughout Daniel Starr's log mansion.

For some inexplicable reason, John Nighthawk felt an affinity with the artist's home. With the disembodied movement of a sleepwalker, Nighthawk left the small den and moved toward the front of the house. Something was pulling him forward, as though guiding him toward his own destiny. He stopped once. A faint chanting came to his ear;

97

eventually it faded with the diminished wind.

"Sky Father," he whispered.

He walked faster … his destination became certain as he stepped into the spacious art studio and stopped as though faced with an invisible wall.

A ray of light slanted across a painting propped against the side leg of the artist's easel. Nighthawk was stunned by the vivid color and the wild beauty of the Indian woman captured within the painting. The birthmark high on her right cheekbone identified Star Watcher as quickly as if her name was painted on her forehead. He stared, mesmerized. It was exactly as Daniel Starr had described the scene in his manuscript.

Her hair had come undone from the braids and was blowing across her face in tresses like black lace. The red of her blanket pressed against the copper of her cheek. The love he saw in her eyes wasn't for him but still made him weak in the stomach and behind his knees.

John moved on unsteady legs to the adjoining table. He stared. A large book was open. Several photos were on display. The top of the page gave the date as 1898. Scrawled in white paint across a dark portion of the page was the legend:

Beef Issue Day at the Pine Ridge Agency, S.D.
... Fall of 1898.

His heart began to palpitate as he peered at the Indian woman in one of the pictures. Her back was to the camera and she appeared to be dancing. A blanket was draped over her shoulders, and she was holding it in a way that when she turned it would flare. Two things kept John Nighthawk's eyes riveted on the photo. One was the dark blemish that could be seen high on the woman's right cheekbone as she peered over her shoulder; the other was the light-colored cowry shells that showed a large, five pointed star design that had been sewn onto her dark blanket. It was exactly like Starr's hand-drawn star signature!

Without taking his eyes off the glossy page, Nighthawk pulled a chair over and dropped into it.

His gaze dropped to the text below the photo. It read:

Edges of Time

Photographer J.C.H. Grabill was compelled to photograph this scene because of the charm of the Lakota dancer and her adopted son, Nighthawk, who provided the music for her dance. Information received was that the boy was found wrapped in a blanket on the Wounded Knee Battlefield eight years previous.

John Nighthawk didn't move. He wasn't sure that he could. His eyes raised up to the photo once more. Partly hidden by Star Watcher's blanket was a grinning eight or nine year old boy, happily keeping time with a small ceremonial drum. John Nighthawk stared in awe at the first photo he had ever seen of his great-grandfather.

He had known that his great-grandfather was born a Minneconjou and was raised by another family. The oral history of his family wasn't complete, but he did know that much. There had been talk of Wounded Knee in conjunction with his family, but no one had known for certain because his real family had all been killed.

John glanced at the remaining photos and stood on wobbly legs. He was having trouble believing his own eyes and difficulty sorting through his thoughts. Taking a step backwards, Nighthawk stumbled over the tripod leg of an easel. He glanced up at the painting on the easel; paints and brushes still cluttered the ledge in front of it. His eyes were drawn back to the stark but colorful painting.

The main focus of the painting was centered on a dark-skinned cowboy on horseback. He was herding several head of cattle toward some waiting, poorly dressed Indians. Red dust rose from the mottled earth shades of the cattle; blue tinted shadows testified to the intensity of the midday sun. Beneath the shadow of his hat brim, something about the wrangler's eyes drew Nighthawk in for a closer look. He stared aghast at the familiar planes of the lean face. In a sudden burst of clarity, John realized what Daniel Starr had done. He had painted his own face, blue eyes and all, in place of the cowboy's! Exactly as he had done with Starr's painting at Wounded Knee.

Nighthawk spun around, his gaze swept the open book. There. The same scene on glossy paper stared back at him. His eyes dropped to the lines of copy beneath the photo.

> 'During the issue of government beef, J.C.H. Grabill's camera captured the excitement and festive atmosphere of the day. 'Beef Day' as they called it, was a time to celebrate and meet old friends. The cowboy delivering the 'beeves' is a wrangler -rancher from up by Deadwood. He is one of two sons begot by the late, famed plainsman, Caleb Starr. The wrangler, Caleb Jr., is the twin brother of Nathanial Starr, a former scout for the army, who was killed during the Wounded Knee Battle.'

John straightened and backed away from the table and the large book of photos. All he could think of was *wanagi* (Lakota spirits). If he had been Catholic, he would have crossed himself. But being a traditional Lakota, he grasped his medicine bag from where it hung beneath his shirt and whispered a short prayer to Wakan Tanka.

He turned to step outside onto the deck and stopped dead in his tracks. There painted on the wall was Starr's vision: a winter scene that depicted a night hawk weaving in flight between leafless trees. A figure on horseback wrapped in a red and black blanket was cleverly woven into the background. The artist's star symbol was painted into the lower right hand corner.

Nighthawk became captivated by the stark, winter rendering. While staring at the painting, he thought of the manuscript and remembered how Star Watcher had said that she would use his vision to help name the baby. He smiled softly and thought how surprised his friends would be to hear that he now knew how his family came by their name, Nighthawk. Then and there he silently vowed to take the manuscript and show it to the Gray Feather Society, a highly respected group of Lakota elders.

The young deputy stretched and thought of Daniel Starr. He adjusted the hang of his cumbersome gun-belt and wished that he could have met the artist. It would have been good, he thought, to have looked into the man's eyes and to have thanked him for his life and for the many other Lakota that he had helped.

Stepping out onto the deck, John felt the first hint of coolness in the day's breeze. He stopped. The heavy smell of burning sweet grass and sage hung in the air. The sacred scents lingered in spite of the soft wind.

Edges of Time

For an instant John thought he again heard Lakota chanting; then it was gone, as was the sacred smoke. Along with it went any remaining doubts that John Nighthawk might have had concerning the existence of Lakota spirits.

While regaining his composure, his gaze was drawn to the splash of color across the western sky. *Wi* was perched on the edge of the western world and was about to leave it in darkness until the morning when he would again make his journey across the sky. Nighthawk leaned forward against the peeled and varnished railing and glanced down at the undulating prairie toward Bear Butte. His fingers tightened on the soft pine of the rail. Eagles were there ... a half-dozen gliding, swooping shapes circled the sacred mountain in the day's fading light.

"*Wakan.* (Holy)," he murmured.

Sacred eagles hovering over the Lakota's most sacred mountain can only be the best of signs, he thought. Something, perhaps a flicker of a shadow or the whisper of a wing, made him look up.

His breath caught in his throat. Four hovering, eagles sliced through the air above the deserted Starr home. John Nighthawk watched in silent wonder, marveling at the greatness of his gods, as they paid tribute to the man who had truly been the creator of his own special lineage. He raised his left hand and tried to look beyond the heavens. He said, "*Tunaschila, Amba* (Goodbye, Grandfather)."

He lowered his arm, and looked down on the eagles circling his sacred butte and murmured, "*Ista kiksuyapi nis ohinyan.* (I will remember you, forever)."

***

RAPID CITY GAZETTE
EAGLES BLESS AUCTION

The auction that was held to sell the work of artist Daniel Starr was considered a successful, gala affair. Included among those attending was a fairly large population of Lakota (Sioux) from nearby reservations. A surprisingly large number of Mr. Starr's paintings were purchased by the Native Americans. Speculation is that the sales were a committee or council

101

decision. An interesting side story was the arrival of numerous birds, mostly eagles. The birds circled overhead throughout the entire auction. The Lakota, who consider the eagle to be sacred, claim that the arrival of the birds can only be a sign that Wakan Tanka (Great Spirit) was pleased with the event and was giving his blessings.

CHAPTER TWELVE

Deputy Sheriff John Nighthawk was standing at the last parking level on the southern slope at the base of *Paha Sapa* (Bear Butte). He unconsciously rubbed the scar tissue high on his left chest.

At that moment, however, the Timberline incident was a thing in the past and his mind was focused on something else.

Nighthawk stared up at the peak; he had been standing there for awhile, soaking up the autumn atmosphere. His strong Lakota features showed none of the deep spiritual feelings that were presently coursing through his mind and body. The magic of the Butte always amazed him and rekindled his belief in the spirits. It being a day off from work, the deputy wasn't in uniform. Using the early part of the day to take care of some domestic things, Nighthawk had arrived at the Butte as soon as he could that morning. The unexpected arrival of a fall breeze felt cool on his bare legs. There was enough of a bite in the air that John wished he'd brought a jacket to compensate for his light-weight shorts and tee-shirt.

He hooked his thumbs through the shoulder straps of his back pack and breathed in the strange mixture of power and serenity that emanated from the famous butte.

While John Nighthawk's gaze scanned the summit of the Butte, his mind was at peace. He was watching for *wamblis* (eagles). More often than not there would be one riding the thermals near the peak.

There was a sudden wild burst of derisive laughter that drew Nighthawk's attention. The taunting, distasteful sound came from near the open-sided shelter located at the start of the trail leading up the butte. Irritation brought a slight frown of disapproval to John Nighthawk's untroubled countenance. He stared in the direction of the disturbance. Being off duty John didn't quite know what to do about the trio he thought of as Larry, Curly and Moe.

Although the morning's visitors had been few in number, the three young men had been heckling everyone. At the moment a man and woman who appeared to be in their late fifties were trying to move past them and start up the trail. The largest of the three boys was enormous and wasn't allowing the couple to pass

It was obvious from his body language alone that the huge boy was the leader and the other two his cheerleaders. John thought he had seen the big boy look at him a couple of times, but it was probably just his imagination. But then again maybe the kid had seen him in uniform sometime or other.

The middle-aged couple was clearly upset; the man was angry and the woman appeared frightened. The pair was at an obvious loss as to what they should do about their situation.

Not wanting to have to go back to his truck and collect his badge and gun, Nighthawk decided to try using some diplomacy. Maybe, he thought, they'll get the message and go away. John reluctantly strolled over to the only place on the Butte not currently wrapped in a blanket of serenity.

"Hey, what's the problem?"

Five faces turned toward him: two surprised, three hostile.

A sneer crossed the narrow face of the smallest boy as he snarled, "Hey, yer own self, Chief! Ain't nobody asked to hear any war whoops outta you!" His jibe was followed by a quick smile and glance at the largest of the friend, a look that silently clamored for the companion's immediate approval.

Of course, John thought, it's always the dog with the weakest bite that's going to have the loudest bark.

The other half of the duo, who had been picking at his acne, chimed in with a belligerent, "Yeah, dude!"

Wearing the serious, stoic expression he usually reserved for rednecks and other obtuse or abusive adults, John swiftly closed the gap separating them. Making an educated guess Nighthawk just assumed that the youths were merely the usual mouth fighters, so he ignored the racial slurs.

"You're right, I wasn't asked. But I still want to know."

As he spoke he slipped past the mouthy pair before they were able to decide what to do.

Edges of Time

John noticed that the two were barely out of their teens. All three were dressed in the usual uniform of over-sized blue jeans, tee-shirts and expensive running shoes. One, he noticed, was wearing a high school letter jacket. It was black and red with a large S sewn on the left chest.

The third, the largest and oldest, was still blocking the tourists' access to the trail. As John approached the bully he made sure that he could covertly watch the young man's two friends with his peripheral vision. Without the slightest hesitation Nighthawk slipped his slender form in between the middle-aged couple and the hulking youth. With the youth towering above John's six feet, he had to look up to make eye contact. Catching a whiff of rank beer breath, he thought, maybe I'll have to forget about using diplomacy. Taking the offensive, Nighthawk smiled in a disarming manner. Quietly he said, "You don't want trouble with me."

The youngster swayed and blinked in confusion. He appeared to be about twenty-two or three. An errant puff of wind lifted the young man's long dark hair as he met John's steady gaze. There was something vaguely familiar about the youth; he gave the youngster an educated appraisal.

Judging from the size of his neck and arms, Nighthawk could tell he knew his way around a weight room. But for the moment the boy's size didn't really matter because John sensed he was confused and didn't appear to know what to do next. Maybe, Nighthawk thought, it was because of the beer or his lack of experience. With the quandary brought on by John's contrasting smile and aggressive behavior, he looked even younger. His two mouthy friends, Nighthawk noted, were strangely quiet and acted nervous. Suddenly the youth's confusion was gone and his eyes clamped on Nighthawk with undisguised menace.

Holding the bully's gaze, Nighthawk gestured for the man and woman to slip on past. The hulking youth tried to intimidate them with a look, but they walked on by, taking a wide berth around them. John watched the bully's smoldering blue eyes track them; with an abrupt move he turned and met John's steady black gaze, the anger sizzling behind the boy's bloodshot stare, and something else … he couldn't quite put his finger on what it was but he didn't like it. Not taking any chances Nighthawk willed his body into the tautness of a coiled spring.

In a deceptively gentle voice he said, "I'm Deputy Sheriff

Barry Brierley

Nighthawk from the Lakota County Sheriff's Department."

At the mention of his name and official status the boy's eyes flared and instantly became flooded with intensity. His stare quickly evolved into a glare, looking into Nighthawk's eyes with a thinly veiled menace.

Thinking the youth possibly just disliked authority, John let it pass. But he put a little more weight in his voice as he commented, "This is sacred ground to a lot of people. Those that stop to visit shouldn't have to worry about being hassled. I think it's time for you guys to move on."

Any feelings that were hidden before were now in the open. The youth's stare now evolved into open hatred which mystified Nighthawk, so he said, "Come back after you sleep off the beer, okay?"

Without hurrying John stepped past the bully and moved onto the path that began the gradual climb that culminated at the top of Bear Butte.

"Hey, cop!"

Nighthawk stopped and looked back at the massive youth. The young man was standing in the same place quietly watching him. His two friends were strangely quiet as they observed from the background. John had the feeling that they were more afraid of their buddy than anything else.

"You ain't heard the last of me."

His deep voice oozed of latent violence.

"Is that a threat?"

Instead of answering, the youth continued to stare at him until he slowly turned and walked toward his waiting friends.

John stared after him for a moment then mentally shrugged the threat off as youthful bravado.

Turning away Nighthawk quickly started up the trail. After a short distance, he lengthened his stride while simultaneously adjusting the straps of the back-pack. The pack only contained a single over-sized book, but John wasn't accustomed to wearing a pack and was irritated by the binding shoulder straps. Just before moving up the trail into the trees, he glanced a final time at the summit. When Nighthawk thought of what might be waiting at the top he smiled. With all his heart he hoped the pack would be heavier on his return trip.

Having decided to seize the day and to also work on his conditioning, Nighthawk began to run up the sinuous trail. When he jogged by the middle-aged couple, he nodded and waved off their profuse words of gratitude. He maintained a steady pace and enjoyed the quiet of the wooded path. The only sounds to be heard were occasional bird calls, wind among the pine boughs, and the rustling of leaves from other trees and bushes. Nearly everywhere he looked Nighthawk saw countless ribbons of bright cloth tied onto the branches of trees as prayer offerings to the Lakota Sky Father.

As the gradient increased he shortened his stride making it easier to traverse the twisting trail. Better than half way up he came to a lookout point and stopped.

John's policeman mentality and his proficiency as a tracker didn't always allow him to relax and enjoy himself. At times he felt that he spent too much effort unconsciously absorbing every detail of what he saw and sensed. It was time, he thought, to make a more conscious effort to relax.

The cool breeze soothed his mind while cooling his lightly perspiring body. Out of habit Nighthawk's black eyes probed the lookout area as though it was his first time climbing the Butte.

At a strategic point on the path where there was an abrupt change of direction a wooden platform had been built as a sight-seeing lookout point. The scaffold had been constructed on top of a pinnacle of granite that overlooked the eastern slopes and the southeastern prairie.

While he caught his breath Nighthawk looked back down the southern exposure he had just climbed. His gaze searched the parking lot where he had left the three trouble-makers. At the moment there was no one in sight. All he could see were two cars and his red pick-up truck in the parking lot. He scrutinized an area farther down the slope where the A-frame information center and its black-topped parking facility were located. Since the boys were momentarily out of sight his gaze lifted and he looked further south at the looming panorama of the Black Hills. Although born and raised in and around the Hills, John never tired of looking at them. Their sacred quiet presence was always a comfort to him. He stepped onto the viewing platform and walked to its furthest spot.

Enjoying the vast view Nighthawk placed his hands on the wooden railing and stared over the rugged tree and rock covered slope to the patch-quilt patterns of the tilled prairie land far below.

The wind picked up and moved through the pine with a swirling motion that created a subtle hiss of musical resonance. John listened carefully and allowed himself to imagine that he could hear the voices of his ancestors as they whispered tribal secrets and spoke of long ago.

His thoughts turned full cycle as he recalled why he was there climbing Bear Butte, when he could be having a late lunch with his beautiful, young landlord, Nicole Shaw. Nighthawk's impromptu vision of Nicole's face made him smile, but he reluctantly put thoughts of her aside. He felt that today's reason for being on his sacred mountain took precedence over anything else. John knew when he reached the summit there was a need to focus on his reason for being there. Trying to quell his growing excitement, he sat down on one of the built-in benches, removed his back-pack, and rested. As he happily savored the scent and sound of the sibilant pine Nighthawk allowed his thinking to return to the night before and his marvelous discovery.

***

Five miles south of Sturgis, South Dakota, Nighthawk exited I-90 and followed the road into a growing community called Blucksburg Mountain Estates. The development was sprawled across the treeless, southern slope of a pine-topped ridge that was located on the north side of the Interstate.

He maneuvered his sheriff's department Cherokee along the street that paralleled the many homes and took the first road that led to the top of the wooded ridge. Just over the crest the road curved to the right, and he followed it east for a short distance. Nestled within the pine along the north side of the ridge were several homes, most of which overlooked the prairie. John pulled into one of the driveways with a far-reaching view.

Located on the north side of the road the house appeared much smaller than its actual size. Only a small portion of the dwelling was visible from the road. Most of the home was tiered down the sharp slope of the ridge; John's portion was the top floor. He rented his apartment from the young widow, Nicole Shaw, who lived in the lower level with her ten-year-old son, Mike. Her husband had been killed in an auto fatality a few years earlier. Not having had adequate insurance she had needed to supplement her income to enable her to hang on to her home, therefore Nicole rented out the upper level.

Edges of Time

It was a perfect arrangement for Deputy Nighthawk. He wanted to live within the Hills, but he also wished to be near his peoples' sacred mountain, which he could see from his deck. There was also another, more personal purpose, a reason that could also be viewed from his residence.

John parked the county vehicle in the mouth of the driveway which was level with the top portion of the house. The double garage was down a brief incline from the top of the driveway. Stepping out of the Cherokee the deputy glanced east to where the dirt road disappeared into some trees near the crest of the ridge. Towering above the road and showing through the trees was a portion of a cedar-shake roof and a short span of log wall. The rest of the house that was hidden by trees was perched on the spine of the long ridge. Although unable to see it from where he was, Nighthawk knew that the beautiful log home was still empty and probably just as forlorn appearing as the last time he had seen the house. John remembered exactly how it had looked standing proudly alone and rising above the tree level like a patriarch overlooking his domain.

John Nighthawk's thoughts returned to when, not too long in the past, he had spent some time in the rustic home. Only the deputy and a few elders from his tribe knew and believed what had happened to him. The manuscript was so personal and bizarre Nighthawk was hesitant to tell others about its existence.

While John stared at the exposed portion of the roof he again felt closeness with the man, a man he had never met. A chill went up his back as he thought *wakan* (holy) ... much medicine.

He tore his eyes away and stepped into his apartment. Knowing that Nicole was working late, John hadn't bothered knocking on her door. Besides his wanting to be near Starr's abandoned residence, the deputy had another personal reason for wanting to live where he did. Several months after moving in, Nicole and he had started dating. She was white, but he knew that in many ways her heart was Lakota. His feelings for her were becoming so strong he was beginning to worry about their relationship. If she felt the same they could be in for a lot of problems.

In this part of the county, John knew that white and Indian relationships were almost always looked upon with a prejudiced eye. Nicole was color-blind when it came to relationships, and he didn't think

Barry Brierley

she had a clue as to what they would be up against if they were to get serious. John smiled as he facetiously thought, better be careful, Deputy Nighthawk, or this white woman will steal your heart and you will be unable to arrest her for doing so.

Stepping over to the fireplace, he unbuckled his holstered Browning 9mm and placed it on the mantle. The lingering scent of sweet grass and sage smoke reminded him that his friend, Weasel Bear, had been there earlier in the day and had blessed his home with a sacred ritual.

Dropping his tan, narrow-brimmed, sheriff's department hat onto a chair, Nighthawk slid his patio door open and stepped out onto a small deck that overlooked the steep, pine tree covered slope and a small portion of the sweeping prairie. The pine-scented air was his most favorite of nature's perfumes. He breathed it in and looked down on the Butte.

It stood alone on the very fringe of the prairie; towering above everything nearby. John could see an eagle soaring near the summit; with the distance its size was reduced to a mere speck. A growing tightness in his chest made him lean forward and clutch the railing. Every time he saw *wambli* he was affected in some way. The eagle was very sacred to his people. In his mind he spoke a silent prayer then put his spirituality aside.

His thoughts abruptly turned to Daniel Starr; the artist who had disappeared. He glanced through the patio's open door at the stack of library books on his coffee table. Having scoured nearly every library, museum, and bookseller in the Hills, he dreaded having to go through more picture books, but he'd already put it off for several days. John knew that the continuation of his research was necessary if he was ever to find out what happened to Daniel Starr and his quest.

It had been over a year since John had found the manuscript; however, he was still undecided whether or not to go public with what he knew. If only for his own satisfaction the search would continue until he found proof of Starr's having once again been transported back in time to the 1890's. The fact that, by going back in time, Daniel Starr had become someone other than himself, was a story best left unsaid. Who would believe it?

In the west the sky was beginning to show some color when Nighthawk left the deck and re-entered his apartment. After turning his reading light on, he began to painstakingly page through the books. All

Edges of Time

of the publications had a common denominator; each dealt with Native Americans, and all had photographs from Lakota and other reservations after 1890. Many of the photos were disturbing because they included scenes of poverty and depravations with Indians poorly dressed in cast off white man clothing, or homemade calico dresses.

It was full dark outside when John picked up the over-sized book dealing with a historical incident called the, 'Wanamaker Expedition of 1913.' Skimming through the pages, he saw that it was a photographic record of an expedition that traveled across the country by rail and had visited seventy-five Indian reservations. Most of the Indians photographed were dressed in white man's' clothing, or in beautifully beaded and quilled old-time traditional regalia. Included were many personal portraits and several shots of white dignitaries teamed up with various tribal chiefs for some type of ceremonial document signings. The United States flag was evident in many of the photos; one Indian woman had 'Old Glory' wrapped around herself as though it was a blanket.

Nighthawk didn't bother reading the text. Probably, he mused, just another treaty that was destined to be broken by the whites. He began using his thumb to rapidly flip through the pages. Suddenly he stopped. He quickly thumbed back through pages he had already flipped through. There. His heart seemed to skip a beat. While thumbing the pages, John had recognized the profile of Bear Butte. He stared. His heart rate quickened.

The butte was a looming presence behind a small group of people in the foreground. Excitement moved rapidly through his body, as he studied three of the people in the photo.

In the foreground two Lakota chiefs were dressed in war bonnets, beaded and quilled shirts, and leggings. They were flanked on either side by a couple of grinning, middle-aged bureaucratic-appearing white men. All were seated on what looked like a long, elegant sofa surrounded by prairie grass and sagebrush. Behind the strange ensemble was a scene that, if anything, was even more bizarre. A beautiful Indian woman and a young Indian man, both well dressed in stylish white clothing of the time period, circa 1913. Both Native Americans were standing; they were holding aloft what appeared to be a large, detailed painting of Bear Butte. The woman was smiling and holding the painting with one hand while balancing an open parasol with the other. Her face was vaguely

Barry Brierley

familiar. The young Indian man, his right hand supporting the opposite end of the unframed painting, was smiling broadly at the camera; which in itself was a rare sight because Nighthawk knew that many Indians at that time were still afraid of cameras. They believed that the cameras stole their shadows.

But the most staggering sight in the photo was the older man, who was sandwiched between the woman and young man. He was kneeling on one knee and pointing at a spot in the painting. His rigid forefinger indicated a position near the summit of Bear Butte. The man's features were more Indian than his missing person photos, but Nighthawk knew, without a doubt, that it was the missing artist, Daniel Starr!

Over the years, he had seen Starr's photo on so many missing person police flyers that John knew the man's face almost as well as his own. The difference between then and now was obvious. When the photo was taken back in 1913 Starr's Indian blood was more prevalent and he was a younger man. Nighthawk slowed his thinking for a moment while his heartbeat returned to normal. As he studied the photo, he absently ran a trembling hand over the smooth surface of the glossy page. He pushed his face closer and squinted. Nighthawk carefully placed the open book down and abruptly got up and left the room. When he came back a magnifying glass was clutched in his hand. He peered closely at the magnified face of the woman. Because her hair was piled on top of her head John could clearly see, within the shadow of her hat, the identifiable star-shaped birthmark high on her right cheekbone.

"Star Watcher," he murmured aloud.

Because of her natural beauty John could see why the woman was the catalyst that had pulled Daniel Starr back to the nineteenth century. He was entranced. Even under the close scrutiny of his magnifying glass, Star Watcher's beauty remained undaunted in spite of the years and the grainy, antique photo. She still looked as beautiful as in Starr's painting, rendered when she was twenty-three years younger.

Nighthawk moved the magnifying glass over the face of the young Indian man. He immediately saw the similarity between the young man's face and his own. Their faces were different, but because of the similar features it was obvious they were related. John knew that he was looking at the first adult photo he had ever seen of his long-time unknown ancestral grandfather, Nighthawk. Exhilarated with the excitement of it all, John let his eyes drop to the paragraph beneath the photo. What he read there brought a smile to his lips and an emotional tear to his eye as he contemplated Starr's intuitive move and far-sighted plan.

***

While moving swiftly up the trail Nighthawk's thoughts were still lingering on the photo. At first he hadn't understood what Starr was trying to tell him. It wasn't until he recalled the part in the artist's manuscript where he had added a post script. It was his final correspondence to whoever was reading his story. By rereading his copy of the 'post script' John had been able to figure it out: *"I must add, dear reader, if ever your common sense leads you to doubt my accomplishment, study the work of the 'Shadow Catchers.' I owe them a great deal. Perhaps, in time, my support will repay them in a small way and inform you of my existence in the past."*

It was the last eight words of the missive that convinced John of Daniel Starr's desire to communicate ... the key word being *inform.* His reasoning told him that had Starr not planned to convey more information he would have used the words *prove* or *confirm,* instead of the more flexible *inform.* Nighthawk had known that it was probably a long-shot, but his instincts told him otherwise. Why, he mused, would Daniel Starr be pointing to a specific spot on Bear Butte rather than an open-handed gesture as a presentation of his painting? In his heart, John knew that Starr was telling him to take a close look at the spot he was indicating.

Nearing the summit, his musing was interrupted by a young couple who happily breezed by him on their way back down the Butte.

His breathing had deepened and he was perspiring again, but Nighthawk felt good. Wanting to keep his conditioning, he wrote himself a mental note to visit the gym, do some work on the heavy bag and jump some rope.

Before John got into police work he was considered one of the three or four best super middleweights in amateur boxing. Since there was no place to go after the amateurs except turn pro, Nighthawk quit. The life of a professional boxer had too many pitfalls, so he decided to

113

concentrate on the one other thing in which he excelled, being a tracker. Most law enforcement tracking today was done with teams. John Nighthawk learned his skills by an old Lakota named Two Fingers who taught him the traditional method of tracking both humans and animals.

Finally, he was alone at the peak. With an unexpected decrease in the wind, the silence was absolute. Nighthawk momentarily enjoyed the peace of mind. For him, serenity usually went hand in hand with quiet times. A need to discover if his theory was valid chased away John's usual calm acceptance of the way things are. Curiosity, however, pushed him swiftly to the other side of the crest. It was the spot where the viewing platform projected from the summit. If his calculations were right, Daniel Starr's finger had been pointing at an approximate spot just below where the tourist lookout had recently been erected.

Walking out onto the platform, Nighthawk looked down at the sharply receding slope. His breath caught in his throat and he stopped moving. A mule deer was wildly dodging around trees while running uphill, straight toward him. Apparently something down below had frightened it enough so that the grueling run was deemed necessary. It moved straight toward the base of the lookout point. Nighthawk was careful not to so much as twitch; he barely breathed. The deer, a four-point buck, stopped directly in front and below of the platform. His antlered head lifted and John would have sworn that the deer looked right at him. The buck lowered his head and sniffed at one of several gray rocks that were scattered about. His delicate hoof tapped at the rock like a horse trying to clear snow away from some grass. A resurgent gust of wind swept across the top of the Butte. An unexpected rattle of pine boughs caused John's eyes to lift; when he lowered his gaze the deer was gone. He felt the hackles raise on the back of his neck. The wind rustled the leaves and caused them to whisper softly.

"Spirits," he murmured quietly.

Stepping off the sightseeing scaffold Nighthawk shucked his pack and moved down onto some large stones resting next to the platform support pillars. As he slowly worked his way down the incline the logical side of his brain was at odds with his spiritual side. Being a traditional Lakota, and standing on top of his peoples' most sacred place, logic didn't have a chance.

Nighthawk stepped onto a large flat rock just in front of the vertical support timbers. The spot where the deer stood was on a flat area of terrain just beyond the rock. Taking his time he set the pack down beside his foot and looked at the distant lake two miles off to his right and far below. He absently thought how it would be nice if he were to invite Nicole and her son, Mike, to the ancient lake for a picnic.

Not able to let his thoughts stray too far from his quest John thought again of the deer. He marveled at how unafraid the deer had been and couldn't help but wonder if there was some spiritual reason why he had been there. His gaze drifted back to the flat portion of terrain directly below him. In his mind John transformed the patch of ground into a grid. His searching eyes minutely examined each square before moving on to the next. Nighthawk's total concentration was so centered he became absolutely motionless and barely breathed. Having completed the grid search he tried the complete opposite. He stared at the general area of rocky surface and forced himself not to focus on anything. Had his eyes been camera lenses he would have wanted them adjusted to the infinity setting, putting everything close at hand, out of focus. Something, he thought, does not belong in this clearing. John squinted his eyes to the point where his eyes were almost shut and peered through his eyelashes at the blurred piece of ground. It was then that he saw what had been bothering him. The stones were different. A shiver moved up his spine as he thought; the deer smelled one of the rocks then nudged it with his hoof. Was he trying to give me a clue?

"That is *witko* (crazy) thinking," he mused aloud, "Or is it?"

John moved to the very edge of the flat rock and sat down with his ankles crossed beneath him. He began to re-examine the flat area where the mule deer had paused. His eyes kept returning to the rocks. What made them different from all the others, he questioned? All at once he knew; it was their color. All the other stones nearby were tan; these were gray; like the one the deer touched. Another thing that caught his eye was the size. Most of the gray rocks were of an approximate size of an orange. That in itself was an indication they were brought there. Why, he wondered. And why were several of them lined up one behind the other? Maybe, he thought, the men that constructed the scaffold had used them for something. He rejected that idea when he noticed how many of the rocks were firmly imbedded into the soil, indicating that they had remained in the same place for an unknown number of years, or decades.

It wasn't until he noticed, in two instances, where the aligned rocks formed a V, and in another place an X. It was then that he knew.

Nighthawk slid off the rock and began to gather the stones that weren't aligned with another. He swiftly replaced the rocks in different spots. A pattern began to emerge. In moments he was finished. Jubilant, he stared at his reconstruction. It was Daniel's 'star' made from rocks. The five pointed star design that had been used by Daniel Starr in lieu of a signature.

He recalled how the artist had used the star symbol on paintings, notes and even in his manuscript. John was ecstatic. He knew without a doubt that Daniel Starr had been standing on that very spot almost a century ago.

Nighthawk was staggered by the enormity of his discovery. Who would believe him? No doubt his Lakota elders, the Gray Feather Society, would accept the story. He knew that no *wasichu* (white man) would. With a derisive grunt, John thought if they can't see it, touch it, watch it on TV, or read about it in their newspapers, they won't believe it.

John stared at the crude star and thought about Daniel Starr and the love of his life, Star Watcher. He wondered what it was like to love a woman so much that you would give up everything to be with her. It must be wonderful to love so completely; or is it? What if you were to lose her?

Nighthawk shook off his musing, and looked around. Birds were singing; a warming breeze was sifting through the pines. Others would probably be climbing the Butte. How would he explain his strange behavior? It was then he remembered the middle-aged couple that the young men were hassling. Where are they, he wondered; they should have made it to the top by now. It's possible, he thought, that they had decided not to climb all the way. John knew that many people only climbed as far as the platform with the eastern view. He put the thought aside and tried to relax. It was a futile effort; he could feel the excitement steadily building.

He knew that Daniel Starr would have left something for him, but what? Where? John remembered how the artist always drew his star so that the lines that overlapped were on the lower left point. From where he stood the over-lapping point of the five-pointed star was pointed to the left of the scaffold, aimed directly at a small rocky ledge. There was nothing else nearby, only the shelf of rock. He looked beyond the ledge and to either side. Unless Starr had buried something, the stone abutment was the only possible candidate for a cache or hideaway. Moving closer he saw that the stony ledge was like a cliff in miniature. He stopped only feet away and stared. Nighthawk smiled. Everything looked natural but for one small detail. Starr hadn't known who would find and read his manuscript, so he wasn't taking any chances of his current hideout being overlooked. The largest stone was right in the middle of the ledge and it was sandstone. Starr's five-pointed star had been carved deeply onto its face.

Using his clasp knife, John swiftly scraped away the caked dirt and pebbles that surrounded the stone like ancient mortar. Using a stick for a lever, he pried it free. He quickly stepped back to avoid the path of the falling stone; when he looked up there it was, a hole behind where the rock had fit into the ledge. The first thing he saw was an oblong object wrapped in some strange looking material. He didn't know what it was but it definitely wasn't meant to remain a part of the ledge. Recovering his stick, Nighthawk probed into the dark recesses of the hole to be sure that some rattler hadn't made a home there.

He pulled the object free and was surprised by its weight. The strange wrapping turned out to be oilskin, a material that was applied for waterproofing 'back in the day.' Inside was a metal box. Its surface had been covered with a light oil or animal fat. There was very little rust and no lock. It opened like a trunk. Nighthawk simply lifted the lid.

John felt his heart beating strongly against the wall of his chest. Another oilskin-wrapped package was inside. Seeing what the object was, he felt light-headed with relief; it was a journal in which he hoped contained a manuscript. Although Daniel Starr wasn't aware of it, he shared a special kinship with John Nighthawk, and the deputy was thrilled that the artist had once again decided to share his story in written form.

He removed the box and carried it up to the platform. Assuming the journal was a manuscript he couldn't wait until he got home to start reading. Setting the box on the bench he lifted the lid for a final peek. John was about to shut the lid when he stopped. His curiosity and excitement were too great. He felt that he'd better slow down; he hoped that he was way too young to have a heart attack.

After cutting away the protective covering, he smiled … as with the first manuscript Daniel Starr had left a note separate from the chronicle. The single page was handwritten in cursive; John carefully picked it up and began to read.

Dear Reader,

I must assume that someone is reading my chronicles. If not I'll have to resign myself to the possibility that I'm corresponding with myself. If the later is true I'll simply have to consider my scribbling a form of therapy and continue on. Before I tell you my tale let me first inform you that there has never been a time that I have regretted my seemingly impetuous move. My love for Star Watcher is endless; our happiness is almost too much for others less fortunate than us to endure. Over the years our friends have done one of two things; they either try to stay near in hope that some of our happiness will rub off on them, or they would do the opposite and stay away, our delight in each other being too much for them to handle.

Another reason for my lack of regret is my love for my adopted son, Nighthawk. Being childless in my previous life, my joy in fatherhood has been as bountiful as my love of life itself. Don't misunderstand me; my past life did have its rewards. Most of all were the many friends accumulated over the years, and my painting, which became my passion and eventually my life's work. My interpretation of Native American historical moments resulted in a very profitable and rewarding career.

But let me tell you this, until I experienced and overcame the unforeseen obstacles that I did upon my return to the past and subsequent search for Star Watcher, followed by our numerous years together. I feel I really hadn't lived until now. Perhaps when you read the enclosed manuscript you will understand.

Nighthawk stared for a moment at the inked missive and wondered at the man's obvious courage. But then he remembered how Daniel Starr had written that he had regained much of his lost youth when he time-traveled. That alone would be a strong incentive. Being still young, John thought, I probably can't imagine <u>how</u> strong the incentive was. Put that motivation together with his love for the woman and it sounds like an opportunity the man simply couldn't pass up. He smiled to himself as he remembered the startling information written about Starr in the book on the Wanamaker Expedition. John's respect for the man was becoming endless.

John put the piece of paper back in the box and closed the lid. He let his mind relax and his gaze slide to the west. His eye was again drawn toward the lake two miles away. Nighthawk absently recalled how history recorded that Native Americans had camped there for more than four thousand years. The casual thought stimulated John's intellect. When he thought of all the stories and history connected with that fact alone, it made him hunger all the more for knowledge of the past and of his people. Knowing that he couldn't wait until he got home to read the manuscript, John shook his head at his lack of patience. He sat down on the wooden bench built into the platform's guard rail and once again opened the flat chest; he removed what looked like a leather-bound journal approximately 11 X 14 inches in size. He opened it and eagerly began reading.

Barry Brierley

Book Two

NEAR WOUNDED KNEE CREEK

Barry Brierley

CALEB STARR JR.

B. BRIERLEY

Edges of Time

BLACK ELK

B. BRIERLEY

Barry Brierley

CHAPTER THIRTEEN

PINE RIDGE AGENCY, SOUTH DAKOTA, 1897

I was choking. A red-orange dust and the closeness of milling cattle had created a hell that was hard to ignore. I was flat on my back in dry red clay and pulverized manure while numerous beeves were trying their damnedest to step on me.

Where in the hell, I wondered, had the word 'beeves' come from? Cattle had always been cows to me. My heart thudded with excitement as I struggled to get to my feet. The stench and clamor of the cattle were so overpowering that it seemed to have become a part of me.

Faintly, over the din of the bawling cattle, I heard laughter. Through the haze I saw several indistinct human forms; a pair of whom seemed to be crouching in mid-air. I blinked repeatedly and turned away. My heart gave a lurch when I noticed that a saddled horse, a tall blood bay, was standing close behind me. The cloud of red dust was so thick I could barely breathe. Reaching, I grabbed at a stirrup. For some reason my left hand couldn't grab hold. My horse stood rock solid as I grabbed the leather with my right. With the thick dust roiling and getting in my eyes I couldn't see what was wrong. Through the shifting haze, I saw my right hand as it clutched the stirrup. The dark skin and the strength in my fingers came from a man of much younger years than my former self. It was then that I realized I was back! I'd made it back to the nineteenth century.

Using just my right hand, I pulled myself to my knees. I shook my head and tossed longish, blue/black hair back away

Barry Brierley

from my eyes. The excitement of being back made the sight of my graying brown hair suddenly transformed into a shiny black, seem unimportant. All that mattered was that I would soon be with Star Watcher.

The cattle passed me by, and the swirling dust swiftly cleared out. I noticed that my left hand felt heavy and awkward. Looking to see what was wrong, I stared in absolute horror. My left hand was gone! In its place was a crudely carved wooden hand. I couldn't believe my eyes; how could that be possible? I desperately prayed that I was only dreaming. Fighting down a rising panic, my searching right hand felt straps and a buckle beneath the shirt on my left forearm. How could this have happened? My mind recalled the image of the J.C. H. Grabill photo. I remembered it vividly as only a professional artist can.

Caleb Starr, Jr. was astride a horse in among a herd of cattle, the reins were held in his right hand and his left ... was out of sight behind him. Oh my God, I thought, I had painted myself into the body and life of a one-armed man!

Deputy John Nighthawk was so shocked he didn't realize he had stood up. He stared at the manuscript page with eyes that didn't want to believe. Slowly he lowered the leather bound manuscript and set it down. Trying not to run Nighthawk left the platform, skipped over the stones, and skid down the bank to where he had left the back-pack. He snatched it up and, forgetting his efforts not to run, raced up the incline back to the viewing place. Pulling the Wanamaker Expedition book out of the pack he immediately turned to the marked page with the photo of Daniel Starr. The artist was pointing at the painting with his right hand; his left was out of sight behind one of the seated dignitaries. John suddenly felt deflated. He wished that he had the other book. It was a publication in which Starr had found the photo of Nathanial Starr's twin brother, Caleb Starr, Junior. He remembered that his painting of the photo had been the catalyst that had propelled the artist back in time. Feeling frustrated and defeated by the whole scenario, Nighthawk realized that everything was irrevocably out of his control and had been from the beginning. He set the journal down and managed to sit down himself. He was aware that he was far too involved with something he had no control over. His awe of Daniel Starr was manifesting into borderline hero worship. The man's ability to handle adversity was phenomenal. While his mind was doing flip-flops and threatening to do a reality check, without forethought John picked up the antique journal. He simply couldn't believe the man's fortitude and resolution. Taking a deep breath he opened the journal and found where he had stopped reading, and once again resumed.

***

My mind was so bedazzled and shocked by my new discovery that I was unaware that someone was near until I felt hands slip beneath my arms and hoist me to my feet and then brusquely began to brush the dust off my shirt and pants. I turned and stared into a handsome, middle-aged Indian face. He wore a penny-colored countenance bearing a pair of twinkling eyes, black as coal, and a wide mouth that was struggling not to smile.

Not yet accepting my misfortune, my gaze kept jumping back and forth between my wooden hand and the Indian as he methodically continued to brush me off. To get my mind off my false hand, I absently took stock of my attire.

I was wearing a dark, faded, collar-less cotton shirt beneath a tan vest. A red sash was wrapped tightly around my waist, covering where my suspenders buttoned onto my cotton canvas pants. A long, high plains style knife was sheathed beneath the sash at my back. As I stared down at my worn, shotgun chaps and stupidly wondered how I would ever manage unbuckling them one-handed, the Indian bent down and retrieved a tan, sweat-stained, narrow-brimmed hat.

Handing me the hat the Indian looked me over for any possible injuries. I returned the visual scrutiny while trying to figure out what this man had to do with my new life.

The Indian was dressed in buckskin pants, a dark cotton shirt and was wearing a red bandanna on his head beneath a black, full crowned wide-brimmed hat. His hair appeared to be tied in some kind of a knot on the back of his neck. He wore a bright red sash, identical to my own, around his slim horseman's waist. A beautifully beaded vest completed his outfit.

The Indian looked beyond me and waved to the obscure

Barry Brierley

figures in the settling cloud of dust. While my mind was whirling with a hodgepodge of disbelief, pity and denial that I had lost my left hand, another part of me was accepting my situation. The disfigurement was a fact that I couldn't change. If I was going to find Star Watcher and learn how to survive, first I had to learn how to cope.

While one part of my brain was rationalizing, another area was telling me, 'you're going to die alone, a penniless, crippled half-breed.' In the middle of all my confusion the Indian, whom I inexplicably knew to be named Billy, looked me in the eye and suddenly gestured over his shoulder. He grinned and said, "Long-eye and me believe this is first time you fall off horse since you were a baa-ak-saa-wi-she."

Somehow, I knew immediately that he had said "child" in Crow Indian dialect.

My gaze abruptly swept beyond Billy's smiling face to the rails of a crude corral. I was searching for the person to whom Billy had waved.

A couple of Indians sitting on the fence were the men 'crouched in mid-air' that I had seen through a thick cloud of red dust. While other Indians nearby were stoically watching the proceedings. In the middle of the group of poorly dressed 'blanket Indians' a tall, gray-haired, bearded white man was leaning against the fence.

The man's skin had been burned by the sun as dark as any Native American, but besides the beard and sweeping mustache, it was the older man's dress and presence that set him apart.

His thumbs were hooked in a pair of vest pockets beneath the sweep of a faded bandanna that I was certain, in its day, had been a colorful portion of his wardrobe. A tall-crowned, sweat-stained, light-colored hat with a wide furled brim sat on his head. The hat was so much a part of the man it looked like it had never been removed since the day he bought it. Also looking like it belonged was the large pistol rigged in a holster on his left hip, a set-up for a cross-draw. Ordinary range clothes and knee-high, stove-top boots, and leather wrist-cuffs set off his outfit.

Seeing me look his way, the man, whom I suddenly realized had to be my newly acquired father and actual ancestor, Caleb Starr, grinned and waved. Mesmerized by shock and unexpected turn of events, I clumsily raised my left arm and waggled it to return his gesture. Still grinning, the weathered plainsman grabbed his faded blue neckerchief and wiped the dust free of his bearded face. Something dark and mysterious was bothering me about Caleb Starr's presence. Why was he here? Neither he nor Billy was in the book's photos.

My brain had been so bruised by my misfortune that I hadn't had time to think of Star Watcher and young Nighthawk, nor worry about Starr's whereabouts.

All at once I was choking; bending from the waist I hacked and coughed repeatedly. Billy hovered nearby. While freeing my lungs of the clinging dust I must have spit up more than was obvious, because at that moment I became aware that Billy was a Crow Indian and that I was his nephew.

"Are you well, Strong Arm?"

"I will live, Uncle. But I promise never to fall again. As I grow older and softer the Mother Earth's skin has grown harder."

Billy laughed and slapped me hard enough on the back to raise another small cloud of red dust.

After Wounded Knee, my recognition of my Crow name was no surprise; nor did the fact that we were speaking in the Crow language. Now that I had become Caleb Junior and was slowly adjusting to the fact that my feet were once again firmly planted in the soil of the nineteenth century, minus my left hand, I had to pull myself together. Still shaken by my situation I knew that nothing was ever going to really shock me again.

As Billy walked toward my father, I paused at my horse's left stirrup. Still standing firm, the tall horse turned his head and gave me a baleful look. His arched, swollen appearing neck gave me pause as I sensed the raw power he projected. I had been about to mount when it dawned on me that I couldn't grab the pommel of the saddle or the mane to pull myself up. Somehow, I knew that my horse had been trained a different way. I also knew his name; it was Redman. Without any further thought I circled my horse, grabbed the reins and mounted from the right side, Indian style. The newfound strength in my youthful right arm gave me a brief, if fleeting, comfort. Once in the saddle, there *was such a feeling of confidence and familiarity that I knew instantly that there were not many who were my equal on horseback. Redman danced to the left. With a light pressure on the rein, the big stallion spun in a tight circle raising even more dust. I felt like the mythical centaur must have felt who was half man and half horse. Spiritually, as well a physically, I had become as one with my horse.*

With my head still spinning from my trauma I wasn't quite ready to face a father I had never met. Whirling Red in another circle I threw another wave at Caleb Starr, forced a grin at Billy, heel-tapped the strutting blood bay into a canter, and rode out of the corral through pink clouds of rising dust.

CHAPTER FOURTEEN
ON RESERVATION TRAILS

Aiming the big horse toward the wagon-rutted road, I slowed Red to a walk giving me the time to examine my new appendage.

The artificial hand had been carved in a clever but ugly manner out of a very hard wood. The four stubby fingers had been shaped into a curved half-fist with a larger space between the first and second finger. Useful objects could be carried from the curved fingers, and perhaps reins could be worked into the slot between the two fingers. The only thing that puzzled me was the thumb. The man who carved it had shaped the thumb in an upright, 'thumbs up' manner and, like the fingers, had been fashioned into a more sturdy form than that of a real thumb; I couldn't for the life of me understand why it had been fashioned in such a manner. The surface encircling the wooden member had been worn smooth and darkened with use. While studying the wooden thumb I realized that with the forefinger on my right hand I had been massaging the underside of my real thumb. There was a curious callus formed on its surface. It was cracked and hard as leather, and I couldn't figure out what had caused it. Thinking the hardened skin had probably been formed from roping or some such labor, I put my curiosity aside and touched Redman with my heels and cantered forward.

Almost immediately upon reaching the road I met several Indians riding toward where the cattle were penned. They looked Lakota, but I couldn't be sure. When they passed me, their smiling faces were animated with excitement. This appeared

131

strange because there were Indians everywhere and almost without exception, the riders were the only adults showing any light-hearted emotion. On the other hand, young children were happily running everywhere.

Except for moccasins nearly all the Indians, children and adults alike, were dressed in drab, hand-me-down white man's clothing, or homemade calico, cotton or muslin dresses and shirts.

A pair of running dogs appeared out of nowhere, barked at Red's hooves, and disappeared again into the tall grass. In an abrupt move that was pure reflex, I had reined in my horse using my wooden left hand. Realizing what I had done, I stared in surprise at my artificial appendage. I had automatically slipped my reins into the carved slots on either side of my curled middle finger. The leather ribbons had then been looped over the forefinger before being wrapped around the erect thumb in a manner that would anchor them. Heel-tapping the bay into motion I shook my head at the wonder of it all and refused to get caught up in the illogical aspects of my bizarre situation.

As I rode by the many groups I could hear snatches of conversation that confirmed they were Sioux. Just in case I hadn't mentioned it before, Lakota was a language that I had picked up during my years of painting the Sioux and my relentless fixation on their history and culture. The Sioux that I had known during my career as an artist were a troubled people, and these Lakota didn't really seem to be much different, unless poorer and more destitute. A prevailing pall of hopelessness seemed to be hovering over each group; also, here and there, I heard occasional words of dissension and anger directed my way along with some hostile looks. Being half Crow and half white, the glances thrown my way could have been aimed at either bloodline. Ignoring the rude looks I rode Red through or around many of the groups. Several times I heard the word 'wasichu' (white man) and often I heard the Lakota speaking of food, or how hungry they and their children had been.

A high-pitched yipping made me twist in the saddle to look back toward the corral and stock pen. My mouth opened in surprise as I watched a group of blanket swinging, yelping Sioux horsemen chase a small herd of cattle from their split-railed *confinement. They were the same group of excited Lakota that I had met on the road.*

The cattle quickly spread out with beeves running in all directions, and the hard-riding Lakota chasing them. Gunshots interrupted the afternoon quiet as riders rode alongside of the cattle and shot down on them as though they were buffalo. This was a surprise to me because I thought the Lakota weren't allowed firearms. My wonder changed to pleasure as I watched many smiling, blanketed women and a group of knife-flourishing men appear who seemed to come from everywhere. They ran in a long ragged line toward the fallen cattle and pounced like wolves on the still quivering carcasses. The sun, shining almost directly above, glinted off the skillfully wielded knives clutched in their fists.

Later that year I learned that it was the last time Lakota were allowed to chase the cattle and ride them down like buffalo; nor could they butcher them in the traditional way. After a government order put a stop to the practice meat was to be killed privately by butchers, cut in the white man's way, and issued out in hunks that cut right into the natural pieces which the women were used to leveling out into jerked meat. A meat house was erected and brought so much resentment that one night someone burned it down. I was told an Oglala did the deed.

Seeing the random killing brought back some vivid, unpleasant memories of Wounded Knee. I was getting flashes of unarmed Lakota running toward the gully while being ridden down soldiers on horseback. It was time to leave. I turned Red and rode away from the scene.

Redman's smooth, loping gait carried me down a dusty road that led toward a scatter of buildings that were mere dots far in the distance. Roughly two miles separated the buildings from the beef rationing. In the far distance the dark, looming presence of the Black Hills dominated the horizon.

The dwellings I was approaching had to be the town and agency of Pine Ridge. I had learned in my research that it was where the other rations were distributed; bacon, cornmeal, flour, coffee and sugar were the added rations.

Barry Brierley

Although eight years have passed and they appear different in the summertime, some of the buildings I recognized from Wounded Knee when I bought food and other rations for Star Watcher and me to take to the Stronghold.

All along the narrow road Lakota were walking or riding in wagons with an occasional horse-backed rider pacing alongside. They were either going toward or coming from the beef slaughter. I couldn't help but speculate on what an interesting painting the scene would make. I passed a stream where I knew women would soon be rinsing and cleaning the slaughtered animals' intestines. Like with the buffalo of olden days the Lakota didn't waste a thing.

Filled to the brim with anticipation my excitement level began to climb. At any moment I expected to see Star Watcher and young Nighthawk walking toward me along the rutted dirt road. My expectations were put on hold as I encountered a handful of blue-coated, horseback Indians riding toward me on the same road. A young, thin army officer sporting a mustache led them. The day was getting warmer and the pink haze rising from their horses' hooves hung in the still air all but hiding the horses' legs. At first I thought the Indians were what other Sioux called Metal Breasts, the Sioux police who were recruited to work for the Bluecoats enforcing the white man's laws. When they came closer I saw that I was mistaken; there were no badges. I remembered from my research that they were Oglala Sioux soldiers. While passing the group I heard a muttered curse followed by another insult, "... egg-sucking, Crow dog."

When I looked to see who had spoken, several pair of black Lakota eyes were staring at me with open animosity.

Strangely unruffled, I returned their looks with equal venom then spurred Red into a hard gallop and let them taste some of our Crow dust.

The village of Pine Ridge wasn't much to look at, a scatter of buildings and houses that appeared as desolate as the rest of the land. A long line of women and children and a handful of elderly men coursed along the length of a feed ramp and dock into the shadowed confines of one of the buildings. Nearly all the women, in spite of the day's heat, were wrapped in blankets or white cotton wrappings. Later I learned that the white garments were

134

bed sheets used in lieu of a blanket in the summer heat.

After walking Redman the length of the line and enduring more unfriendly glances I concluded that Star Watcher wasn't among the gathering. Confused and filled with a growing fear I reined my red horse away from the buildings toward the open prairie. Here and there were scattered dwellings that looked like one room sheds or log storage shacks until closer scrutiny revealed them to be the actual homes of Lakota families.

My heart was filled with pity for these defeated people. Not only were they forced to live in such cramped housing, but also having to live in square boxes was an abomination. These people considered the circle to be sacred; they built their lodges and even formed their villages in circles. Was housing them in square dwellings ignorance, or was it truly calculated? My head reeled with indignation at the possibility that it could have been done on purpose ... anything to force this wild, wonderful people into a domestic therefore manipulative frame of mind. If indeed it was premeditated, it was probably considered necessary by those in control.

After aimlessly searching I wheeled Redman and headed back to town. Once there I again rode the length of the main street watching, hoping for a glimpse of a dark blanket decorated with a large star. Remembering the photo in the book I was again impressed with Star Watcher's ability to capture the likeness of my child-like overlapping star.

I considered stopping and inquiring at some of the homes but decided not to. Why would a Lakota help an unknown Crow breed? I was momentarily at a loss as to what I should do. It was obvious that Star Watcher wasn't anywhere nearby. A horse's soft nicker perked Redman's ears and brought my head around. An army officer was riding up the road. Not having any other options I turned Redman and we cantered over to intercept him. It was the blade-thin officer I'd seen earlier leading the unit of Lakota soldiers. He slowed his horse to a walk as I came abreast. I reined in and the officer followed suit. His gelding, a dapple-gray, gave Redman the eye which, of course, the red horse ignored.

Barry Brierley

Up close the lieutenant appeared to be made of a stern stock, a no nonsense kind of guy. A lean, almost bony, sunburned face was the background for his hard, yet expressionless gaze. Even his trimmed, full mustache was serious looking. His dark eyes locked onto mine and appeared to do their damnedest to see all the way into my soul. I sensed that if I didn't speak soon I'd be dismissed and left sitting beside the trail eating the dapple-gray's dust.

"Sorry to bother you, Sir... I was wondering if you could tell me where that photographer, Grabill, is set up. I'm trying to ..."

"That would be in Deadwood."

The officer's interruption startled me. I was about to ask what he meant when he spoke again.

"Unless he's on one of his expeditions looking for truth with a camera lens ... where there isn't any to be found."

"He hasn't been here taking pictures of 'Beef Day'?"

"You're the rancher Starr's son ... got that horse ranch up near Deadwood."

It wasn't a question, but it was enough to startle me again. I nodded, grateful for the information of where my home was located. I was getting a little agitated, however, with the man's abruptness. But if it wasn't for this rude lieutenant, I thought, I'd have to ask someone where I lived.

"Grabill hasn't been here since last year during 'Beef Day'."

How can that be? My heart plummeted, and my stomach was now tumbling like a hand-pumped butter-churn. I envisioned the date, 1898, beside Star Watcher's photo.

The soldier must have seen the disbelief on my face because all at once he felt inclined to explain.

"The picture taker comes every other year on the even numbered year dates. This being '97, he won't be back until next year. When he was here last year, Grabill was taking photographs of all the squaws and any of the bucks that'd let him."

How can that be? In my mind I once again quickly reviewed what was in the book. I distinctly remembered the date for Star Watcher's photo as well as Caleb Junior's as being 1898. My mind was a whirl with all the confusing dates. All I could ascertain was that the dates were wrong in the book. God knows when or how the photos were compiled and cataloged.

Before I had time to get depressed about what must have happened the lieutenant was speaking again.

"You'd think that Grabill or some other picture taker would have showed up on this beef day; some of the Wild West show-people came through earlier."

I barely heard the man's last words ... my thoughts were focused on Star Watcher.

"Have you seen a young Lakota woman wearing a dark blanket decorated with a star design made from cowry shells or elks' teeth?" I asked. As the lieutenant thought my query over, I added, "She has a young son with her; he's about seven years old."

The lieutenant slowly shook his head and replied, "I can't help you, Mr. Starr." He raised a gauntlet-gloved hand and pointed in a southerly direction. "You will find a wagon road over there that will take you a few miles south to Black Elk's cabin. He's an Oglala medicine man. If anyone would know of her it would be him."

Refusing to give in to sorrow or worry my heart began to beat faster knowing that I was about to once again meet the famous Lakota holy man. I became inexplicably nervous. Would he remember me as ... or not at all? Suddenly, I realized the army officer had extended his hand and was speaking to me. I gazed into his dark, intelligent eyes and shook his hand.

"... A great admirer of your father's scouting exploits. Please tell him, Lieutenant John J. Pershing sends his regards. Good day to you, sir."

I was so surprised when I heard his name; his last words came to me as though through a tunnel. I became momentarily speechless and silently watched the man ride away. My gaze fixed with fascination on the soldier who was eventually to become the Supreme Commander of the United States Army, and be known throughout the world as Blackjack Pershing.

Barry Brierley

CHAPTER FIFTEEN

The eagle's scream startled Nighthawk. Directly above him a golden eagle soared. My God, he thought, he's less than fifty feet above me. Without taking his eyes from the eagle, the deputy got to his feet. Miraculously, the bird wasn't alarmed and seemed to be looking straight into his eyes. A chill swept up John's spine as the golden eagle swooped to the left and planed down the southern side of the butte. Far down the butte it began to circle once again.

Because of the angle of his view, John couldn't see what was below the soaring eagle. If he were to guess he would say it was where the upper parking lot was located.

He stared in disbelief as the great bird began to flap its long wings and work its way up the side of the butte until it was once again able to hover and soar above. Again, the eagle's golden eye appeared to make contact with his black gaze before sweeping into a graceful glide that carried the raptor down the southern flank of Bear Butte. A gust of wind rustled the nearby pine boughs causing them to whisper in a rhythmic manner. John listened until he was certain. His mind faltered as his hearing focused on what sounded like a subtle incantation. Were the spirit voices beckoning?

Nighthawk was sorely tempted to shelf his common sense and go with his instincts. When he again saw the eagle begin to circle over the same area he threw away any lingering, rational thoughts and reluctantly began to pack the manuscript back into the compact box.

His mind reeled with mixed thoughts of Blackjack Pershing and his spirit eagle. He knew without doubt that the eagle's spirit was trying to tell him something. Balancing the flat chest across his shoulders and pack, John held on and started jogging down the trail.

When he reached the half-way viewing platform, John carefully lowered the chest and worked at regaining his wind. His breath rattled in his ears as he breathed, pulling huge amounts of air deeply into his lungs. Sweat added sheen to his face and dampened his black hair. Hearing a faint motor noise he looked downhill toward the upper parking lot.

Nighthawk's pick-up was the only vehicle remaining in the lot. A pair of motorcycles was circling it while a pedestrian was pelting something at his red 4X4 truck. All that John could hear were a few incoherent yells and the tenuous motor noise of the bikes. A sleeping rage awakened deep within the belly of John Nighthawk; it kindled a fire then coursed through his veins with the quickness of mercury. Forgetting his tired back, John practically threw the chest on top of his backpack. Eyes still locked on the scene far below, he set out at a fast jog that rapidly developed into an all-out run. Rather than risk a fall and damage to the contents of the chest, Nighthawk forced his eyes to fix onto the serpentine trail. While he ran, the passing air cooled the rivers of sweat streaming down his body and gave him the lift he needed to continue.

When he rounded the last bend before the straight-away to the parking lot, he saw the white blurbs of their faces as they turned his way. Unintelligible shouts of defiance were thrown in his direction. Nighthawk's body vibrated with fatigue and fury. Sweat was in his eyes, burning and blurring his vision. All he saw were three men, or kids; two on motorcycles; one of them sounded like a Harley. Still too far away to identify the vandals, he watched as the one on foot hopped onto back of one of the bikes. John stopped and helplessly watched as the two motorcycles roared out of the parking lot, leaving in their wake the faint sound of shrill laughter that lingered in the air like a haunted memory.

The lump in his stomach grew larger with each faltering step that brought him closer to his ruined truck. The vehicle's windows were broken; all four tires were slashed; the paint job had been thoroughly keyed; dents from rocks covered the body and hood. In John's mind, one word amply described an assessment of the damage to his lovingly, pampered truck. ... trashed. They had all but totaled his new truck.

Nighthawk slid the chest carefully into the back of the truck and shut the tail-gate. He stood there leaning against the gate as a slight breeze cooled his overheated body. Suddenly his head lifted and he lunged for the cab door. When it opened to his urgent touch, John knew that his worst fear had been realized. He threw open the glove box anyway, but his hope was merely a pipe dream. Both his gun and badge were gone.

CHAPTER SIXTEEN

When Nicole pulled up in front of the Mobil station in her beat-up Buick station wagon *Wi* (the sun) was ending its day long journey crossing the sky. Seeing John lift a flat chest out of the bed of his truck she quickly got out and opened the back-end of her car for him. As she stepped out of John's way she paused, staring in disbelief at the damaged pick-up.

"Oh, John, how awful ... I am so sorry."

John set the chest on the end of the tailgate. Not wanting Nicole to see the anger that still lingered in his eyes, Nighthawk didn't meet her gaze.

"That it is ... thanks for coming down. I really appreciate you coming down to pick me up."

John paused, looked in the Buick and asked, "Where's Mike?"

Pleased at Nighthawk's query she answered, "He's staying overnight at a friend's."

With a graceful move Nicole smoothly slipped into the back of her station wagon and began moving things out of the way.

Although being mentally and physically drained Nighthawk couldn't help but admire her lithe form and graceful movements. As she worked to make room for the chest John watched *Wi's* lingering fingers of gold and orange play with the red highlights in her long, wavy dark hair. The pleasant sight made the deputy want to do nothing more than stare, enjoying her beauty. But instead he forced himself to look away and busy himself with the careful placement of the chest.

Nicole stepped down from the back of her Buick, leveled a pair of eyes as black as any Native American.

"John? Are you sure you're all right? You sounded so different on the phone. I've never heard you so angry."

Nighthawk smiled slightly and slid the chest into the back.

"I think most of that anger you heard was directed at myself. It was foolish of me to leave my gun in the truck ... even though it was locked"

John and Nicole slid onto the front seat and shut the doors. As Nicole pulled away from the station and headed south toward the freeway, Nighthawk resumed, "What worries me the most is that, because of my dereliction of duty, I now have a possible loose cannon running around the Hills with a 9mm Browning with a full clip of thirteen rounds. And, he has my badge and I.D. to get him through any door he wants."

"Don't be too hard on yourself, John. You'll find him."

John looked at Nicole, and smiled.

"Thanks."

Nicole glanced his way.

"For what?"

He scrunched down in his seat and shut his eyes.

Nicole sneaked another glance before returning her eyes to the road. Just when she thought he wasn't going to answer, he said, "For not asking how I got myself into such a stupid situation. Let me shut my eyes for five minutes. I promise you'll hear the whole sorry tale before we get home."

Nicole smiled to herself.

"Sounds fair to me."

She tried to concentrate on her driving but found that she couldn't get John's last four words out of her mind, 'Before we get home.'

When Nighthawk finished his story the headlights of the old Buick were showing the way up the Blucksburg Mt. Estate road. In telling his story John had left out the part about Daniel Starr. It was bad enough if she thought he was a poor excuse for a deputy sheriff, he didn't need for her to think he was also crazy.

John lifted the box out of the back of the Buick and headed for his door. Nicole opened it for him. As he slipped by she gave the chest a cursory look. Nighthawk saw the look.

"I'll tell you the rest of the story later. Okay?"

John stepped inside his door and set the flat box down.

"Sure, John. It's your business, you don't have to explain. I'd better get downstairs. I told Mike I'd give him a call when I got home."

Edges of Time

As she turned away Nighthawk quickly reached and gently pulled Nicole back through his doorway and into his arms; her arms slipped around his neck and held him close, and he could feel the warmth of her body pressed against him. Through the thin weave of his tee-shirt he felt her warm breath quicken as she pressed her face against his chest. John held her tight and absorbed the clean scent of her hair. He buried his fingers in her thick dark tresses and gently tugged until her head raised and he could see the pale oval of her face. In a voice soft as the night breeze, he said, "Thank you for being there. It means more than you know."

Nicole's smile was bright in the dim light.

"But, I really do know how much it means, John Nighthawk, and I'm happy that I'm the person you thought to call."

Holding John's gaze she gave him a hug and slowly stepped back; her hands slid from behind his neck, down across the flat planes of his chest.

"I know you have a lot on your mind, so I'd better leave."

Nicole turned to go, then stopped and looked back.

"Mike said to tell you he would have come along to pick you up except he's with his friend. I think they were playing some video game."

Nighthawk smiled.

"Tell Mike that I'll try to find the time to take him up in the hills sometime tomorrow or Sunday. And thanks again for the lift. You're a life saver."

With a covert glance Nicole saw the hard light lurking in her friend's ebony eyes. Concern showed briefly on her face.

"Are you going out tonight, John?"

"I have to. My automatic pistol needs to be found before someone gets hurt with it being in the wrong hands."

Nicole slowly backed to the door and smiled.

"Come down stairs for a cup of coffee before you leave."

Just before pulling the stairway door closed, her eyes silently beseeched Nighthawk.

"I want you to calm down so that you'll be careful, John Nighthawk. I also wish to see you tomorrow."

She paused, then said, "If not later tonight."

Barry Brierley

Chapter Seventeen

Nighthawk stepped from the brightly-lighted cafe and looked both ways on Main Street. He was surprised by how deserted the Sturgis streets were. Usually at this time of evening there were at least a few vehicles on the move and a pedestrian or two. The deputy slowly began to walk east on Main; his dark civilian clothing made him appear almost formless in the murky, dark night. A nearby streetlight was flickering, creating strange night shadows. While John moved east along the sidewalk toward the post office where he had parked the sheriff's department Cherokee, his mind was sorting and stacking the small amount of information he had just received about some of the local youth. The Sturgis police officer he caught on break was eager to help but had little to offer. More importantly he was debating whether to inform his boss about his situation now, or wait until morning. Technically, he was off duty ... but he knew that with his semi-automatic pistol and badge having been confiscated Nighthawk was duty-bound to contact the sheriff immediately.

Since the very roots of their relationship Nighthawk always thought first before calling Sheriff Hoage. Their association had always been strained, to say the least, and it didn't take much to cause the hackles to rise on Sheriff Hoage's red neck.

Still walking east he crossed the street. At first Nighthawk didn't pay any attention to the four Harleys parked side by side across the street, but when he saw the shadowy figures leaning against the building on his side of the street he was quick to make the connection. As he approached them he became more aware of the solid weight of his back-up automatic. It was holstered in the small of his back beneath his brown leather jacket.

"Hey, Geronimo. Where the fuck ya goin'?"

Nighthawk abruptly stopped opposite the three dark silhouettes. The building they were leaning against was set back from the others and put them several feet away from John's sidewalk. A match rasped and the ensuing flare briefly illuminated a broad, bearded face surrounding two tiny, blue eyes ... a face that was living proof that Darwin's theory wasn't simply a wild guess.

It was the shorter man to the smoker's right that moved from the shadows first. As if on command the other two stepped forward joining the first. When the smoker stepped into the clear Nighthawk saw he had the body to back up the face's claim to fame.

"You wouldn't by chance be one o' that Sheriff Pig's boys, would you ... a certain Injun fuzz that goes by the name of Hawk-shit, or some other such thing?"

The ape-like throwback wasn't the voice. It came from the least tall of the three men. As they strolled toward him Nighthawk stood his ground. They walked abreast reminding John of the scene from the film, The Wild Bunch, when the outlaws strolled through half a Mexican army while on their way to their final, bloody confrontation.

The short one wore a bandanna tied onto his head like a pirate and a black leather vest strung with chains that jingled when he walked. He had an arrogant strut and a solid body whose burly width made up for his lack of height. The last of the three outlaw bikers was of average height with the nervous eyes and the blade-thin body of the habitual drug user. Up close he also had the filthy personal hygiene of one who cared little for the opinion of other more pristine humans.

The three bikers stopped several feet away as the talker accepted a light from his hulking friend. The flare of the lighter illuminated his face just long enough for Nighthawk to see the open hostility in his dark eyes. The look belied the gap-toothed grin he gave the deputy.

"My name's Deputy Nighthawk. Who are you?"

Still wearing his picket fence grin, Talker stepped closer. Like wolves the others followed their Alpha leader's example. In close the street-light revealed the talker's battered features. His face bore witness that he was a man who had seen many battles and hadn't won all of them.

Talker shrugged.

"What's in a name, anyhow? One thing sure ... I ain't one o' them

Edges of Time

sissy RUB dudes."

The biker's two sidekicks laughed appreciatively.

John, like most law enforcement officers, was aware that RUB stood for Rural Urban Bikers … a label pinned on the many doctors, lawyers, and other professionals who had become motorcycle riders for a hobby. In recent years the part-time bikers have increased in number by leaps and bounds.

Obviously about to share another joke, Talker turned his smile onto his friends as he glanced at Nighthawk.

"I hear you lost something … that so?"

While Nighthawk felt the hair tingle on the back of his neck Talker and the druggy laughed uproariously. As the shock of what was said hit home it caused waves of apprehension and anger to immediately move through John's body; and for the first time the deputy speculated on the whereabouts of the owner of the fourth Harley.

Trying to remain calm, Nighthawk threw a glance at the hulking biker that he thought of as 'Throwback' who hadn't joined in the laughter. He simply continued to stare hard at John and drag on his cigarette. Using humor to lighten his mounting concern, Nighthawk thought, I wonder if he's waiting for a hand sign command or a banana.

As suddenly as it began the laughter stopped. The deputy's eyes locked in on Talker.

"If you know where my property is, you had better speak now."

Talker's grin didn't falter nor did his arrogant gaze.

Nighthawk thought briefly of making an arrest but quickly changed his mind. He knew he wouldn't get information from either of them unless they wanted to give it. It would just be a case of traveling down a road he was sure they'd all been down before. Stalemate, he thought. John decided he would wait for the man to speak or make some kind of move … if it took all night.

From the corner of his eye the deputy saw the emaciated biker he identified as Junky glance at his leader then back at him. Pretending he didn't notice, Nighthawk continued to match stares with the leader in a stubborn attempt to break his 'tough guy' resolve.

Talker took a deep drag on his cigarette and blew the smoke toward John. The biker's gaze abruptly shifted then returned.

"I ain't got your property, Injun. I'm just a messenger. But I know

147

who's got it."

Nighthawk, excitement tingling through his veins, waited. He knew he would be wasting his breath to tell 'Talker' that saying what he did would make him an accessory to a crime. He could tell that Talker was tiring of the game and couldn't wait to give him the message. John held his gaze and remained silent.

Junky began to get fidgety. He poked Talker and exclaimed, "Come on, Crab, tell 'em so we can blow this dump."

Crab (Talker) pinned Junky with rage-filled eyes and jabbed him in the chest with a threatening, sausage-sized finger. He then aimed his smoldering gaze at Nighthawk.

"Does the place Timberline ring a bell?"

John Nighthawk felt his stomach clench like a fist as nausea caused saliva to flood his mouth; he swallowed ... only pride and pure determination kept his face impassive and his mouth closed. Was it his imagination, or was the scar tissue on his left chest really beginning to tingle?

"What about Timberline?" John quietly asked.

"You killed a man there ... busted a whole handful of caps on the dude." Crab leered as he added, "Story is ... he wasn't armed."

"He was armed. He shot me with an arrow then tried to kill me with a tomahawk."

The nasty group laughter that followed his remark chased away any guilt that might have been hovering in the back of his mind. Choking back a snigger, Crab sneered, as he said, "Ain't you the one that's supposed to be swinging a hatchet and launching arrows?"

Crab's reply as well as the accompanying laughter rekindled John's simmering anger. He quickly controlled his emotions before they ignited and began to burn out of control.

"You got something to tell me ... you had better say it soon."

"Or what?"

No phony grin this time ... Crab's eyes blazed with animosity.

"You better listen close, pig, or ya won't have a chance 'n hell a getting your gun 'n badge back!"

Keeping his gaze locked onto Nighthawk the biker abruptly grinned.

"And the son of the man you killed will meet ya at eight in the mornin' at the Butte parkin' lot. Said for me to tell ya he's gonna kick yer ass, then just maybe he'll give back your gun 'n badge. If ya don't come <u>alone,</u> he said, whatever happens it'll be on your head."

Frump's son! Nighthawk's mind staggered with the revelation of the youth's identity. He had known from his investigation that the man had an ex-wife and a pair of sons but had never dreamed of any type of reprisal. The story he had heard was that James Frump had completely alienated himself with the family. Having been in the hospital when the ex-wife was informed of his death, John never met the family.

That explains the hateful look the youthful bully gave me at the Butte, he thought, when I mentioned my name.

The overpowering roar of a Harley being kicked to life wiped out any questions Nighthawk might have wanted to ask. John's quick look made instant eye contact with James Frump's son who was calmly sitting astride the fourth Harley. Even with the distance between them Nighthawk could see the hatred in his eyes and notice, for the first time, that he had the same general features as his father.

Still holding Nighthawk's gaze the young Frump grinned. As the grin evolved into a sneer, he revved his Harley, peeled out and roared up the street as though he didn't have a care in the world. His long, dark hair whipped out behind giving an illusion of great speed.

John fumed. He knew he didn't have a chance in Hell of catching up with him. Hiding his emotions from the bikers, the deputy impassively watched him go. Even seated on the huge motorcycle he thought Jimmy Frump easily looked as big as his father.

With a calculated insolence in their motion the bikers stepped past Nighthawk into the deserted street. Crab, trailing behind, stopped next to him and lit another cigarette. This time he turned his head and blew the smoke away from John. When he looked back he said, "You know what, Deputy? From what I've heard and seen at the way you Indian people are treated I'd think you'd be more inclined to be a rider like us than hang with the hogs as yer doing."

Startled by the man's change in conversational attitude, Nighthawk spoke from his heart.

"I believe in the law, but I also believe I can do more for my people serving it ... rather than fighting it."

Crab gave him his gap-toothed grin.

"Figured you'd say somethin' like that ... you may not believe this, but we riders are mostly law abiding. Leastwise, we don't break any big

149

laws. Thing is we just don't like cops an' stupid rules. There's getting to be way too many pigs that shouldn't have the authority they got ... 'cause they sure as hell abuse it."

"Hey, Crab!"

The biker looked at his buddies who were crouched on their bikes waiting. Crab casually flipped them the bird. When he turned his head the street-light exposed more of the biker's ravaged face. Crab caught him looking. Nighthawk expected him to say something, but he was shocked by what he did say.

"Ya know some of these scars I had coming, but most of them were given to me by my old man after Ma left. He was mean and one crazy sonuvabitch! An' I hated his guts ... which reminds me ..."

Crab gestured up the street toward where the fourth Harley had gone.

"... Jimmy's just as crazy mean. He's capable a doin' anything. You watch your back... man."

Stunned, as much by the biker's willingness to give him information as he was by his warning, Nighthawk watched him cross the street and straddle his Harley. The three bikers fired up their machines.

Head swimming with all the new information, the deputy stood still and quiet as one of the pine trees in his sacred Black Hills. Suddenly on impulse he shouted over the revving cycles'

"How well you know this Jimmy?"

Crab signaled his cohorts to stop revving their engines. He gave Nighthawk his picket-fence grin as he shouted back at Nighthawk.

"Better than anybody, Man ... Jimmy's my baby brother!"

This information stunned Nighthawk; he watched as the three bikers drove away encompassed within a bubble of their own ear-pounding, cacophony of sound.

CHAPTER EIGHTEEN

Back at his apartment, Nighthawk paced back and forth on his narrow deck. The prairie far below was shrouded in darkness, except when a distant thunder storm illuminated the land with an occasional flash of heat lightning.

His mind was in turmoil; he knew he should contact the sheriff's department, but guilt over having killed the boy's father was getting him personally involved. The deputy wanted to find a way to protect him rather than have the young man start his life with a criminal record

Lightning flashed and briefly illuminated Bear Butte. The sudden display of natural light distracted Nighthawk, and he thought of Nicole downstairs reading a copy of Daniel Starr's first manuscript.

He had finally decided to trust that Nicole won't think him crazy when she discovers his belief that Daniel Starr had truly managed to travel back in time. When Nighthawk returned from town she had met him at the door with questions that could be only answered if she knew the whole story. He had paused for only a heartbeat before rushing inside and returning with a leather briefcase, which he thrust into Nicole's hands with the words, 'Read this manuscript and then I'll tell you where it came from and everything else I know and believe.'

John remembered having softly added, 'I want to be with you later. My hope is that I won't be working all night. I must decide what to do about retrieving my pistol and badge.'

Nighthawk stopped his pacing. He abruptly decided to gamble and wait. He felt assured that he could safely delay making his final decision. John knew there would be no sleep for him, so there was time enough to think the problem through. But first he had to find a way to relax. One of the first things he learned after becoming a deputy sheriff was not to try to force a solution when confronted with a serious situation. If time allowed, what had always worked for him in the past was to get his mind off the problem for a few hours. Almost always the answer would be there when he needed it.

A balmy night breeze stirred his black hair and soothed his perspiring body. The scent of pine and leaf mold filled Nighthawk's senses while his ears heard the rustle and scratch of aspen leaves and the click and scrape of branches rubbing together. Inexplicably the breeze suddenly developed into a stronger flurry of warm air. His awareness became stronger and more acute. Carried on the wind he heard the subtle thump of a nighthawk's wings as it made an abrupt change of direction. Mixed with the scent of pine John caught a whiff of what had to be burning sweet grass and sage. The logical part of his brain dismissed the fragrance as being his imagination, but his spiritual side knew better.

He looked through the glass of his patio door where a lamp glowed beside his worn sofa. Inadvertently his gaze drifted beneath the halo of light until it fastened onto the exposed metal corner of the chest. It lay on the floor in the shadows in an imagined shroud of mystery. Its near magical allure was too much for John to resist.

Nighthawk stepped over to the sofa, pulled the flat chest free of the end table, and placed it on the coffee table. Glancing at the time he loosened his collar and sat down. Planning on only reading for an hour before looking in on Nicole, Deputy Sheriff Nighthawk cleared his mind, then carefully opened the chest and removed the manuscript. He began to read.

CHAPTER NINETEEN
HOLY MAN REUNITED

I rode south along the rutted road; out of habit my artist's eye searched for scenes in the barren terrain that would make attractive landscapes. Except for the wide blue sky there wasn't anything colorful enough to capture my interest. The land was as bleak as any I'd seen. It must have been late summer or early fall; except for scattered patches of green trees the rolling, featureless land had been burnt to shades of brown and tan by the summer sun.

Still on the road, Redman carried me over the lip of a wide but shallow depression. Off to the right there was a stretch of land that harbored a small tract of small trees and brush in its center. At the eastern edge of the foliage, I detected a small cabin beside the road. As I approached the dwelling a sweat lodge constructed out of brush and blankets could be seen behind the cabin. The ceremonial hut was setting near a narrow, swift running stream. The waterway meandered parallel to the dirt road before disappearing among the natural folds of the prairie.

Stepping down from Redman, I approached the open door. A familiar voice from within stopped me in my tracks.

"Washtay (Greetings)! I have been expecting you, Crow Bluecoat."

My heart began beating like a trip-hammer and seemed to be lodged in my throat. He had called me by the same name he had at Wounded Knee when I was Nathanial Starr, Caleb's twin brother. While I struggled to suck in enough oxygen the Holy Man of the Oglala spoke again.

153

Barry Brierley

"Come closer, Starr, so I may see you. I have dreamed of your arrival."

While he was speaking, I quickly stepped through the doorway and peered about the gloomy interior. There was very little furniture, only a potbellied stove, blankets hanging on the walls, a rickety table and two chairs. Some boxes and parfleches (painted and beaded, rawhide containers) were leaning against the back wall. Black Elk was seated on a blanket on the dirt floor facing away from the door; there were no windows. He was sewing cowry shells onto a linen garment. Strings of thin sinew, shells, and beads were gathered into the cloth on his lap. Nearly forgetting my manners, I finally spoke.

"Washtay, Black Elk. My heart is pleased to see you are well."

Black Elk carefully gathered his items, got to his feet, and faced me. We exchanged nods and brief smiles. The Oglala Holy Man's lean, dark features were expressionless as his steady gaze slowly swept over me not missing a thing. I couldn't help noticing that he had aged in the seven years since we had met. He looked older than his documented mid-thirties. He obviously had carried much of his peoples' burden since the massacre at Wounded Knee.

As he looked me over I quickly tried to figure out how he could possibly have seen me coming. His cabin was situated in a dip in the terrain; when I first saw his cabin it was a mere heartbeat away. With his lap full of beads and things he couldn't have gotten up and peeked outside without spilling some of his paraphernalia into the dirt. He wouldn't have had the time! My eyes snapped toward the ground where he'd been sitting ... there was nothing there but the blanket and dirt, not one tiny bead could be seen. My eyes jumped up to Black Elk's face. His penetrating black eyes were fixed on mine. Suddenly he grinned, turned aside, and set the cloth and other items onto the old table. Disarmed by his radiant smile, I remained silent. With a sweeping gesture toward the out-of-doors, he said, "Come, sit and smoke with me."

We stepped outside. Black Elk pointed with his thumb toward a stump that had been sawed level. As I sat down I briefly wondered whom the white fool was who cut down what had to have been a glorious tree. Judging by the diameter of the trunk it would have been a landmark in this nearly treeless, barren land.

The holy man produced a short pipe from a pocket in his worn, white man's' clothing. My hand automatically went inside my vest to my shirt pocket. I removed a leather pouch, some corn shuck cigarette papers, and a folded piece of paper. I was flabbergasted. Caleb, Jr. must smoke ... and roll a cigarette with only one hand? I was astounded! Suddenly, I felt foolish. I had remembered reading about cowboys who were able to roll a smoke with one hand. And in those days it wasn't considered an uncommon skill.

I quickly handed the tobacco to Black Elk and said in Lakota, "Please accept this small gift."

Black Elk smiled and nodded.

"Palamo (Thanks)."

He accepted the offering with dignity and grace. Thankful to be rid of it, I felt I had enough of a handicap with a missing hand; I didn't want to have to worry about lung cancer as well. Digging into my pocket once again I was able to produce a couple of wooden sulfur matches and a stub of a pencil. I set the matches in front of him and put the pencil back in my pocket with the paper. Black Elk gracefully proffered the pipe in offering to each of the four directions above to the Sky Father and to the Earth Mother below. While he fussed with his pipe I studied the great medicine man and was saddened because of his obvious poverty. His shabby cloth attire helped me to remember the last time I had seen him. I will never forget the first look I had of his startling demeanor. He was a vision of Lakota splendor.

The rasp of a match on stone brought me back from my memories. Black Elk puffed. The smell of tobacco was soothing, much more so than the puff Black Elk insisted that I take. I bravely managed not to choke and wondered at the strangeness of my being able to adopt some of Caleb, Junior's traits and memories but not all of them. I silently chided myself for my foolishness. There I was, a hundred years back in time ... and I was concerned because some detail of my having absorbed the life of one of my ancestors didn't make sense? Whoever wrote, 'Therefore lies madness' could have been writing it for me. I must be careful not to try to rationalize all that has happened. God knows, it would be an impossible task.

I mentally set aside all my random thinking knowing that all my thoughts need to be focused on finding Star Watcher and our adopted son, Nathaniel.

A light touch on my arm interrupted my thoughts. Black Elk was looking intently into my eyes, if not my very soul. As he began to speak in melodious Lakota, I became instantly mesmerized by his ethereal beliefs. Then later I was amazed by what he had surmised. It just didn't seem possible that the man was able to convincingly explain what he knew, and did, without some kind of unearthly guidance.

"Before I tell you of my vision I must speak of times past. I have seen you many times over the past winters. You did not know me. It was you, yet it was not your spirit. You came with your father, he who the Crow call Long Eye. With each passing winter you would bring the spotted buffalo for we Lakota and also many horses for the Bluecoats."

Black Elk reached out and touched my wooden hand. At the time I would have sworn that I felt a tingle surge through my artificial appendage. As he resumed speaking he gently cradled my carved hand in both of his.

"After the Bluecoats had stopped the killing at Wounded Knee there were stories told that several of the Crow scouts had been killed up near the Stronghold. Star Watcher told me that your name was mentioned as one of those killed. Yet, she also saw you when you came with the spotted buffalo many moons later. After seeing you for that first time, she came and talked with me. Star Watcher said that at first she thought it was you and that you had lost your hand during the blizzard. She tried to speak to you in Lakota, but you did not fully understand. She could see in your eyes that you did not know her. She told me it was your face, but it was not you. For a long time her heart was on the ground."

Black Elk released my wooden hand and paused. A slight breeze could be heard moving through the leaves among the trees behind the cabin. His head turned slightly as he listened. He looked at me and smiled sadly before he continued.

"When I saw her again another winter had passed and she had stopped grieving for you. She said her heart told her that you *would return to her and her son. She knew this to be true and that she would wait forever."*

A lump formed in my throat, and my eyes became misty. At that point, I tried to interrupt. I didn't have a clue what I was going to say or how I was going to explain. But somehow I had to find Star Watcher, and Black Elk was my only hope. Unexpectedly, my thoughts became morose. I worried that she was dead and that Black Elk was trying to tell me so. Before my courage completely left me, I was determined to ask if she was still alive. As I was about to ask, my hand involuntarily raised in a beseeching manner.

Before I could speak the holy man stopped me by raising his own hand. His voice filled with faith and conviction.

"Last night I had a vision. Part of the dream told me that Wakan Tanka brought your spirit here. He brought you back to be reunited with your woman. In the vision you suddenly appeared in a cloud of pink dust falling from a large red horse. You were surrounded by Lakota and Crow who watched you while floating inside the red dust clouds."

I sat there stunned, and also relieved that he hadn't said Star Watcher was dead. With those amazing words being said the holy man carefully knocked the dottle out of his pipe and stood up.

"Your spirit went inside your brother, the man with the wooden hand, and you have become that person."

Head spinning with the wonder of it all, I was about to ask where Star Watcher was, but I waited. In his eyes I could see there was something else he wished to tell me.

"I think Wakan Tanka also brought you here to find Star Watcher and her son, Nighthawk." He paused for a moment, thinking. Then he looked at me and said, "They are no longer here at Pine Ridge. No one knows where they have gone."

I couldn't breath ... there was a roaring in my ears that shut out the world around me. I didn't know whether to laugh or cry. Part of me wanted to shout, 'She's alive!' The rest of me wanted to murmur, 'I'll never find her again.' The shock of the sudden information hit me like a hammer and for some unknown reason,

Barry Brierley

I could not begin to pull my eyes away from Black Elk's sympathetic gaze. After what seemed an eternity, I could breathe again and the roaring in my ears diminished until I heard the soothing, reassuring sound of Star Watcher's voice ... in my mind it whispered, asking me to come to her.

The imagined voice faded as Black Elk's voice broke through my self-pity and longing and made me think once again of the moment at hand.

"This woman's heart belongs to you, Wooden Hand. If anyone can find her, you can. She has not been seen since near the end of the Moon of the New Grass."

Black Elk's use of what was apparently my Lakota name barely registered. I was excited and trying to recollect what month entailed 'New Grass.' Then I remembered; it was May. I turned to Black Elk and asked, "What Moon are we in now?"

"The next moon will be the Moon of the Falling Leaves," he replied.

That starts in September, I thought, so this must be August. She disappeared in late May or early June. She's been gone at least two months. As the excitement continued to build I once again became aware of the palpitations of my heart. Maybe, I reasoned, she went to nearby towns, such as Deadwood or Sturgis, to look for me.

Black Elk added a new sense of urgency when he said, "Near the time she went away there were wasichus from what the whites call 'Wild West shows.' They were looking for Lakota to travel with them and go to the large wasichu villages. This was not Pahuska's (Buffalo Bill Cody) show. I was told this one had fewer wagons."

Black Elk's words brought back the half-heard words of Lieutenant Pershing; voiced a second time the words rang in my ears, tolling doom and despair. I forced myself not to listen to the ringing and prayed to God she wasn't taken.

In my research while looking for a way to return to this century I came upon information that stated that from time to time Native Americans were kidnapped and forced to travel both in this country and abroad with the shows ... some not returning for several years, others not returning at all.

Time became essential. I remembered the pencil stub and

Edges of Time

scrap of paper in my shirt pocket. Not knowing if he lived alone or even had transportation, I pinned Black Elk with my gaze and asked, "Could you get a message to Long Eye for me? I must leave now; each wasted moment could make a difference."

Nodding in agreement, Black Elk watched as I clumsily unfolded the piece of paper. There were tiny, vertical pencil lines in groups of five covering one side. Turning to the blank side I used the stump for a tabletop and secured the small paper with my wooden hand. The medicine man stood quietly waiting as I wrote a quick note to the father I had yet to meet. The writing was unexpectedly awkward because of the misplaced callus perched on my good thumb. Overcoming my clumsiness I finished the note. As I passed it to Black Elk, I remember thinking how everything was becoming weirder with each passing second.

Meeting Black Elk's concerned gaze, I said, "Le mita pila, kola, (Many thanks, friend). Someday I hope to be worthy of your friendship."

The medicine man stepped forward and clapped his hand onto my shoulder and squeezed as he proclaimed, "You are a good man, and a friend, Wooden Hand. Brave up! Wherever your path takes you, Wakan Tanka will guide you."

Filled with anxiety yet taut with resolve, I was at Redman's side in less than two strides. Remembering to mount from the right I swung into the saddle. The big red horse came alive beneath me. I reined him away from the cabin and touched my heels to his ribs. With a surge of power he lunged forward, only to have me haul back on the reins after galloping up the road but a short distance. As our own dust enveloped us, I spun Red around until I once again faced Black Elk. Forty or fifty feet separated us, yet the affinity I felt for this man was such that it felt as though he was standing right before me, gazing into my eyes. Standing in the stirrups I shouted, "Where was the last place she was seen?"

Black Elk stepped forward, cupped his hands around his mouth and shouted back to me.

"Near Wounded Knee Creek!"

Barry Brierley

CHAPTER TWENTY
DISCOVERY

Redman and I traveled northeast of Pine Ridge across a tan, barren wasteland that had bends and crevices on it like a crumpled piece of cardboard. The land we traversed entailed a generous portion of the reservation; nearly all was treeless and almost devoid of water. In my previous life I had traveled much of this same land while compiling research for my many paintings of the Lakota. For some reason, perhaps because of the many homes and roads, it didn't seem nearly so desolate. Yet the pervading sense of hopelessness was just as strong.

Eventually we came to a tiny, flowing stream protected from obscurity by a few scrub pines and some green brush that bordered the thin waterway. Wondering if the trickling stream was a portion of Wounded Knee Creek, I reined Redman in, stepped down and led him to the water. The dust lodged in my throat had made further travel unbearable without some fresh water. When he had had enough I moved Red back away from the stream. Somehow, I knew the blood bay was cowboy trained to 'ground rein.' I gambled and dropped the reins. Redman rolled a large brown eye my way but didn't so much as twitch. I knew then that he wouldn't move as long as his reins were on the ground.

Before quenching my thirst I refilled my canteen. Tired, but happy to have reached a probable area to begin my search, I slapped my dusty hat on my leg and looked around at the desolate land. Peering in all directions nothing really caught my eye that was familiar except for the far away blue/gray profile of the Black Hills in the far northwest. I was standing at the foot of

161

Barry Brierley

a low ridge that was sprinkled with pine. It seemed strange after the many miles of flat featureless land to have my view interrupted and made me anxious to see what was on the other side. I sensed that the place of the fighting or battleground was close by. Of course the last time I was at Wounded Knee it was winter; I'm convinced the terrain at that time would have looked quite different.

Swiping at the perspiration on my face, I threw my hat on top of a clump of sage, stepped to the creek and had a drink. The water was cool and refreshing. For some reason it seemed important to keep my wooden left hand dry, so I knelt and scooped the water with my right and splashed my face, washing away the sweaty dust and the days wind burn. I dried my face on my shirt's sleeve and moved to Redman's side. For some unknown reason I stopped beside the saddle bag. Something compelled me to open it and reach inside. To my surprise, my searching hand found and removed a heavy cartridge belt. There was no holster, but the loops were filled with brass cartridges. Using my wooden hand for a prop I examined the bullets and saw they were forty-five caliber. Without thought I grasped one end of the heavy belt and with an obviously practiced swing, whipped the belt around my hips and trapped the buckled end with my false hand. With the ease of a process done many times, I buckled the belt just above my shotgun chaps over the sash and the suspender buttons that supported my canvas trousers. For the first time I noticed the free end of the sash hanging on my right hip. On the end it was lightly beaded above a short fringe.

I paused for a moment and reflected on the buckling maneuver as a whole. It was obvious that what I had just accomplished, with one hand, had been done countless times by Caleb Starr, Jr. With increasing anxiety I slipped around to Red's opposite side and reached inside the other saddlebag. Cool metal met my warm fingers as I grasped and removed the weighty object. Light reflected off spots along the barrel's shiny length where the bluing had been rubbed away. I stared in disturbed wonder at the revolver that fit so comfortably in my hand.

This was no cowboy's snake gun or a soldier's issued sidearm. I was looking at a modified, factory-fashioned killing machine. It was a Cal. 45 Remington, Model 1875 revolver; even more disturbing were the carefully calculated personal modifications that had been applied to the pistol. After briefly studying the changes that were applied I quickly itemized them. Brass wire had been wrapped around the trigger and flattened so that it molded the firing mechanism smoothly to the steel trigger guard. The revolver could no longer be cocked before firing. To fire the gun the hammer had to be pulled back and released.

Another alarming change was that the barrel had been shortened; therefore there was no front sight. An alteration that hindered the pistol from being accurately aimed only pointed. Yet, unbelievable as it must sound, I was able to handle the unusual, heavy revolver with accustomed ease. Therefore, the pistol must have been effective for Caleb, Jr. This unusual awareness of the firearm's capabilities must have come from some unknown recess in my brain or Caleb's memory.

For the first time since becoming Caleb, Junior, I noticed the large size and uncommon strength of my right hand. A growing fear was slowly oozing its way into my awareness. What frightened me the most was the familiarity with the way I handled the weapon and how everything seemed to fit. As I held the pistol my thumb didn't wrap around the hand grip; instead it comfortably rested on top of the hammer ... just behind the previously mentioned callus that had been such a mystery to me!

The growing sheen of sweat on my brow wasn't entirely caused by the afternoon heat. I was beginning to worry about the person I had become. It was great regaining a youthful body, but had I now taken on the persona of a man killer, a gunman?

Pushing the distressing thought aside I stepped forward and collected Redman's reins. I must continue my search for Star Watcher, I thought, and forget everything else. Foot in stirrup I hesitated. I felt the hard edges of the revolver press against my mid-section. Without thought I had slipped the Remington in behind my belt just in front of my right hipbone where the butt of the pistol was in a handy proximity to my right hand. These actions that I took without conscious thought were very distressing. If these alarming personality revelations hadn't been

Barry Brierley

experienced before, I would have been concerned for my sanity.

Wondering if my adjustments to my new life and new self were ever going to end, I swung up on Red and urged him up the slope of the low ridge. Topping the hogback the first thing to catch my eye was the ravine at Wounded Knee. It was still quite a good distance away, but I knew immediately that it was the very gully in which the blood-crazed soldiers had pursued and killed so many of Big Foot's band of Minneconjou Sioux. In my mind's eye I could still see the stunted pine that were scattered along the crests and slopes mixing with the shabby, blanket-wrapped bodies.

My recollection of that day was so vivid that, in spite of the August heat, shivers ran up my spine. During our escape in the bitter cold I remember how we witnessed acts of brutality that defy description, but cannot be forgotten.

A faint sound of far away laughter snapped me from my musing. Below the long bluff on my left front, my sweeping gaze caught a flash of green trees and movement near a distant, ramshackle shack. A strange tingle of expectation passed through my body. Relishing the hope the feeling hinted at, I touched Redman's ribs with my heels and rode along the spine of the ridge seeking an easy way down. Almost immediately I found a slope with a gradual incline. While Red slowly picked his way down the sandy shelf, I carefully studied the terrain below.

At the base of the ridge there were a few trees and another small tributary of the creek that paralleled the low ridge. The shack was faced away from the ridge, fronting the distant gully. The meager stand of trees below was between me and the shack so there wasn't much to see. Upon our reaching the bottom of the shelf a faint, raucous laughter appeared to be coming from the front of the dwelling.

As we slowly approached the building from the right-rear, apprehension began to mount. Not knowing what was waiting around the corner had me strung-out and taut as a stretched wire. With resolution guiding my false hand, I held Redman to a sedate walk.

KA-POW!

The unexpected gunshot caused Redman to jump sideways like a cat! My newfound skills on horseback served me well and

164

kept me in the saddle. Once again another of young Caleb's talents became instantly apparent. While bringing Redman back under control I noticed that the Remington was in my hand yet I had no recollection of drawing the pistol. The familiarity I had with the gun was disconcerting. As I had mentioned in my first manuscript while at Wounded Knee, I had never handled a revolver in my life, only an automatic.

I felt more nervous sweat escape the sweatband of my hat as I quickly slipped the revolver into its spot behind my belt. I didn't want to suddenly appear in front of an armed man with a gun in my hand. Recognizing the flat sound as that of a pistol shot, I assumed someone had either shot a snake, or was merely target shooting. Somehow my spontaneous rationalizing didn't really help. I was filled with a sudden inexplicable apprehension as I once again heel-tapped Redman into motion. Holding the big bay to a strutting walk I advanced toward the front of the building.

Like a curtain being opened from right to left, the area in front of the shack slowly came into view like a scene from a play. The first thing to grab my attention was a covered wagon; a team of mules in full harness was attached. The wagon had blue wheels and its canvas sides were rolled up and fastened fully, exposing a pair of large, wooden barrels lashed to the support struts that arched over its bed. The wooden sideboard facing me had been lowered, much like the tailgate of a truck. Wooden taps were prominent near the base of the barrels.

Instinct caused me to rein Redman back to a slow walk. All at once a man stumbled into view, approached the wagon, and filled a cup at one of the taps. His back was to me, but it was obvious he was white and very drunk. His greasy blond hair spilled over what appeared to be a grimy, white, removable collar. Half the man's blue-striped shirt was pulled free of his trousers. I jerked on the reins in surprise when more crude laughter came from the cabin. I managed to stop Redman before the front of the cabin was revealed.

The man at the wagon drained his cup and fumbled with the lashings on one of the barrels. Again, some sense of pending endangerment alerted me that I was entering a very dangerous situation. *All my senses came immediately alive. I knew there was at least one other man out of sight. The one in view was armed, but I had no way of knowing if he was the one who had fired the gun.*

A pistol was holstered in a cross-draw rig on his left hip, and a lever-action rifle was leaning against the wagon bed. Who were these men? Without forethought, it was then that the truth hit me. Whisky peddlers! I should have known right away when I saw the taps in the barrels.

Sometime during my years of research for my paintings, I had read that whiskey peddlers would sneak onto the reservations and sell illegal whiskey to the Indians.

"Dance ... you sonuvabitch!"

More laughter followed.

"Get up, damn ya!"

The man at the wagon didn't even turn around. But the vicious bully's voice added anger to my growing apprehension. I heel-tapped Red's ribs. When Redman's walk carried me around the corner of the shanty the whole dreadful scene unfolded before me in little more than a handful of heartbeats.

A burly, filthy white man was standing in the doorway, pistol in one hand, a bottle in the other. An old Indian wearing nothing but a loincloth and moccasins was slumped on his hands and knees in the powdery dust of the front yard. His wrinkled, dust-covered skin was a pathetic sight. The blood smeared across his wizened face and his discarded clothing scattered in the dirt made me instantly ashamed of my white blood. As the stocky man's body straightened with awareness of my presence, I felt a sudden rage tighten my muscles, preparing me for the action that I knew was soon to follow. The expression 'white trash' flashed through my mind like a bolt of lightning.

"Abel? We got us some company!"

My focus was on the man with the gun in his hand, but by turning my head just a hair, my side vision was able to see the blond one at the wagon clumsily turn around. When he saw me the tin cup dropped from his hand.

The man with the revolver kept his eye on me and stepped away from the doorway. He moved closer to his drunken friend then stopped.

Edges of Time

While they hesitated I let Red continue walking, bringing the dirty blond closer into my range of vision. Although the man by the wagon was drunk, I instinctively knew that both men needed to be closely watched. Keeping my left side facing them so they wouldn't see my pistol, I reined Red to a halt.

"Who in hell are you?" the stocky one asked.

In the shadowed area beneath the brim of my hat, my eyes were searching, looking for some sign that the pair weren't alone.

"Just a stranger drifting on through," I said.

A flash of color caught my eye and my gaze lifted to the roof. What I saw became a spark that inflamed my smoldering fury. It took all the restraint I could muster to conceal my rage. It was at that very moment that I realized that Nathaniel's twin brother had a completely different personality ... whereas Nathaniel was frightened most of the time he was at Wounded Knee, Nathaniel's brother was a whole different story.

As Caleb, not only was I not frightened, I couldn't wait for one of the filthy, two-legged animals to make some kind of threatening move, or even look like they were going to hurt the Lakota elder again. I would then burn them down and even enjoy doing so. And somehow I knew that I could do it with absolutely no regret.

Pinning me with angry eyes, the burly man stepped toward me. He didn't point his revolver at me, but he hadn't lowered it either.

"Best keep on drifting, mister... if ya know what's good for ya."

Ignoring the threat, I held a tight rein on my wrath and spoke in Lakota to the old man.

"Brave up, Uncle. This will soon be over."

The old one didn't look at me but while still on all fours he seemed to straighten with a new found pride, fiercely attentive to my friendly words.

At my voice the stocky one hunched his shoulders and tensed up, while on my right Blondie straightened and although drunk, still had the good sense to look frightened. The old one gazed in my direction with unseeing eyes. Disgust caused bile to rise in my throat. He was blind! My fury was held in check by a very thin thread of humanity.

"What'n hell did you say? You'n Indian?"

The stocky one's voice had an abrasive edge to it. I knew he'd be the first to react. I saw his pale eyes flicker toward my wooden hand.

With my right hand resting on my thigh, I flexed my fingers, loosening them. I had no idea from where all my self-confidence came from, but I wasn't the least bit intimidated by my new adversaries. A strange calmness settled over me and everything appeared brighter, more distinct.

"I have a question for you. Where is the woman?"

"Go to hell, cripple!"

With his words his eyes went wide and his gun hand began to lift. I have no recollection of reaching for the Remington; like magic it appeared in my hand and I thumbed the hammer. With a strange grim satisfaction I felt the double recoil in my fist. The twin explosions seemed far away; all objects became crystal clear as my bullets struck the stocky whiskey peddler in the right arm and shoulder, causing him to pirouette into a lazy spin which carried him to a sitting position on the ground. Through the slowly drifting smoke, I saw Blondie frozen in place with his hand on the butt of his still holstered revolver. To my surprise, the barrel of my pistol was already pointed straight at him, and it remained so while I deftly controlled a dancing, spinning Redman with my false hand.

"Get those fingers up high where I can see them!"

Eyes bugging, mouth agape, Blondie raised his arms. The wounded man was still sitting up, coddling his bleeding shoulder and shattered arm. Closely watching them both, I swung my leg over the pommel, kicked free of the remaining stirrup and slid down from Red. Leaving his reins resting in the dust I walked toward the wounded man. At my approach I saw the fear grow in his eyes and spill from his trembling lips in a whining drool.

My God, I thought, he thinks I'm going to finish the job. Ignoring his pathetic whimpering, I kicked his pistol far out of reach and walked past him to the old Lakota.

"It is over, Uncle. You are safe."

Edges of Time

My Lakota must have been reassuring for he lifted his blind eyes toward me and tried to smile as I helped him to his feet.

In a voice dry as corn husks, he croaked, "Le mita pila."

The old one's whispered 'thank you' caused a wave of pity that engulfed my heart. Quickly I mentally pushed the emotion aside before the lapse destroyed my defensive thinking.

Keeping a wary eye on the two, I gathered up the old one's clothes and placed them in his hands. He clutched them to his chest and continued to murmur his thanks as he allowed me to guide him to the shack's open door. I only went as far as the doorway, foolishly waiting to see if he was able to find his way inside his own home.

I glanced at Blondie, who the stocky man had called Abel, and saw he still had his arms raised as high as he could reach. Approaching him from behind, I threw a look at the wounded man who was still groaning. Watching me closely, he rocked back and forth carefully cradling his shattered arm. Slipping the Remington behind my cartridge belt, I snatched the rifle from where it had fallen into the dirt and threw it as far as I could. Keeping a close eye on the wounded one, I drew my revolver again. Stepping forward, I moved up beside Blondie. Hearing my approach, his head whipped toward me. Still drunk, he staggered but managed to keep his hands in the air.

"Where's the woman?"

My voice crackled with authority and anger.

Blondie stared at me in terror. His mouth opened but no sound came out. Using my left hand's curled wooden fingers, I deftly hooked his gun out of its holster and dropped it into some debilitated appearing bushes.

"Where's the woman who lives here?"

Blondie looked at me with frightened eyes.

"Honest to God, Mister... there weren't never no woman hereabouts."

Relief liberated some of my tension. There was no doubting the man. He was too afraid to lie. Still watching the sorry pair I walked to the wagon. Because of the gunfire the mules had spooked but had been unable to pull the heavy wagon far with a set brake. Just the same they still lunged forward several more feet when I put a couple well-placed bullets through the base of the two whiskey kegs. Facing the shack, I shouted in Lakota.

"Do not worry, Uncle! The bad wasichus are leaving. They no longer have reason to stay!"

With grim satisfaction, I watched the amber liquid pour from the holed barrels into the reservation dust. I felt tired. I wished Lieutenant Pershing were nearby so I could give him the two whiskey merchants. What the hell, I thought, I might as well just chase them off. For all I knew the army would probably just slap their wrists and send them on their way.

With a heart heavy with longing for Star Watcher, I thought briefly of Black Elk's parting words, 'Near Wounded Knee Creek,' and how auspicious they had been. I lifted my gaze to the roof of the shack and the object that had triggered my rage. An old blanket had been spread and fastened to the sod roof with stones. Although faded and torn, the red and black blanket Star Watcher had wrapped around her almost seven years ago still had enough color to have caught my attention. Although the design didn't stand out as well as in the black and white photo, my star signature was clearly visible on the blanket where Star Watcher had meticulously recreated it with white cowry shells.

CHAPTER TWENTY-ONE

Nicole Shaw sat upright and peered at the clock on the mantle. It was eleven-fifty. She wasn't sure what had awakened her; perhaps she had heard John return. After reading extensively in Starr's manuscript she had put it aside when she became sleepy and decided to take a nap until John returned. She hadn't left a light on, but the moon was up and was spilling blue light through her windows creating a surreal illumination while forming deep patches of shadow.

Listening carefully she could hear no sound coming from upstairs, but something wasn't right ... she sensed something was wrong. Barely breathing Nicole listened. She slowly moved her head as her eyes scanned the room concentrating on the many shadows. Suddenly her breath caught in her throat. There appeared to be a large, dark shape down low where there shouldn't be shadows. She felt her body tighten as fear wormed into her very essence. Nicole could feel her pulse palpitating in her neck as she stared at what she was certain was a threatening presence. The large formless shape was so close she was afraid to move.

During the Gulf War, Nicole had been in the army and had extensive training for night combat. One of the many things taught was how to determine movement on a dark terrain. It was believed that movement could be more readily seen if watched without looking directly at the object. She was also trained to watch for shadows that appeared darker than others nearby.

This object didn't move. Desperately hoping it was all just a figment of her imagination Nicole kept one eye on the shadow and quickly reached up and turned on the lamp. She stared, frozen in horror!

A figure straight out of her worst nightmare was crouched only a couple of feet away. As he leaped toward her, Nicole's mouth opened to scream. Her reaction was too late; his large, heavy hand smashed into her face leaving her dazed and tasting her own blood. Vice-like his right hand clamped over her mouth. A waft of stale sweat engulfed her. She caught a glimpse of hate-filled pale eyes raging out of a wide band of black paint.

Although still dizzy and hurt, Nicole tried to fight back. His left hand quickly tightened on her throat. Before encroaching darkness took away her senses, she saw a vivid flash-frame of bared teeth and long hair that was greased and twisted tightly into an upright position on top of his head; the rest of his face, distorted by fury, was covered with a greasy red paint. Nicole's last lucid thought was, 'Thank God, Mike isn't here.'

**

With a sudden move, Nighthawk's head lifted from the manuscript. He had fallen asleep! He glanced at the clock. It was almost midnight. How, he wondered, could he have fallen asleep, captivated as he was with Starr's tale? Forcing his mind to return to the here and now, he thought immediately of Nicole. John knew she was expecting him but figured she would probably have given up and gone to bed.

Running his fingers through his hair, Nighthawk sat up and fought off his need for sleep. His incisive mind quickly confronted what needed to be done. Relentlessly, he reviewed the events of the day: the discovery of the manuscript, his truck being trashed, his gun and badge stolen, and the unexpected trauma of the revelation of the perpetrator's identity. The one-and-a-half-year old Redfoot incident returned to his mind with a rush of trepidation and horror. With the case having been solved in less than twenty-four hours didn't diminish the trauma of the bloody climax or the occasional misgivings he felt deep inside.

John stood up and stretched. He wondered what had awakened him. Ignoring the passing thought, the deputy thought again about Frump's son and his threat. He knew he had stalled long enough; the time had come to call the sheriff's department. When he put on the badge, the oath he had taken meant something more than just a job. Facing reality Nighthawk had known all along that the situation was nothing to mess with. If the youth wound up with a record it was simply a fact he'd have to deal with. Time was needed for the department to decide how the situation was to be handled.

While stepping lightly to the phone he rubbed the sleep from his eyes. A sound brought his head up. He froze; scarcely breathing, Nighthawk closed his eyes, shut down his other senses and focused on listening. The subtle noise seemed to have come from downstairs. John's eyes snapped open, and he quietly moved to the patio door. Carefully, he slid it open and stepped out onto his deck. Leaning over the railing John peered down towards Nicole's window. Yellow light spilled out illuminating the shrubbery beneath the window sash. She's still reading, he mused, and Nicole must be caught up in Daniel Starr's narrative. A smile had just begun to form when he heard her Buick station wagon's engine turn over. The smile disappeared. Where would she be going at this hour? As John stepped back through his open patio door the motor revved then quickly settled into a steady roar. The sound abruptly diminished as the vehicle surged up the driveway incline.

Sensing something was wrong, Nighthawk lunged to the door and threw it open and ran outside. His heart sank as he saw the Buick's taillights disappear over the crest of the road that led down off the ridge. Apprehension was sounding an alarm inside his head. Mentally pulling the plug on his unfounded fears, he turned and stepped toward the door. John stopped as suddenly as if he had struck an invisible barrier. Dread momentarily immobilized him. A piece of paper was attached to his redwood door. Filled with foreboding he swallowed his fear and stepped up to the note. It had been pinned to the wood with a small handmade knife, apparently fashioned from a file. The missive had been quickly scrawled in pencil. Heart thumping, he began to read.

Been a change in plans, chief! Your lady friend asked to see where it was you murdered my old man. Better hurry if you want to see her alive.

P.S. COME _ALONE_ OR SHE'S DEAD MEAT!

Nighthawk's heart seemed to pause in mid-beat as he examined the thumb print that had been used in place of a signature. The smeared print had been made by first dipping the thumb in fresh blood.

Barry Brierley

Chapter Twenty-Two

Nighthawk's anger was threatening to overcome his judgment. The thought of Nicole being in danger because of him was almost too much to bear. He did thank *Wakan Tanka* that her twelve-year-old son was not involved.

With a Herculean effort Nighthawk cleared his mind of worry and concentrated on what he must do to safely get Nicole free of the madman. He no longer thought of young Jimmy as a boy. The youth relinquished that consideration when he stepped over the line. In Nighthawk's way of thinking, his use of violence was enough for him to now be dealt with as an adult. By assaulting innocent Nicole and forcing her into his private war, Jimmy had become just another criminal and had ruined any chance he had for leniency because of his youth.

The moon was up. Nighthawk had been driving without lights for the last mile. He estimated Timberline was about a mile further up the grade. Pulling off the road onto an old logging road John stopped the Cherokee and got out. The interior lights didn't go on when he opened the door, because he had taped the button down inside the doors frame. After removing the Mausberg twelve gauge pump, Nighthawk eased the door shut and made ready to enter the blue, gray and black world of a moon-lit forest.

Having prepared his weapons before leaving, he just needed to double check to be certain they were loaded and ready to be used.

The shotgun when loaded with a magnum load of buckshot was considered to be one of the most powerful ever manufactured. He hoped he didn't have to use it, but considering the size and mental state of his adversary he wanted some stopping power if he was justified to use it. Moving quickly, he slipped a camouflage jacket over his T-shirt and

Barry Brierley

some baggy camouflage-fatigues over his jeans.

When John stepped from the moonlight into the shadows he virtually became a part of the underbrush. He paused, then slipped his hand inside his shirt and grasped his medicine bag. He breathed a brief prayer.

Nighthawk had worn the medicine bag on a thong around his neck since he was a small boy. Inside there were items known only to him; they were his 'medicine' talismans that would help guide him along the right paths of his life.

A slight breeze stirred some nearby aspen leaves. Taking advantage of the subtle movement Nighthawk moved quickly but silently through the moonlit forest. As his forefathers had before him, John moved with the wind. The smell of pine was strong on the night breeze, as was the scent of aspen and leaf mold. Because each of his moves was calculated, he became all but invisible to the untrained eye.

Marlon Spotted Horse, his friend who fought in Desert Storm, had given him the camouflaged military fatigues he was wearing. In John's wildest dreams he had never thought that he would be wearing them while attempting to save the woman he loved. Knowing that Nicole had also been a part of Desert Storm during the brief war, he fervently hoped that her training would help her through what must be a terrifying experience.

***

Nicole Shaw opened her eyes and thought she had died and gone to Hell. Golden light flickered up on the earthen walls that encompassed her, splashing the interior with an orange, red, and yellow glow. The frightening realization that she was bound and gagged swiftly brought Nicole back to harsh reality. The distorted light came from countless candles set in hand-hewn shallow niches that were carved at random out of the surrounding dirt walls. There was nobody else in the small room. She was lying on a dirt floor among a scattered accumulation of paper, discarded magazines, and other refuse. She stared in wonder at the unbelievable array of candles that adorned the dirt walls. Memory of the abduction arrived in a rush of horrific images.

As Nicole grit her teeth and dauntlessly hung on to her will to live, a strange smell seemed to hover just beyond the reach of Nicole's ability to identify it. Then she knew. It was the smell of old sweat ... and something else. A slight scraping noise came from behind her. Terror instantly consumed her.

Her muscles tensed as a pair of rhythmic sounds evolved into muffled footsteps and heavy breathing. A large hand seemed to reach inside her chest and squeeze her heart as her captor's stooped form stepped into her hand-hewn hovel. He straightened to his full height and seemed to fill the room. Through terror-filled eyes Nicole peered up at a six-foot-five young man who was a living, breathing nightmare. She'd never seen a young man so large up close, or one so frightening!

He ignored her; his head was poised in an attitude of listening. Fighting down her fear, Nicole quickly took the opportunity to size-up her kidnapper.

He was winded from running. Sweat glistened on his painted face and chest. He was completely naked except for a cotton loincloth and poorly tanned moccasins. A large homemade bow and arrows were strapped across his broad, weight-lifters back. A tomahawk was in one hand and Nighthawk's semi-automatic pistol in the other.

Nicole's heart seemed to catch in her throat as she realized that he's the one who stole John's gun and badge. Realizing that the youth had to be completely insane made her fear almost too much to endure. As she stared at her captor her revulsion escalated and her sudden lack of confidence left her breathless.

Nearly every inch of his massive body was painted red and black. In the flickering light she saw that something wet was hanging from his belt.

Suddenly Nicole made a choking sound and her black eyes bulged in horror.

Upon hearing the slight noise Frump's scarlet painted top-knotted head turned and he stared down at her with a savage, pitiless regard.

The unexpected sight of what hung from Frump's waist had caused Nicole to nearly choke and vomit. She fought down her nausea, knowing full well that if she did regurgitate with a gag in her mouth, she could easily choke to death. Even so, she couldn't take her eyes off the bloody, gray-haired scalp dangling from his belt.

While regaining his breath, a smile that didn't reach the pale eyes crossed young Frump's broad face.

Barry Brierley

"So you're the Indian's white whore."

His manner of speaking made his comment more an observation rather than a question.

Within the black band of paint Nicole saw hatred darken his light blue eyes as he leaned forward and whispered, "He's coming to us." Still transfixing her with his eyes, he softly repeated, "He's coming to us."

He looked away from Nicole, listening.

Still not looking at her he added, "I was waiting for him along the road. When he came he had his lights off."

His head suddenly whipped toward her and he pinned her once again with his madman's eyes.

"He's coming through the woods ... thinks he'll catch me off guard."

He laughed. The laugh was more frightening to Nicole than his words. His insane laughter had a wet, gurgling sound like something unseemly being slowly withdrawn from slimy, clinging swamp muck.

"Thinks he'll catch me off guard," he softly repeated, then laughed again.

His laughter filled Nicole's head with visions of horror. Finally finding the courage to admit to herself that the young man was totally insane, terror was escalating with each heartbeat. The repetitive thought of him being completely out of control consumed her.

He was staring at the wall less than a foot away from her when Frump abruptly began talking to himself. He did so in an incoherent manner while slowly rocking his huge frame back and forth. His actions reminded Nicole of a troubled child she had once seen sitting on a sofa crying totally distressed while rocking back and forth. When her gaze picked up the dried blood where it had run down his leg from the gray-haired scalp, Nicole looked away.

Suddenly young Frump's face was inches from hers; startled she quickly recoiled from his rank body odor before fear rendered her motionless.

"Maybe I'll surprise him!" he roared, splattering her face with his spittle.

Nicole cringed. Squeezing her eyes tightly shut she waited for the pain of the blow that she was certain was coming. It never came. Instead, Jimmy Frump whispered her name. Nicole stopped breathing. Keeping her eyes shut she waited, dreading the touch of his hands. The touch never came. Instead, she felt his breath on her cheek as he repeated in a whisper, "Maybe I'll surprise him."

With an abrupt move, Jimmy Frump straightened.

Nicole opened her eyes just enough so she could covertly see through the fringe of her lashes. She watched as Frump slipped the automatic pistol behind the thong belt that secured his loincloth. He abruptly stooped and stepped through the low opening and was gone from her earthen jail.

Relief washed over her as she battled her fears. She had no idea who he was or why he wanted to kill John. For the moment fear kept her from asking why.

She breathed in clean air that almost overpowered the smell of his sweat and the clotting blood but not completely. Horrified by even the thought of the gray-haired scalp she tried hard to put it out of her mind.

Nicole knew the room wasn't very far from a source of fresh air, because the candles would have eaten up the room's oxygen, but she wanted to be sure he had left before attempting to find out.

Nicole listened. She waited to hear him leave the dirt tunnel. When she no longer could hear his movement she would know he'd left the cave and would have some idea how far underground she'd been taken. Nicole knew her idea was sound but she never heard a thing. Releasing her breath, she thought, the man moves like a ghost. Her concern abruptly switched to John and she became even more afraid as she thought, perhaps John won't hear his movements either.

***

Nighthawk moved soundlessly over the uneven ground like a *wanagi* (spirit). A whooshing sound nearby caused him to freeze in place. He immediately realized that it was a great horned owl. Disturbed by his presence, he had left his perch in a dead pine tree that was close by. John watched as the owl soundlessly glided between the clumps of spruce and aspen then disappeared into a dark mass of towering, ponderosa pine.

John waited motionless until he was certain that there was no one around who would be curious as to what had alarmed *heecha* (the owl).

Cautiously, Deputy Nighthawk resumed his stalk. He knew he was getting close to the old logging community, so he reviewed in his mind the layout of the secluded camp.

He remembered there were more than a half dozen deserted cabins at Timberline. The camp was in close proximity to the paved county road and the cabins were arranged in a three-sided rectangle, with the road on the south side completing the box. A large, grassy clearing was in the center where several permanent picnic tables had been placed in a random manner. When Jimmy's father, James Frump, had been the caretaker his cabin was the further-most building on the west end.

When secretly approaching a nearby enemy camp, or outpost, the Lakota of old always advanced from downwind; Nighthawk used the same tactic. He made a swing to the west so that the slight breeze would be in his face. When he felt the soft kiss of air on his cheek John faced the breeze and glided like a wolf through some blue spruce and sparse underbrush. Suddenly he stopped. Something was wrong. At first he didn't know what it was. He listened and waited. His black gaze swept his perimeters then fixed straight ahead. Through the trees where Timberline should be Nighthawk saw a faint, fluttering glow reflecting off the shimmering leaves. Why would Jimmy build a fire? Is it simply bait?

Apprehension sent a shiver up his spine as he stealthily crept forward. Like a wraith the Lakota lawman slipped soundlessly between the slender white trunks of a clump of aspen. As close as he was, John wasn't taking any chances. The glow which he assumed was a fire had evolved into a flickering, yellow light. He would move only a few feet at a time, then stop and listen; proceeding only when he was certain he was unobserved. Nighthawk was pretty confident that if someone was watching him, his sensory perception would feel the man's eyes and he would know. A sudden urgency spurred him to a greater speed. He now knew for certain that the illumination was coming from some type of fire.

At the very edge of Timberline, John stopped and peered through some bushes as he studied the old logging camp. Every muscle in his body tightened as he stared at the horrific scene unfolding in the open ground in front of the cabins. Suddenly Nighthawk threw all caution aside and was up and running. In two strides he was across the road and onto Timberline property.

He ran without any attempt at concealment. John Nighthawk had never run so fast in his life. It wasn't Nicole Shaw's burning station wagon that triggered his reckless run; it was the sight of a figure slumped over the steering wheel. Through the rear window amidst the flickering flames and smoke he had seen Nicole's dark hair splayed across her shoulders.

In mid-stride Nighthawk saw movement from the corner of his left eye. Instantly he dove forward, sliding across the top of a picnic table on his stomach! Almost simultaneous with the resounding explosions of three gunshots, John heard one round snap by his ear while another plucked at his jacket. He hit the grassy turf hard, rolled, came to his knees and fired the pump from the hip. The first shot wasn't aimed and he wasn't prepared for the solid recoil. He quickly recovered and jacked in the second shell. Nighthawk involuntarily ducked as two more bullets snapped past. He fired a second and third deafening blast as fast as he could work the action. With the third boom still reverberating in his ears, John was up and racing for the burning car.

The image of Jimmy Frump's nightmarish, painted form spinning and falling back beyond the fringe of light was still planted in Nighthawk's head as he ran toward the car. When he reached the burning pyre the heat was like a slap in the face. He tried in vain to approach the front door; the flames were simply too intense. Because of the roiling smoke and flames he couldn't see Nicole clearly. Out of desperation, John quickly raised the Mausberg and fired point-blank, twice ... knocking out the windshield on the passenger side. The smoke rolled out of the gaping hole like burning trash from an incinerator barrel. By then the car was almost entirely wrapped in fire. Nighthawk shielded his face from the heat with his left arm and got as close as possible to the opening. Bracing himself for what he was about to see he peered inside. Through the flames and smoke the body was still slouched over the wheel. Dead eyes stared back at him. There was a bullet hole above the right eye. It wasn't Nicole! It was a man.

Nighthawk swiftly backed away. What he had mistaken for hair across the person's shoulders was in reality blood that had exploded from the huge exit hole in the back of the man's head. He had also been scalped!

Suddenly the station wagon became completely engulfed in flames! Nighthawk staggered back then ran for his life in a full sprint. A

Barry Brierley

thunderous explosion nearly ruptured John's eardrums; the blast from the automobile's burst fuel tank propelled him forward, then slammed him down onto Timberline's grassy turf. In the midst of chaos and pain all Nighthawk could think of was that Nicole was still <u>alive</u>. His heart soared.

In his mind's eye the unexpected image of an only slightly wounded Jimmy Frump brought him instantly to his feet; silently he screamed, 'Where is he?'

Ignoring his newly acquired aches and pains Nighthawk avoided the flaming wreckage and stumbled in the direction where he had last seen young Frump. He saw him spin and fall back into the darkness but didn't know how badly he was hurt.

John suddenly stopped. He had just noticed that his hands were empty. The pump shotgun was gone! He must have dropped it when the explosion knocked him down. Frantic, his hand slapped at his holster. Relief that the Browning automatic was still in his holster immediately slowed the sudden hammering of his heart.

By pulling the slide back and releasing it, he cocked the weapon. Knowing that he was presenting a silhouette target against the backdrop of the burning car, Nighthawk swiftly dropped to the ground and crawled toward the spot where he had seen Frump go down. With the fire's heat at his back, John slipped out of the ring of firelight into the darkness beyond. He didn't move until his eyes readjusted to the gloom.

A blink of light glanced off a metal object. Nighthawk was drawn to the spot like an ant to sugar. It was his stolen Browning automatic! Probably in light of the pistol's potential danger to innocents, John took a single, reflexive step forward. He immediately stopped and knelt. A darker patch of ground was directly in front of him. His hand moved forward into the area and felt moisture. John smelled his fingers. It was definitely blood. Quickly scooping up his 9mm automatic, Deputy Nighthawk got to his feet. His gaze swept the gray and black terrain with an intense scrutiny motivated by desperation. Disbelief nearly brought the deputy to his knees as he saw the empty, moonlit field and the surrounding deserted cabins.

The disappointment the deputy felt was almost painful; it made the recovery of his pistol a hollow victory. Although seriously wounded … Jimmy Frump was gone. With the realization came a pregnant, debilitating fear; Nighthawk still did not know Nicole's whereabouts. Frump did.

CHAPTER TWENTY-THREE

Nicole Shaw jumped! Air sucked in through her nose and lodged in her throat. She heard distant gunfire! The sound terrified her. She held her breath listening. Then there was more shooting; some of it from a different type weapon. In spite of being tied hands and feet, she shuddered. In her mind's eye she could see bullets tearing John to pieces.

The image was one she had carried with her for years, not of John, but of a young soldier from her unit who was literally torn apart right in front of her eyes by Iraqi machine gun fire. It was a reoccurring nightmare she brought back from the Gulf War.

She released her held breath. All at once the fear left her and she became angry; bound and helpless, rage became her only friend. It was something new to focus on instead of just waiting for rape or death … or both. She knew John Nighthawk was alone in the dark trying desperately to save her from the giant madman and there wasn't a thing she could do to help. She instinctively knew John would not have brought in the sheriff's department. He wouldn't trust Sheriff Hoage to do the right thing and still keep her safety as his number one priority.

Suddenly the air shifted. She smelled wood smoke and something else, leather. A sound at the very extreme edge of her hearing caused her to stop breathing and listen. There, she thought. She heard it again. The slight, unidentifiable sound seemed to enter the very essence of her being. She tensed and resumed breathing in a very shallow manner. The strange sound was quietly repeated.

All at once she thought she could identify the sound. It was a hushing tone that reminded her of gentling a horse or the comforting of a frightened child. The sibilant sound had come from behind her. Nicole's back was to the tunnel, but the manner in which she was tied didn't enable her to face that direction. She flinched as she felt something, or someone, touch her bound hands. Again she heard the calming shush. The sound was followed by a soft voice that spoke words that were welcome as a breath of fresh air in hell.

"Do not make a sound. I am a friend of Deputy Nighthawk. While he is making war I will get you away from here."

The voice, with a Lakota accent much like John's, sent a soothing wave of relief wash over her exhausted body.

Nicole felt the cords fall away from her wrists, then her feet. As she slowly moved her cramped arms and feet, he touched her arm and said, "I will jerk the tape from your lips. By doing so it will hurt less."

Nicole nodded. Straight long hair, smelling of wood smoke and black as a raven's wing, spilled over her shoulder and brushed her cheek as she felt his fingers gently work underneath the tape. In spite of his soft touch she smothered a gasp as he ripped the tape free.

"Thank you. Whoever you are. Where ..."

Abruptly his hand closed over her mouth. She smelled damp earth mingled with wood smoke. She once again heard his whispered, 'shush.' His head raised and he listened.

She studied his chiseled profile and the lean planes of his youthful Lakota face. Then his head turned and he pinned her with obsidian eyes that made her instantly think of John Nighthawk.

"Who are you?" she asked.

"Later. First we must get you safe," he breathed the words.

Swiftly, without making a sound, the Lakota moved back into the dimly lighted tunnel. Nicole started to follow, then stopped. Something shiny caught her eye wedged into a recess in the wall. Instinct caused her to grab the object and thrust it into a back pocket of her jeans.

When Nicole stooped to step into the tunnel she stopped. Her rescuer was crouched in the fluttering light waiting. Seeing the Lakota almost naked, dressed the same primitive way as the madman, she hesitated. In the candles' blinking light his dark skin had a soft coppery glow. His midnight eyes peered at her from his dark, unsmiling face. He reached out with a hand toward her and beckoned with a subtle gesture. Not having another option, she followed.

Edges of Time

After advancing but a few feet, Nicole smelled the fresh night air. They immediately rounded a sharp corner, squatted, and duck-walked through the bottle neck of the tunnel. They reached the outside after brushing past a large bush that covered the entrance. After the candlelight she couldn't see a thing but thought she could hear the subtle trickle of moving water. The clean freshness of the outside air was invigorating. The man took her by the hand and led her down an incline into some pine trees. The scent of crushed pine needles floated in the air like a fine cologne mist. Her eyes were still adjusting, but Nicole could see the man's darker form squatting beside her. She wondered who this man could be and why is he dressed like a Lakota of the olden days?

"How did you happen to be here?" she whispered.

He took so long responding, she didn't think he was going to answer.

While watching the top of the slope he said, "Earlier I heard a single pistol shot. No one hunts with a pistol ... and would never shoot after dark. I came to see."

Nicole saw him slowly turn his head and look to their rear. Satisfied no one was there, he turned back and continued watching the skyline at the top of the incline. His voice, when it came again, was without inflection, no sorrow, no judgmental tone, but merely the facts. To Nicole's ear the Lakota sounded like a man at peace with himself, a person who had seen life at its fullest and at its worst, and remains true to only his own beliefs and laws.

"I was there when Jimmy Frump put the body of Timberline's new caretaker into the Buick station wagon, then set it afire."

Nicole gasped, clapping her own hand over her mouth so no more revealing sound would escape. Her mind recoiled at her rescuer's words. But her thoughts rolled right over the fact that her car was burning.

Jimmy has already killed, she thought, was I to be next? Nicole swallowed her fear and took a couple of deep breaths. A light touch on her arm gave her pause.

"I am sorry to frighten you, but you needed to know," he paused, "I wondered who the Buick belonged to. I knew it wasn't the dead man's. His Ford is still behind his cabin." He looked at her, then added, "I found you because I knew of Jimmy's hiding place. He has always liked to play Indian. It took him many nights to secretly dig his hideout next to his

185

father's dig." His voice turned bitter as he added, "Now his mind is gone. He makes war on women and by his dress and actions makes a mockery of my people."

Night vision intact, Nicole watched the woods as she listened and wondered at the harshness in his voice.

"But, how do you know all this?"

With a sweep of his arm, indicating everywhere, he answered, "This is my home."

She thought about his words. When she turned to make a comment he was gone.

Concerned with his sudden departure, her fear returned. Nicole tried to relax but worry and fear wouldn't allow it. Anxiety had placed a burning in her chest that felt like acid eating its way through her heart. Although she knew there was nothing she could do, her fear for John was consuming her.

She looked back the way they had come. Peering through the dark trees she thought that here and there many of the autumn leaves appeared to be kissed by moonlight. Beyond the leaves Nicole saw a dark mass that looked like a small hill rising from the slope of a wide, wooded incline. Then she thought she heard a faint trickle of water. At the base of the hill, to the right, she caught a glimpse of reflected light glistening off what looked like a small pool of water nestled in the middle of a few birch and pine. Beyond the nearly bare hill at the top of the incline the sky displayed a mystifying orange glow that showed through the back-lit trees. She swallowed, thinking it must be the Buick.

Suddenly Nicole tensed. She thought she had heard the motor noise of a vehicle. Then, quickly as it arrived, the sound was gone, and her hopes were gone with it. From the top of the slope, there came the noise of someone recklessly smashing through the underbrush. She knew it wasn't John; she would wager anything that he had never in his whole life wildly stomped through the woods.

Briefly silhouetted among the trees, Nicole saw the unmistakable image of a running man. As the figure started down the incline he slowed his headlong run to a stumbling walk. She saw immediately that it was Jimmy.

Through frightened eyes Nicole noticed that he was staggering, holding his left side. Worry and fear joined forces and tried desperately to take away her courage and faith. If that happened she knew it would leave her defenseless and without hope. Dear God, she thought, where is John?

Her self-preservation instincts had Nicole frantically look once again for her rescuer. She didn't know if she should run or stay. Wisely trusting her rescuer's advice, she stayed.

The moonlight did nothing to soften the impact of the frightful image Jimmy Frump projected. Light from above gleamed across the flat planes of his large pectorals and the sheer bulk of his muscular arms and legs. Nicole shuddered with revulsion as she watched the red and black painted figure pause, then pull the bushes aside at the tunnel's entrance. Flickering yellow light spilled from the opening. She couldn't pull her eyes away from Frump's injured side. His skin glistened with sweat and light also reflected off the dark blood trail that ran down his left leg. He tugged at his uninjured side. Nicole gasped as she saw light reflect off the steel of his tomahawk. She suddenly realized that Frump was planning to kill her!

"She is gone."

Young Frump abruptly turned, grasping his injured side as he did so, and looked toward the small clearing that faced the tunnel opening. Nicole looked also. Unable to believe her eyes, she stared. Her Lakota rescuer was standing a few feet away from Frump. Although several inches shorter and much lighter, he appeared to be unafraid and completely relaxed. Apparently without a weapon, dressed in a leather loincloth and moccasins, he stood motionless, arms at his sides. Mesmerized by the moonlit confrontation, Nicole stared, certain that Jimmy would hear the beating of her heart.

"Who the hell are you!?" Frump roared!

Instead of answering the question, Nicole's rescuer asked one. "Where is Deputy Nighthawk?"

Nicole's breath seemed to be caught in her throat, fearing Frump's reply.

Inexplicably the Indian's words infuriated Frump; he suddenly raised his hatchet and rushed straight at the unarmed man.

Wide-eyed, Nicole watched as Frump's tomahawk sliced through the air. The Lakota somehow avoided the killing stroke and disappeared from sight behind young Frump's bulk then reappeared like a conjurer's trick! Before Jimmy could recover from his wild miss, the Lakota's moccasin encased foot snaked out and struck his bloody wound a solid blow.

Frump dropped his hatchet, clutched at his wounded side and howled like a gut-shot coyote.

The debilitating kick had connected just above Frump's left hip where two of the magnum-propelled buckshot from the deputy's shotgun had ripped through his tender flesh.

Nicole could almost feel his agony. His pain seemed so severe he appeared unable to move. She watched as the angular Lakota immediately spun in a circle and struck Jimmy high on the jawbone with the back of his swinging fist; the meaty sound of fist connecting with jaw echoed across the small clearing. Frump's legs buckled as he staggered backward.

The Lakota crouched before him like a wolf about to spring.

Within the time frame of a double heartbeat, Nicole's gaze ripped from the scene in front of her to something picked up by her side vision.

Random shifts of movement and light were coming down the slope. Hand-held flashlights were sending eerie shafts of illumination in every direction. Nicole instinctively counted the hand-held lights. Her quick look had registered two flashlights and three figures tearing recklessly down the incline.

Nicole focused again on the moonlit gladiators just in time to see Frump's unconscious body hit the ground. The impact sent a scatter of fallen aspen leaves floating upward on cushions of air. Suddenly, the young woman's eyes darted everywhere, but her search was a waste of time. Her rescuer was gone! Nicole felt naked and vulnerable. The inane thought, where did a man like him learn karate, passed through her mind and then was gone.

John, she thought, where are you? She cringed among the leaves, trying to make herself appear smaller and more difficult to see as the probing shafts of light neared the clearing.

CHAPTER TWENTY-FOUR

In a daze Nighthawk slowly picked himself up, brushed bark and leaves off his face, and struggled to collect his bearings. It came back to him in a muddled rush of fact and speculation.

After finding the blood, but no Frump, Nighthawk thought he knew where he went to hide, the place where Jimmy's father, James Frump, had died at the base of the hill near the small waterfall. John guessed Jimmy would have known about his father's attempt at gold mining and his excavation into the side of the hill. Near there would be the perfect place to hide Nicole. Not wanting to risk a Frump ambush, John had decided to make a wider swing in his approach. That was when it happened.

For the first time in his life John had recklessly run through the dark woods and had run smack into a ponderosa pine tree. The impact had knocked him off his feet and rendered him momentarily senseless.

With time growing short, fear for her life became his impetus. Once again throwing caution to the wind, Nighthawk ran. With an automatic in each hand he raced recklessly through the dark shadows of the forest determined to stop Frump. Up ahead he saw light bouncing off the trees. Flashlights! Nighthawk's mind became a swirling vortex of confusion. He quickly slowed his pace to a walk and it evolved into a skilled, stealthy approach. Who could it be? John's thoughts were reeling as his mind tried in vain to come up with a rational answer.

***

Nicole held her breath and watched as the three men reached the small glade and their flashlights picked up the still form of Jimmy

Barry Brierley

Frump. She mentally kicked herself for not running when she had the chance. She didn't know who the men were, but she didn't like their looks. The short, broad one crouched over Jimmy's inert form.

"Holy shit!"

Nicole jumped, startled by the short one's sudden exclamation. The other two, one very thin and the other, whose hulking presence was enough to give her the creeps, crowded in close.

"He's still alive, man."

The thin one's announcement sent a chill up her spine. They know him! The realization that they could be friends, or cohorts, of Jimmy made her skin crawl with apprehension.

"Look at him! He's got more paint on his face than a two-dollar whore! The crazy bastard has really gone 'round the bend."

With the short one's words the ape-like third man began flashing his light around. Suddenly, the flashlight's beam struck her full in the face, and stayed there. Blinded, she froze!

"Hey!"

His grunt-like shout brought the other flashing beam to join his. Nicole, heart thumping, brought her hand up, shielding her eyes from the bright lights. She felt like a deer caught in a poacher's spotlight. Still unable to see, she relied on her hearing.

"I'll kill the first man that moves!"

Nighthawk's voice cracked with the authority of a man who meant exactly what he said. Nobody moved.

"Slowly lower your flashlights."

With John's voice Nicole's relief was instantaneous. The sensation was so intense; it felt like her bones were melting ... this was a John Nighthawk she had never witnessed before. As John's command was obeyed she rubbed her eyes and turned away, blinking crazily to get her vision back. Hearing a slight noise to her rear, Nicole's look was in time to catch a fleeting glimpse of long hair splayed across a bare back before the moving image disappeared into the underbrush. A feeling of good will washed over her with the knowledge that he hadn't left her alone, after all.

Nighthawk was cool as ice as he stared at the three bikers over the barrels of his twin automatic pistols. His focus was on the brother, Crab. He knew that if there were to be any trouble it would start with him.

"This ain't what it looks like, Chief."

190

Edges of Time

Crab's voice displayed no fear.

"Keep talking. I see any movement other than your lips, you're a dead man."

"That's pretty harsh, Dude. Look what ya did to my brother."

Before John was able to reply, Junky intervened.

"Who's the 'crispy critter' in the car, Man?"

Ignoring the callous question he glanced at Jimmy's sprawled form. After noting the steady rise and fall of the massive chest, his gaze returned to Crab. He stuck one pistol behind his belt, grabbed his handcuffs and threw them at Crab, who caught them along with the words, "Put those on your brother ... behind his back. But first, bring me your flashlight ... slowly."

The stocky biker, picket-fence grin flashing beneath his hard eyes, stepped forward, flashlight extended.

Pistol aimed straight at Crab's head, Nighthawk said, "Stop!" He reached and took the light from the biker's reaching hand. "Now, step back and do as I said!"

As Crab crouched beside Jimmy and turned him over, John waited to hear the click of the cuffs before he added, "When he comes around we don't want him killing anyone else."

"Ah, man ... Jimmy did the dude in the car?" Junky whined.

"Shut up, Stick! I'm sick a yer loose mouth," Crab exclaimed, as he stood up.

Nighthawk flashed the light at Stick and said, "You! Stick. Bring your flashlight over here and set it on the ground."

After the scrawny biker had complied and returned to the others, John said, "Now sit down ... all three of you. Hands behind your heads."

After they did as he ordered he glanced toward where he'd seen Nicole and called, "Nicole? Are you all right?"

"Yes, John," was her soft reply.

"Please come over here and get the other flashlight."

Nighthawk kept his eyes on the three scowling bikers and listened as Nicole Shaw walked through the long grass of the clearing. His side vision picked up her blurred entry into the sphere of artificial light. Seeing her, even in a peripheral manner, eased his tension.

Nicole quickly picked up Stick's flashlight and moved to John's side. She immediately trained her beam on Jimmy's hand-cuffed form.

Barry Brierley

Flying insects attracted to his sweat and blood flew in and out of the light's dazzling orb.

To Nighthawk's tired eyes, Jimmy Frump, with his bulging muscles, war paint and bloody wound, looked like he had just fallen off the set of a bad Western.

Feeling the warmth of Nicole's breath through his shirt made John's knees feel weak. The reality of her being truly safe hit him hard. He glanced at her. In spite of her stained jeans, disheveled hair and large frightened eyes, she looked wonderful. When she smiled tentatively at him, Nighthawk's heart soared.

"It's going to be all right," he said.

"This is all real touching, but I got somethin' to say."

Crab's grating voice snapped John back to the reality of having four prisoners and no way to transport them.

"Say it," John retorted.

"Me 'n Stick and Monkey ain't involved in this shit."

At Crab's mention of Monkey, Nighthawk glanced at the oversized biker realizing he had only said one word since he arrived.

"When we couldn't find Jimmy earlier, we got worried. He'd been talking some crazy shit. But he didn't say nothin' 'bout no kidnapping."

"What did he say?" Nighthawk asked.

He felt Nicole move in closer and lean against him.

"He said somethin' about not waitin' 'til morning to get even. We thought it was just talk, him bein' not much more than a kid 'n all. But, like I said before, we got worried when we couldn't find him. So, we cruised on up to yer place ..."

"Hold it. How did you know where I lived?"

"He showed us earlier tonight before we saw ya downtown, man. We were just cruising, ya know? Jimmy said he wanted to show us where the cop lived. I said, 'What cop?' Jimmy said, 'the one who's ass I'm gonna kick.' So he took us up there for a drive by."

Crab glanced at his two buddies, then back at John and said, "Can I take my hands off my head, Chief? I have trouble talking without using my hands."

"No," Nighthawk exclaimed, "and don't call me 'Chief!'"

"Okay, okay!" The hard light was back in the biker's eyes as he continued, "Anyway, we went back and yer door was open ... and Jimmy's note was still stuck in the door."

Edges of Time

"John?"

Nicole's nervous voice pulled Nighthawk's attention over to Jimmy Frump, who was beginning to regain consciousness. His unexpected movement captured everyone's attention. The three bikers watched his efforts with as much interest as Nighthawk.

The deputy suddenly brought his head up. He listened. Faintly, in the distance, he could hear the impossible. It was the pulsating whip of a police cruiser siren. He didn't understand. How in ...

"It's what I been trying to tell ya," Crab asserted, "We used the phone in yer house 'n called the sheriff!"

John aimed an ear toward the sound. His hearing confirmed that the sirens were drawing closer. He looked up toward the cabin area where he knew the sheriff would arrive. Yes, he thought, it's the sheriff. Only Sheriff Irwin Hoage would use a siren on one of the most lonesome roads in the Black Hills.

"Look out!"

Monkey's warning shout was only a fraction ahead of Nicole's startled whimper.

For just an instant everything seemed to be in slow motion. Nighthawk's eyes followed his turning body. Like a dancer practicing a routine rotation, his body revolved and the Browning slowly came into line. He felt Nicole's hands on his arm and shoulder as she blindly grabbed at him for protection. Her movements appeared to be made with sloth-like inertia. In the bright beam of John's flashlight Jimmy Frump's mad eyes surrounded by his twisted, garishly-painted face, bored into his own. His mad eyes were rapidly growing larger.

Nighthawk blinked and suddenly the action was alarmingly normal. Teeth bared, hands still cuffed behind his back, the living nightmare bore down on him with the imagined speed of a runaway truck. John had just managed to swing Nicole out of the way when suddenly young Frump was smashed sideways out of the flashlight's powerful ray of light.

When John again illuminated the scene he saw young Frump had been hammered to the ground by his older brother, Crab. Who was almost half his size,. He lay there, arms cramped behind his back, and screamed obscenities until Crab released him and stood up. Jimmy turned his face away and began to cry. The stocky biker swayed over his brother's sobbing form and wiped away some tears of his own as his voice, shaking with emotion, murmured, "This wasn't supposed to happen, Jimmy. I'm the black sheep remember? Me, Crab! I'm sorry I hurt you, but ya can't be running around killing people. You need help, Man."

Nighthawk stared, and certainly not for the first time wondered at the complexity of human nature and the ties that blood binds.

As Crab Frump continued to talk, trying to reach beyond the barriers erected by his brother's dementia, Nighthawk lowered his pistol but continued to watch the four men. The arrival of the shrilling pulse of the cruisers' sirens was a welcome sound but pitifully out of place in his sacred hills. He saw the strange biker, Monkey, watching him. John nodded a 'thank you' for his warning shout. Monkey looked away and spat into the weeds.

Nighthawk felt the gentle touch of Nicole's hand on his arm. In the deflected light from her flashlight, her eyes looked twice their normal size as she said, "John, I'm sorry I grabbed your arm. You could've ..."

"You're sorry? This whole thing is my fault. I'm the one ..."

This time Nicole interrupted.

"Let's wait until later to talk about it." Carefully avoiding John's gun hand, Nicole moved in closer and said, "I have a present for you."

Nighthawk's attention was abruptly pulled away by a distant shout and flashing lights coming from the top of the incline. Shadowy figures were moving down the trail; their flashlights were bouncing powerful beams of light in all directions. A hard object was pressed into his hand. John looked and saw his Lakota County deputy sheriff badge shining up at him. John glanced at Nicole and smiled self-consciously.

He knew that with all the current pain and sorrow the loss of his gun and badge had caused, he had no business feeling happy but he couldn't help it. Somehow, thinking of the future victims who would have suffered or died because of Jimmy's mental disorder seemed to help. Nighthawk met Nicole's steady gaze and held it.

"Thank you."

She nodded and slowly smiled.

With the arrival of the sheriff and his deputies, Nicole's thoughts turned inward. In a dream-like state she recalled the horror of her recent experience. A tremor moved through her whole body as she relived the nightmarish terror in her mind. For some strange reason the cerebral replay seemed to help pull herself together. In spite of not having been physically injured Nicole felt emotionally violated and exhausted and she knew that good luck had played a major role in her survival. Her thoughts, unexpectedly, focused on her son, Mike. The awareness that he was spared the horror she had experienced became an instant stabilizing factor.

Almost before she knew it was happening, the sheriff's deputies were everywhere demanding assistance and recognition of their importance to the case in question. And John's help seemed to be needed at each and every one of the countless places needing assistance. Every few moments she heard the startling bellow of Sheriff Hoage, shouting for Deputy Nighthawk.

Silently and covertly Nicole watched the rotund sheriff as he managed to constantly get in everyone's' way without ever really accomplishing anything.

Her respect for John grew in giant leaps and bounds with each new departmental crisis she was forced to witness involving the Lakota County sheriff's comic antics.

Her eyes searched and found John Nighthawk's lean form ... the only calm, solid figure on the scene. While surrounded by mounting chaos and flashing lights, he appeared a pillar of stability.

Something made her decide to wait until they were alone to tell John about his wild friend, who had probably saved her life. She watched him for a moment, thinking they both were in need of some tranquility after all this. Nicole smiled inwardly as she looked about her and facetiously thought, maybe we should rent a cabin up here in the Hills where we can get some peace and quiet.

Barry Brierley

CHAPTER TWENTY-FIVE
RECOLLECTIONS, STRANGE WAGON WHEEL TRACKS, AND A CONFLICT OF INTEREST

My first night back in the nineteenth century Redman and I idled the time away beside a small stream while still on the open prairie. It was a garrulous creek that did its level best to keep me awake half the night. It gurgled and babbled throughout our whole stay. I also suspect that there was some dormant water nearby for there had to be hundreds of mosquitoes wanting to share my space.

Up at the crack of dawn, I was anxious to resume the search. There's only one thing worth mentioning about that first morning and my preparation before leaving. I discovered that my Crow name 'Strong Arm' was aptly applied. I must have lost my left hand when I was very young. The power I had in my right arm was phenomenal. With a boost from my right leg I was able to swing my heavy, leather saddle onto Red's back with astonishing ease. While making the other essential tack adjustments I did notice that the saddle had been stripped down of all unnecessary paraphernalia that added weight. But in spite of that, it was obvious that my right arm had abnormal strength.

Confidence fulfilling my quest, I gave Red the lead and headed northwest. One good thing about traveling to the Hills was that there was never any danger of making a wrong turn; the Hills loomed on the horizon like a dark island on an undulating sea.

Before the day was spent we were in the southern foothills of the Black Hills, the smell of pine was tingling my nose, and the temperature had lowered by several degrees. As the elevation got higher so did Redman's spirit, becoming as frisky as a colt.

Barry Brierley

Perhaps it was just the Hills doling out some of their magic. My spirits were also on the rise, and memories from the recent past added to my euphoria and sense of purpose.

Preceding my leaving the reservation, I had learned several things of real value from the old one. Like a tumble-weed returning to the beginning of its journey, my thoughts backtracked to the shack near Wounded Knee Creek.

After making sure that the wounded whiskey peddler wasn't going to bleed to death before he reached a doctor, I had helped Blondie load his partner onto the leaking wagon and sent them on their not-so-merry way. I watched for awhile as they paralleled the ridge north before heading west toward the Black Hills. Just to be on the safe side, I decided to bring the elderly Lakota outside to question him, enabling my suspicious gaze to track the whiskey wagon's retreat.

Feeling a special compassion for the blind elder, I gently led him from the shack into the sunshine. While keeping one eye on the dust of the wagon, I was pleased to see that the old Lakota had managed to dress himself and clean the blood from his face. Taking care not to frighten him, I began a conversation with him. When I told the elder my name he became so excited I felt the need to calm him. Speaking softly in Lakota, I suggested we sit down and have a small council. He smiled and complied. Once seated, he told me his name was Small Dog and that Star Watcher had asked him to stay there in case a mixed blood named Starr was to appear asking for her. Small Dog's story poured from his lips like water from a canteen. He told me that Star Watcher had used the shack as a place to wait for my return.

"She had no doubts that you would return," he said, "but she had no idea when it would happen. She thought Wounded Knee would be the place for your return and said that when she comes back she will wait for you here, near Wounded Knee Creek, no matter how many winters it will take."

Small Dog stopped talking and faced the northwest. The afternoon sun made his face glow like burnished copper as he brought his left arm across his body, from right to left, pointing in the general direction of the Hills. "She took her small son and left for the Sacred Hills. She spoke of the wasichu village called

'The Place of the Dead Wood.' She will seek you there."

While Small Dog went inside after insisting on practicing the Lakota custom that decrees a visitor is always fed before leaving, I mused about what had been learned.

Knowing Small Dog's referral to the 'place of the dead wood' was the town of Deadwood Gulch, I was excited by his words and had to compose myself and wait as good manners decreed. After the old one returned from his cabin where he had prepared a simple meal for me, I thanked him profusely and gulped my food like a hungry wolf not tasting a thing.

By the time I had finished, my excitement level had risen to an alarming plane. Before it reached the point that might bring on a coronary I asked Small Dog one final question about Star Watcher. Speaking very slowly so that he would be sure to comprehend my humble Lakota, I tried to establish how long ago she had left. Having lost the true concept of time passed, Small Dog was vague in his reply. All he would say was, 'Many suns ago.'

As I thanked him and rose to leave, his gnarled fingers reached out and touched me. He said, "Star Watcher gave me something for you." His hand opened.

Resting on Small Dog's withered palm was a stained and torn piece of paper. It had been folded several times and the creases were soiled and yellowed with age. With a thumping heart, I carefully took it from his hand.

"Palamo (Thanks), Small Dog. You are a true friend of Star Watcher." The old one beamed a nearly toothless smile as I slowly opened the missive. A lump formed in my throat as I recognized the note I had left for her so many years ago.

DO NOT WORRY, I WILL RETURN.
I LOVE YOU.

 Nathan

Barry Brierley

My star signature seemed to leap off the page, bringing with it all the wonderful memories of the love Star and I shared during our brief tryst inside the cave. Once again I mentally experienced the steamy atmosphere and our loving embraces. I also remember the bitter cold of the blizzard that raged outside our haven's natural stone walls, and the absolute stillness of the white world I explored after leaving her the note. Most prominent of my recollections was the heartbreak of being unable to return.

Suddenly, I found that I had difficulty swallowing. I turned the piece of paper over. There were some words painstakingly written on the back. Knowing that Star Watcher couldn't read or write, I wondered who had written it for her. While I devoured the short message, Small Dog's voice came to me as a hollow, distant echo as he unknowingly answered my silent question.

"She had the wasichu at the trading post make the marks for her."

I KNOW YOU WILL COME. WE WILL
WAIT FOR YOU. PLEASE HURRY.
I LOVE YOU.
STAR WATCHER

I stumbled to my feet and looked at the ridge that blocked the view of the Hills. My mind imagined the blue mass hovering in the distance where hopefully I would find Star Watcher and the boy, Nighthawk. While carefully refolding the note, heartfelt tears blurred my vision until I was momentarily as blind as Small Dog.

***

Redman lunged up a short grade of the wagon road and my thoughts returned to the present. Even so, the warmth that seemed to come from the note in my pocket made me pause and marvel at the power of my vivid imagination ... or the spiritual strength of the Crow deity, The Maker of Everything.

We were now deep into the pine and after the dust and sameness of Pine Ridge, the aromatic scent of the many trees and various flora was like an expensive perfume meant to be bottled and savored at leisure. In spite of the pleasant atmosphere, my gaze kept returning to a certain set of wagon tracks on the old road. There was something curious about them. There were several sets of them ... all had a certain width of track and narrowness of rim that was different from all other wagon trails I had encountered. Not to mention hoof-prints the size of pie-tins, obviously tracks of some very large horses.

Suddenly, a covey of quail was flushed by Redman's hooves. The small but swift flying birds scattered in every direction; as I fought to control Red's abrupt skittish behavior, my concern over the strange wagon tracks flew away with them. It wasn't until much later after I left Deadwood that my attention would be once again drawn to them.

After an uneventful night beside a quiet lake deep in the Hills, I was up and ready to go shortly after first light. Once in the saddle, I quickly urged Redman into a canter, and we quickly moved along the shaded forest road toward Deadwood.

My search for Star Watcher wasn't the only reason I was so eager to be on the trail. The other reason was a growing hunger. Like a fool, after yesterday's discovery of the pistol and cartridge belt and having been fed by Small Dog, I had neglected to see if there were any food supplies that I missed in the saddle bags. When reopened, what it had to offer wasn't exactly stimulating. Several apples and a couple pieces of tough jerky weren't what one would consider a balanced, staple diet. And I strongly suspected that the apples were for Redman. I realized that it was my own fault. At least I knew that when we reach town or a settlement I'll be able to buy a meal.

While searching for anything edible, I had found a couple of twenty dollar Double Eagle gold coins and some lesser change in my trouser pocket. How they wound up in my left hand pocket, I'll never know. I went through hell trying to fish them out with my false hand; I finally had to resort to dropping my pants to get at the damn coins with my right. In the world of the physically challenged time-traveler, if there is memory of how to handle oneself in a gunfight, why isn't there recollection of how to do something simple as buttoning your pants properly with one hand? After realizing that not a soul was near at hand to answer my foolish cerebral complaint, I put aside my petty grievances and shoved all thoughts of food behind me. With my new found ability to joke about my handicap and other perplexing situations, I did experience a certain amount of satisfaction. It was the knowledge that I was quickly adapting to my new role in the nineteenth century and had become as one with Caleb Starr, Jr. Being still troubled by my frightening skills as a gunman, I was confident that my Daniel Starr persona was still in control. But then, in all honesty, I was quick to embrace anything that helped to fortify my resolution to find Star Watcher and Nighthawk.

Later that morning we met a fast moving wagon that forced Redman to leave the road or we would have been hit. I hollered at the muleskinner, but he was too busy whipping his mules into making a stronger effort to reply. For that matter, I doubt that the man even noticed us. Swallowing my displeasure we regained the road and resumed our climb deeper into the Hills. Whenever the terrain would allow it, I alternately rode Redman at a trot, a canter, and a walk. The more miles traveled, the more impatient I became, yet time did pass swiftly.

In spite of my growing fatigue the day developed into a beautiful, sunny one, and the higher the road climbed the fresher the air became and the more yellow were the tree leaves.

Later in the day, through a clearing in the pine and birch, I caught a brief glimpse of what had to be the mining town of Deadwood. It was nestled in a deep gulch between some tall, nearly treeless, hills.

Back in the future I had spent a good number of years drifting around the Black Hills but their overall natural appearance was quite different now than in the twentieth century. I believe it was because the tree distribution was different. In spite of the advance of civilization there appeared to be less foliage now than in the future.

Fearful that I'll be too late to catch Star Watcher in town, I encouraged Redman into a swifter pace. Except for passing an occasional miner and the continued presence of the deep, narrow wagon tracks, I thought that the rest of my approach to

Edges of Time

Deadwood was going to be without a noteworthy incident. Unfortunately, such was not the case.

Not far from Deadwood a narrow trace cut through the pine in a more direct line toward the mining town. I reined Redman onto the obviously less used route. Except for when I had to slow for an occasional deadfall sprawled across the road we made good progress along the new tree-shaded passage. Grouse and quail were everywhere; the game birds exploded into flight whenever we approached too close for their comfort. Eventually, the trail narrowed and when we passed through a rocky draw it quickly widened dramatically into a relatively treeless area.

About the same time I slowed Red to a walk, my ears perked. I could have sworn I heard someone shout. I noticed Red's ears were pricked also. When I glanced back there was no one to be seen.

I convinced myself that the sound we heard was merely a creak of my saddle leather and concentrated on maneuvering Red around a finger of rock partially hidden by a bush of red sumac.

After the whiskey runner incident, I had thought it prudent to continue to carry my revolver in my belt in case there were other unsavory characters about that would impede my search. As it turned out, I was either a prophet or my Caleb Junior instincts were good ones.

"Hold it right there, mister!"

Instantly, I reined Redman to a stop. The angry, nasal voice came from my immediate right.

We were in a small, treeless gorge which nature had carved out of a hill. The slopes on either side of the ravine were covered with a giant's handful of large boulders scattered here and there.

I noticed that there was a slight breeze fanning the back of my neck, which explained why Red hadn't given any vocal warning.

"Keep them hands where they are an' look at me."

That strange phenomena I had experienced near Wounded Knee Creek was once again in control. I was relaxed and ready for anything. My false hand held Red in check, while my right

203

Barry Brierley

rested at the junction of my thigh and hip. Behind me I could hear the rhythmic approach of a person wearing spurs. That makes at least two of them, I thought.

Fully conscious of the Remington's grip resting just above my hand, I slowly turned my head to my right and looked for the source of the voice. The first thing I saw, less than ten feet away, was the business end of a rifle with a hexagon barrel pointed straight at my heart. The man's face behind the rifle was in deep shadow because a patch of sunlight was hitting his battered, narrow-brimmed, gray hat. Except for his hands, bearded chin, and wrists cuffed in scarred leather, the rest of him was hidden behind a granite boulder.

"Is this a holdup?"

Before the rifleman could answer my question, a wheezing, youthful voiced grumble came from the rear.

"Sorry 'bout that, brother I was off in the bushes, lightening my load, when this jasper showed."

Before the rifleman could reply a gruff new voice came from the opposite side of the trail.

"Don't worry 'bout it, Lonnie. Just a fella passing through."

Except for straight ahead, I was boxed. I slowly turned and looked toward the new voice. Two more men had stepped out of the shadows into the sunlight and were walking toward me. No spurs on this pair, I thought, as they move quietly. The tall gent in the lead had a curious, pigeon-toed walk, but as I was soon to find out, he had a straight-forward manner of speaking.

"This ain't no holdup. But we need ya to get down off that blood bay."

Not having any choice, I slowly freed the reins from my wooden hand. Being more than a little conscious of the rifle I kept my hand clear of the Remington and cautiously stepped down from Redman. The tall gent ducked under Red's head, took the reins, stepped in close and pulled my revolver free. I glanced at the rifleman and was relieved to see him lower his weapon and step clear of the rock. He was joined by another man who moved out of the deep shadow of a boulder. Both were heavily armed. These men, I thought, aren't mere cowhands.

The fellow in front of me was about my height, which I estimated to be about six feet. He sported a full-trimmed

204

mustache and wore a suit coat over range clothes with a big revolver holstered just below his hip-bone. He had a melancholy, serious air about him. Beneath the moderate brim of a weathered hat, the hard look in his dark eyes belied his dispirited demeanor. I decided this was not a man to mess with.

"Where ya headed?"

Before I could answer I was distracted by the rifleman who the fellow, Lonnie, had called 'brother.' With an exaggerated swagger, he stepped up close and handed his rifle to the man behind him. The man, who was much smaller than me, grabbed my arm and jerked so that I faced him. He stuck his face up close to mine.

"Leave him be, Kid."

The voice of their apparent leader calling the man in front of me 'Kid' sent chills down my spine. Hearing the nick-name and him having a brother named Lonnie made me think I should know him. With the projected knowledge came the realization that I was very close to having a 'near death experience.'

The 'kid' was short, about five feet six or seven, with dark skin and a short, shaggy beard and a mustache that covered his mouth. He had a dead serious look about him and a curious light in his eyes that made me pay close attention to his every move. He glanced at the leader and then looked up at me. With his short stature my six feet must have felt threatening. Eyes black as coal, and just as lifeless, peered into mine then rudely crawled across my features like a pair of black beetles.

"Yer Injun, ain't ya?"

His nasal twang grated on my nerves yet the calm was still with me. I experienced no fear but could feel the tingle of growing anger surging through my veins. I held his hard look.

"I'm half Crow. What tribe are you from?"

Rage widened his eyes and his right fist swung up at my face. My left hand got there first to block his punch, and his balled fist smashed solidly into the hardwood of my carved left appendage. He howled like a coyote. Strange as it may seem, he clutched his arm instead of his bruised fist. Quicker than thought, he released his arm and his hand went for his holstered revolver; the taller

Barry Brierley

man behind the leader pinned his arms to his sides, and for a heartbeat the taller man's eyes met mine. It was a disconcerting experience; the man had double pupils in one eye. My side vision picked up a blur of movement. Suddenly, the muzzle of the leader's pistol was a couple of inches from my nose. It wasn't until then I became aware that my hand had automatically reached for my own pistol which was no longer there.

Like myself reflex had the dour-faced fellow draw his pistol. Apparently remembering he had my pistol, he lowered his revolver and threw a hard glance at 'Kid' as he said, "Back off, Harve! We have need a' this fella. Bob would be right upset if you put a hole in this drifter just cause he asked the same question you asked him."

The name 'Bob' seemed to calm the bearded one. It didn't have the same affect on me. My heart was thumping and my head was spinning as my mind grasped what, and who, I was dealing with. Hearing 'Kid' called 'Harve' didn't help any; all it did was confirm my suspicions.

The black-eyed hothead stopped struggling in the arms of the tall man, but his eyes never left my face, as he said, "I know Bob left you in charge, Harry, but don't crowd me."

The man's dark face moved to within inches of my own as he nasally intoned, "Hear this, Injun, if our trails cross again yer a dead man."

He stepped back absently rubbing his sore arm. When my dazzled brain put the names Bob, Kid, Lonnie and Harry together, I knew my hunch was right. I had to be very careful what I said and did.

All my years as a painter, and before that, I was a voracious reader and researcher of the Old West ... and not just about Native Americans.

In this group they were all dangerous men, each and every one of them, and I was almost certain I knew who they were

The leader, Harry, put his gun away and looked my Remington over with interest. His eyes lifted and fixed on mine as he asked, "Who the hell are you, Mister?"

"My father has a horse ranch near Deadwood ... I work for him."

Harry stared at me.

Edges of Time

"Rigged like it is, this ain't the revolver of a ranch hand."

I didn't answer him. His eyes dropped to my false hand as he added, "How'd you lose yer hand?"

I shrugged and continued to meet his piercing gaze. Without lowering his eyes he asked, "What's yer name?"

When I told him, he continued to watch me without expression.

"Heard of your father... never met him, but heard tell he's a good man to ride with."

He looked past me and gestured to someone behind me. The man moved up next to me. It was the other taller man that was with Harry when I'd first seen him; he patted then pushed on Redman's rump to get him to move so he could slip on by. I tensed as he took Red's reins from the leader and led him aside. I made a mental note that Lonnie, with the spurs, was still at my back.

"We ain't stealing your horse, Caleb. We need you to deliver a message for us in Deadwood. An' we need to be sure you do it without running off and talking to someone else ..."

While he talked, my eyes never once left Redman. At that moment, I didn't care who they were, there was no way I was going to let them take my horse.

"Reckon we'll just have to hang on to yer horse and your Remington 'til you get back."

Something told me that losing Red would be like losing my other hand. No matter what, I would not let it happen.

"I'm in a hurry. My wife and boy are missing ... I'm trying to find them."

The leader shook his head at my words and without expression said, "That's a shame, Caleb. Peers to me you'd best hurry so you can collect your horse and gun and start hunting for 'em again."

I glanced at the one called 'Kid' who was grinning at my hopeless situation, and I felt a renewed awakening of anger deep inside my guts. I made a promise to myself that one day my retribution would be sweet.

"How about one of you ride with me to the edge of town ...

Barry Brierley

with my horse and gun? That way, if your friend has a return message, I can save us both time by passing it on and they can meet with your man without my taking the time to ride all the way back."

I held my breath, hoping they'd take the bait.

Before Harry could say no, Kid spoke up.

"I'll take him, Harry. You know god-damned certain he ain't gonna get away from me ..."

I looked at Kid. Those lifeless eyes were staring at me. Clearly defined in his hard stare, I could see the scenario of my own death. Kid's next words confirmed his intent. At least they did in my mind.

"A dead man can't ride away."

He looked at Harry and laughed as though he was joking. Harry handed the Remington to Kid and turned away. Pulling a piece of paper and pencil from his pocket, Harry began writing his note using my saddle for a table. Over his shoulder he said, "Harve, after Caleb comes back 'n you swap horses, I want you to wait for McCoy and our friend so you can lead them to where we'll be."

I knew, instinctively, Kid was going to kill me. I wasn't sure when, just knew he was going to try. I couldn't understand why Harry didn't see it. Maybe he didn't care.

Knowing the attempt was futile I tried anyway.

"How come one of you don't take the message to town?"

Harry quit writing. He handed the note to Kid, who must have been smiling beneath his ratty beard. Harry looked at me and grinned as he said, "Hell, I thought ya would've guessed by now, Caleb. We're bank robbers. Them town folks know all our faces."

TWENTY-SIX
POOR JUDGEMENT AND SWEET REVENGE

I led the way along a narrow, sun-dappled trail. The hot-headed outlaw, who they called Kid, followed behind on Redman. I was on a long-legged sorrel that showed a lot of promise but was no Redman. The deep seated anger burning inside me was constantly threatening to surge to the surface. It was something I had to keep in check constantly if I wanted to live. I knew, without a doubt, the bearded outlaw would have no reluctance toward killing me, if given an excuse, before I delivered their message. His murderous reputation was well documented.

When the trace widened, Kid carelessly moved Redman up until he was close behind. He probably thought because I was minus an arm I posed no threat. I hoped to show him that poor judgment can sometimes cause a man a lot of pain, and even death.

Before we left, Kid had to shorten the stirrups on Red's saddle. Judging from the way my horse acted up, he hadn't had too much to do with other men. And when the outlaw attempted to mount him from the left side, Redman put him on the seat of his pants. The fiery killer didn't appreciate the good-natured guffaws that came from his gang. When he covered his embarrassment by whipping my horse with his reins, I vowed then and there that the outlaw would pay for Red's pain with some of his own.

To save Redman from another whipping I explained how he was trained to be mounted from the right. The diminutive Kid had fixed me with one of his snake-eyed stares. It was a look that

Barry Brierley

had 'payback' written all over it for not telling him before.

We were fast approaching the buildings on the fringe of Deadwood. I knew it was now or never because I was convinced that when I returned from town the man his cohorts called 'Kid' was planning to kill me. I was convinced that my hot-headed captor was the infamous killer, Harvey Logan [alias Kid Curry], who had escaped from the Deadwood jail less than a month ago.

A few years ago, when I was still Daniel Starr, I had been commissioned to paint a mural inside the Butte County Bank in Belle Fourche, a river town which was located just northwest of the Hills. The mural was to commemorate the robbery of the bank that had taken place there in the summer of eighteen ninety-seven. The old bank had since been moved to a neighboring town so the panoramic painting was done on the wall inside the new bank.

The robbery had been pulled off by the notorious 'Wild Bunch.' Many historians are convinced that the gang's leader, Butch Cassidy, wasn't with them at Belle Fourche. Some believe that he, Sundance and Elzy Lay were robbing another bank in Montana at the time. After the robbery, several of the Wild Bunch had been captured and incarcerated in Deadwood's jail because the Belle Fourche jail had burned down a week earlier. In my research for the painting I read where three of the outlaw prisoners had escaped from the jail. The remaining two inmates, a man named Ponteney and another, Tom (Peep) O'Day, were not so fortunate.

What solidified my belief that 'Kid' was the infamous Kid Curry was when I remembered that during his escape he had been shot in the right arm. Earlier, when Kid had thrown his punch and I blocked it with my wooden hand, I noticed that he had grabbed his arm, instead of his hand, in pain. The injured right arm, plus my memory of a few photos of Kid Curry, alias Harvey Logan, was what validated my suspicion. Come to think of it, he was probably wearing the leather cuffs as protection for his slow-healing gunshot wound.

Since we were quickly approaching the edge of town where we would soon part company, I decided that here and now would be the best time to make my move. From somewhere in Caleb Junior's memory bank there occurred to me that a certain *communication existed between the man and his horse, Redman. It wasn't much but it was something that could possibly give me the edge I needed.*

Since we had left the others the kid had trailed behind, well out of my reach, yet still able to keep an eye on me. Trying to appear casual, I threw a glance back at Kid Curry. What I saw caused my heart to beat in triple-time; I knew the moment had arrived. We were walking our horses along the sun-dappled trail and Kid had just pulled out his tobacco and paper to roll a smoke. In doing so he had allowed Red to catch up and pull up along my left side. I waited until both Kid's hands were occupied in rolling his smoke. Switching my reins to my right hand, I tightened my grip on the leathers and let out a piercing whistle. Redman blew-up! The big bay exploded into action by going straight up in the air and fish-tailing on the way down. Even while fighting to stay in the saddle, Kid Curry's right hand was closing on the butt of his revolver. I believe the pistol was already clearing leather when the hardwood of my false left hand smashed against the leather cuff that encircled his wounded right arm. He screamed in agony but tenaciously hung onto his gun. His cry of pain stopped abruptly as another sweep of my wooden hand landed solidly on his high forehead with a sound reminiscent of a length of oak kindling striking a hollow log. His eyes rolled back and he toppled off Redman as though he were a ruffled-grouse knocked off a branch with a hickory stick.

Swiftly I quieted my own spooked mount and grabbed Redman's reins while continuing to watch the stunned outlaw. When I stepped out of the saddle, the creak of saddle leather was loud in the silence of the clearing, but Kid Curry didn't so much as twitch. He was sprawled out among the branches of a shattered deadfall, suspended a few feet above the ground like a sailor in a hammock. Without hesitation I approached him then stopped in my tracks. Kid's snake eyes were half open. He wasn't quite unconscious but he was thoroughly dazed. Breathing a quick sigh of relief, I stepped forward, and twisted the gunman's revolver free of his grasping fingers and tossed it in the bushes. Moving quickly, I retrieved my Remington from Kid's belt. I hesitated

Barry Brierley

then snatched the note from his shirt pocket. A livid patch of red marked his domed forehead, a certain precursor to a multi-colored bruise. The outlaw didn't move, nor seem capable of doing so. I bent from the waist until my face was mere inches from his.

"Haven't you heard? Smoking can be very hazardous to your health. Any hurt you're feeling now is pay-back for whipping on my horse."

I knew he heard me because, muddled as he was, Kid Curry's glazed, hate-filled eyes lifted toward mine. I readjusted my stance and added, "Any new aches you wake up with you can put on my tab."

My balled fist lashed forward and struck him squarely on the point of his chin, snapping his head back. His compact body abruptly relaxed and he slumped, swinging in his sagging bed of dead tree branches.

After adjusting Redman's stirrups to where they belonged, I rode up a slight grade between two buildings and into Deadwood without even a backward glance. As far as I was concerned, Kid Curry had been an obstacle that suddenly became a nonentity. I didn't even check to see if his neck was broken or if he was still breathing. Harvey Logan, alias, Kid Curry, was a mean little man who was very lucky to still be alive. I can't abide a man who willfully beats a helpless animal, especially if the animal happens to be my horse.

CHAPTER TWENTY-SEVEN
FRIENDS AND RELATIVES,
A PIECE OF HISTORY AND A LIVING LEGEND

When I rode into nineteenth century Deadwood it was a sunny afternoon filled with movement and color. The main thoroughfare was clogged with miners, horses, mules, wagons, and Chinese. In contrast to the sun's cheerful ambiance the air was as congested as the street. The stench of manure, sewage, and garbage hovered in the atmosphere as though it belonged there. Of course, the heat of the late summer sun certainly didn't do anything to diminish the problem. Names leapt out at me, familiar names of buildings that I knew were still standing a hundred years into the future, like Bella Union, the Fairmont Hotel with its two story windowed turret. Then there is the famous Nuttel & Manns' Saloon No.10 where twenty-one years earlier Wild Bill Hickok was killed in a poker game holding a pair of aces and eights. In draw poker, one hundred and twenty-two years after the murder, two pair made up of aces and eights is still known as the 'dead man's hand.'

While keeping one eye open for Star Watcher the other was busy looking for the Silver Dollar Saloon. While my roving eye took in the scenes, I let Red pick his own way up the street. Back in the glade, I had decided to actually deliver the short message I had been coerced into delivering. Part of my purpose for doing so was because I instinctively knew that Harry, whom I figured had to be the much celebrated Harry Longabaugh (alias the Sundance Kid). I was certain that he had nothing to do with Kid Curry's plan to kill me. From all I'd read about the Sundance Kid,

213

Barry Brierley

it was believed that he would readily kill but never in cold blood. On the other hand, Kid Curry (Harvey Logan) was a different breed. He was one of only a few riders associated with the Wild Bunch that were considered to be killers. Another reason for passing on the note was pure and simple, curiosity. Research can be very rewarding, but it can also be captivating.

I knew what it was the man Bob McCoy was doing for the Wild Bunch in Deadwood, and I decided I had to have a look at the man Butch Cassidy entrusted with three thousand dollars to hire a defense lawyer for the two outlaws. In my research all that was known about Bob McCoy was that he wasn't an outlaw but was a rancher friend of Cassidy's and could be trusted to handle such a delicate situation without drinking too much or getting into any other type of trouble. I have to admit that my curiosity can be a tiresome thing.

In spite of the heat of the day and an all but cloudless sky, the street was a mud bath. Because of the stink and the countless wagons being pulled by mules and horses, I was certain that part of the quagmire was caused by animal body waste. The street, I reasoned, must be the runoff for whatever rainwater cascades down from the surrounding hills. I shrugged off my pointless musing, yet was still intrigued with the town's unusual layout. Of course I had visited the modern Deadwood many times, but somehow at its current size the strangeness seemed more apparent.

The town had been built in a gulch, a long ravine where the slopes of the near-treeless hillocks seemed to end at the town's back door. Although new foliage growth was apparent, it was obvious that the nearby hills had endured a forest fire many years ago. I remember reading that the town of Deadwood Gulch had been founded in eighteen seventy-five, or seventy-six. Because of the town's descriptive name, the fire had to have been before then.

Spying the false-front of the Silver Dollar Saloon, I avoided the street traffic and reined Redman over to the hitching rail into a space between buckskin and a fine looking steel-dust gelding. After stepping easily from the saddle, I automatically shifted the Remington into a more accessible position in front of my hip bone. At that moment my mind abruptly displaced my thoughts, and memory of my previously aging body filled my head. I have no idea why it hit me at that particular time but suddenly the weirdness of it all was overpowering. I felt momentarily weak.

Ignoring the hustle and turmoil that encompassed me, I leaned forward between Redman and the other gelding and allowed my arms to support my weight against the hitching rail. Dizziness and nausea fought for dominance while the familiar smell of horse did its best to rescue me from the overall stench of the town. As the discomfort eased, my eyes slid across the gouged and scratched surface of my wooden hand, then slowly shifted and fastened onto the back of my right hand where age spots were once so prevalent. The smooth, unmarked, copper skin of my hand seemed to mesmerize me. How can this all be possible? My head spun with the same unanswered questions I had faced and dealt with at Wounded Knee. I truly thought I was past all that. Yet, again I tenaciously battled to accept the inexplicable.

My peripheral vision picked up head movement from Redman. I looked and found myself being studied by the bay's large, brown eye. Holding eye contact for a beat the gelding swung his big head so close his whiskers tickled my cheek. Red then nibbled at my cheek with gentle, velvet lips before abruptly shying away from my reaching hand. Strangely moved by the bay's apparent affection a change came over me. If his horse believes that I am Caleb, Junior, I thought, why can't I also accept it?

Because of my need to find Star Watcher, I was able to put aside my concerns and focus on what needed to be done. It was at that moment that I decided to forget about delivering the message. More than anything I wanted to get back on Redman and continue my search for Star Watcher. It wasn't to be, however. I reached for the reins. Laughter rolled from the saloon's door.

The conversation and laughter coming from the saloon's bat-wing doors worked like a lure, a mystical Pied Piper that stimulated my curiosity and enticed me to enter its domain of merriment and mystery.

I climbed the steps to the boardwalk and tried not to envision

Barry Brierley

the possible repercussions of my rash move. After avoiding the swaggering bulk of a departing hunter swathed in smelly, greasy buckskins, I pushed through the swinging doors into a world I had only read about, written by authors who through research and speculation painted their own pictures with romantic words and hopeful, educated speculation.

In the contrasting gloom, I paused until my eyes adjusted. There were maybe eight to ten people inside, all of them men. It was obvious from their dress the patrons were from all walks of life. Conversation was loud and boisterous and felt as though it was as much a part of the saloon as the Victorian decor. On the left, smoke hovered near the high ceiling in a drifting cloud. It was poised above some of the clientele who were standing at a long, beautifully polished mahogany bar complete with brass foot rail and shiny spittoons. To the right of the bar were a few tables only one of which was occupied by two men, who appeared to be either cowhands or ranchers. Behind the elegant length of mahogany were arched, half-moon shaped mirrors framed in carved and varnished wood that matched the rest of the saloon's elaborate decor. My eyes were drawn to the wall space above the glass. I believe my chin actually dropped. There was a large, framed painting of a reclining, over-weight nude woman. The painting covered nearly a fourth of the wall. Being an artist I had always wondered if most saloons in the Old West really did have such paintings adorning their walls, or if it was some romanticized Hollywood thing.

Movement pulled my gaze toward two men who were seated at a nearby table. One of the men had his chair tipped back so that his back was touching the wall. His narrow-brimmed hat hung down his back from a leather thong giving him a boyish, carefree look. His eyes met mine. I was startled by the brightness of his blue eyes that were framed by a sun burnished face. His sandy hair was cut short and bleached by the sun. Still watching me, he smiled. The man was oddly familiar; there was something about his square jaw. I started walking toward him.

"Hey! Injun!"

I was so startled by the shout I practically stopped in mid-step.

"Get the hell out! We don't serve yer kind in here."

Edges of Time

The bartender was leaning with his fists on the bar glaring at me; a bar rag was slung over one meaty shoulder. The hum of conversation and laughter had come to a sudden halt and every eye in the place was fixed on me. Before I could react there was a thud of wood on wood and a friendly baritone exclaimed, "Hold on there, Pard. This gent's a friend a mine."

When the bartender looked toward the voice, I looked too. It was the man at the table I'd made eye contact with. The thud was from his chair legs hitting the floor. The talker, who I figured for a cowhand, stood up and with slow deliberation kicked his chair back out of the way.

"You toss him out, me and Bob are out of here with him. Best think on this … you don't want word getting around this ain't a friendly establishment. Get my drift?"

My patron placed his hands on his hips and stared hard at the bartender.

The man behind the bar stood up straight. He gave his handle-bar mustache a twirl, and then threw a nervous glance at the boys at the bar. With a begrudging nod at the ranch hand, the bartender reluctantly agreed.

"All right. But he ain't gonna be staying … understand?"

My benefactor grinned and replied back.

"Sure thing, Clyde. We'll make it short."

Stunned by my unexpected help I threw a quick glance at the other man seated at the table who he had called Bob, realizing that the Bob McCoy I was instructed to give the note to was probably him.

The helpful cowboy beckoned to me and sat down. During the brief confrontation with the bartender I had taken the opportunity to take a closer look at my new, self-proclaimed 'friend.'

The cowboy appeared to be about average height, five nine or ten. Like Bob, he was dressed in range clothes and wore a holstered revolver that hung so that the grip was a few inches below his hip-bone.

Bob appeared to be friendly, too; however he seemed nervous and his eyes, shaded by his big hat, darted everywhere at once.

217

Barry Brierley

At my approach, the talker once again tilted back in his chair. He met my gaze, grinned and absently fiddled with his hat's thong knotted at his neck.

With casualness I didn't actually feel, I glanced at the bar and saw that talk had again resumed. When I looked back the fellow with the sandy hair was still watching me. The grin was gone.

"Sit down, friend. Take a load off ... I got a feeling you got a message for me."

Why, I wondered, would he think I had information for him. I hesitated, and then sat at the round table. My message was for Bob and I didn't know if I should give it to him in front of the other cowboy. I noticed that Bob hadn't said one word and continued to appear nervous.

Strange behavior, I thought, for a member of the Wild Bunch. My fingers pulled the piece of folded paper from my pocket; I hesitated again, and then extended it across the table toward Bob. I glanced at the other cowboy as I said, "The message is for Bob."

Bob didn't move. The cowboy let his chair legs thump to the floor and grinned.

"My name's Bob, too," he said and took the piece of paper.

In spite of the grin his piercing gaze left no doubt as to who was in charge. He read the note while my head spun with the confusion that can derive from two people having the same name.

When his head raised after reading the message, he wasn't smiling. Once again I was hit with the feeling that I should know the man, or of him.

"My people done you wrong, Pard. Instead of forcing you, they could've asked."

His people? That was when it hit me ... Bob, or Robert, as in Robert Leroy Parker, alias Butch Cassidy.

Strange things seemed to be happening with my body at the same time. With awareness that I was talking to Butch Cassidy, my body over-reacted ... I was not breathing normally. It was probably because Caleb Junior was just as awed as Daniel Starr.

Butch Cassidy was one of a select few from the Old West who became a legend in his own time. Shoving aside my foolish awe, I *was able to recover my lost breath.*

Cassidy looked at me and passed the note to Bob. All at once I realized he had asked me something and I missed it.

"What was that? I didn't hear ..."

Cassidy pinned me with his strange eyes and asked, "Did you read this note?"

I returned his hard look with one of my own.

"No. Why would I?"

Cassidy's gaze dropped to where the walnut grip of my Remington was showing above the table's edge. His bright eyes flicked toward my false hand then settled on my Indian face as he leaned back in his chair. The other Bob still hadn't said a word and avoided eye contact like a boy caught with his hand in the cookie jar.

Cassidy held my gaze.

"It says in the note that Harve's waiting on the edge a town with your horse and gun."

His eyes snapped toward my revolver than back to my face.

"That right?"

It was right about then that Caleb Junior's personality took over. Bizarre as it was, I was grateful that whenever danger reared its ugly head, Caleb's personality and expertise intervened and handled the situation.

Outwardly, I don't think it showed, but on the inside my whole body became taut as a bowstring. I looked into Butch Cassidy's disturbing eyes and knew that no matter what the consequences I wouldn't lie to him, nor would I back down. A calmness came over me, just as it had with the whiskey peddlers.

"That was the idea, but Kid Curry had other plans for me."

The two men exchanged glances at my mention of Harvey Logan's alias.

"Like what?" Butch quietly asked.

"Like leaving me as coyote bait along some lonely stretch of the trail."

At first Cassidy didn't say anything, just continued to watch me. But the other Bob was looking everywhere. Either he was a nervous wreck or was keeping watch for the unexpected.

Barry Brierley

Still holding Butch's gaze I added, "Curry was the one who stopped me on the trail at gun point; we didn't become immediate friends."

Still transfixing me with those damn eyes, Butch asked, "He still breathing?"

"He was when I left him. He's riding a deadfall out back of Hodson's General Store. He was snoring and sporting a new knot on his forehead ... of course, he could've choked to death on his own meanness."

A slow grin spread across Cassidy's face as he said, "That sure sounds like old Harve. Always trying to be a huckleberry instead of the persimmon he was born to be."

Then Cassidy began to laugh. His laughter was so infectious that nearly every head in the saloon turned and had to add a chuckle or two. Butch Cassidy took a swipe at his tearing eyes and pulled himself together. Bob just sat there, peering out from beneath his big hat and looking worried.

"Sorry boys," Butch said, as he slowly shook his head, "just the thought of the look on Kid's face after being bested by a drifter is enough to give me the belly laughs for a week a' Sundays."

Caleb's personality was still in control as I said, "I ain't no drifter. Name's Caleb Starr, Jr. I live near ..."

"Hell, I know your old man. He's got a horse ranch a few miles southwest a' here." Butch was staring at me with new respect as he added, "He helped me out of a tight spot once. Damn good man."

There it was ... just like that ... I found out where I lived. Sometimes, although there was nothing I could do about it, I felt like an amnesiac on drugs.

Cassidy gave Bob a surprise slap on the shoulder. Silent Bob nearly jumped out of his chair. Butch grinned and said, "Relax, Bob. Don't be so jumpy. We're in good company here ... do you remember that summer I had that Pinkerton detective shadowing me? It was Caleb's pa that hid me and fed me for a few days."

Bob nodded, gave me another weak grin and looked nervously at the weathered faces of the men crowding the bar. My glance over there was in time to see a few hostile faces aimed my way. I decided it was time to leave and stood up. With a quick look, Cassidy saw the men's faces at the bar and was on his feet in an instant. Without taking his eyes off the hostile faces, he spoke in a voice just loud enough to carry to the bar.

"You're staying put, Starr. If anybody's leaving it's a couple a' them jaspers at the bar."

The faces quickly disappeared, replaced by the back of their heads as they hovered over their drinks and cigars. I smiled at Cassidy.

"Thanks anyway, but I have to leave."

With a few short sentences I described Star Watcher and young Nighthawk and asked if either had seen them. Neither had, so I reminded Butch where I left Kid Curry, shook hands and turned to leave. Bob McCoy's voice stopped me in my tracks.

"You know what? I think I might've seen the Indian woman."

Hardly daring to breathe, I slowly turned and faced Bob McCoy. It was like I had stepped into a vacuum; the noise in the saloon was pushed back to the very edge of my awareness. I scarcely dared utter a sound. When I did speak it was just above a whisper.

"Where did you see her? Was a boy of about seven or eight with her?"

Bob pushed his big, sweat-stained hat up out of his eyes and rubbed his chin as he thought it over.

"She was alone and on foot. It was west of here, on the road past White Water Creek. I remember 'cause it was a couple hours after meeting that rundown Wild West Show that was on the same road. They said they was heading south toward Cheyenne."

He paused long enough to readjust his hat and think about what he was going to say.

"I recollect now how sad she looked. She had a mark on her face, a bruise. I remember 'cause it looked like some fool raised a hand to her. That was two days ago when I was heading for this here town."

Somewhat taken aback by Bob's sudden bout of gregarious behavior, I hesitated. Why would someone hit her? I wondered. Shaking off the thought, I thanked Bob McCoy while still musing over the mystery. With Star Watcher on foot, I reasoned, I should catch up with her sometime tomorrow. Suddenly, it felt like a weight had been lifted from my shoulders. But where, I wondered, was Nighthawk?

The three of us shook hands again and I turned to leave. Cassidy grasped my sleeve, stopping me. I looked into his clear eyes and saw real concern shining from within as he said, "If ever you see Kid Curry again, watch him close. He never forgets ... or forgives."

"Thanks. I'll remember."

I left him standing there beside his table, a friendly, solidly built man, who was probably the most charismatic and well-liked desperado this country had ever produced.

As I stepped into the stirrup and swung up on Red, I couldn't help wondering why Butch Cassidy would risk being seen by the law in Deadwood when he had Bob as an emissary. Why would he take a chance like that? I continued to think about it as I reined Redman around and pointed him toward the late afternoon sun.

While I rode up the muddy street's incline, the cacophony that rose from shouting voices, neighing horses, and the clatter and bang of mule-drawn wagon traffic, only added to my growing excitement. My empty stomach growled adding a gastric contribution to the street noise and reminded me of my hunger. In spite of all the bizarre sights and smells I looked around me and found it hard to believe that this was actually Deadwood, South Dakota in 1897. Everywhere I looked I would see something new that dazzled and fascinated. The pure raw, roughness of the town, however, kept me alert and on a constant lookout for unexpected pitfalls or dangerous men. It was that thought that gave me a plausible explanation for Cassidy's presence.

All the books written about Butch and the Wild Bunch suggest that he wasn't there at that time and place that the wild bunch pulled the bank job in Belle Fourche without him. In all probability their belief was based on the risk he would have been taking of being recognized. I say, he was there for that very reason. Everything I've read about Butch Cassidy implies the same thing; the man loved adventure and living on the edge. He *thrived on being able to thumb his nose at his adversaries. Also, Butch Cassidy struck me as the kind of guy that never looked on the dark side of a situation. He was an eternal optimist.*

Just having been around the man increased my own optimism ten-fold. For example, I knew without a doubt that I would find Star Watcher and Nighthawk before another day had passed. Much to my chagrin, it didn't quite turn out that way.

Barry Brierley

CHAPTER TWENTY-EIGHT
HOMEWARD, TO NIGHTMARES
AND LOVED ONES

Almost from the moment I left town, Redman was in control. I needn't have been concerned about finding the ranch, Red knew every step of the way. Along with getting early directions from a rider leading a mare carrying the Starr brand, I found the place easily.

Redman shifted his weight, snorted through his nostrils, and shook his head. Under my breath I murmured, "It's kind of scary coming home, Red, especially when I don't remember ever having been here before."

With a small sense of disappointment I stared hard at the sprawling ranch, searching for something that appeared familiar. I couldn't say what caused it, but there was something disturbing about the corral. It made me feel uneasy. I shifted in my saddle and began to sweat; my hand involuntarily moved to my stomach. But then, I thought, maybe my discomfort was because the meal I'd bought on the way out of town wasn't riding too well in my belly.

None of the places that served food in Deadwood was inclined to serve someone with Indian blood. I was so hungry and angry by the time I'd reached the edge of town I was considering returning to one of the restaurants and using the Remington as a meal ticket. Fortunately, I came upon an Indian family who were hunkered around some delicious smelling meat cooking on an iron spit. Everyone was watching the fat drip onto the camp fire. The family consisted of a young man, a pregnant

Barry Brierley

woman, and an elderly man. After first trying Crow, then Lakota; neither was any help, and I was about ready to give up.

Then I remembered our universal language. By the use of hand sign, I was able to communicate with the Indian family and purchase a meal for a few coins. Never did find out what tribe they were from, or exactly what I was eating. When I asked, the young man grinned and made the sign for dog. The old one took one look at my face, threw his head back and cackled like a witch who had been asked what she was brewing in her pot.

For the remainder of the meal the old one swapped grins with the young man. In between bites the old fool found great humor in entertaining us with an occasional bark, or howl. To this day I'm not sure whether I was simply the butt of a joke or a victim of some exotic cuisine.

Over the jagged tops of the ponderosa pine horizon, the sky was just beginning to lose some of its blue color. I heel-tapped Red and he slowly walked me toward the rambling, single-story log dwelling. As we drew closer the buildings took on a clarity that gave me a brief glimpse of my history on the horse ranch. Wherever I looked there was a certain familiarity. My gaze swept the grounds. There wasn't much activity that I could see. But when my eyes once again rested on the corral area, I inexplicably became very nervous and experienced a strange shortness of breath.

When the arena came into view my heart began pounding and tremors made my hand shake. I couldn't understand why. I also wasn't sucking in enough air. I realized that I was afraid. But, strange as it sounds, I didn't know why!

A sudden flash-frame from Caleb Junior's memory told me the arena was where we trained the young horses. A strange feeling overcame me. Everything around me seemed to slow down, colors dimmed and lost intensity. Involuntarily, I shut my eyes.

It began like the opening scene in a movie theater. The only difference being there was no sound. I simply continued to hear the muffled hoof-beats of Redman as he carried me closer to the apparent, frightening memories of my past. In my head I imagined that I could hear the hum of the film rotating on the reel as the images began to roll.

Edges of Time

***

Inside the arena there was an unbroken horse tossing his head, trotting and strutting. He was frantically lunging and bucking wildly at the end of a rope. Dust was rising everywhere, softening the moving images and the color. Suddenly I could see where the tight rope looped around the horse's arched neck. Strange as it may sound I could see myself. I was on the other end of the rope! My God, I thought, I was just a small kid! I saw myself stumble backward keeping the rope taut as a stretched cable. Situated in the middle of the arena, a solitary post taller than I was abruptly came into view.

The familiar sight of the snubbing post had me reeling in the saddle, shaking with fear. Everything went black and I thought I'd fainted. But then everything began to spin. Through it all I could feel Redman's muscles shift as he continued walking. I hung onto the saddle horn until the darkness lifted.

Like a bad dream the scene returned. Once again I was back wrestling with the stretched rope; the cloying dust hovering in a thick cloud around me. I jerked on the rope with all my strength then lunged forward to pick up the slack and throw a loop around the post to snub the horse down. I did something wrong! An extra loop had formed and caught my left hand between the horse and the post. The action slowed to a frightening crawl as I watched the unbroken horse leap away and my youthful right hand fumbled as it quickly tried to free my left of the tightening loop. Then, at that very moment, everything sped up and the thousand pound mustang bucked and lunged, jerking the rope into a quivering, taut line. I silently screamed as the tightened loop of rope pinched off my left hand and a fountain of blood erupted from the severed wrist. Clutching the stump I saw my brother running toward me, then I was on the ground and I saw other legs running at me through the dust and the red rain.

***

227

Barry Brierley

Redman stopped. I wiped the sweat from my face and opened my eyes. Clarity had returned with everything having a sharper image. Where my left hand had been there was a sharp, throbbing pain. Unwinding the reins from my pulsating false hand, I slipped my feet free of the stirrups and slid to the ground. In spite of my wobbly knees I started walking toward the house leading Redman.

The big bay walked behind me like a pet dog. My heart was palpitating like a trip-hammer gone berserk. By the time I reached the yard in front of the ranch house my body had almost returned to normal. Once again I wiped sweat from my brow. A sigh of relief quickly followed. It was over. Now I know.

"'Bout time you got back. We were getting a little worried."

I looked up and saw my new father, or should I say, ancestral grandfather, as he stepped through the main ranch house's open door. The analytical portion of my brain momentarily convulsed with the absurdity of it all; then it passed on and I felt fine, so I told him so.

"I'm fine, Pa."

Caleb Starr stopped and leaned against the verandah roof's weathered support pole.

"Sorry I didn't make it back for the return trip. I've been looking for somebody."

During my search for the ranch I thought about my first verbal exchange with my father and had decided to be truthful, to a point, for my reason for not returning with them. It looked like I was going to need all the help I could get to find Star Watcher.

"Good thing you sent that message on the back a' the 'tally sheet.' We would've been hard pressed to collect what they owed us without it. Hell, we would've been still sitting on our backsides down at Pine Ridge."

Tally sheet? Then I remembered the pencil marks on the paper. Damn, I thought, the pencil marks were the head count of the cattle!

I stopped squarely in front of Starr. Since he was standing on the verandah, I had to look up a bit to meet his gaze.

Up close, Caleb Starr was one hell of a rugged looking individual. His face was burned dark with crevasses and creases interlocking into a crosshatch pattern like an old piece of leather.

Edges of Time

But the twinkle in his blue eyes belied the rough, tough image. In spite of his grizzled features, gray hair and beard, he looked to be in genuine fighting form. He was still wearing the weathered hat and tall boots he had on at the Pine Ridge corral. The only noticeable thing missing was the large, holstered revolver that had been angled in front of his left hip.

"Glad yer home, Son."

Starr abruptly stepped down to my level and pulled me into a tight embrace. Startled, I returned the hug and stepped back. I didn't know what to say. Starr saved me some embarrassment by speaking first. And after all these years, what he had to say still rings in my ears with the pure clarity of a new bell.

"Funny you should mention you were looking fer someone, 'cause someone's here looking fer you ... said she'd been waitin' near Wounded Knee Creek fer a long time."

I stared into Caleb Starr, Sr.'s washed-out blue eyes in absolute astonishment. I didn't speak. I don't think I could have.

Caleb certainly didn't have that problem. He frowned, looking uncomfortable as he asked, "She ain't in some kind a trouble ... is she, Son? Looks like she took a lick alongside her head."

He grinned when I automatically shook my head.

"Sure is a purty little thing. Puts me in mind a yer mother, bless her soul. I tried to get her to ..."

His voice sort of slipped into some kind of receptive void and it slowly faded away. My head became filled with memories of Star Watcher and our short time together. Can it be true, I thought. Is she really here? Suddenly, I felt a hand on my shoulder and heard Starr's voice once more.

"Caleb? You all right, Son?"

I cleared my dazzled mind and stared into the aging plainsman's concerned eyes.

"I'm all right, Father. Where is she?"

"Father? Son, you ain't called me that since you were still filling yer britches. Why are you ..."

Barely holding my excitement at bay, I interrupted. "Sorry, Pa. I ... Where is she? She's still here ... isn't she?"

229

Barry Brierley

Caleb, Sr.'s expression was a quandary of confusion and concern.

"She's camped over yonder on the other side of the ridge, near the spring; I gave her a blanket coat for the night chill. Like I was 'bout to say before, I tried to give her a room, but she ..."

Already stepping into Redman's stirrup, I interrupted my new father a second time, in almost as many seconds.

"I'm sorry, Pa. I know I'm acting strange. But I promise I'll explain later."

As my leg swung over the cantle I spun Red around and kicked him into a gallop. I left Caleb, Sr. staring after me through a rising cloud of red dust. The worried expression on his face was that of a parent who had just discovered that his only remaining son had gone soft in the head.

Chapter Twenty-Nine
REUNITED LOVERS AND
A TALE OF LOSS AND DETERMINATION

Redman cantered up the gradual slope of the ridge while I rode on his back completely unaware of the short ride. My mind was whirling with thoughts of Star Watcher and what I would say to her. My concern for the whereabouts of the boy, Nighthawk, was eating away at my soul. Have we lost him or has she put him in someone else's care while searching for me? I slowed Red as we approached the tree line near the top of the ridge.

When we reached the top I reined the bay in among some scattered lodge pole pine. There was a cool breeze and the scent of pine engulfed me with its subtle aroma.

At first I couldn't see the spring. Looking for a view with a different vantage point I walked Redman along the skyline. There. I saw the fading sun reflecting off water. I slowly worked Redman down the southern side of the ridge. We angled in and out between orange-barked pine and moss-capped rocks while I constantly searched for my first glimpse of Star Watcher.

The spring was at the bottom of a short slope nestled in among some red willow. There were the remains of a recent fire and a bundle, securely wrapped in tanned skins, but no Star Watcher. The whisper and patter of the small spring seemed to be talking to me, perhaps mocking my concern with its carefree tone and incoherent babble. Worry began to dominate my fading optimism and my enthusiasm began to falter. My gaze swept upstream, then down. Through an opening in some pine boughs,

Barry Brierley

I spied a splash of white. All at once, my breath caught in my throat.

A lonely figure wrapped in a Hudson Bay blanket capote stared out over the eastern hills from a prominent finger of rock. Even with the distance between us I could see her long hair lift and fall from a contrary gust of wind. Star Watcher, I have found you. Even as I stepped down from Redman, my mind kept repeating the words like a litany, 'I have found you.'

She didn't hear my soft, quiet approach. I stopped where the flat promontory of stone began and watched her. It was a scene I would always remember, and I knew I would one day paint.

Her back was to me and a slight breeze was gently rippling through her raven hair. She was wearing the blanket coat my father had given her. It was a white, hooded capote with three bright colored stripes along its cloth-fringed hem and sleeves. She was staring across the timbered hills toward the far away plains. The simple fact that she was staring to the southeast instead of the sunset in the west caused a slight tightening and palpitating in my chest. It was obvious that her thoughts were once again near Wounded Knee Creek, watching and waiting for my return.

The sun was at her back casting long, dark shadows across the land; the distant sky was a deepening copper, much like the color of her skin.

Softly, so as not to startle her, I spoke in lilting, rhythmic Lakota, "Star Watcher."

Her back stiffened as she sat up straight. She didn't turn right away. She waited and listened.

"I thought I would never find you."

My words were barely above a whisper, but she heard them. She slowly turned and peered at me over her right shoulder. The star-shaped birthmark was evident high on her right cheekbone, emphasized by the fading discoloration of a bruise. Her large eyes captured mine and in their liquid depths I could see the smile beginning to form there. A wayward gust of wind rippled her hair, lifting it so it floated like black silk away from her shoulders. Still holding my gaze she got to her feet. Everything slowed and became a picture of rare clarity and beauty as she moved toward me like a wanagi from the spirit world.

Edges of Time

Then she was running!

She flung herself inside the sweep of my open arms. I staggered backward clutching her tightly to my chest while spinning her in a circle. My eyes blurred with tears, and my throat thickened, as I buried my face in the familiar sweet grass scent of her hair. She was sobbing and trying to speak at the same time. I whispered, "I love you," over and over. She stopped crying, lifted her tear streaked face and peered into my eyes ... searching, staring, as though trying to see into my soul.

"It is really you? Awicakeya (Truly) it is so. This I can see in the depths of your eyes."

With her words Star's voice broke. Her penetrating gaze swept my face as though searching for something she hoped wasn't there. When her eyes captured mine once more, all doubt was gone. She spoke quietly, "I thought I had lost you forever."

She buried her face in my chest and squeezed with her arms as though she would never let go.

"You will never lose me again," I said, "I swear it."

Although I had spoken Lakota with Black Elk and, more recently, Small Dog, the eloquent language suddenly felt clumsy on my tongue. In my heart I knew why. I didn't know how to ask about Nighthawk. The words that I would probably use, no matter how carefully offered, would not sound adequate in any language.

Star Watcher, with her acute perceptiveness, saved me from asking. With her face still buried in my chest she began to speak. Her words came to me softly, muffled by my shirt, yet the message rasped across the soft core of my heart.

"My son ... he is gone. He was taken from me by the wagon show people."

Her words sent my heart plummeting to the ground. All at once, I remembered my conversation with Butch Cassidy's friend. It was people from the 'rundown wild west show' that Bob McCoy had mentioned. It was they who had kidnapped our adopted son!

Still clutching each other, I lowered Star to a soft pocket of pine needles formed on the pocked surface of the massive granite outcrop. We sat close together on the sun-warmed stone, our bodies touching. While my mind frantically searched for an easy solution for getting Nighthawk back, we were as one, providing comfort and compassion for each other in the cooling air. Her eyes beseeched my own, seeking an answer to our misfortune. I clasped her hands tightly.

"Tell me how it happened. It might help to know when we go to get him back."

With my words, a spark of hope glimmered in Star Watcher's sad eyes. While I watched, the spark faded and disappeared as she lowered her gaze and squeezed my hands. Without raising her head she murmured, "I have not been a good Ina (Mother). I have lost our son."

She kept her head lowered and her eyes averted. My heart swelled with love for this caring, wonderful woman. I watched tears spill down her cheeks and silently vowed to return young Nighthawk to her or die trying. I thumbed her tears away and lifted her face. My thumb carefully caressed the fading discoloration near her eye as I peered into her midnight gaze and said, "You judge yourself too harshly. It is I, Starr, your 'Crow Warrior,' who you are speaking too. We found him together as a baby, and once again we will find him. He is our son. We will take him back. Do you understand? We will not let anyone stand in our way. Tell me you believe."

Star nodded her head but again lowered her eyes. Gingerly, I touched beneath her chin, lifted her face and kissed her trembling lips. The words that passed my lips were as gentle as a whisper of the wind.

"Now is the time to speak; tell me of this terrible thing and how it came to be."

Softness stirred the dark depths of her eyes as they peered into mine. As Star quietly began her story, the rhythm and melodious flow of her Lakota captivated me.

"Our son, Nighthawk, and I were picking berries on a ridge in the foothills of Paha Sapa. Because of the late afternoon quiet we heard the squeak of the wagon's wheel before we saw the strange wagons. I remember there were four of the wagons with the tall wooden boxes setting on them. All of the wagons had tall wheels and the boxes were painted with many bright colors; horses and mules were pulling them. Wasichus and mixed bloods were sitting on seats in front of the wagons from where they could guide the four-legged ones.

Nighthawk and I stood among the yellow-leaf trees, and we watched them pass by. Most of the wasichus did not look at us, and those who did peered at us with eyes that made me want to hide my son behind my skirts or tell him to run like the wind and hide. I don't remember much about the first four wagons, but I will never forget the last one. It stopped near us while the others continued on. Wi (the sun) was a large orange circle behind them. They were so close, I didn't know if we should run or stay. With Wi shining behind the two wasichus that guided the four-legged ones, I couldn't see their faces. I did feel young Nighthawk squeeze my hand. He must have sensed they were bad men. The larger of the two men had stepped down from the tall box and walked toward me, spurs jingled, branches snapped as he came closer. I held my son close behind my leg while my other secretly loosened my skinning knife in the belt behind my back. My heart wanted us to flee, but I was afraid that we both would not get away. I held my breath as the big wasichu came close.

Beneath a big hat the tall wasichu had a red face and a big mustache that looked like the horns on the white man's spotted buffalo. His belly was large, as was the shiny pistol holstered on his hip. The wasichu spoke to me. His voice was loud and frightening. I had to hang on tight to Nighthawk's arm or he would have run away. I wish now I had let him run. Perhaps I would have slowed the wasichu enough and he would have gotten away.

Not understanding what was being said my fear began to move me backwards. The wasichu followed. He jabbed his finger at me and waved one of the thin, white skins with marks scratched on it, in my face. It was what the wasichu call paper.

The other white man shouted at Red Face from the painted wagon. This angered Red Face and he shouted back at the smaller man. While they were shouting our son squeezed my hand, pointed at the side of the wagon box, and slid further behind my dress. When I looked, what I saw made my eyes open wide like heecha (the owl).

Barry Brierley

On the wagon box, above the tall wheels, there were painted horseback Indians chasing funny looking buffalo; everything was painted in bright colors. And in front of that was a large picture of a wasichu with a big hat and two, large, smoking pistols. I quickly gazed at the Indian's hair-styles but could not tell what their tribe was.

Red Face shouted, frightening me. I flinched and tensed as the white man stepped closer and reached for Nighthawk. I pushed my son back out of reach. The smaller man shouted again at Red Face. He stopped and angrily faced the smaller man. Quickly, I pulled my knife from its sheath behind my back and held it ready between my son and the wasichu. My fear for my son had grown so great I thought the beating of my heart would cause it to burst.

Another shout came from the wagon. Red Face looked and saw my knife. He roared like Mato (the bear) and his arm was a blur of movement overhead. From the corner of my eye there was a flash of blue-white metal and a sharp pain near my eye and I knew nothing more.

I must have 'walked in darkness' for a long time. I believe the red-faced one meant to kill me and thought that he had done so.

Next thing I knew a coolness was in the Yata (North Wind), as it stirred the leaves beside my face. Before opening my eyes I listened but could not hear the squeal of the wagon box's axles. When I did open my eyes Wi was gone; darkness had settled in and I could hear the sounds of night creatures moving nearby. I found my blanket and wrapped it about my body while I waited for the moon to rise. I knew its blue light would show me the tracks of their wagon boxes. I was determined to follow our son forever if need be. But I would be careful not to be seen. A dead mother can do no good for her captive son."

After Star finished her heart-breaking story I didn't move. I watched the tears slide down her copper cheeks as a wayward breeze caught a loose strand of hair from her bowed head and caused it to blow free. I couldn't speak; only my arms would move as I pulled her into an embrace. I held her close, my face buried in her fragrant hair until her trembling stopped and the setting sun had us pursue a secluded shelter less exposed to the chill of the night.

CHAPTER THIRTY
HEAVENLY BODIES, LIES, AND A SEARCH FOR REDEMPTION

I awoke to a symphony of night noises. The wind whistled softly through the pine and aspen while a chorus of insects and frogs from the nearby lake added their own special music. We were on the southwestern edge of the Hills. It was our second night on the trail in our quest toward recovering our kidnapped son. Dwindling patches of trees relieved the undulating prairie in all directions except north. A canopy of stars was our ceiling; a soft mound of prairie grass was our mattress.

I affectionately looked at Star Watcher asleep beside me, remembering. During our first night together our lovemaking had begun with shyness. I remember pulling her close into my embrace. We remained thus for mere moments. I felt her hand press hard over my heart then slide across my chest to my left arm. By the time her fingers reached my false hand, my heart was beating in triple time. Star lifted her head and stared into my eyes. The stars overhead were reflected in her gaze as she slowly struggled with the buttons on my shirt. Once it was removed, Star touched the buckles securing my wooden hand and lifted her face to mine. Her Lakota was like a song, written especially for me. It caressed and soothed my soul as she asked, "Strong Arm, may I remove your warrior hand? I wish to rub the muscles and ease the aches caused by its confinement."

I wondered briefly where she had heard my Crow name, but my heart was so full I merely nodded. Star smiled, lowered her eyes and put her fingers to the task. Unable to look away, I

237

watched her face, remembering each and every mark and flaw from before. The heart-shaped birthmark high on her right cheek-bone was as I remembered when painting it. It bothered me to see new lines and creases from the passing of time. The years were forever gone; the anguish or the joy in acquiring the marks and laugh wrinkles were never to be shared.

I felt the constriction ease on my arm. Star's touch was gentle as the touch of feather down, then strong and soothing as she massaged the tendons and stroked the tired, tense muscles of my shortened arm. Before being conscious of what I was doing, Star's blanket-coat was open and falling free from her shoulders. Star Watcher's eyes met mine; they were filled with a gentle but loving intensity. Her hands left my arm and reached for me. We embraced, holding each other as though we would never let go. When we made love it was without urgency but with an unspoken conviction that our union was a natural, physical declaration of our love.

My thoughts unexpectedly returned to the present and once again my gaze lowered to peer down on her sleeping form. I thought how child-like she looked in repose. Her eyelashes fluttered as she dreamed what I hoped were happy images. I let my fingers trail softly across the velvet skin of her hip and down into the tiny valley of incredible softness that lies between the top curve of a woman's hip and the bottom of her ribcage. She did not stir as my fingers drifted away seeking new adventures across the hills and slopes of her small breasts. She stirred, moving sinuously like a cat. As she settled I half expected to hear a contented purr pass her lips. Reluctantly, for fear of waking her, I stopped my caresses and lay back beside her. As my gaze swept the heavens and marveled at the millions of stars that hovered overhead, I felt the warmth of her body along my left side and was at peace.

As I relaxed I cast my thoughts adrift. Waves of contention lurked nearby; they appeared to be waiting to capsize my happiness with second guesses. But it wasn't to be. My heart regretted costing Star Watcher the seven years of solitude, but there had been no other way for me to return. I thank God she had the faith to wait, and the belief and conviction that one day I would come back to her. The love that reunited us in such an unbelievable manner was stronger than ever before. I knew without a doubt that our bond would be as timeless as the stars and sky above and the prairie below. Young Nighthawk has forged an unbreakable clasp between us that will link us together, always.

With the sibilant sounds of Star Watcher's breathing serving as a lullaby, and the warmth of her body a comfort for the night air, I settled back and allowed my mind to drift back to the Starr ranch and Caleb Sr. and how I was going to explain everything that happened between Star Watcher and myself.

***

As I finished my story, the creases and wrinkles on Caleb Starr's bronzed face seemed deeper and more plentiful. His faded blue eyes stared into mine with the intensity of a much younger man. I gazed back praying he wouldn't see the lie.

"So you're saying that back in the year 1890 your brother, Nathaniel, and this woman, Star Watcher, were fixing to set up housekeeping in the same lodge?"

I nodded, still holding his gaze and wondering how I was going to manage getting a convincing story through to him without repeatedly lying through my teeth.

We were sitting on the front verandah, Caleb Sr. in a rocker, me on the front steps. The moon was up and it was the third night of my foray into the wild west of the nineteenth century. My thoughts strayed back to when I left Star Watcher to wait for me among the pine and aspen. She said her heart was too full of me and heavy with sorrow for Nighthawk for a confrontation with Caleb Starr. With her conflicting emotions she knew she would not find the proper words to properly thank my father. Star Watcher begged me to speak for her. I had done so earlier and of course Caleb had accepted her explanation and thanks with grace and understanding.

***

Barry Brierley

Suddenly, the porch scene faded. I was in a room with soft shadows. It was quiet and I was very young and sitting on the lap of a beautiful Indian woman. She was slowly rocking in the very same rocking chair Caleb, Sr. was occupying. My head was resting on her soft bosom as she gently held my hand and stroked my forehead while brushing my unruly hair from my eyes. She was wearing bleached doeskins trimmed in porcupine quills, flattened and dyed orange, white, light blue and green. I could smell the comforting mixed aroma of wood-smoke and sweet grass. I felt her warm breath on my cheek and heard her melodic voice singing softly in Crow.

*****

The squeak of the rocker brought my thoughts back. It had been my first memory of my ancestral Crow mother and it had left me breathless. The chair's rhythmic creak and the hum of an occasional mosquito were the only sounds to interrupt the peaceful quiet of the night and my dreaming. My ancestral grandfather stopped rocking, leaned forward and spat a stream of tobacco juice into the red dust beneath the hitching rail. I saw Redman shift his feet. In my present state of creating fictitious stories, I imagined that Redman gave Caleb Starr a ruinous look.

"Son?"

I slowly turned my head until our eyes met.

"So what your saying is that you and this same Lakota woman that wanted your brother, now wants to share your blanket?"

I nodded, held my breath for an instant, then lied again, as I said, "I met her a few years after Nathan was killed. He had talked to me about her but we'd never met. He probably didn't mention her because of the Lakota and Crow thing. What with Billy and Ma being Crow ..."

With a casual wave of his hand, Caleb, Sr. let me know of the disdain he felt for the ancient feud that existed between the two great nations. Another indifferent gesture encouraged me to continue.

"But the important thing now is that we have to find her eight-year-old son and get him away from the Wild West show

people before something bad happens to him."

Caleb, Sr. leaned forward as he said, "An' this boy a hers ain't Nathaniel's son, or yours?"

I shook my head as I replied, "No, sir. At Wounded Knee he was a baby Star Watcher and Nathan found hidden in the snow. Since then she has raised him as her own son at Pine Ridge."

Now it was Caleb, Sr.'s turn to shake his head. Shifting his chew to another spot, he said, "Peers I'm getting old. I don't remember loving between two young people as being so confusing.' Seems to me it used to be a simple question, followed by an answer of saying I will, or I won't, and then they usually did."

While Caleb Sr. took the time to spit, I managed to wipe away a smile that was threatening to develop into a full-sized grin. And I didn't want my new father to misinterpret anymore actions on my part.

"What I need to know," I asked, "Can you give me the loan of a horse and grubstake for the trip?"

Caleb, Sr. stared hard at me for a moment. He turned his head and looked for a place to spit. Changing his mind, he pinned me with those washed out blue eyes that still had steel and grit in them. I managed to remain impassive under his scrutiny, but it wasn't easy. Still watching me, Caleb, Sr. looked aside, found a likely spot, and spit. After wiping his mustache left and right with a gnarled forefinger, his gaze returned to me. Once again he leaned back in the rocker and pushed it into motion. He rocked silently for a moment, thinking. With a sudden move he stopped rocking and said, "Son, am I getting soft-brained or are you actin' kind of strange lately?"

Momentarily at a loss for words I had to look away. Before I could react, Caleb, Sr. had more to say.

"Boy, you should know by now that everything on this ranch will be yours someday. It don't matter to me what you need, or take. Like I said, when I'm gone it'll all be yours anyhow. Peers to me this gal is muddling your thinkin' ... but, I understand. Your mother did the same thing to me."

With a sudden move that belied his age, the old plainsman

was up on his feet looking down on me. I followed his example but got to my feet at a more leisurely pace. Eye to eye we took each other's measure. Caleb Sr. placed his large weathered and callused hand on my shoulder and said, "Son, anything I have is yours to take."

He paused for a beat and I felt his hand tighten on my shoulder. "Son, I know for a fact that more than anybody I know, save one man."

Caleb then paused looking as though he was remembering something from days gone by.

I watched as the old man seemed to mentally shake his head and add, "His name was Raven and he was a white man that rode with the Lakota during their war with the blue bellies. He became a good friend."

The pale blue of his eyes captured mine as he frowned and added, "Hell of it is, he disappeared, haven't seen him for almost twenty-year."

A twinkle appeared in his eye.

"I know that you can take care of any violent situation you'll be faced with. But, with that said, if you feel you need me or Billy to go along to ride shotgun all you got to do is ask."

A small spark of anticipation glowed in his eyes, as he added, "You don't know what long odds you might come up against. Me and Billy, we're still willin' and able, son."

I looked deep into the aging plainsman's eyes. At that moment I truly felt like Caleb Starr's son. Something strange but wonderful seemed to pass between us. Once I thought past the surface bonding I realized what that 'something' was. It was pride. A pride of family bloodline that was unlike anything I had felt before.

"Thanks, Pa. I knew I could count on you and Billy."

I broke eye contact for a moment, blinking away the moisture his love and loyalty had brought to my eyes.

Looking him in the eye once more I said, "It's a small outfit we'll be dealing with. I can't imagine them putting up much of a fight over a small Lakota boy."

Caleb Starr stared over my shoulder for a brief instant; the glint in his eye made me think he was reminiscing.

"Sometimes, Son ... the why and why not of a situation just

don't add up but still happens. There just ain't no telling what a passel a' no-accounts are apt to do."

His faded blue gaze found me again. I smiled and nodded, knowing he was right. He turned aside and spat into the dust. I thought bringing him and Billy along would be the smart thing to do, but I felt their days of sticking their neck out should be over. I thanked him for the offer but turned it down. His final words to me were, "If you change your mind, just give us a holler."

***

In no time at all, I had collected the necessary gear and Uncle Billy had run out a horse for Star Watcher. It was a long-legged buckskin gelding that Billy said had a fast start and a lot of bottom. After our good-byes, I left my father and Uncle Billy standing on the verandah watching me ride off. I'm sure they felt what Star and I were doing was a foolish, perhaps reckless, venture to undertake alone. Later on I came to realize that they were right.

By the time I finished with my retrospect clouds had moved in obliterating our starlight ceiling. My thoughts turned to young Nighthawk, who I hadn't seen since he was a baby. Would he accept me? Would there be room in his young heart for a one-armed wasichu? Thoughts of the danger he could be in at that very moment were a torment.

Successive distressing thoughts, such as the latter, and a whole chorus of serenading coyotes kept me from sleep until far into the prairie night.

Barry Brierley

Chapter Thirty-One
BUSHWHACKED, BEGUILED, AND KIDNAPPED

We were up before daybreak and well on the trail by the time Wi cleared the pine-topped peaks to the east. The night time clouds passed on and the morning looked to be a fine one. Once on the trail, I left any ill effects from my near sleepless night behind me. By afternoon we had left the Black Hills behind us and had entered rolling grassland as we moved south toward Cheyenne. Open country stretched to the far horizon and looked as though it would go on forever.

Without forethought Star and I rode white man style, side by side, rather than the usual single file used by Indians. We couldn't seem to bear letting each other out of sight. With Nighthawk's fate still unknown, however, our joy in being reunited was far from complete. We rode through high grass that touched our stirrups at a ground-eating lope until our mounts began to tire; we then slowed to a trot, then a walk. By alternating our mounts gait we were able to span large tracts of land in the least amount of time and still spare our horses.

The big sky overhead and the undulating plain far ahead of us left me feeling impotent yet breathless with anticipation. Where is my son, Nighthawk?

I wondered endlessly of his whereabouts. In spite of my optimism, I worried. The possibility that we might never see him again, however, never entered my head. We knew our search would never end until his fate was resolved. There was no need to confer with Star Watcher. On that subject, our hearts were as one. Our life together would not truly begin until after we have

Barry Brierley

found Nighthawk.

The trail we rode curled and dipped but seemed to always head in the same southerly direction. Caleb, had told me of an abandoned military post, Fort Laramie, situated between the Hills and Cheyenne. It was located at the confluence of the North Platte and Laramie Rivers. I was hoping to reach the abandoned fort early the next morning. Caleb had said that we might pick up some information about the traveling show from settlers in the area. He assumed that some of them had chosen to stay in the area when the army moved out.

Upon leaving the tall grass into a more arid, stony land we came upon a wide stream. Our trail then joined another trace that was apparently an often used rugged road that followed the twisted course of the waterway. After passing between some grassy hillocks the trail dropped down into a terrain foreign to the surrounding plains.

Subsequently we soon entered a low valley where trees and sandstone bluffs were a common sight along both sides of the trail and stream. I was pleased to see that Star Watcher's eyes were busily watching the many rocky abutments, brush, and tree covered canyons we encountered. I also quickly became more watchful and conscious of the upcoming lay of the land. It wasn't as though we were expecting trouble. At that time and place, it was a natural reaction to new terrain if one expected to stay alive. Of course my actions and reactions were probably those of my other self, Caleb Junior; and from all that I've experienced so far, his instincts were rarely amiss.

After traversing a wide bend in what we thought of as the wagon trail we approached a narrow ford of the stream. Splashing across the shallow area, I heel-tapped Red up the opposite bank. Suddenly, I reined to a stop. Star Watcher, close behind, reined her mare in beside Redman.

There in the dried mud were the strange wagon tracks, and pie-tin sized hoof-prints, I had seen near Deadwood. How can they not be the same tracks we hunted? My silent query was quickly answered.

Following my line of sight, Star looked at the tracks, then at me. Her voice trembled with either anguish or fury as she confirmed my thoughts by saying, "It is the tracks of the

246

wasichus who stole our son."

When I looked in her eyes I knew the catch in her voice wasn't caused by sorrow. Within their black depths lived the rage of all mothers who had one of their children taken from them. Determination and pain were etched into her striking features.

My heart reached out for her but my focus and resolve stopped me from physically consoling her. More than anything else we needed our son back. And we needed him returned as soon as possible. The longer he was gone the bigger chance of him being harmed.

Without advance warning young Caleb's personality came to the fore. Just as it had happened near Wounded Knee Creek, I felt a self confidence I'd never experienced before. When my eyes met Star Watcher's something unusually strange happened. Somehow, without having to even voice our intention, or discuss it, we both knew what we needed to do.

It was time to ride!

With an escalating urgency, Star and I urged our horses into a ground-eating lope as we followed the distinct trail. To our right the setting sun was painting the landscape a glowing orange, casting long, dark shadows toward the eastern horizon. The stream, situated on our left, became gradually larger, dropping down from our ground level sweeping away the red clay and gradually eating into the rising land. For countless decades it had cut through the red soil steadily deepening the cut-bank channel until it evolved into a high red wall on the far, eastern side of the swift moving stream.

After slowing our gait to a walk, I slipped my canteen free of the saddle's pommel and looked back at Star Watcher prior to passing it over to her. Without warning, I felt the bullet slam into my stomach. Through the jolting pain in my right hand and stomach I heard the sound of the rifle shot. I couldn't breathe! As I began to slip from the saddle my sliding gaze caught a glimpse of Star's shocked expression framed by the sun's blinding, golden rays. Then I was falling, falling! All I could think of was, 'Please God, not again! Don't let me lose her again!'

I bounced off the edge of the tall cut-bank and fell toward the

Barry Brierley

stream several feet below; landing with a great splash and a burst of agony at the very rim of the water. A biting pain chewed its way through my side and stomach with a relentless passion.

With a survivor's instinct, I knew immediately what must be done. Gritting my teeth against the forthcoming effort, I sucked in a mouthful of air. Without thinking about it I painfully rolled out of the water into the shadow of the overhang. My goal was to get as close to the clay bank as was physically possible. Agony had me squeeze my eyes shut and clench my fists. While waiting for the pain to diminish, I listened.

I heard shouts and the hammer of horses' galloping hooves. A grating voice shouted, "Stop that bay stallion! Don't let her slide by on the buckskin! Grab her red ass!"

I heard another shot! My heart lurched inside my chest. Please God, no! My silent plea lodged in my mind like a splinter from my broken heart. A darkness from within swiftly consumed me and I knew no more.

Then I must have quickly regained consciousness for once again voices came from above. I'm alive! Silently, I rejoiced but was afraid to move. I slowly opened my eyes to an orange and yellow world. Sundown, I thought. Red-orange earth, dark roots and stones loomed overhead.

Frighteningly near, a man's familiar gravelly voice quietly suggested, "He must a' got swept downstream! He's a goner. That was a center shot, ever I seen one!"

A thought swept through my being with lightning speed. They can't see me because of the bank's overhang!

My optimism faded with memory of the shouted reference to Star, followed by the gunshot. Another, somehow familiar, voice answered the first. "Who do ya think you are, Tom Horn!? Hell! I'm surprised ya hit him at all!"

The vigorous noise of a horse's snort startled me. I gasped and sharp pain swept through my side! Trying in vain to breathe slowly, I heard the sound of an approaching horse. When I turned my head aside, I blinked. Not quite believing what I was seeing. I stared at the orange, earthen wall across the stream.

Clear as day was the dark silhouette of my would be killer! Back-lit by the setting sun, his shadow was fully cast against the far wall of the red clay bank!

Edges of Time

He looked to be a slender man carrying a rifle and wearing a narrow, curled-brim hat. There was something different about his hair. It was longish but didn't seem to want to lie flat where it stuck out beneath the brim of his hat. The silhouette of his head moved this way and that searching for some sign of me.

While I watched, he leaned forward in his saddle. That, and the coordinating squeak of saddle leather, told me he was looking for me in the shadows beneath the bank. I barely breathed. Another shadow rider joined the first. The muffled sound of his horse's hoof-beats matched the animal's animated, dark image. The silhouette of the man's lanky frame looked familiar but the narrow-brimmed, tall-crowned hat didn't. Usually a man's hat is as identifiable a part of him as his face.

"Leave it. If he's not dead he will be soon. His body must have swept downstream." The marked voice of the second man pricked my ears as I tried in vain to identify him. He added, "The boss caught the young squaw. Peers like after her buckskin spooked, she got him under control and was trying to get back here to help her Injun friend. He's got her now ... he'll throw her in with the others."

My heart soared. Star was alive! The first voice spoke again and caused a new chill to shimmer its way down my spine. "Glad to hear she ain't dead. Though, after I have me some fun, she might wish she be dead."

I wouldn't soon forget the leering, cruel voice. Their ensuing laughter stoked the coals of my simmering rage back into life and gave me even more incentive to live.

The shadow riders reined out of sight and I listened as they spurred their mounts into a canter and rode away, leaving my mud-wall movie screen blank. Hardly daring to breathe, I listened to the diminishing sounds of their horses. In an effort to gather my strength, I rested. My right hand had stopped hurting; it cradled my wound while the wetness of my clothes made me worry about blood loss, and my inability to move. The last image I saw before consciousness left me was my blanket-covered canteen lying beside the stream with the sinking sun glinting off the bent, burnished metal where the bullet had ricocheted, *tearing the cloth cover. It was at that moment that I knew that I would live to reap my revenge.*

CHAPTER THIRTY-TWO

NEW TRAILS AND SOWING THE SEEDS OF VENGEANCE

I awakened to the whisper of owl's wings. The great horned owl glided over me so closely I felt the caress of air caused by its passing. My thoughts scrambled for purchase in an effort to regain my bruised memory.

Having momentarily forgotten how the canteen had deflected the bullet, I was somewhat surprised to still be alive. I don't know how long I was unconscious, but it was long enough to give the moon time to rise.

My gaze swept the surrounding, colorless landscape while the moon's pale light caused dark shadows to be displayed beside all objects, hiding all or nothing. My lingering discomfort had lessened considerably and I was able to move slowly with no debilitating pain. With great anxiety I lifted my shirt exposing the pale skin of my chest and injured side to the moon. There was no gaping bullet hole; in fact the skin wasn't even broken, only darkened with a huge dark bruise. It was then that I remembered the scarred canteen; and shortly thereafter I noticed that the little finger on my wooden hand was missing. I couldn't believe my good fortune.

Like a man bent and twisted with age I slowly got to my feet, hand gingerly pressed against my bruised ribs.

Straightening up, I once again silently rejoiced at my luck. My jubilation was short-lived, however. I suddenly remembered the bushwhacker's intent concerning Star Watcher. My hand went to the cartridge belt at my waist. My revolver was gone! Frantically, I looked everywhere near at hand. Nothing. All at

Barry Brierley

once I stood up straight and looked behind me toward where I had been hiding in the shadows beneath the overhang. Because of the moon's blue light the shadows were no longer there. I smiled when I saw that the moon's pale light caused the revolver to glisten as though wet. It was lying right where I had been sprawled on my back unconscious.

With great relief I hobbled over, picked up my pistol, and worked the action while brushing it free of sand and dirt.

I stopped moving. Barely daring to breathe, I listened carefully. While unconsciously absorbing the normal night sounds, I listened for anything that didn't belong.

My concentration was so complete that I felt the blood pulsing in my neck. At first I couldn't hear anything unusual. Then realization sharpened my senses; it was too quiet to be natural. Something big was moving around in the night silencing the lesser creatures. With gun in hand I ducked and eased back underneath the overhang and resumed watching and listening.

There. I heard the muffled sound of a horse walking in sand. Someone was coming back for another look! My reasoning caused my heartbeat to feel as irregular as the sounds created by a small boy beating on his first drum.

Tightly clutching my revolver, I listened. I was totally convinced that they had returned to make sure I was dead. The hoof-beats stopped right above me! My heart seemed to pause in mid-beat as something touched by moonlight dangled in front of me from over the edge of the overhang. I stared, in wonder, at the two slim, indistinct objects. The horse snuffled! The sudden sound was so startling I reflexively lifted the Remington and thumbed back the hammer. Suddenly, I knew what was happening. I eased the hammer back down and lowered the pistol. There was something way too familiar about the noise that erupted from that horse. When I was absolutely sure a rush of pure relief eased the pain of my battered body.

Ignoring my aches and pains, I abruptly stepped into the open. Red was so surprised he shied, jerking his head up and away. The picture Redman's actions had painted inside my head was perfectly clear. The shadow image I had seen was Red stretching his muzzle toward the edge of the overhang to smell for me. With the lowering of his neck the trailing reins had slid

252

over the edge creating the 'dangling' mystery.

Redman slowly stretched his muzzle down toward my outstretched hand. I believe he was trying to catch my scent or re-establish contact with a familiar scent. The reins once again followed his muzzle's lead and when they tumbled toward me I grabbed them.

Wrapping the reins around my wrists I commanded the big horse into backing up. Redman pulled, and backed up. Using his great strength he pulled me upwards until I was once again on top of the cut-bank. After retrieving my trampled hat, and a moment or two spent showing my gratitude to Red, I painfully swung up onto the saddle. By the blue light of the moon, I reined Redman once again onto the trace that displayed the distinct wheel marks and the bushwhacker's fresh pony tracks.

Thinking back, I believe it was at this particular time that my Caleb Jr. personality began to take control. Earlier he had taken charge and tightened my resolve, but as the danger increased so did his power. I remember as the final confrontation grew closer I did things and made instant decisions that I know I wouldn't have been capable of making had I been thinking in my normal rational manner. The action taken and the decisions made had to have come from an experienced, ruthless survivor who had been in the same situations many times.

Keeping Red at a walk, I carefully removed all cartridges from my gun-belt and revolver and dropped them into my saddle bag. While opening a new box, I thought, there's no way I was going to ride into a shooting situation that could mean life or death using potentially unreliable ammunition. While painstakingly refilling the loops and chambers with dry loads, I could feel my confidence rising in step with a growing anger. It was a quiet fury; it simmered inside and eventually caused me to become as patient and confident as an old mountain lion stalking his prey.

I readjusted Red's reins on my wooden hand and spurred him into a lope.

With a beautiful harvest moon showing the way, I relentlessly followed the riders hated tracks that I knew would

Barry Brierley

eventually lead me to Star Watcher and young Nighthawk.

CHAPTER THIRTY-THREE

Deputy Nighthawk carefully closed the journal and rolled onto his back. A towering rampart of cumulus clouds slowly rolled by with the bright blue sky creating a perfect backdrop.

He could smell the damp grass and the richness of the soil beneath the blanket he was lying upon. More importantly he was aware of Nicole's light perfume and the warmth of her hip pressed against his own. She was sitting up watching her son, Michael, wading along the edge of the lake.

Nighthawk, his thoughts shifting, turned his head to the left and stared at the majestic presence of Bear Butte a mile away. Without consciously biding it to do so, his mind abruptly returned to Daniel Starr's journal. He was completely fascinated by the man and by his determined quest to reunite his family. John let his mind drift; it bounced here and there like a tumble-weed, as he remembered the impediments of Daniel Starr just as well as his extraordinary achievements.

"What do you think will happen to him?"

The question caught John off guard. His thoughts were riding south toward Cheyenne, with a man who had lived a hundred years ago.

"Who?" He asked with a puzzled frown.

Nicole lowered herself onto him; she rested her upper body and right arm across his chest.

"James Frump, silly."

Pretending that Nicole's minimal weight was too great to bear, John wheezed, "Who ... what ... where?" He gasped.

Nicole laughed. John's answering smile was smothered by Nicole's impromptu, passionate kiss.

"Mom?"

Barry Brierley

Michael's faint shout from the lakeside brought Nicole's head up. She listened, apprehensively. When she heard him call again, inquiring about lunch, a slow smile crossed her face. She looked down at John. Seeing his mischievous expression, she queried, "What?"

Using a combination of hand sign and bad English, Nighthawk rubbed his belly in a circular motion and poked his finger in his open mouth.

"Me heap hungry, *wikoskala* (pretty woman). Bring me food!"

Nicole's happy laughter echoed throughout the deserted picnic area. All at once her expression changed, and she became serious; rising quickly to her feet she looked for her son. She saw him immediately.

Michael waved at her and Nicole grinned, returning a wave; then with hands on her hips, she once again faced John's reclining form with a smile still lingering on her lips.

"Be careful now, I'm not your woman yet, John Nighthawk!"

John grinned. An impish gleam was in Nicole's eyes as she spun and walked away. With an admiring eye he watched Nicole's lithe body stride through the sea of golden, autumn leaves toward her waiting son.

John's thoughts, however, were elsewhere. Rolling onto his back, his thoughts lingered only briefly over Nicole's question. Unless there was some outrageous miscarriage of justice, he thought, James Frump would no doubt be institutionalized. What did concern him was the roll of the dice for Crab and his biker cohorts. In John Nighthawk's mind they had not broken the law. If there was any guilt it was through association. With Crab being the guilty party's brother, and if he wasn't aware of James' intent, where was the brother's criminal act?

He mulled the pros and cons over in his head, knowing that he had practically no say over whatever the outcome of the judge's decision.

Nighthawk stared absently at the clouds overhead. As though in a dream he heard the shouted yet strangely muted conversation between Nicole and Mike.

The defused sound echoed in the back of John's mind while he focused on nature and listened to the wind rustle leaves and the latticework of branches rub against one another in the trees overhead. With less effort than one would imagine he blocked out everything except the clouds above enabling him to give his imagination free rein. One oddly shaped cumulus eventually became the arching neck and noble head of the young Caleb's stallion, Redman; another became the wind-blown tresses of Star Watcher as she rode away from those who he thought would probably capture her. Once again, in his mind, John Nighthawk was back riding on the vengeance trail with the young gunman, Caleb Starr, Jr.

Barry Brierley

CHAPTER THIRTY-FOUR
LONELY TRAILS AND TORRENTIAL WATERS

In the moonlit hours before first light I crossed many rolling hills and a nearly tree-less, undulating grassland. After the tracks led me away from the diminishing stream my progress was forced to slow down dramatically. In the lingering predawn darkness I feared that I might lose the trail and waste precious hours.

Resting my horse I waited for what seemed like an eternity for enough light to enable me to follow their tracks. When there was barely enough light Red carried me through a world made eerie by the gloom and the indistinct shapes caused by the false dawn.

When Wi peeked above the horizon I found we had entered a basin scattered with stands of trees and several deserted homes that had the look of having been vacant for years. Leaving the abandoned homes behind, Redman cantered us across a vast empty landscape. Yet far ahead through the dimness, a scatter of tiny, yellow lights flickered on and off.

With an abruptness that was equally startling as it was frightening I was forced to stop, speculating on the unusual lights. Thunder and lightning crashed and flashed, lighting the surrounding terrain with a macabre show of eerie lights that could have been performed by a roving band of demons from Hell.

With each crack of lightning Red danced as though possessed. I looked up to a sky filled with cobalt thunderheads that roiled overhead like the vanguard of a black and blue herd of

259

stampeding buffalo.

Conscious of my belted Remington and the fresh cartridges, I quickly unrolled my slicker from behind my saddle's cantle as the first large drops of rain began to pelt down and play a drum roll on the brim of my hat. The rain came down in buckets but was unable to deter my focus, nor squelch the fire that was rapidly growing inside of me. God help them, I raged, if Star Watcher or Nighthawk is harmed in any way.

While riding at a canter through the driving rain I saw we were fast approaching a line of trees that bordered a narrow river. Although cramped in size the river was a turbulent brown force. Somehow I was certain that it was the North Platte. I also knew that if I followed it west I would find its junction with the Cheyenne River and the location of the abandoned Fort Laramie.

Moving west, I followed the serpentine coils of the North Platte. As I rode on, the storm showed no sign of lessening yet the gloomy sky appeared to grow considerably lighter. The beat of raindrops on the brim of my hat was abruptly drowned out by an exceptionally loud crash of lightning. Within the brief, bright flash of the lightning I saw a strange sight. Straight ahead was a bridge unlike any other I'd ever seen.

The near side of the bridge had three arches, or half circles, parallel to a matching trio on the opposite side. As Redman carried me closer I saw that the unusual structure was constructed of iron, wood and cable; the iron parts were the arches with vertical steel cables running about a foot apart, within the multiple archways.

The falling rain muffled the hollow clatter of Redman's hooves as he trotted across the bridge's wooden passageway; the syncopated rhythm of his hooves seemed to be in tune with the palpitations of my heart. Because of the approaching sunrise and the driving rain, which shortened the range of my vision, I sensed the closeness of Star Watcher and our son. Overshadowing my escalating excitement my increasingly inept grip on reality added fuel to my wildly simmering rage, as Caleb's personality continued to assert itself and began to completely dominate my every move. The pulse of adrenaline that coursed through my veins became a catalyst pushing me onward like an avenging angel.

CHAPTER THIRTY-FIVE
FAMILIAR ADVERSARIES AND A MOUNTING FURY

Abruptly as it had started, the rain stopped. I rode on ... but I was no longer alone. The hatred for those who had separated me from my loved ones had evolved into a living monster that I carried inside me every step of the way.

The rising sun peeked above the horizon with the shyness of a pubescent boy covertly peering at the face of his first love. For one lingering moment I broke free of the Caleb Junior spell, enchanted by the beauty of the long, searching rays of light as they spread rapidly across the land touching all with a gentle radiance. I watched the distant flicker of lights blend then disappear as the sun magically painted all within its reach with a golden brush.

Feeling the warmth of the sun I removed my slicker. As I fumbled to secure the rain gear behind the cantle, Redman quickly crested a small hill. After doing so he immediately slowed his pace. One glance up ahead and I reined Red to a stop. The slicker fell unnoticed to the wet ground. Less than thirty feet away a familiar canvas covered wagon with four mules harnessed to it was setting unattended among some stunted cottonwoods. The unexpected appearance of the wagon was as startling as a vision or some form of unearthly presence. My first thought was how the blue painted wheels looked familiar. I knew I'd seen them before. But where could it have been? The canvas side of the wagon had a legend painted there in bright colors:

INDIAN JACK'S SNAKE OIL MEDICINE
A Sure Cure for All that Ails You!

Barry Brierley

Suddenly, realization hit me right between the eyes ... those damn whiskey peddlers! At the very moment of my awareness the sun glinted off metal from something poking from beneath the lower edge of canvas.

It was almost like a magic trick when the Remington suddenly appeared in my hand pointed at the wagon, and immediately it exploded and bucked as I thumbed the revolver three times!

The cacophony of sound launched two buzzards and a magpie, perched on trees near the wagon, into the early morning sky. While Redman danced and turned I kept the Remington poised and my eye on the three new holes in the canvas. There was a choking sound succeeded by a tearing noise as the coarse material bulged and a wine-colored stain oozed down the wooden side of the wagon. The bulge diminished as there sounded a hollow thump followed by a sibilant rattling sigh.

The stench of burnt gunpowder was in my nose as I spun Red in a circle searching for a new target to appease my growing blood-lust. Resting my revolver on my thigh I reined the big bay around, pointed him at the wagon, and gave him a gentle heel-tap. As Redman sidled toward the garishly painted wagon my gaze, peering from beneath the narrow brim of my hat, was flitting everywhere on the lookout for any new danger.

With the barrel of the Remington, I cautiously pushed the canvas covering the rear of the wagon aside. The stocky whiskey peddler who was already carrying two of my bullets had two more souvenirs. He stared back at me with sightless eyes from his make-shift bed in the wagon; what was left of his face was ashen and his skin was already taking on the waxen sheen of the newly dead. The skin of his bandaged arm and shoulder was dark and stained with old blood and yellow infection while the Colt revolver he had pointed at me remained cocked and at rest beside his leg. The stench of gangrene emanating from the wagon told me I had probably done the man a favor by putting him out of his misery.

I maneuvered Red around until I was able to reach his pistol from the saddle. Lowering the hammer, I stuck the Colt's revolver behind the cartridge belt in the small of my back.

Craning my neck I took a closer look at my less than innocent victim. With the cold deliberation of a hardened killer I apparently had become, I was pleased to make note of the fact that two of my three bullets were less than an inch apart just below the bushwhacker's left ear. His right ear had now become a part of the canvas wall's new decor.

Wondering at the present location of his cohort 'Blondie' I abruptly allowed the canvas flap to fall back shutting off the staring eyes forever.

Quickly reining Redman away from the wagon my gaze slipped into and around the surrounding terrain. From behind came the sudden, startling thump and scrape of running hooves smashing through underbrush. The snap and pop of crushed branches barely preceded a glancing blow to the outside of my left shoulder; the simultaneous explosion of the gunshot and the burning pain from the bullet racked my senses before registering in my brain. Instinct had me instantly haul back on the reins! Redman reared and turned; the move had him spin on his hind legs like a dancer's pirouette. I gripped hard with my legs and managed to maintain my balance while seeking out my new target. The move surprised 'Blondie' so completely that instead of completing his attack by getting in close where he couldn't miss, he hauled back on his reins. The whiskey runner's horse squatted back on his sliding haunches while Redman laid his ears back and lunged forward.

Neck out-stretched and teeth bared, the big red horse charged the off balance horse and rider. Terrified by Red's attack, the man named Aaron, whom I thought of as Blondie, froze. By the time he recovered he had all he could handle just staying in the saddle. Before he could raise his pistol again, my Remington bucked and roared as I placed my pistol's remaining two rounds one inch to the right of his dirty shirt's pleated panel. He crumpled and toppled backwards over his struggling mount's rump. Before I was able to rein him away, Redman managed to slash the neck of the dead man's hapless horse as it struggled to get to its feet. While I fought to pull Redman away from the struggling horse, I noticed the flat, narrow-brim and tall crown of Blondie's hat lying crumpled among the broken branches. Grim, smug satisfaction coursed through me as I recognized the hat from the red wall silhouette of the bushwhacker with the familiar voice.

Reining Red back from a lope into a fast walk, I pointed him in the direction where I'd last seen the lights. My blood was up and pumping hard; I was eager and more than ready for a final confrontation. Conscious of the bay's muscles shifting beneath my thighs, I methodically punched the empty brass casings free from the Remington's cylinder.

While slipping new loads in the revolver, I thought briefly of Redman's surprisingly aggressive behavior. I closed the loading gate and eased the gun into its place behind my cartridge belt. I then pulled the whisky peddler's Colt from behind my back, exchanged the two empty casings with new load and returned it to its place behind the cartridge belt.

Urging Redman into a lope I stroked his neck and remembered Uncle Billy's remark as he handed me the reins to Star's horse. He had said, "This a good horse ... plenty of bottom, and she will fight for you, Strong Arm."

At the time, I was so anxious to return to Star that Billy's remark struck me as a joke. Now, after seeing Redman in action, it was obvious what he meant. I was told that at one time, many years ago, the Crow were famous for their 'war horses.' Redman had been trained as a war horse and I'd forgotten. All the memory I retained concerning the training of Caleb's horse was when I was a boy. I remember absolutely refusing to allow my horse's ears to be notched (which were the Crow custom for their war horses). Remember it or not, I couldn't have been any happier with Red's performance. He just might have saved my life.

CHAPTER THIRTY-SIX
WILLFUL BLOOD-LETTING AMONG
HISTORICAL SITES AND ANCIENT RITES

After topping a slight rise, I could not believe the panoramic scene spread out before me.

The deserted Fort Laramie sprawled across a large, flat, nearly treeless area. It was composed of twenty to thirty dilapidated wooden buildings constructed in many different sizes and functions; they surrounded a vast parade ground and was bordered on the far south side by what was called the Laramie River, but in truth was probably a tributary of the North Platte. Like the one I'd recently crossed, this river had plenty of cottonwood and red willow spread out along its banks.

With my overview I was able to clearly see how both the North Platte and Laramie River came together on the west side of the wall-free fort.

The large building seen before reaching the bulk of the buildings surrounding the parade ground was where most of the activity was focused. The action seemed to center around a pair of tents near the building's frontage.

A couple of fires were burning nearby in front of what appeared to have been long barracks. I counted six or seven men moving around the campfires and tents. I could faintly hear a fiddle being played. The fiddler was playing a lively version of a vaguely familiar Spanish tune while castanets joined in with a measured cadence.

Knowing the odds were heavily stacked against me, I tried desperately to think of a plan that would improve my chances.

Barry Brierley

Strange as it may seem the normally distracting music helped to clear my head while I studied the closest building and grounds.

The impressive barrack-like dwelling was a very long two-storied building with a full verandah running the length of both levels. In back of the building were several wagons, formed into a circle. When the one characteristic that they all shared became obvious I wasn't all that surprised. All of the wagons had blue painted wheels! The knowledge that the whiskey runners were involved in one, or both, of the kidnappings made my killing them almost excusable, filling me with a certain grim satisfaction.

Apart, yet near the circle of wagons, were several shabby, canvas tipis. Keeping a wary eye on the people near the fires I steered Redman into a route that would take me close to where the wagons were setting.

If at all possible, until it became clear what I was up against, I chose not to be seen by anyone. Without bothering to think why, I abruptly reined Redman to a halt. Nearby were some red rocks still wet from the rain storm. In some inexplicable way I was drawn to these particular stones. Staying out of sight I stepped down drawing my knife.

Finding the red rock to be soft sandstone, I was compelled to mix it into a serviceable war paint. Working quickly, I scraped and pulverized some of the stone and mixed it with stagnant water until it formed into a paste. It wasn't until I began applying the red paste that I remembered why. Somewhere, stored in Caleb's memory of Crow beliefs, I found the answer.

It is believed by my Crow ancestors that by using paint made from a certain ground red stone, which is part of the Everlasting Earth, the wearer will be protected by The Maker of Everything.

I didn't have a mirror, yet I knew that within the shadow of my hat brim my freshly painted forehead above the nose and cheekbones gave my countenance a new ferocity. For the present it being in the shadow of my hat brim it also couldn't be seen from a distance. Settling my hat firmly in place I was ready to make war. I mounted Redman and angled to the right toward what looked like a wash bordered with some scrub juniper, oak, and wild plum.

Red traversed the dry wash to an area near the edge of the

wagon circle. After making sure we were alone, I heel-tapped Redman and he carried me up onto the plain where the wagons were setting. Pleased to have arrived without incident, I spoke softly to Redman and stroked his sleek neck. To my left I could hear boisterous voices and laughter coming from the front of the long building, the barracks. I was a little north of the building, but the wagons were behind. On my right were three long, narrow structures with fenced in areas in between. A small herd of mules and riding horses were enclosed inside. Keeping a tight rein on Redman my eyes were constantly on the move as I approached the wagon train.

To the right were the Indian tipis. Smoke came from a couple of them. Ignoring them as any type of threat, I focused on the tall wagons with the narrow rims and rode slowly into their midst as if I belonged there. I reined Red to a halt.

Except for a team of gigantic work horses corralled in a special pen, there was no sign of life. While studying the huge horses I marveled at their great size. Not knowing anything about the breed, I guessed that they were either Clydesdales or Perchon draft horses. The huge powerful beasts were probably used to pull the supply wagon carrying the show's enormous canvas tent and accessories.

With an increasing sense of foreboding I heel-tapped Redman into slowly moving forward. Most of the wagons had wooden, roofed boxes mounted on their bed rather than the conventional canvas covering. Nearly all of the vehicles were painted in broad, garish lettering and figures with the legend **INDIAN JACK'S WILD WEST SHOW** displayed in bold letters. In vivid color a boisterous, two gun cowboy, riding a flying Indian lance appeared to be the show's logo. There was one wagon, however, that was truly different. It pulled me to it with the same inevitable certainty as a buzzard is drawn to a dying animal.

The iron bars were about six inches apart and ran vertically on three sides giving the wagon the same look as those vehicles used in a circus to cage tigers and lions. The bottom and back platform of the empty cage was plastered with garbage and reeked of feces and urine. When my gaze saw the legend written along the upper edge of the cage a chill seemed to pass right through me as though I wasn't really there. My inner rage was rising with each heartbeat, growing and forming itself into some nameless monster, bloodthirsty for my inevitable revenge.

Near the wagon I spied the remains of a cooking fire. In seconds I was crouched beside the charcoal residue. Dipping into the dark mess with two fingers I smeared a greasy black line across the bridge of my nose just below the red. Black paint for revenge, red for protection ... I was ready for anything. But all I could think of was how, for the first time in my life, I truly wanted to kill another human being.

Somewhere on the other side of the building, the fiddle and castanets had stopped to make way for a new diversion. A drum began a rhythmic beat and a male Indian voice began singing an Oglala prayer in Lakota.

Jeers and laughter surrounded the thump of the drum and each throbbing beat and derisive yell threatened to break my heart. I knew I had found Star Watcher and Nighthawk but was somewhat confused by the man's voice ... another unwilling participant?

The music was coming from the front of the barracks. I reined Redman around and encouraged him to move forward at his own gait. While I made ready to make war, the big horse carried me at a walk toward my destiny, and with each step Redman took my confidence climbed. There was no way, I mentally raged, that an antiquated bunch of poor circus performers was going to continue to imprison and humiliate my family.

A cold, detached feeling came over me as I covertly double checked the loads in the dead whiskey peddler's .45 Colt. Making sure all six chambers were filled, I stuck it out of sight behind the gun belt at the small of my back. Also double checking the Remington I nestled it into its usual spot in front of my hipbone and limbered up my fingers. I was making ready while the random jeering and derisive laughter pulled me forward as surely as if on a tether.

Just before rounding the northern edge of the barracks building I made a final check that Redman's reins were firmly slotted between the wooden fingers of my left hand and that the balls of my feet were solidly entrenched in the stirrups. My hat was scrunched down onto my head with the brim pulled down, keeping my painted upper-face in shadow.

At a slow walk, Redman and I rounded the corner of the barracks. As we did so the sun peeked across my left shoulder illuminating a startling, pagan scene that shook me to my very core. I was stunned.

I remember thinking at the time, while struggling to control my fury that this unbelievable sad setting could possibly evolve into being the last one I see.

Approximately a hundred feet from me was Star Watcher. She was dancing, head bowed in shame. She moved listlessly to our young Nighthawk's uninspired drumming. Seated on the boy's left was an Indian with streaks of gray in his long hair, passionately singing a Lakota prayer song. I stared, shocked by the bestiality of mankind.

All three of the Indians were stripped completely naked! Nighthawk and the man, who had been captives much longer, were smeared with dirt, rotten food, and other refuse. Star and young Nighthawk's forced nudity would make the killing that much easier. Behind the performers, in a couple of the cage-like wagons, were other Indians who had become a captive audience to the three Lakota's' inhuman degradation.

I had no difficulty identifying the enemy; they were every-where. At first, with the distance between us, I was ignored. The troupe members were focused on the captive entertainers; they ogled the naked trio with the same glee and obscene exuberance the Romans must have exhibited at the gladiator games in the coliseum.

Through eyes misted with empathy and rage I peered at the display of callous disregard for humanity; I watched them with jaded eyes and I felt shame at being a part of the human race.

Of the ten or eleven people there, four or five were the ones doing the bulk of the heckling. A handful of women in the group were keeping busy by using loud verbal ridicule and throwing rotten fruit and vegetables at the performing prisoners, or as the painted legend above their inhuman cage which I had read *earlier, identified them: 'Behold, The Sioux! The Murderers of George A. Custer!'*

After witnessing such a pointless array of cruelty I can only imagine how the populace of visited towns would have reacted toward such an exhibit. Those without compassion would have the very object of their hatred and prejudice within reach. There is no doubt that their misplaced retribution would be just as disgusting as what I was currently witnessing. Both fury and shame of my white blood made it impossible for me to gaze any longer upon their humiliation; for the moment, I pretended they weren't there and looked beyond them.

The troupe audience was mainly seated in a half-circle and fortunately, the performers were closest to me. My roving gaze quickly searched the group for the man Star Watcher described as being Nighthawk's abductor. After searching in vain for the red face with the big mustache, I began to look for the leader of this pack of wild dogs. I zeroed in on the sunburned, sneering face of a man located in the approximate center of their crude amphitheater. While moving closer, some primal instinct kept me focused on that one man. Because of his lack of a big belly and his somewhat moderate mustache and goatee I was certain that he wasn't Star Watcher's abductor, but his arrogant body language alone told me he was the leader of the troupe.

The man was sprawled between two women who seemed eager to serve his every need. Instead of reclining on a velvet robe trimmed with ermine fur like a king, this self-made potentate lounged upon a hairy buffalo robe.

His long, dark curly hair was greasy and oily with brilliantine and it sprouted from beneath a flat crowned, wide-brimmed, white hat. The man's pampered hair set off the fancy stitched, silk shirt that was sloppily tucked into fringed, buckskin pants. More important to me than his fancy attire was the sneering expression on his ugly face. Twin, silver mounted pistols were in Mexican loop holsters, on crossed gun-belts just below his narrow hips. I would've bet all my worldly possessions that I was looking at Indian Jack, owner of this so called 'Wild West' abomination.

By reining Red's slow approach more to the right I had the sun at my right shoulder and in the enemies' eyes, while putting my family out of the direct line of fire.

With the sun's glare to deal with, I was still ignored by most. Keeping Redman at a walk, I saw Indian Jack's head slowly turn as his cruel eyes followed my every move.

One of the troupe members, while watching me with confused eyes, was cradling a long, iron-pointed staff with the flag of Indian Jack's Wild West logo embroidered on its silk surface. Several of the others were also watching me in a suspicious manner.

I heard Star's voice as she hissed, "Heyah!"

The drum and chanting stopped. I knew then Star had seen me, but I didn't dare take my eyes off my adversaries. Providing the only movement in sight I became the focal point of every eye there. I reined Redman to a stop.

Keeping my left side facing the enemy, I quietly sat and waited, letting Indian Jack's nerves and curiosity do their work.

If everyone here chooses to fight, I mused, then I was probably going to die. The thought passed fleetingly through my head and then was gone. The fury in my soul, generated by what I had seen, and by the cruelty of the man seated before me, took precedence. For the anguish he had inflicted on my loved ones, I elected myself both judge and jury. The man was going to die if it took my last breath to accomplish it. It was as simple as that. But first, I thought, Star, Nighthawk and the other Lakota must make their escape.

From beneath the shade of my hat I threw a glance toward Star. She must have covertly told them who I was for all three were standing close together watching me. I believe their physical closeness was as much for drawing strength from each other as it was out of modesty. My heart went out to the older man when I saw how he had taken a warrior's stance, placing himself between them and the pending danger.

Without looking away from Indian Jack, I said to them, "Do not run, but slowly begin walking away toward the wooded gully behind you."

Upon hearing my words spoken in Lakota the people seated before me reacted with confusion. It was obvious that they didn't understand my words; they also didn't appear to know where my voice was coming from. Indian Jack knew.

Gaze still locked on me, he immediately got to his feet; the large spurs on his over-the-knee boots sounded loud in the unusual quiet. With a hand resting on the butt of one of his revolver's he glared at me with disdain. When my peripheral vision picked up movement to my left, Indian Jack caught it also. He threw a quick glance toward the departing Lakota then refastened his gaze on me. I felt the full impact of his hatred across the twenty feet that separated us. He sneered and loudly exclaimed, "Who in the hell you think you are?"

I didn't answer. I was busy watching the four men who stood up and walked forward to join their leader. All were armed and three of the four looked very dangerous, especially the tall one who looked to be of mixed blood; he practically bristled with weapons. And there was Red Face! He must have been lying down out of view. Star Watcher's description fit perfectly, right down to the big belly, mustache, and hat.

"Mister!"

Indian Jack's whispery voice pulled my gaze away from the red-faced bully. When my eyes met his, Indian Jack continued.

"You don't just sashay in here and tell people who work for me to leave."

"I just did."

With my words Indian Jack's lean face became flushed with anger. He managed to control himself long enough to reply.

"You weren't invited to this party. Since you be here, ya gotta pay the piper."

I didn't answer. Some of the troupe watchers began to fidget.

I could see that my silence was eating at him. He controlled his anger long enough for his gunmen to spread out flanking him but still facing me. I made a point of marking that Red Face was on my left.

The dark side of Caleb's personality was completely in charge, for I was filled with confidence and rage. I wanted their blood. His next words sealed his fate and those who followed his lead.

"Bein' painted and all, you just another fucking Injun or a squaw man? Or you be some kind a clown who wants to join our

Edges of Time

traveling' show?"

His gunmen and one of the women laughed at his wit. Indian Jack laughed along with them, appreciating his own repartee. To my jaded ear their chortling meant no more to me than the yapping of a pack of demented coyotes communicating with a full moon.

All at once the whole scene seemed to become brighter; each object and person became crystal clear. It was time.

Indian Jack grinned as he added, "Since ya spoiled our fun, my friends 'n me could use a few more laughs."

I smiled at him.

"Well, here's your first laugh."

I felt the buck of the Remington and heard its loud report before fully realizing that I had drawn and fired. Indian Jack's head snapped back, causing his hat to fall off as if to show off the new hole in his forehead. Hands still empty of weapons, he toppled backwards like a felled tree. Before Indian Jack hit the ground, Red Face on his left was already falling with a .45 slug lodged deep in his chest.

I was so focused I barely heard the second resounding report of the Remington or anything else. It was like I was in some kind if vacuum where sound is muted and motion slowed. The stench of burnt gunpowder stung my nose while the snap and hum of a bullet passing my left ear jerked my head to the left. I instinctively reined Redman into a spin in the same direction, while thumbing a shot at the third man who was about to shoot again. Luck was with me as my snap shot hit the man in the throat. He fell back out of sight clutching at his neck and making horrible choking sounds.

While I was on the lookout for the mixed-blood, Redman lunged forward just as another gunman stepped in front of him and put a round through my sleeve, burning my arm on its way through. As the man staggered backward away from Red's hooves and snapping teeth I shot down into the crown of his head, bursting it open like a dropped melon.

I was a killing machine; whoever got in my way died. Motion caught my eye as Indian Jack's flag flapped high in the air like a

Barry Brierley

banner held high bravely leading a cavalry charge. The man who carried the staff was running like a flushed rabbit toward the protection of the gully. Those remaining seemed afraid to move. My wild eye swept the grounds looking for new targets and especially Indian Jack's mixed-blood shootist.

Not knowing if my last shot had been the revolver's final cartridge, I slipped the Remington back into its usual place and snatched the Colt from the belt behind my back. The big bay spun like a child's top as I sought out a new target. More gunfire erupted! A bullet tugged at the brim of my hat. Simultaneous with the reverberating sound of the shot, I spurred Redman toward a pair of men who had appeared from the far end of the barracks and were firing at me with rifles. Another bullet buzzed by my ear like a killer bee searching for a home.

Instinct told me if I didn't close with these men they would kill me. Several men and women, having seen the blood I'd already spilled, were scattering before me like quail flushed by a wildcat. Several ran east toward another long building that looked more like a storehouse than barracks. To my great relief, the riflemen at the far end of my building saw me coming and got nervous, or simply had a change of heart and ran away.

Reining Redman around, my eyes were everywhere watching for danger. As I cantered the stallion toward where I'd last seen Star and Nighthawk, I breathed a sigh of relief.

My respite was short-lived. A ricochet caromed off a nearby rock and went screaming away into infinity. Blood sprayed my face as a rifle bullet gave Redman the notch in his ear I had saved him from years before. He blew up!

His reaction was simultaneous with the sound of the gunshot. His sudden move was for the best because another .44 bee hummed by my ear while I was getting Red back under control. His pain made the big horse wild and eager for action, so when I jerked his head around and spurred him he didn't falter in the least bit. He lunged forward while I relentlessly searched for a target. Another loud discharge that came from the second floor of the barracks had me haul back on the reins and snap a quick shot that knocked the man down and out of sight. As Red slid and hopped to a halt I saw two men on the ground floor armed with rifles, throwing down on me. Red had barely stopped when I slammed my spurs into his ribs. Not used to such cruel treatment the big horse responded with exceptional quickness. As we all but leaped forward, I felt the hot breath of a bullet as it briefly kissed my cheek; another plucked at my shirt!

I hauled back on the reins, stabilizing Redman. I fired twice, as fast as I could! The Colt bucked and jumped in my fist like a live animal. Still on the building's lower verandah were two more; one man dropped his rifle and fell back out of sight, the other grabbed his wrist and spun away. I turned and, with no time left to even blink, stopped moving. I was looking directly into the large muzzle of a repeating shotgun held at hip level by the missing mixed-blood gunman.

In spite of my desperate situation I was able to notice that something was vaguely familiar about him. Up close I saw that he had to be of both Indian and black blood. And judging from the look in his eye he wasn't planning on inquiring about my heritage. His longish hair stuck out from beneath the brim of his hat in all directions.

My mind raced as I concentrated on finding a way to stay alive.

"Who'n the blue blazes are you? Ye sure ain't God Almighty!" he rasped.

The voice was that of the bushwhacker! It was his wild hair that had first caught my eye; I recalled his animated shadow on the red wall.

Remembering, I had to admire the man's presence. With all his weapons the gunman was a sight to behold; he wore two cartridge-belts with holstered revolvers, a large knife, and shells for his lever-action shotgun in a belt across his chest.

Suddenly the sky darkened; clouds shut down the early sunshine, swiftly cooling the atmosphere. His words were still hanging in the air when a cold rain began to fall as if the clouds inexplicably decided to unload all their excess moisture from the earlier storm. Normal sound was instantly washed away by the sudden deluge.

Time stood still as I noticed how the autumn rain caused white steam to rise from the breed's sweaty clothing. It gave him the frightening appearance of the devil's advocate risen up from Hell determined to stop me. His crazed, wild-eyed look, short beard and sweeping mustache added to his menacing image as he slowly raised his scatter-gun.

Still driven by young Caleb's blood lust, I was on the brink of testing the breed gunman's reflexes to see if they were mortal, or otherwise. Instead I inexplicably paused and listened. The gunman was also listening.

Besides the steady beat of the falling rain on the brim of my hat, there was a loud rhythmic thudding. It was a sound that was felt more than heard and was challenging my senses. The strange, heavy sound was muffled by the rain but was becoming stronger by the second. I didn't dare take my eyes off the man but my side vision picked up rapid movement close-at-hand to my left! Indian Jack's gunman and I simultaneously glanced toward the sound and a movement that was sensed more than seen. My eyes widened in shock at the phenomenal sight!

At a later time, I would once again reflect back on the violent happening and wonder again at the courage and resourcefulness shown by a man who had lived through an unknown length of time, suffering unbelievable degradation and humiliation. But in the moment, when it did happen, it occurred with a subtle swiftness that was beyond immediate description.

When I first looked the giant horse was at full gallop and was almost on top of the gunman swathed in black. Wearing an expression of bitter resolve the Lakota singer with the gray streaked hair was crouched over the massive neck of one of the huge, work horses.

"HOKA HEY!"

His passionate war cry resounded in my ears, sending a chill up my spine.

Because of the pelting rain and the horse's bulk the Lakota looked unnatural, undersized like a child, on the broad back of the huge horse. A rope had been rigged around the horse's jaw for a bridle. He was no longer naked; he had improvised and fashioned a loin-cloth from some bright material. In lieu of war paint, charcoal foraged from some dead fire striped his determined face.

Rain bounced off the Lakota and horse alike as though

poured from a bottomless bucket. Indian Jack's flag no longer flapped beneath the glistening, pointed iron tip of its staff; the Lakota warrior was extending the wooden staff like an old-time lance.

I raised my Colt at the same time the gunman swung the scatter-gun away from me and pointed it toward the onrushing Lakota. Before I could shoot, the iron point of the lance bit into the wooden butt-stock of the Winchester shotgun, wrenching it from his hands.

BOOM!

At such close quarters, the ensuing blast of the ten-gauge shotgun sounded like a cannon! The accidental discharge hit no one but startled everyone!

With the loud noise the giant horse had abruptly shied to his left, splashing water in all directions. Either his shoulder or his leg struck the man in black; the glancing blow sent him flying!

I was too occupied calming a dancing, twisting Redman to see the details, but I was in time to observe the gunman land in a sopping heap not ten feet away. He struggled to his feet, swaying and dripping mud and water. Before I could level my revolver the warrior was there on foot, arriving like a runaway force of nature. The mixed-blood gunman was straightening with a pistol in each hand when the running Lakota slammed into him. His momentum smashed the gunman back onto the wet turf, sending mud and rainwater flying in every direction.

Through the driving rain I saw the unarmed Lakota, his long, graying hair whipping around his face, climb astride the squirming killer's chest. A hand grasping a revolver raised up, the Lakota slapped it away like a pesky fly.

As I stepped down from a skittish Redman, my quick glance was in time to see the Lakota snatch his would be killer's remaining pistol out of his other hand, stand up, and fire down into his chest. The gunman flopped once and then was still. A cloud of smoke rose and engulfed the shooter's head and shoulders before being absorbed by the falling rain.

The Lakota stood still staring at the gunman impassively while the rain slicked his long hair and ran down his nearly

Barry Brierley

naked body in rivulets.

I tore my eyes away and with revolver leveled, let my gaze span the rain-swept clearing. I couldn't believe it, there was no one in sight. The immediate danger was gone. Just in case it wasn't, I lowered the Colt, held it against my chest with my wooden hand, and began to reload, my hat brim serving as an umbrella for the job. Reloading the Remington was next.

While it was still in my hand I looked again at the Lakota who had saved my life and probably Star Watcher's and Nighthawk's as well. His eyes lifted and met mine as I said, "Kola, le mita pila (Many thanks, friend)."

With an almost imperceptible nod, his Lakota soft and lyrical, he replied, "Your woman has told me of you, Crow warrior. After this day songs will be sung about the Kangi (Crow) warrior on the red horse who makes war like the tokala."

At first I didn't understand 'tokala.' The rain's patter on my hat was distracting my thought process, but then I remembered research done for one of my paintings of the Lakota. Tokala means Kit Fox. It was an old time Lakota warrior society similar to the Cheyenne Dog Soldiers. In both societies, in one way or another, its members pledged to fight to the death to protect their people.

For an instant I felt pride in my deed, but then I recalled the relentless killing machine I had become and felt ashamed. It was at that moment that I realized that Caleb Junior was no longer in control. With the passing danger his much darker soul receded into some temporal recess of my brain.

The aging warrior's gaze shifted. When my eyes followed his line of sight I saw he was looking through the rain toward the Wild West Tipi Village. His gaze returned, raising his voice to allow for the smothering rain.

"I must tell the other Indians to leave before Bluecoats come and blame them for the killing."

As though in coalition with his words the sun chose that moment to break free of the clouds and for the rain to cease. While symbolizing a new beginning, the yellow light brought with it a freshness and a thankfulness for being alive.

For the first time the Lakota smiled. Rain was dripping off his nose as it was from the brim of my hat. His black eyes met my

278

blue ones as he slowly gave me the hand sign for brother.

"My name is High Bear."

There was movement beyond the wagons. For a moment our attention was once again drawn to the Indian camp. Several of the indigenous people from mixed Indian tribes were coming out of hiding looking frightened and concerned. High Bear, his smile being but a memory, turned away from the unpleasant sight. When his eyes found mine, the smile returned to his eyes as he continued, "If ever you need help, warrior, come to the Yellow Bear Camp at Pine Ridge. How are you called among your people?"

When I told him he nodded and said, "To me you will always be, He Who Kills With One Shot." He glanced toward the distant wooded ravine and added, "Your family waits for you there ... near the wild plum tree. Your son, Nighthawk, is very brave. One day, Wakan Tanka willing, he will be a great warrior."

"Pila maya. (Thank you.)"

Our eyes locked for a mere heartbeat. He turned and with a surprising abruptness walked away toward the tipis; his long, wet hair lifting and falling with each purposeful stride. I discounted his abrupt manner; in my heart I knew an unspoken bond had formed between us. I paused, then I realized what I was seeing, I had to smile at the irony in spite of the nearby death and destruction. The make-shift loin-cloth had been created from a portion of Indian Jack's flag, which had previously been fastened to the lance's wooden staff. The embroidered Indian riding a lance logo bounced in soggy rhythm on High Bear's buttocks as he walked toward the distant tipis.

Barry Brierley

CHAPTER THIRTY-SEVEN
CLOSING THE GENERATION GAP

How do I begin to write of my first meeting with my son? I know how strange that must sound. But believe me, after having known him as a baby for only a brief hour or so near Wounded Knee Creek, in the very center of chaos and violence ... how could that possibly be considered a first meeting? However I never forgot the special feeling I experienced when those sparkling black eyes first touched mine.

Ducking beneath the dripping canopy of cottonwood branches I reined Redman to a stop and stepped down near the outreaching limbs of the wild plum. A rustle of leaves brought the Remington to hand and my body into a crouch. I slowly straightened, my heart tight within my chest as Star Watcher came running into my arms, the red skirt of her cotton dress fluttering behind. I wondered briefly where she had found clothing, but I knew High Bear must have foraged and provided.

While I breathed in her familiar scent and felt her body so close to mine, something wasn't quite right. There was another feeling, a gentle nudge from the past. Once again I felt the strange weight of unknown eyes watching me. I looked up and saw him step slowly forward. Staying beneath the emotional armor of the sprawling branches of the plum tree, Nighthawk stopped. Our eyes met and held. Rain water dripped steadily from the leaves and branches, enshrouding him in slivers of silver light.

Completely unaware of the tableau being played out nearby, Star was hugging me and murmuring words of endearment; we were both wet and splattered with mud but unaware. I held her closely, somehow fearful to let go. But at the same time, I stared, captivated by the presence of Nighthawk, my son.

***

Deputy John Nighthawk slowly closed the journal, noting as he did so that there were a few pages of manuscript left. His heart was too full to continue. He knew that one day he would finish it, but first he had to savor what he had already read. For the moment reading about his ancestral grandfather was almost too emotional for him. Silly as it seemed, even to himself, he was afraid this might be his final link with his family's past and he wasn't ready for it to end. The sound of a car's motor brought his head up. Thinking it might be Nicole and Mike returning from Sturgis, John carefully set the journal on the metal box, propped it against the leg of the picnic table, and quickly got to his feet. The motor noise was from a Ford sports vehicle not his Jeep Cherokee. Disappointed he watched the vehicle pass the tall, chimney-like stone outcrop across the road from the park's entrance and continue down the road.

Earlier, Nicole had borrowed his Jeep to 'go shopping' as she had described it. In reality, Nighthawk knew she was giving him time alone to finish the manuscript. Having read Daniel Starr's first manuscript Nicole knew how important it was to him.

A subtle rumble reminiscent of a truck crossing a wooden bridge lifted John's gaze to a blue expanse of sky. The towering cumulus had grown dark and animated. Thunder again rolled overhead and the clouds began to tumble and move in from the north.

Nighthawk quickly gathered their blanket, the journal and other paraphernalia and hurried to the nearest gazebo. While carefully setting the journal on a clean spot on the picnic table inside, he remembered the steel box. John hurried back through the first raindrops, scooped up the box and ran back inside the shelter. Rain began to fall in large drops, then in sheets. Nighthawk stared up at the gun-metal sky in awe. The rain was falling so hard the clouds all but disappeared in the deluge. He looked across the two miles separating him from Bear Butte; the sacred mountain was a mere pallid silhouette through the falling rain. The deputy's thoughts began to drift and turn inward as his mind created a surreal image. The clouds and the Butte disappeared completely as the Lakota Sky Father wept and millions of cold tears fell, cleansing the earth and purifying the water; the land once again became virgin, acre upon acre of buffalo grass untouched by plow, nor harvested by man.

Nighthawk absently set the tin box on the table; the metallic sound of the box on wood caused the illusion to vanish. He looked down at the oblong tin box; the sudden return of reality was confusing. Is his mind playing games, he wondered, or was there something false about the sound the metal made as it touched the wood surface. To his ear it didn't resonate as an empty, metal container should. Nighthawk slowly sat down and opened the box. The falling rain formed a gray curtain of privacy around the open sided gazebo as John held the empty, open box up to whatever diffused light he could find.

Totally unaware of the isolation created by the surrounding screen of water, he stared at the tiny screw-heads barely discernible in the four corners on the bottom of the metal box. His breathing increased to the point where he worried that he didn't have a paper bag handy. He got his breathing under control, set the container down, and fished a clasp knife from his pants pocket. With shaking fingers Nighthawk pulled out several multiple-use blades until he found the one with the tiny screwdriver point. While using his finger to guide the tool to the slotted screw, John felt a greasy residue. A smile spread across his lean face. He silently rejoiced knowing that some type of rust deterring lubricant had been used.

Setting the last tiny screw aside Nighthawk produced a thin, pointed knife blade and pried at the apparent lid to a false bottom. Lifting the lid free he set it aside and removed what looked like a block of wood wrapped in a waterproof oilskin with leather thongs tied around it. Unable to untie the thongs, John reluctantly used his knife to separate the binding from the wood. With great care, he held the object up to the best light available and examined it. It appeared to be two flat, pieces of wood treated with some unknown substance and tied together. A wax had been used to seal the seams where the wood joined to form a perfect fit. With a surgeon's precision, Nighthawk used the point of his blade to break the sealant running the length of the groove formed by the joining of the two pieces of wood. Very carefully he removed the top piece of wood. In between the twin pieces of wood were several sheets of paper of an approximate eight by ten size. Nighthawk's breath seemed permanently lodged in his throat; he was flabbergasted. John counted six pieces of paper. Each sheet was a letter. But each was a special letter, a missive unlike any other and all six were of great monetary and historical value.

Nighthawk's head was rapidly spinning. He felt light-headed. What other surprises, he wondered, will this amazing man come up with next? He thought back to when he discovered Starr's photo and what was written about the man's business venture beneath his photo. As if it wasn't enough that Starr, knowing the future, had become a silent partner with Orville and Wilbur Wright, and for several years had financed the brothers and had been the mainstay that kept their flight project functioning. John mentally shook his head knowing that even by 1913, Starr had to have become wealthy. Cradling the letters, he thought, now this. Overwhelmed by it all, Nighthawk slowly sat down and carefully placed the box back on the picnic table.

Dazzled, yet in total awe of the man, John knew in his heart he had to finish Starr's chronicle. And, he told himself, there is no chance of my waiting until tomorrow. In the world of Daniel Starr, he mused, tomorrow is the same as yesterday and the past becomes today. Whatever it is he has to say, John decided, if it's here with me now it must be dealt with today.

John quickly but carefully put everything in its place and out of harm's way, everything, that is, except the journal. A cool breeze moved through the open dwelling. Nighthawk closed the box, sealing the valuable letters from the weather. He tightly held the book in his hands, completely unaware of the cooling atmosphere. He did notice, for the first time, that the rain had dwindled and blue was once again peeking through the gray clouds. John looked down the road toward Bear Butte. He knew that Nicole and Michael, when they come, will approach from that direction. The road was empty. The deputy opened the journal and began to read.

Edges of Time

***

My heart swelled with pride and love as I gazed at my son. Star, feeling a new tension in my stature, pulled free of my embrace. Seeing Nighthawk she gestured to him and softly said in poetic Lakota, "It is the warrior, Cay-leb, who the Kangi (Crow) call Strong Arm and we Lakota, Wooden Hand. This is the man who has now saved our lives twice. He has traveled a long way and fought many battles to once again become my husband and your father. What say you, my son?"

With his glittering, obsidian eyes still fastened on mine the boy stepped clear of the wild plum; he walked toward me stopping a few feet away. Nighthawk's gaze broke away from mine and began to size me up. Being Lakota he couldn't resist giving Redman equal time. While he looked us over I felt compelled to do the same.

In the morning light his attire could only be described as 'desperate.' Except for lightly decorated moccasins peeking out from beneath muddy, rolled up pants legs, nothing fit. At the waist his cotton trousers were so large they were folded over and held together with what looked like a sliver of bone or some kind of awl. He wore no shirt, was splattered with mud, and his hair was braided into two plaits from which several strands of hair had loosened and drifted in the slight breeze. In spite of all the desecration and the humiliation, he stood unafraid and with pride. In his tiny seven-year-old body he stood before me with the composure and bearing of a chief.

I was so moved and delighted by his youthful courage that tears momentarily blurred my vision. By the time I had blinked them away Nighthawk had again stepped closer. His ebony eyes were again fastened to mine. I saw the smile enter his eyes before it reached his lips and my heart soared.

"Welcome home, my father."

Before I could reply, he added, "What is your horse's name? Can I ride him?"

Barry Brierley

CHAPTER THIRTY-EIGHT
AFTERWORD

So, Dear Reader, my meeting with my son was a success. We did stop at the North Platte to clean up. While Star and our boy stayed at the river, I rode back toward the fort. Meeting some of the Indians released from the show I was able to barter for more appropriate clothing for them. But High Bear was nowhere to be found. When I asked of his whereabouts, a spokesman for the group of blanket Indians made a vague gesture to the north. High Bear and I were destined to meet again, however. It came about a few years later in the Yellow Bear Camp at Pine Ridge. I was on a spiritual quest at the time and considering my coincidental rescue of him from the Wild West Show, the Oglala people befriended me. Because of High Bear's stature among those of the camp, he was very influential in allowing me, a mixed-blood Crow, to be given permission to participate in one of their secret Sun Dances.

It was a great honor. In those days it was against the white man's law to practice their most sacred dance, and the Yellow Bear Camp had the reputation of being Pine Ridge's den of malcontents.

Our return trip to the Hills was uneventful. Upon reaching the Starr Ranch, Star Watcher and our son were welcomed into the family by one and all. Even Uncle Billy took Star into his heart, and into his arms.

In no time at all, we were an important part of everything that made the horse ranch work. I don't want you to think that I completely settled down to ranch life. As you probably know by

Barry Brierley

now, Caleb Junior's temperament was too volatile to keep him completely out of trouble. Perhaps one day I will write of my adventures up Montana way and tell about a cowboy who became one of my best friends ... and about a run-in with an old adversary of mine, and a great adventure that made me decide to be satisfied with a tamer life.

Before I go I must confess that Star Watcher thinks I'm witco (crazy) writing to someone I'll never meet, or perhaps, to someone who will never read what I've written. Be that as it may, Dear Reader, I'm convinced my words will be read and shared and hopefully what I have given you will be put to a worthwhile use.

***

Nighthawk lowered the journal, disappointed that it ended sooner than he expected. Noting there were several pages remaining in the book, he casually began to thumb through the pages. He stopped and gaped. Nighthawk quickly scanned the remaining pages. Because of his excitement he could feel his heart palpitating. On almost every page there was a sketch done in pencil, all signed with the Star symbol as a signature. Beside each sketch there was a printed notation of some kind or other ... either a name, quote, or message. Returning to the first page after the manuscript John paused. The first sketch was a head and shoulders rendering of Star Watcher grinning, her eyes alive and dancing with happiness. Turning the page, he froze. He knew instantly it was a pencil portrait of his ancestral grandfather,

Nighthawk, as a young man in his early twenties, the young Lakota is wearing a narrow-brimmed cowboy hat and a collarless shirt. In the drawing his head was turned slightly away, but his eyes were fastened onto the artist. John could see love and respect in the boy's expression. Knowing Daniel Starr's skill, he was certain he would sketch only what he saw.

Nighthawk flipped through the other pages, noting that he only recognized some of the figures and scenes. John carefully closed the book, deciding to wait to examine them until he had the time to savor each detail. His mind began to drift thinking about what he had read and what he could do to help his people with Daniel Starr's wonderful gift of the antique letters. John decided he would once again confer with the Lakota elders. He would contact Weasel Bear as soon as possible.

Something brushed against Nighthawk's shoulder!

He recoiled, startled by the contact. Nicole was standing over him, her hand at her throat looking almost as surprised as John. He had been so wrapped up in his thoughts he hadn't heard Nicole's approach. Mike's cheerful, ten-year-old face peered around his mother's slim form; he grinned at Nighthawk.

"We scared you ... didn't we?" Mike exclaimed.

John grinned, and said, "Well ..."

Mike laughed, pointing at John.

"I thought you can't sneak up on Indians."

"Michael!" Nicole admonished.

John's hand whipped out grasping Mike's arm; with a swift jerk he had the boy inside his embrace and on his lap, entrapped by his long arms. Mike giggled and struggled in vain as John smiled up at Nicole.

"That's all right. Mike and I fully understand one another."

Still hanging onto Mike's squirming body John added, "Mike knows if he teases too much I won't let him play with my scalps."

Mike stopped laughing and wiggling. He looked deeply into John's eyes and with mock seriousness the boy replied, "Oh, no! Come on, John, that ain't fair."

Staring at the two of them as though they had lost their minds, although secretly pleased at their rapport, Nicole automatically said, "Say, *isn't*. Ain't is not a word, Mike."

Unable to control himself any longer, Mike laughed and lunged up and forward, trying to break loose from the deputy's grip. John pretended to lose his hold and Mike broke free. Staying just out of reach, and by using taunting facial expressions, and staying barely out of reach, he blatantly dared John to catch him. Nicole smiled and shook her head at their playfulness.

Nighthawk then made a sudden move at Michael who leapt out of range laughing.

Nicole and John suddenly made eye contact. Seeing the happiness in Nighthawk's eyes, Nicole asked, "You finished it, didn't you?"

Nighthawk nodded and smiled.

"Yes I did. You won't believe his story and what I have to show you later."

"Come on, John. Bet ya can't catch me!" Mike taunted.

Together they watched Mike's silly, antsy, bouncing figure as he tried to entice John into action; then they simultaneously looked at each other and froze.

Their ensuing spontaneous laughter was equally as much for young Michael's silly antics as for their timing with their corresponding glance.

When Nighthawk's laughter faded he met Mike's exuberant gaze.

"Tell you what, you load up the Cherokee without stepping in any of the rain puddles," John said, as he pointed toward the rock formation just beyond the park's gate, "and I'll race you to the chimney rock."

Mike's face lit up like a Christmas tree. Without a word he gathered an armful of their things and sprinted for the vehicle.

Nighthawk's black gaze met Nicole's.

"Remember in school when you had Art Appreciation?"

Nicole nodded, looking puzzled.

"Do you recall the famous cowboy artist, Charles M. Russell?"

"Yes, of course. But why do you ask?"

Nicole's scowl was thoughtful, not angry.

"Why are you grinning? Or should I say beaming?"

Nighthawk dropped the smile and silently watched as Mike entered the gazebo and grabbed another armload and carefully avoided a mud puddle on his return trip to the truck. John again met Nicole's gaze.

"Did you know he used to write to friends often? Sometimes he would do a small watercolor on the letter itself and mail it to the friend." Before Nicole could say anything, John added, "We now have in our possession, five original Charley Russell letter paintings addressed to Caleb Starr, Jr., with the heading, 'Friend Caleb.' And is signed, 'C. M. Russell.' A couple of the paintings are of Caleb Jr. on his horse Redman. Even the wooden hand is visible. There is also another piece of paper that has one of his poems and a small still-life painting."

Nicole appeared stunned.

"But, how is that...?" she began.

Nighthawk, barely able to keep his rising excitement in control, interrupted, "There's a false bottom in the box."

Seeing young Mike's approach, John stood up and carefully picked up the box containing Daniel Starr's gift. He glanced at Nicole, who was watching him with a small smile on her face, and added, "Later. Okay?"

Edges of Time

Nicole nodded. But as she watched John Nighthawk walk slowly to his vehicle Nicole wasn't thinking about his wonderful discovery, she was thinking of how twice in the past week John had suggested, by his not thinking about his choice of words, that they were as one. When he said, 'We now have in our possession,' was his latest slip.

Nighthawk, on the other hand, was thinking of the discovery. He was remembering the hand-lettered words in the poem Russell had hand written for Starr:

The West is dead my friend.
But writers hold the seed.
And what they saw
Will live and grow
Again to those who read.
C.M. Russell

Nighthawk stopped. A gentle breeze touched his cheek. There was still coolness in the air from the rain. He barely noticed Mike's hurried passage back to the gazebo, nor heard his teasing remark. John's gaze was inexplicably pulled toward the east, to Bear Butte.

The sacred mountain towered above as though only a couple hundred yards away instead of the two miles he knew it to be. After the rain the clouds were much lower; a large cumulus currently enveloped Bear Butte's high summit. Somehow, the fact that the clouds were touching the mountain made John feel that much closer to the Sky Father. The fresh smell of wet grass and damp earth made him aware of the Earth Mother and the essence of his self.

Inexorably his thoughts once again turned to Daniel Starr; a willing captive inside an unbelievable vortex of living on the edges of time. Although they didn't share the same blood, through his manuscripts Nighthawk had become the man's kindred spirit. He stared upward toward the hidden summit and felt the power of his mountain, *Paha Sapa*. Under his breath, Nighthawk whispered.

"Wherever your heart takes you, Strong Arm, my prayers ride with you."

THE END

Barry Brierley

Author's Note

Much effort has been put into this novel to make it as historically accurate as possible. Besides using the obvious written research available, my wife and I have traveled over the land covered by my time traveler protagonist in his search for the Lakota woman. I also lived near Sturgis in the late seventies and my residence was in the same approximate location as the fictitious artist, Daniel Starr's home overlooking Bear Butte. I have traveled by snow mobile into the Black Hills and discovered an abandoned lumber camp. I have hiked to the summit of Bear butte several times and have roamed the Wounded Knee Creek area. While researching Butch Cassidy, I concluded that the Wild Bunch was in the Black Hills during the time indicated in my story. My wife and I also visited and did research at Belle Fourche and the Butte County Bank, the place the Wild Bunch robbed that same year as the events in my story imply.

BB